The Snowdonia Killings

by Simon McCleave

A DI Ruth Hunter Crime Thriller

Book 1

2019

Your free book is waiting for you

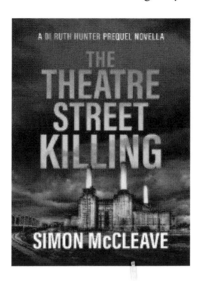

Get your FREE copy of the prequel to
the DI Ruth Hunter Series NOW
at www.simonmccleave.com
and join my VIP Email Club

For Mum and Dad

'An eye for an eye will only make the whole world
blind.'
Mahatma Gandhi

'Revenge is sweet and not fattening.'
Alfred Hitchcock

'Before you embark on a journey of revenge, dig two
graves.'
Japanese Proverb

CHAPTER 1

MARCH 2017

It was nearly midnight as officers from Peckham CID moved into the rancid concrete stairwell of Crane House, SE15. It stank of piss and weed, and used crack vials crunched under foot. The walls surrounding them carried the names of heroes of the local gang, the Peckham Young Guns, recorded in thick, rounded white graffiti – *Dwain G, Bailey, Dukes, Choke ...*

Four Armed Response Officers, carrying Glock 9mm pistols and dressed in their black NOMEX boots, gloves, and Kevlar helmets over balaclavas, moved purposefully to the bottom of the stairs, awaiting instruction. Their goggles and ballistic body armour gave them an eerie, futuristic appearance.

Detective Inspector Ruth Hunter was taking no chances as she motioned silently for CID officers and the AROs to head up the stairs to the fifth floor. She heard the thudding of her pulse in her ears and felt the grip of anxiety in her stomach. She adjusted her tight, heavy ballistic vest. Even though it was there to save her life, Ruth cursed how uncomfortable and restrictive it felt. *It's worse than Jane's bloody bridesmaid's dress,* she thought.

Thirty minutes earlier, Peckham nick had received a call to say that someone had heard a gunshot in Flat 127 of

Peckham's Pelican Estate in South East London – a notorious hive of drug gangs, violence, and murder. Ruth knew the flat was home to Kossi Asumana, aka Taz, a drug dealer and member of the infamous Peckham Boys, who had been linked to murders and crime for decades. Asumana had been on CID's radar for a while now, even though he was only a minor dealer of crack cocaine on the estates. However, Ruth was more concerned about the fact that Asumana lived in that flat with his wife Zaria and their two young children. She prayed that none of them had become collateral damage in a deadly trade. Already that year, London had seen the deaths of four innocent members of the public, caught up in the crossfire of gang warfare – and it was only March. *It's turning into South Central.*

The officers moved quietly along the concrete walkway and arrived outside the innocuous red door to Flat 127. Ruth motioned, and one of the AROs stepped forwards with what they liked to call 'the big red key' – a steel battering ram that would break down the door in one hit. Ruth knew that a dry sense of humour was the only way to survive in the job.

Ruth clicked her radio. 'Three-seven to Gold Command. Officers in position at target location.'

The radio crackled back. 'Three-seven received. Gold Command order is '*Go!*''

Ruth paused, her mind racing through the various dark scenarios they might find behind that door. *Right, let's go.* She nodded at the AROs and moved back against the wall.

Bang! Ruth flinched as the door swung open with an almighty thud and the officers moved in, weapons trained in front of them.

'Armed police!' they bellowed as they stormed into the flat. 'Armed police! Everyone get down!'

Ruth followed, heart pounding in her chest. The flat was tidy, and she noticed African wall-hangings and the smell of spicy cooking. Ruth spotted children's shoes neatly lined up in the hallway, and two pink coats hanging from hooks. It didn't look like the usual squalor she had come to expect of a drug dealer's home. The officers spread out throughout the flat, searching the rooms. In the hallway, Ruth carefully stepped over a discarded child's game, pieces thrown haphazardly across the floor. She had a sinking feeling in the pit of her stomach. *Please let the kids be okay.*

'Armed police! Drop the weapon!' an officer cried from the next room. It was followed by a woman's scream.

Following the noise, Ruth went into the compact living room and immediately saw a body. Kossi Asumana. His white t-shirt was soaked with blood, and there was a shocked expression on his face. He was dead.

Ruth turned to see the AROs training their guns at Zaria Asumana, who was also covered in blood. She held a 9mm Baikal handgun, but her hand was shaking uncontrollably. Her box-braided hair, fashionably held by a brightly coloured scarf, belied the look of terror on her face as she stared wildly at the officers who'd just stormed into her home. Her eyes jumped between all the strangers in front of her, around the room, out of the window, but her stare was blank. She was in shock. Something terrible had happened here.

Ruth glanced at the AROs and calmly said, 'It's okay.' She moved forwards, looking at Zaria, establishing eye contact. 'Zaria?'

'Ma'am?' an ARO said in a concerned tone, but Ruth ignored him. She knew what she was doing.

'Zaria? My name is Ruth. I'm a police officer,' she said in a well-rehearsed and gentle tone.

Zaria came out of her trance, looked up at Ruth and then down at the gun in her hand. She clearly didn't know how it had got there.

'Drop the weapon!' the ARO commanded again, but Ruth gave a hand signal to give her a moment. *Shouting at her isn't the way to do this!* It would be sod's law if she died tonight.

'He's dead. But I don't know how ...' Zaria's Sierra Leonean accent was thick.

'Zaria, I need you to give me the gun.' Ruth's tone was soft. 'Zaria? Can you pass the gun to me?'

Zaria looked at Ruth but was still in a daze. Then she nodded, put the gun down and slid it across the table. One of the AROs came forwards, took the gun away and made it safe.

They had the gun, but they had a new problem. Ruth crouched down and looked at her. 'Zaria. Where are your children?'

Zaria shook her head, her eyes suddenly wild. 'I ... I don't know.'

Ruth looked at her detective sergeant. 'Check the flat.'

The DS nodded. 'Guv.'

Ruth glanced at a female detective constable. 'Keep her here until we find the kids.' She didn't want Zaria trying to roam around the flat in a frenzy.

Ruth quickly manoeuvred herself out of the living room, down the hall, and found what looked like the children's bedroom. Two small single beds with pink princess duvet covers, dolls and teddy bears neatly lined up on the pillows. She checked, but there was no sign of any children. *Where the hell were they?*

The DS hurried towards her down the hallway. 'Nothing, guv. No sign of them.'

'Shit,' Ruth muttered. Were they lying somewhere dead? Or had they simply fled and were now out there on the estate, terrified and alone? *This isn't good.*

Then, from inside the children's bedroom, a noise and some movement. Ruth turned and walked over to where she thought the noise had come from – a narrow, pink wooden cupboard that had been built into an alcove.

She carefully opened the doors and immediately saw two young girls cowering, looking utterly terrified. *Thank God!*

Kneeling, Ruth looked at them. 'It's all right. No one's going to hurt you, okay? We're going to look after you.' The first girl blinked, then shifted herself and stood up. 'Good girl. Come here.'

The girl's face was streaked with tears as Ruth took her hand and gently guided her towards the DS. Her little fingers were icy and still shaking with fear.

Ruth turned back to the alcove and asked, 'Do you want to come with me, darling?' The other girl nodded, held out her hand, and Ruth helped her out of the cupboard. 'There we go. You're safe now.'

Ruth watched as the girl wandered over to her sister, still lost in the trauma of what had happened. What would the events of the last hour do to them as they grew up? She had seen it so many times before. The ongoing cycle of crime, poverty, and addiction in places like this. There was nothing they could do except try to hold it all together.

Lives could be ruined in a split second, especially in SE19. And that's why she was leaving the Met at the end of the week.

THE DARK, HEATHER-CLAD moorland of Denbighshire, North Wales. Its acidic heathland was home to yellow gorse and green bilberry. Behind these uplands, the ominous, mountainous landscape of Snowdonia National Park and then Mount Snowdon itself. *Fynydd Snowdon.* 3,600 feet above sea level. It was a dark, looming and timeless presence. Watching. Judging. Sometimes it felt like a strong, protective, and even reassuring boundary. A geographical shielding arm. Other times it seemed to suggest a hidden danger, anger, or even malevolence. A wronged past or resentment that would eventually be settled. Dark in summer, dusted with snow in winter, Snowdon is known as *Yr Wyddfa* in Welsh – the Tomb.

Uneven grey mountain walls seemed to dissect the landscape randomly. Made from local dry stones, they date back to the end of the nineteenth century when the nearby Penrhyn Quarry was in its heyday. The walls had weathered and formed a rich growth of lichens, thriving in the clean air and fresh westerly winds. A rabble of butterflies also inhabited the mountain walls, including wall brown butterflies patrolling their territories, migrants such as the red admiral and painted lady, and the peacock butterfly observed on the wing as early as mid-February.

Further up the mountain, moraine and esker gravel banks and pingo depressions had been formed by the melting of buried ice at the end of the last ice age. It felt like a forgotten landscape. Not on the way to anywhere; just here. Somewhere where time stood still, and nothing changed from century to century. Epic in scope, and the final refuge against invading Romans and Normans, Snowdonia was where Owain Glyndwr, the last native Prince of Wales, had been crowned.

Across the hills below, DS Nick Evans cursed the uneven ground below his feet. Lithe, handsome with a dark beard, he had an authority beyond his years. *It's far too early for this much running*, he thought as he chased after a man twenty years his senior.

The older man puffed and grunted as he ran and slid, but Nick still wasn't gaining any ground. Nick had known the man, Dewi Jones, since he was a boy. He had taught Nick geography at the local secondary school, Ysgol Dinas Padog, until he took early retirement and worked on the family sheep farm that covered 1,600 acres. The Joneses had run the farm for generations. Snowdonia was that kind of place. A series of tightly knit communities where everyone knew everybody, and their business.

However, three days earlier, Dewi Jones had been impli-
cated in an ongoing investigation into the production and
circulation of child pornography in North Wales. When
Nick arrived to ask him a few questions, Dewi simply ran. If
he had doubts over Dewi's guilt, then they had been crushed
by the older man's immediate dash for the back door. Nick
had no idea where Dewi was going, or how he thought he
was going to escape. Step in Detective Sergeant Nick Evans
of the North Wales Police, *Heddlu Gogledd Cymru. Gogledd
Cymru diogelach* – A Safer North Wales.

The ground steepened, and they were now 1,200 feet
above sea level. Even in spring, the wind could be icy and
Nick felt the cold sting on his hands and face. He thought
what a tough, unforgiving place it was to farm. That the
Welsh had farmed sheep here since medieval times seemed
beyond amazing, veering on insane. Nick allowed himself a
small smirk of national pride and patriotism, but right now
he had a suspect to catch.

Nick ploughed on, slipping on the bumpy ground before
regaining his footing. He was stunned that Dewi was still going. He didn't strike him as being particularly athletic but
Nick had hardly gained any ground on Dewi in the past few
minutes. Nick's calves were burning with the effort of running and keeping balance. His hangover wasn't making the
chase any easier. *This is getting ridiculous,* he thought.

As he glanced up ahead, Nick spotted a chestnut-
coloured horse tethered to a wooden gate in the approaching
field. Dewi was heading straight for it. Nick had a sinking
feeling as he watched Dewi untie the horse and heave himself onto its back.

'You've got to be kidding me,' Nick muttered as he sucked in air.

Dewi kicked his heels, and the horse galloped noisily up the steep mountainside, its hooves throwing clumps of earth into the air.

Where the hell is he going? Dewi's escape seemed directionless, and an educated man like him must have known it was only a matter of time before he was caught. He would have to come down from the mountains, eventually.

Nick knew he had no chance of catching Dewi. Maybe he should just radio for help. For a moment, he thought they could get the police helicopter out, but he knew that since the budget cuts it was hardly likely.

He stopped and looked around, thinking what to do next. Then he spotted a mud-spattered, green Syma quad bike in the adjacent field. *Bingo!* A moment later, he jumped over the fence, got on, pressed the ignition and gave chase uphill. Nick had ridden quad bikes as a kid. He rode the vehicle skilfully, like a jockey, taking the bumps in the natural suspension of his knees. *This will even out the odds*, he thought.

Dewi was out of sight but, a minute later, Nick came thundering over the brow of the slope and then slowed the quad bike as he reached the rocky terrain that led up to an old rusty feed shed. The horse ate grass outside, unaware of the unfolding drama.

Was Dewi in the feed shed? If so, why? Nick stopped, seeing that he would need to travel the rest of the way on foot. He jumped from the quad bike and steadied himself. The bumpy ride had destabilised his balance, and he waited momentarily for it to return. Plus, he was hungover, so at least the icy wind numbed his headache a little. In truth, Nick suspected that he was still drunk.

He navigated the uneven ground. His foot slipped on some wet moss and he nearly fell. As he clambered over the rocks, he remembered how Dewi used to meet up with Nick's father, Rhys, when he was home on leave from the army. That was until Rhys became too entrenched in 'the illness' to travel or even leave the house. Dewi and Rhys belonged to the same masonic lodge over at Chirk.

Nick also remembered sitting on the banks of the River Dee, just up from Llangollen, with his father and Dewi. A glass bottle of pop and a red straw. Crisps with the blue square packet of salt. Halcyon days shot in the soft focus of childhood. Summer evenings that went on forever.

Just as they began to wander along up to The Cornmill pub, Nick had seen a salmon leap from the water. The sun caught its pink-orange tail and, although he probably imagined it, Nick remembered the salmon seemed to hang in the air for seconds. Rhys and Dewi, who were in the middle of arguing about the latest cricket test against the West Indies, missed it - but Nick knew it to be true.

Boom!

Nick's train of thought broke. He knew exactly what the sound was. A shotgun. His heart sank as he let out a breath. *Oh Dewi, what have you done?*

Constructed from grey corrugated iron, the shed was rusted where the bolts held it together. Nick quickly unhooked and opened the iron gate, which creaked as it swung on its hinges. Inside it felt damp and dark, and the air smelt thick and musty. There was a twelve-foot feed passage down the centre with a steel barrier for silage or hay. The wind hummed against the iron structure, which reverberated with a low, deep, eerie moan.

Nick clicked on his torch as he went deeper into the barn. Casting its light across the floor, the torch beam stopped short as it lingered over the sight that Nick feared most. Booted feet and muddy trousers in a sitting position. Straw that was black and sticky from blood. Nick blinked and then forced himself to look up. He recognised the chin with the greying stubble. The mouth that had laughed and told crude jokes that Nick didn't understand. But above that bloody top lip, the head was gone. Shattered into a thousand pieces against the corrugated iron behind. Streaks of blood, brain and skull fragments had spattered ten feet up the metal wall.

The stuff of nightmares, Nick thought to himself. Of his nightmares. And he knew exactly how to take those nightmares away. He pulled a small bottle of vodka from the inside pocket of his jacket, unscrewed the top, and took a long drink.

THE NORTH WALES COMMUNITY of Dinas Padog lay about twenty miles west of Llancastell along the A493. The edges of Snowdonia National Park were only ten miles away to the east and visible; the dark, looming plum presence of the Llyn Llydaw ridge cut across the skyline.

Though easily explained, the deep purple colour still stunned its many visitors. Because of an optical effect called 'Rayleigh scattering', the refraction of blue light is more visible in the spectrum than the wavelength of red light. At sunrise and sunset, the light passes through the atmosphere at a lower angle and travels a greater distance through a larger volume of air. Much of the green and blue scatters away, and more red light comes to the eye, creating the colours of the sunrise and sunset and, to the human eye, painting the mountains a vivid purple. But the tourists didn't want to know the technicalities as they marvelled at the splendour of the sight.

A large new-build detached house was located on a small road on the outskirts of the town. As the light faded, Arabella Dixon strode authoritatively across her garden and into the evening glow.

With shoulder-length braided hair, Arabella was mixed race with a nose and chin that seemed too small for her face. However, she was proud of her slim, elegant figure. There weren't many fifty-three-year-old women who went running in figure-hugging, black Sweaty Betty lycra. Sometimes she even sported a crop top. She would make self-effacing comments in the staff room about squeezing her 'enormous bottom' onto the long, burgundy sofas that lined the walls of the room, and then lap up the 'Oh shut up, Arabella. I'd kill for a figure like yours' comments, claiming she still had five pounds to lose.

Originally from Merseyside, the Old Swan part of Liverpool, she'd worked hard to get where she was today, a career teacher in her early fifties aiming for a headship. Arabella's mother's family originated in Trinidad, Jamaica, and came to Britain in the early 1950s.

Arabella's mixed-race heritage often made her feel like an outsider. At St Oswald's Secondary School, a group of lads used to tease her, call her a 'half-coon'. They even dropped her on her head once to see what colour her blood was.

At university, earnest, politically correct students asked her where she was from and when she replied 'Liverpool', it would be followed by, 'No, I mean where are you originally from?' as though she had to justify the colour of her skin.

Arabella flattened and then virtually lost any Scouse lilt in her accent, thinking that being 'a coloured Scouser' might hold her back in her career. Anyway, she hated the adenoidal twang of her family's accent – a blend of Irish, Welsh and ca-tarrh.

Headteacher Neerav Banerjee, late fifties, came out into the garden with a bottle of beer in hand. He was tall and handsome with black swept-back oily hair. Charming and friendly on the surface, Banerjee was in reality ruthless, ambitious and controlling. He was the perfect politician, which is what a headship required in the modern era of the education system.

'More thoughts on staff tattoos, Neerav?' Arabella asked. It was her pet hate.

'I agree with you. They do need to be covered at work,' he replied.

'I just don't get it. Middle-aged wobbly flab covered by permanent drawings that would have failed a GCSE in art,' she quipped. Neerav chortled, looking her up and down. Arabella didn't mind. In fact, she loved it as it confirmed what she knew to be true of Neerav, and most men in her experience – an erection cut off the blood supply to their brains. And sex for her was all about power and control.

Arabella sat down on the expensive garden furniture and looked out as the sun faded and darkness came. Things in her life were good. A new job on the horizon. The sexual attention of various men in the village. Beautiful house and garden.

'What's happening with Bronwyn Wright?' Arabella asked, sipping her drink. The internal politics of the school were everything to her. And skilfully manipulating them was her forte.

Neerav's voice lowered a little. 'She didn't come to the meeting yesterday. She has "work-related stress".'

'Occupational Health?'

'Next Thursday,' Neerav replied.

'She'll resign. She's a lazy wanker who's frankly had more chances than she deserves. As far as I'm concerned, she's gone. I'll send you the advert I've written for her job.' Arabella's tone was one of cold focus and she knew it turned Neerav on. She knew he wanted to shag her right there and then. And that was fine. He was good in bed. But it was no more than that. If he wanted to delude himself there was something deeper, that was his problem.

'Thanks, Arabella. Always one step ahead,' Neerav noted gratefully.

'That's what I'm here for. You know that, Neerav.' Arabella's tone was confident. 'Do your job properly or go. That's my motto.' Arabella made no attempt to endear herself to 'ordinary' members of staff. She didn't care that her haughtiness rubbed everyone up the wrong way. In fact, she liked it.

Arabella's phone vibrated in her jacket pocket. She took it out and glanced at the lit screen. A text message.

YOU'RE A BLACK NIGGER BITCH!

Arabella didn't react. Another prank text, but she looked up at the undergrowth at the rear of the garden anyway.

Was that a noise? No, she was just being paranoid. But it wasn't the first time she had heard something.

She put the phone away.

'Let's go inside. It's getting cold,' she said, and they went back into the house.

CHAPTER 2

A RED LONDON BUS TRUNDLED along Whitehall and stopped with a bursting hiss of air brakes. It was early spring, but winter still lurked, trying to cling on. The heavy traffic edged forwards at an interminable speed. Ruth turned into Richmond Terrace, passing a young bearded homeless man in a woollen hat asking for change. She stopped, crouched and gave him some coins and a smile.

'What's your name?' she asked. She could see that one of his eyes was completely red and bloodshot.

'Mark,' he replied.

'Where's home, Mark?' she asked.

'Halifax.' His northern accent was pronounced.

'Long way from Yorkshire. Are you getting any food or shelter, Mark?' she asked.

'Sometimes. I had a B&B for a bit but I started using again,' he explained.

'Do you know about Skylight Crisis?' she asked.

'No ...'

'Do you know Commercial Street, by Liverpool Street station?' she asked.

Mark nodded, his eyes widening in surprise that someone was trying to help him.

Looking at her watch, Ruth saw it was ten o'clock. 'Get there at eleven. There's a free drop-in session. They'll look after you and try to find you somewhere to stay.'

'Thanks,' Mark said, looking a little embarrassed.

'You take care of yourself, all right?' she said, and looked at him until he nodded.

She wished she could stay longer and do more. He was somebody's son. What did he dream he would be as a boy? What did his parents and family say when they predicted what that little child, playing beside them, would do when he grew up? She imagined how she would feel if her own daughter Ella, also in her early twenties, was living on the streets. *How does anyone think this is okay?*

Ruth pulled the collar of her dark raincoat up as an icy wind off the Thames swept against her. The screech of an ambulance's siren burst through the air and made her jump as it tried to navigate the heavy traffic. She watched as the emergency vehicle mounted the crowded pavement for a moment to bypass a stationary car and nearly hit a speeding cycle courier.

The very process of existing in London was stressful. Tension and anxiety hung in the air like a toxic nerve gas. Some people got off on it, but she didn't, and that's why she was glad she was leaving. In fact, she couldn't wait. London had changed so much. And there were too many ghosts. Too much hate and violence. Ruth dipped her hand reassuringly into her leather case that hung from a strap over her shoulder and took out a packet of Marlborough. She pulled out a ciggie and lit it, dragging deeply. *That's better.*

Two Chinese school children in blue blazers and ties whizzed past her on Segways. Ruth looked up at the building she was now stood in front of. For some, Scotland Yard evoked foggy nights, Sherlock Holmes, and wholesome 'Bobbies on the Beat'. However, the new home of the Met since 2016 – a state-of-the-art three-hundred-million-pound glass-fronted building – looked more like an advertising agency, which for her said it all about modern policing. Style over substance. It housed the Met's senior management team along with the Met's crime database – the Home Office Large Major Enquiry System, more commonly referred to by the acronym HOLMES – a nod to the literary traditions of London policing. They even knowingly called the training programme Elementary.

Ruth finished her ciggie, stubbed it out on a bin, and walked towards the entrance. She pulled out her ID warrant card at two security checks. Concrete barriers in front of the ground-level windows were a countermeasure against car bombing. A protective concrete wall surrounded the entrance to the building. The armed officers from the RASP – Royalty and Specialist Protection – patrolled the exterior of the building holding ISG MCX sub-machine guns at their sides. It was still unnerving even though it had been a daily sight for her for the last twelve years.

Ruth got to the revolving glass doors and entered. Passing through another security check, she strolled down to the plush canteen that smelt of cooked food and coffee.

Over in the corner, Chief Inspector Jess Gallow, whom she had worked with in South London, waved. If she was honest, Ruth had always had a crush on Jess. She could gaze into her big brown eyes forever. Now part of the Counter Terrorism Unit, Jess was based at Scotland Yard. She had done well for herself and Ruth was pleased for her.

Jess got up with a broad smile. 'Jess.' They hugged for a moment as people looked over. Police officers weren't known for their touchy-feeliness.

'*Chief Inspector* Gallow? Do I have to curtsy or bow now?' Ruth teased.

'Oh, shut up and get yourself a coffee,' Jess said with a laugh.

Ruth got an Americano and returned. 'God, what happened to the days when you could sit and have a coffee and ciggie?' Ruth could feel the craving for nicotine as soon as the coffee touched her lips, and it made her uncomfortable.

'That's progress, apparently. Anyway, I've given up,' Jess bragged.

'Have you? How long?' Ruth asked, impressed and jealous at the same time.

Jess looked at her watch, 'It's nearly eleven hours now.'

Ruth laughed. Jess was funny and had the ability to put her at ease within minutes, no matter how long it had been since they last saw each other. They would have made a brilliant couple if only Jess hadn't been straight.

'When's your last day?' Jess asked.

'Tomorrow. I'm all packed up and ready to go.'

'North bloody Wales Police force? Now that's not progress is it?' Jess raised a quizzical eyebrow.

'I've had enough. It's got so bad that I don't even register that I'm looking at another dead young person anymore. And North Wales is nice and quiet. Nothing wrong with that,' Ruth said defensively, though part of her suspected there were other reasons for her transfer. She knew, however, she was too long in the tooth to ever make it to detective chief inspector. Taking a back seat in the rural beauty of Snowdonia was what she needed.

'Why North Wales?' Jess asked.

Ruth shrugged. 'I spent a lot of time there when I was a kid. My dad had family in Conwy. His Auntie Dolly married a Welsh bloke called Charlie. They didn't have children, so they spoiled me and my brother rotten.' In that moment, Ruth remembered all the presents at Christmas, Easter, birthdays, and even just for arriving on their summer holidays. Barbies, Action Men, Buckaroo, Mousetrap, and even an Atari one year. *Asteroids*. Ruth was fantastic at *Asteroids* on the Atari and no one could beat her.

'You'll get bored. Unless you're happy to be a big fish in a small pond?'

'Oh God. I don't want to arrive as some cockney know-it-all from the Met,' Ruth said pulling a face.

Jess shrugged. 'Regardless of its problems, there's nothing like the Met.'

Ruth had thought the same thing frequently. But her life as a copper in London had made her cynical. Watching human beings at their worst. The amount of death, destruction and mayhem she saw on a daily basis. She also had to contend with the covert bullying of DCI Jim Parsons at Peckham CID who had managed to chip away at her confidence and morale in the last two years. But it wasn't something she could ever report. The Met wasn't like that.

'Honestly, I need boring. I'm running on empty. It's beautiful up there. And technically I wouldn't be here if it wasn't for North Wales.'

'How's that?'

'My grandmother took my dad up to Conwy at the height of the Blitz. He was only three. They stayed with her sister. And when they got back two years later to the house in Balham, it had gone - along with half the street. Direct hit from a Luftwaffe incendiary bomb. So, if they hadn't gone up to our family in North Wales, I wouldn't be sitting here talking to you today,' Ruth explained.

'Right. Well, it's the Met's loss.' Jess gave her a sympathetic look. 'I'm only jealous. You've been through a lot. And nicking speeding tractors until you can claim your pension might be just what you need. It will be a whole lot better than all that mayhem you deal with down in Peckham.'

"Couldn't get any worse, could it? I'll take speeding tractors, poaching and sheep rustling for the next few years." And then Ruth thought of her daughter. 'And Ella is over in Liverpool so I'll get to see more of her.' She sipped her coffee for a moment and then said, 'It won't solve what happened with Sarah. But it'll be a new start which might help.'

The ghost of Sarah followed her everywhere. And it was exhausting.

At around eight on the morning of 5 November 2013, Ruth's partner and love of her life, Sarah Goddard, got on a train at Crystal Palace station but never arrived at the other end at Victoria. She vanished. She disappeared off the face of the planet and had not been seen since.

'There's no news on that, is there?' Jess asked.

Ruth shook head. There had been no news for over four years. They had trawled every frame of CCTV, every possible witness and sighting. There had been extensive news coverage, appeals, social media and posters. Nothing.

'I don't know how you've got through it,' Jess confessed.

'Sometimes I don't get through it. Sometimes I just sit and cry. But I have to keep busy or I'll go mad,' Ruth said.

'Is it why you're going to Wales?' Jess asked.

'Maybe. A new start can't hurt, can it?'

'I don't want to burst your bubble but just be careful. Ghosts have a habit of following you wherever you go,' Jess said.

Ruth knew that was probably true, but she was going anyway.

HAD HE FORGOTTEN SOMETHING? What was it? He thought he could grasp it but it was out of range. Restless and agitated. And now it had gone. Christ! A horse seemed near and its nostrils flared with hot breath that steamed in the cold, which he could feel on his face. And now a funeral procession from a bygone era. A Victorian Welsh street with wet cobbles, dark and icy – thick fog obscured anything in the distance. Four black horses, resplendent with ostrich feathers and velvet drapes, proceeded slowly. A hearse trundled and shook as it rattled along the cobbled road. Gold leaf writing, Bisset & Sons, *and flowers that spelt the name* Nicholas. *Men with top hats and tails and the sound of the wooden elm wheels clattering. Nick turned trying to get his breath, fearing he would suffo-*

cate. The more he ran towards the funeral procession, the further away it seemed to get. A church tower that had a clock with no hands. Dewi Hughes, the man he'd seen dead and headless the day before, smiled from the crowd on the pavement. Beside him stood Nick's father Rhys, dressed in the smart red ceremonial military uniform of the Welsh Fusiliers. Nick tried to punch him but was dragged away.

He saw a medieval gallows appear out of the fog. A solemn-looking man, grey beard and a crooked nose, walked forwards. Dressed in a dark purple robe, this was St Thomas Glynn. They put a noose around Nick's neck and he crossed himself. Looking to the sky and God, he plummeted through the trapdoor with the crack of wood hitting wood. He hung for a moment, kicking his legs almost comically, and then died.

Nick woke with a start, took a deep breath and held it for a moment. He exhaled with an audible sigh. The pulse in his carotid artery, to the side of his windpipe, thudded like a drum. He lay still in the darkness, cursing the anxiety in the pit of his stomach. Even a tingling in his testicles. That's when he knew his anxiety was high. Processing the dream for a moment, he stared at the ceiling. A dream that reminded Nick that one day he would die.

He put his hand to the left of the bed and patted the duvet. No one beside him. Good. The sheets and mattress were dry, which was another positive. He hadn't wet the bed that night. The back of his neck was covered in sweat and so was his pillow. Why was he wide awake? He reached for his watch but knew from the darkness outside that it was still early. A quarter to five. He lifted a full glass of water and his hand trembled a little. Alcoholic shakes. He lay back and listened intently to the darkness. *How did I get here? To this point?* His pulse slowed a little.

Nick got out of bed and crossed over to the window. The curtains were open, as they were every night. When he couldn't sleep, he felt more comfortable looking out at the night sky. In Alcoholics Anonymous they called it his 'Higher Power'. A spiritual connection to something greater than himself. It was less claustrophobic maybe? However, his Higher Power was failing him miserably at the moment and he needed a drink. It's the first drink that gets you drunk. Not the fourth or the fifth. The first. But he knew that. He didn't need self-righteous slogans reverberating around his head at this time of the morning. Already his body had tensed with anger.

He peered over at the house opposite, trying to penetrate the darkness. An old retired couple lived there. Nick knew them to wave to, but they were God-bothering Presbyterian Christians and their smugness made him want to do them physical harm. God had abandoned him long ago and Nick held grudges.

And then he caught his reflection in the glass and didn't like what he saw. In fact, 'didn't like' wouldn't cut it. He loathed what he saw.

As a boy, everyone said that Nick looked like his mother. Dark, hooded eyes, slim nose and a strong chin. Now everyone claimed that Nick was the 'spit' of his maternal grandfather, Bryn, especially now he'd grown a beard. Nick wondered if he would look like his father when he grew old. His super at work declared it happened to everyone. 'One day you wake up, look in the mirror and you realise you're shaving your father.' Maybe that's why Nick grew the beard? He had no desire to be like his father, ever, or anything that looked like him. The hate and resentment were still there and, no matter how much he talked to his AA sponsor, it never seemed to dissipate.

His super, John Jones, told CID two days ago that a new detective inspector would be arriving today from the Met in London, which was just what Nick needed. Some arrogant cockney know-it-all 'giving it the big one' and putting all their backs up. Bloody English. They were short of DIs but if she patronised anyone in CID, then Nick was all ready to set her straight. He had already rehearsed what he would say to her as soon as she started. He'd played that conversation out in his brain a few times already. That's just what he was like.

Nick felt bitterness towards the London Met since Thatcher sent them to police the striking Welsh miners during 1984. His whole extended family worked at the Bersham Colliery. He had heard their stories of how the Met had arrived boasting they were 'up for it' and antagonising them into fighting with them. When the Met Police coaches passed through lines of his striking uncles and cousins, the officers waved five-pound notes – 'Lady Godivas' – at them.

In the evenings, while Welsh miners were at home with no money, the 'cockneys' went on the piss in local pubs, bragging about all the overtime, labelling the miners as 'Commie Taffs', and bought the local women drinks and shagged them.

Only one thing for it, Nick thought as he trudged towards the kitchen, opened the fridge and pulled out a half-bottle of vodka. He put it to his lips, took a breath and swallowed two large mouthfuls. A few seconds later, it hit his stomach. Then his abdominal muscles and diaphragm contracted powerfully, he retched and threw up the clear liquid onto the floor. Nothing new there. He tried it again and began to dry retch. Salt. He needed something salty to keep the vodka in his stomach long enough to pass into his blood stream. Taking a piece of thickly-buttered bread, he shook salt onto it and ate a mouthful. He crunched the snack, waited two seconds, and then gulped a mouthful of vodka.

A minute went by. So far so good. He risked another mouthful and then another, plus more salt which was doing the trick. The warmth of the vodka radiated from his stomach and there was relief in his head and body. Thank God for that. Slumping against the kitchen counter, he took a deep breath before falling back into bed with the vodka bottle beside him.

CHAPTER 3

RUTH HAD BEEN DRIVING for two hours. It had been twenty years since she last visited North Wales. Now it would be home for a while. Along the M54, she passed the turnings to Telford and then Ironbridge, making a mental note she must visit one day, but knowing full well she had been making the same promise for years.

Soul II Soul's *Back to Life* played on the radio and Ruth sang along. *Club Classics Volume 1* was the sound of 1989 and she knew every word of every song. She had seen Soul II Soul live at The Fridge in Brixton in 1991 and it was her favourite gig ever. Taking ecstasy for the first time, she had popped a Dennis the Menace – so-called because the capsule was black and red – and remembered she never wanted the night to end. Sitting in Brockwell Park smoking weed and drinking wine from a bottle, Ruth and her friends watched the sun come up.

The Shropshire countryside stretched away on both sides of the road with not a building in sight. It was mid-morning and, to the right, the sun threatened to burn away the cloud cover, giving the sky a strange white light. To the left, a more leaden sky headed her way. If she squinted, Ruth could see rain falling on the ridges of Myndtown Hill and the top of Black Knoll in the distance. Without taking her eyes off the road, Ruth delved into her handbag on the passenger seat and pulled out a cigarette and lighter. She put the ciggie in her mouth, lit it, and took a deep drag. *That's better.*

The sprawling countryside gave Ruth a lift. The pain of London life and what had happened with Sarah haunted her daily. People told her it would get better, but it just didn't. In fact, it got worse. She had tried to rise above it and not let it affect her, but that was impossible. So, this was a new start. A quieter life.

Ruth was heading for the beauty and simplicity of North Wales. It had been a family ritual for their summer holiday to come to this beautiful part of the world every year, its hills and valley now so familiar. Long, interminable journeys in the family mustard-coloured Rover 2000, an old tape recorder playing Culture Club or Lionel Richie until the batteries ran out, or their parents decided it was time for Cliff Richard or Neil Diamond. They couldn't afford a car stereo but when they belted out *Dancing on the Ceiling*, it didn't seem to matter.

Someone once wrote that 'youth is wasted on the young'. Now she knew exactly what they meant.

NICK PULLED INTO A narrow space in the car park at St Mark's Church. He turned off the engine and continued to listen to Rag and Bone Man.

Hesitating for a moment, he pursed his lips and looked over at the closed glove compartment. He leant back in the seat and glanced around. The clattering rain was getting worse and the covering of raindrops now gave the car's windows a protective shield. Nick was becoming invisible inside, which was a good thing. Away from the prying and judgement. The song *Human* continued, its lyrics seeming to justify his need for a drink.

Nick reached over and opened the glove compartment. The clunk of glass against solid plastic as the bottle of red wine rolled into view. *Thank God. That's a relief.* There was nothing worse than forgetting how much was left, seeing an empty bottle and realising you were totally screwed.

Nick grabbed the bottle, spun the cap and pinged down half a bottle in three aromatic gulps. Nick liked the sound of the verb *ping* in his head. *I'm just going to ping down half a bottle of red.* Supermarket Shiraz, £3.99. And more importantly 16% abv; not quite sherry but close enough. It wasn't going to stay in the bottle long enough to buy anything decent.

And then the absolute relief and joy as the alcohol zipped through his neurotransmitters and brought calm to his brain stem. *God, that feels good already.* Blood vessels dilated, serotonin and dopamine did their stuff. Nick exhaled. *I'm back in the game.* Back to 'normal'. The clock inside the car told him he still had ten minutes.

He sat back and looked up at the church that nestled on the corner of the high street in Dinas Padog. It had been originally built as a parish church in 1887 and designed in a fourteenth-century Decorated-Gothic style. From the car, Nick could see the modern stained-glass window, made at the local college of art in the 1960s in memory of the martyr St Thomas Glynn. Glynn was a schoolmaster who refused to become a Protestant and was hanged, drawn and quartered for his faith by the English in Llancastell's beast market in 1564. For revenge, his ghost haunted the English soldiers who executed him, driving them mad and eventually suicidal. Nick loved the idea of a Welsh ghost getting his own back on his English oppressors. He felt a great affinity with the ghost of St Thomas Glynn and greater affinity with his vendetta. Nick had once even asked his sponsor if St Glynn's ghost could be his Higher Power, before realising how crazy that made him sound.

When Nick was eleven, and on a school trip, he had seen a model of St Thomas Glynn, which was mounted on replica gallows. Nick was fascinated by the story even as a boy. The gallows in the church were the gallows from his dream.

Nick took his car keys from the ignition, got out, and jogged towards an open door, shaking water from his coat. He chucked two extra-strong mints into his mouth and crunched. *That'll hide the smell of booze,* he thought.

This was it. Today was the day he would stop drinking. *This time I've had enough. I'm going to tough it out with the sweats and shakes. Even if I have to take a few days off work and just lie in bed suffering. I'm going to fight it and stop.*

Nick thought the meeting room to the side of St Mark's Catholic Church was a reassuring time warp. The room was being used for a Thursday midday Alcoholics Anonymous meeting. It had changed little since the 1970s. The walls were painted two tawdry shades of green – lime and emerald – separated by an old picture rail. A huge fireplace dominated the far wall. It was framed with Victorian ceramic tiles, and across the worn oak mantel were small ceramic statues of Our Lady and the saints.

Nick sat in his regular grey, plastic seat at the back. That way he could avoid too much chit-chat and no one would smell the booze on his breath. He also knew he had no intention of 'sharing' today. His voice tended to slur with this amount of alcohol in his bloodstream and it was a total giveaway.

To one side, a grey-bearded man in his late sixties, Will, was sitting with his legs crossed. Nick thought he was a pompous twat. That was the perfect word for Will. Not very holistic or karmic but he didn't care. Total twat.

As a middle-aged woman stopped her 'share', Will sat upright a little. 'Hello, my name's Will and I'm an alcoholic.'

'Hello, Will,' the room responded like a congregation.

Nick prepared himself to hear the same share that Will trundled out with regularity. *The man lacks any self-awareness*, Nick thought to himself, despite being over twenty years sober.

'Thanks for your share, Yvonne. I always enjoy hearing what you've got to say. And I found myself ...'

Blah, blah, blah. Nick had already drifted away and switched off. *What the hell am I doing here? It's not working. 'Keep coming back,' they always say. 'It works if you work it.' No thanks. Just piss off!* Nick's anger was already rising. He was wasting his time and getting angry, so he waited for the tea break, left, and sat in the car finishing the wine. That was more like it.

That was the terrible truth. The world was a better place when he had booze in his system.

CHAPTER 4

IT WAS HALF PAST SEVEN and the car park at *Ysgol Dinas Padog* was emptying. Year 11 parents' evening was over. A few students, in bottle-green blazers and loosened ties, lingered awkwardly with chatting parents.

The school's sports hall was what you would expect of a seventies build. High ceiling, open-brick walls, basketball hoops, and a complicated intersection of multi-coloured lines to mark out a variety of sports. Desks and chairs were being stacked and put away by the caretakers, with a metallic clatter.

Caretaker Mike Gardner had worked at Dinas Padog for nearly thirty years. He was small, not much over five foot six. He was wide without being overweight. An ex-paratrooper, someone once quipped that he was so barrel-chested that it looked as if he'd swallowed a fire extinguisher. His skin, especially on his face, seemed to have a permanent tan. A dark oak colour. No one knew why and neither did he, so he was 'Mike Tan' to his local friends. He put it down to gypsy ancestors although there were always jokes about his secret supply of man tan.

He stacked the chairs onto the red iron trolley. After what he'd seen in Northern Ireland, he liked the simple life. No stress. No bother.

Between 1971 and 1996, fifty-one men of the Parachute Regiment were killed while serving in Northern Ireland. The first was Mike's friend, Sergeant Ashley Willet, 3rd Battalion. He was killed during a bombing incident at the Springfield Road Police Station in Belfast. The IRA left a hand-carried bomb in a suitcase at the front of the station. Sergeant Willet held open a door allowing members of the public and police officers to escape and then stood in the doorway, shielding those taking cover. For his actions, Willet was awarded the George Cross. Mike felt scant consolation - he had helped put bits of his friend into bags. So, it was for good reason that Mike wanted life to be quiet and mundane.

Suddenly, there was a commotion as chairs and a desk clattered to the floor on the far side of the hall. Mike looked over to see Dylan Wilkins, a general handyman and caretaker, a tall young man in glasses and a floppy fringe, looking blankly at the fallen chairs and desk. *Oh great! Now what?* Mike wondered as he watched Dylan blink for a moment, not knowing how to react but looking shaken by the event. Dylan clasped his hands together and rocked. Mike needed to go over to him. Dylan was on the autistic spectrum so it didn't take much for him to get freaked out.

Mike walked over with a fatherly smile. He was fond of Dylan. 'Don't worry, Dylan. Come on, lad, I'll give you a hand.'

'Sorry, I'm sorry, Mike. I dunno what happened ...' Dylan's tone was that of a worried child.

'No harm done,' Mike said, trying to reassure him. He knew that Dylan was easily upset.

Arabella Dixon entered the sports hall, ignoring Mike and Dylan tidying away the evening's event. They weren't worth acknowledging. She was wearing a black, fitted business suit, with a laptop bag swinging down by her side, and knew she looked the part. Marching over to a table where a small red plastic sign bore her name – *Miss A Dixon* – she picked up her forgotten planner and placed it into her bag.

Arabella had left the rest of her department in the staff room, scoffing the sandwiches and cakes provided at the end of parents' evenings. It made her angry to watch them gorge, as many of the female teachers were bordering on morbidly obese already. She listened to them explain their latest diet regimes but refused to join in. It pushed all her buttons because what she hated was others' lack of self-control. She watched colleagues dive in for second or third helpings of cake during department meetings or coursework moderation. And when they complained of guilt and talked of 'sins', she would target them in her imaginary cross-hair sights, give a withering look and let fly with, 'You could just not eat it.'

'Arabella?' a confident male voice. It was Neerav Banerjee. She made a show of being pleased to see him, especially as she was relying on him for an outstanding reference in the next few months.

However, next to him was Graham Williams, the rather eccentric assistant head, whom she couldn't stand. He had flowing grey locks and a natty blue suit and orange tie. Everything about him was affected.

'Hi Neerav. Graham.' Arabella forced her smile. 'I think tonight was a success.'

'Except for our most disadvantaged students who were no-shows again,' sniped Graham. His voice was deep with a strong North Wales accent. *He is such a twat,* Arabella thought. There had been little love lost between her and Graham. He thought she was a bully and only interested in her career. She thought he was a dinosaur. Arabella also thought there was something distinctly creepy about him. She had flagged up to Neerav the time Graham spent unofficially 'counselling' sixth formers with emotional problems and that it was inappropriate. Neerav shrugged it off, saying that Graham was a well-meaning, Bible-bashing Baptist who thought he could save the souls of troubled young people.

'Well, goodnight, gentlemen. I'll see you in the morning.' She spun on her heels and left.

Arabella knew that Neerav was watching her as she walked away. She ensured her hips moved and rolled just enough to cause him to stiffen a little. *That's the game, and I'm bloody good at playing it*, she thought.

It was now nearly eight o'clock and dark outside. Arabella made her way out of the school, striding purposefully along the empty maths corridor and then through the rear car park, secure in the knowledge she'd handled everything superbly. She thought about the new potential headship at Neston on the Wirral that she had identified in an advert in the *TES* last week. A good school, but she already knew where she would make changes. After a year or two, she knew they would think they were lucky to have her. *Bring on the new challenge,* she thought with a modicum of excitement.

The sound of heavy rain broke her thoughts as it clattered off buildings and car roofs, bouncing and splashing on every surface.

As Arabella used her security card to open the glass doors, her phone buzzed with a text message. She clicked her phone to read.

Southern trees bear strange fruit
Blood on the leaves and blood at the root
Black bodies swinging in the southern breeze
Strange fruit hanging from the poplar trees.
Nigger bitch!

Arabella ignored this and gazed up at the night sky, now filled with large, falling raindrops. She saw an indistinguishable figure emerge from the shadows of the corrugated iron bike shed. She pulled her black umbrella from her bag. Always prepared. Unfurling the umbrella up with a decisive snap, she went for a walk-run across the wet surface of the car park. The splash of water was cold against her ankles.

It was dark and there was too much rain for Arabella to see anything, but the hooded shape seemed to move to follow her. Or was that just her imagination? She stopped a moment to look and then resumed her trot for her car, assuming it was another member of staff.

The figure approached, splashing through the emerging puddles. Something about this person's hurried movements annoyed Arabella. This was not the time or the weather for any conversation. She turned to see what the hell they wanted. It better not be one of those over-keen parents ...

Arabella frowned when she saw the figure up close. 'What are you doing out here?' she asked, indicating the rain and sounding surprised.

The figure didn't respond but aimed a punch that connected sharply with her mouth and cut her lip. She staggered back but remained on her feet. Now dazed, she dropped the umbrella, bewildered about what was going on.

'What the hell are—'

A gloved hand reached out. Arabella instinctively went to protect her throat. She backed away, going into survival mode. What the hell was happening? She turned, and the hand tried to pull her back by the plastic identity badge she wore around her neck. However, the force with which the figure pulled snapped the lanyard against her neck, leaving a small burn mark against her skin.

'What are you doing?' she shouted as she shoved the figure backwards. Was this really happening? Her disbelief and anger was now escalating into fear.

Arabella turned and ran, breaking the heel on her left shoe. She panicked and looked for an escape, but was surrounded by cars blocking her way. Sprinting through the narrow gap between two cars, her hip bone banged hard against a metal door handle. Normally it would have hurt, but her overriding emotion was now terror. The gate to the back of the school was closed and locked. It had been a long shot. *Shit!* She was trapped. She flicked off both shoes in a mad bid to run faster barefoot. Her whole body burnt with fear.

Glancing around in panic, she ducked and hid behind the school minibus. She fumbled frantically to open the pink leather case of her mobile phone, then pushed the power button. Looking at the screen that carried the white Apple logo, she begged it to load quickly. *Come on, come on.* Her pulse thumped noisily in her ear. The phone was still turning itself on. Where was her attacker? Maybe they had gone? She could call the police and hide until they arrived.

'Come on, for God's sake ...' her quiet, terrified voice urged the phone to burst into life. It didn't. Seconds of eternity. The rhythmic bang of her heartbeat. She took out her car keys and held the ignition key between her thumb and forefinger like a weapon. It had a fob hanging from it that read *Save Water – Drink Prosecco.* Her hands were shaking, and the terror was making her feel sick.

She could plunge the key into her attacker's face or even eyeball?

Please don't let me die, she thought.

Out of nowhere, strong hands spun her around, pushed her roughly against the wire fence, and a forearm crushed her windpipe. She coughed, gasping for air, tears running down her face. The other gloved hand covered and pinched her nose and mouth.

'Get off me!' She could feel her voice weakening. She was sucking desperately for air. She snatched at a handful of clothing, hair, anything, but only grabbed air. Her head was starting to swim. *Don't faint,* she told herself. She lashed out with the car keys and hit the figure's body, but the force jolted the keys out of her grip and they fell onto the wet concrete. Her vision was now blurring and losing clarity.

Arabella smashed her phone as hard as she could against the assailant's face, connecting with bone, but the killer was unmoved and her phone dropped with a sharp crack.

She was fighting for breath and for life. *Please someone help*. She clawed at the figure's face but she just couldn't breathe. They were whispering something.

She lashed out again and struck bone and flesh but it was too late.

Everything went black.

CHAPTER 5

IT WAS GETTING LATE, and outside it was dark and raining. The raindrops pattered on the large glass windows of the sixth floor of the North Wales Police Eastern Divisional Headquarters. The dotted lights of Llancastell stretched away into the distance before the shadowy ridges of Snowdonia loomed into view on the horizon.

Ruth had been in the CID office for over an hour for an informal induction. She was tired and hungry and looking forward to getting to her hotel. Gazing around at her new surroundings, she felt a little disappointed about what would now be her place of work. Everything looked dated and old-fashioned compared to the modern CID offices of South London.

The office was open plan with twenty or more work stations, computers and flat-screen monitors. Desks were covered in box files and paperwork. To one side the Robbery Team, another area for the Burglary Team, and a more discrete area for the Family Crisis Intervention Unit which dealt with domestic violence and child protection.

The chief superintendent had briefed her on how North Wales Police worked, the make-up of CID, and what he was expecting from her in her role. He was impressed by the level of her experience. Yet, Ruth still had that nagging twinge of imposter syndrome. Whatever she had achieved in her –

not insubstantial – career, Ruth never seemed to build any internal surety of meaningful confidence. She knew she was a good police officer, she always did her job as best she could, but no matter her success rate, she still feared that one day she would be 'found out' as a fraud.

It didn't take long for Ruth to get the measure of Chief Superintendent John Jones as they sat in the CID office. He was one of those unattractive men, thick-set, balding but smart, who seemed to have an abundance of wit, confidence and charisma that some women found very appealing. He believed his own 'publicity' and, because of that, it seemed to make it true. She guessed that he had been divorced three or four times, with countless affairs, but women still believed that they would be the one to rescue him from himself.

Ruth had met men like this before. In fact, it seemed to be a prerequisite of the higher ranks of the Metropolitan Police. Relationships, marriages, affairs were just tidal – one rolled in as another rolled out. That was just human nature.

Ruth ignored Jones' attempts at charm and glanced around the office again, watching a young male CID officer through the glass having a quiet 'discussion' with an older female uniformed officer. The arrogance of CID officers to-wards uniform was often a source of conflict. It had always been that way and Ruth remembered exactly what it was like when she was in uniform. Being treated as a glorified assis-tant, expected to take statements, and other 'menial' tasks. Ruth had worked with police officers who, once they had transferred from uniform to CID and bought their Matalan suit, thought they were Inspector bloody Morse. Far too im-portant to leave the office unless there was a major incident.

She thought about her first skipper in CID, Detective Inspector 'Uncle' Terry Harrison. His motto was *Deprehendo Deprehensio Vitum,* which translates as 'Overtime Solves Crime'. Terry was a big drinker in the days when that was a requirement of CID. After a stressful day, which was most of them, he'd sink eight pints, a doner kebab with extra chilli sauce, and then take 'a blue-light taxi' home. But his man management was brilliant, and he could read what you were thinking in an instant. He had no qualms about publicly bollocking an officer, but he would also make you feel a hundred feet tall two minutes later. She bloody loved him, but coppers like Uncle Terry were thin on the ground these days. Especially if the Tory government got their way and every copper would need a degree to join the force. They didn't have a clue.

'Well, DI Hunter, it seems that should be about everything.' Jones said, picking up some paperwork. 'Having a hugely experienced detective from the Met in our CID is going to be just what we need. I think you should be able to head to your hotel to get some beauty sleep before the big day tomorrow—'

Before the Chief Superintendant could finish, there was a rap at the door and a young officer stuck his head in. 'Sorry, sir, but you'll want to see this.'

Beyond the glass, the whole mood of CID had completely changed.

As Jones came out to see what was going on, DS Nick Evans approached and said, 'Sir, we've got reports of a suspicious death at the school in Dinas Padog.'

'Any details?' Jones asked.

'Could be a teacher. And first responders say it looks like she was attacked,' Nick explained.

Jones looked at over at Ruth. 'Sorry to ruin your evening but I've got all three of my DIs working on the county lines project with Merseyside and the NCA. I'll need you to step in on this as the SIO to start off with. If I get one of my DIs back, we can take a view then.'

Ruth couldn't believe her luck. She just wanted a hot bath, a gin and tonic, a ciggie and bed.

She could see that Nick was visibly bristling. 'Sir, with all respect DI Hunter has just arrived. And Dinas Padog is my old school and where I live. I'm more than happy to lead the investigation as a temporary measure.'

'Thanks, Nick, but DI Hunter has twenty-five years' experience in the Met. I'm sure that she's more than capable of hitting the ground running,' Jones said in a withering tone. 'If you can go along with her, show her the ropes, that kind of thing.'

Nick gave them a look like he'd been asked to clean out the toilets and walked away without saying anything.

'He'll grow on you,' Jones said sardonically.

Just what she needed on her first night. A murder and an angry Welshman whose toes she had stepped all over.

TWENTY MINUTES LATER, Nick and Ruth were racing along the B127 at speed. The CID dark blue Astra CDTi's blue LED lights were flickering and siren shrieking – 'blues and twos' – to clear what little rural traffic there was. However, Ruth spotted a labouring John Deere tractor, with its distinctive green and yellow colouring, lumbering into view. Nick pulled onto the opposite side of the winding country road and flew past. Ruth's heart was in her mouth.

'For God's sake!' Nick said under his breath and gave the farmer a glare.

Ruth ignored Nick. She had already taken a dislike to him. She looked up at the sky above them. It was true what they said. No city light pollution out here, and the moon seemed big and bright now that the storm had moved on. It cast patterned shadows on the hills and countryside.

She wondered where her gentle introduction into rural Welsh policing had gone?

'Been in the job long, Nick?' she asked after a few more minutes of stony silence.

'A while,' Nick mumbled.

'And when did you do your sergeants' exams?' she asked.

'I think it's best that I just concentrate on driving, don't you?' he snapped.

Ruth could see they weren't going to do the whole 'getting to know you' thing. She had made an attempt to break the ice. Sod him if he wants to make things difficult. She could always pull rank on him if he acted like a prick. The atmosphere in the car felt a little tense, and Nick had made it clear earlier that he resented her arrival in CID.

Ruth clicked on her Tetra radio. 'This is DI Hunter to Control. In terms of the scene at Dinas Padog High School, are the exits secure? We need an inner and outer cordon set as soon as possible. No one leaves the school site.'

The CAD operator crackled back on the radio. 'Yes, ma'am. Victim's name is Arabella Dixon. Looks like there was a struggle. That's all we've got at the moment. Uniformed officers have secured the site already.'

'Okay. Thank you, we're en route.'

Ruth saw Nick give her a sideways glance. Maybe he had just realised that she did actually know what she was doing.

Getting evidence in 'the golden hour' after the crime had been committed was vital. The scene was fresh, it had not been contaminated, and it might not have been there for long. It was imperative that they do things quickly.

They drove the last few minutes of the journey in silence.

The rain had stopped its incessant drumming by the time Nick and Ruth pulled into the staff car park at Ysgol Dinas Padog. Instead, there was a more half-hearted drizzle hanging in the air, as if the energy of the storm had been taken away by the darker events of the evening. A storm no longer seemed appropriate or dignified.

There was already a luminous tapestry of yellow, white and blue lights at the scene where emergency signs, vehicles, an ambulance, four squad cars, uniformed officers, and two SOCO vehicles with *Heddlu/Police* markings had already been set up. Ruth could hear the crackle of a radio but otherwise the area was still and quiet. The chilling, unreal atmosphere at a murder scene that made stomachs turn.

Nick took the key out of the ignition. 'Bet you thought you'd escaped up here for a quiet life, ma'am?' Nick's tone was darkly sardonic.

Ruth ignored him. She knew he was having a pop. She opened the door and eased herself out of the car. It was true.

She hadn't planned on being launched straight into a murder enquiry, let alone take the lead. She had hoped for the sheep rustling, tractor theft or whatever else the mocking banter of her colleagues at Peckham nick had suggested her new duties would be. Her parting gifts at her leaving do had been an inflatable sheep and a dildo fashioned to look like a Welsh leek. That's subtle cockney humour for you.

'We get one or two of these a year, if that,' Nick explained.

'Good timing on my part then,' Ruth replied in a sarcastic tone.

As they approached the blue and white police cordon tape, Ruth looked over the school buildings. A mish-mash of functional school architecture, if it could be called that, from the last five decades.

'In the Met, it's once or twice a week,' Ruth said in a dismissive tone. She wanted him to know from the outset she was experienced and really knew her stuff.

When Ruth was working in Peckham, there was often more than one murder a week – mostly gang and drugs related. Stabbings mainly, but shootings were on the rise too. London's Operation Trident had been a disaster. The idea to have a dedicated unit targeting black-gang gun crime was progressive. In parts of inner-city London, the culture of gun crime affected whole communities and there were neighbourhoods where ninety per cent of homicide victims were black men. However, Ruth wasn't in the mood to talk the complexities and failings of inner-city London policing now.

'Know much about this school?' she asked.

'Should do, ma'am. I went here. Everyone round here did,' Nick replied.

'You know I'd prefer *boss* to *ma'am,* otherwise I sound like the bloody queen. So ... what's the school like?' Ruth was still looking around.

'Nice rural school. No big problems. The odd farmer's boy who didn't want to be here but nothing nasty. Bit of weed once in a while. It's a good school,' Nick explained. Ruth thought Nick sounded like he was defending his school's reputation.

'Control's report said that the victim was one of the teachers. What kind of person attacks and kills a teacher?' Ruth was thinking aloud.

'I don't know. There were a few teachers at my school I would have gladly killed given half the chance. Some of them were right bastards, you know what I mean?' Nick joked.

Ruth ignored him. He was doing little to dispel her judgement that he was immature and parochial.

Reaching the uniformed officers who were manning the police cordon and crime scene, they showed their warrant cards.

'Detective Inspector Hunter and Detective Sergeant Evans. Are you the FOA, Constable?' Ruth asked, immediately taking the lead. The FOA was the 'first officer in attendance' at the scene of a crime.

The female constable, slim, dark haired, who was holding her notebook, nodded. 'Yes, ma'am, I was first on the scene,' the constable said, looking pale and shocked at having found a murder victim.

'Are you okay?' Ruth asked. Seeing your first murder victim was always traumatic and she could see the constable was struggling.

'Bit shaken, ma'am, but yeah, I'm fine, thanks.'

'If you're sure?' Ruth gave her a kind smile to reassure her.

'I'm sure.'

'So, what have we got?' Ruth asked.

'Victim is an IC3 or M1 female. Arabella Dixon. She's the deputy head teacher at the school. Looks like there was some kind of struggle. Marks around her neck. Broken heel on her shoe. Some scratches or cuts on the back of her hand. Might be defensive wounds.'

The Police IC codes were used to identify race. IC3 meant black Caribbean. M1 signified black and white mixed race.

The constable walked with Ruth and Nick as they ducked under the tape and made their way over to the white scene of crime tent that had already been erected over the victim's body.

Ruth could see that scene of crime officers had just arrived. Two forensic halogen arc-lights on stands burst into life and dazzled her for a moment. Other SOCOs were taking crime scene photographs and a video. She was pleased that everything so far was in hand just as she would have expected it. Maybe Llancastell wasn't quite as provincial as she had feared ...

'Dixon? Name doesn't ring a bell. Who found the victim?' Nick asked.

'Mike Gardener, sir. He's the caretaker here. He thought she had collapsed, so he attempted CPR and then when there was no response, the other caretaker, Dylan Wilkins, dialled the emergency services,' she replied consulting her notebook.

'We'll need to speak to them both. Preferably tonight, constable. Take separate statements from them both and see if they match.' Ruth was calmly getting into her stride.

'Yes, ma'am. They both seem very shocked though.'

'Mike Gardener's my uncle,' Nick ventured under his breath, too quickly.

'Right?' Ruth looked at him quizzically. 'Small world.' This was a tightly knit community. She didn't know if that made things easier or more difficult.

Nick shrugged defensively. 'Thought I should flag that up in case it becomes a conflict of interest, that's all.'

Ruth ignored him again. 'What time was the victim found, Constable?'

'Just after eight, ma'am. He couldn't be precise.'

Nick took this in for a moment. 'Seems late. Why was the victim here?'

'Parents' evening, sir.'

Ruth nodded, thinking out loud, and said, 'So, the place would have been busy. What time did the parents' evening end?'

'Seven thirty, ma'am. But only staff had access to park their cars in this rear car park. Parents had to park out the front,' the constable replied.

'Okay. Constable, could you make sure there's a proper scene log? Everyone needs to sign in and out, whatever rank they are. Okay?' Ruth said politely and turned to Nick. 'Let's see what SOCO has to say.'

They put on a set of white SOCO overalls, purple latex gloves, paper shoes, and a face mask.

Ruth walked over, then took a moment, gazing only at Arabella Dixon's feet that were shoeless and in black tights. Her feet were splayed at an unnatural angle. She could feel it in the pit of her stomach. Death.

Nick took an audible breath and Ruth noticed.

'All right, Sergeant?' she asked, wondering if there was a chink in Nick's tough Welshman act.

'Yeah, of course,' Nick replied dismissively.

Ruth moved her gaze up the body and to the pallid skin of Arabella Dixon's face. Her eyes were open, glassy and dark. For a second, she felt sucked in and compelled to look into them. Into that emptiness where death lay.

Walking closer, Ruth squinted in the harshness of the SOCO lights. It reminded her of dozens of crime scenes from before. She looked at the victim's colourless face, neck, and the position of her body. She had been murdered. There was no doubt in her mind. And Ruth knew she was now responsible for Arabella Dixon. For her family, for her friends, and for those in the community.

Ruth turned to the chief SOCO and said, 'As far as I'm concerned this is now a murder scene.' She then turned to Nick, 'Sergeant, I'm going to need everyone in CID in so I can brief them as soon as possible.'

As Nick walked in front of her, Ruth looked up at the inky blackness and the stars that glistened above her. She had been in Snowdonia for less than twenty-four hours and was running a murder case.

Welcome to bloody Wales!

Four years earlier ...
Snowdonia

It was winter and the ragged hills, valleys and lakes of Snowdonia were snowbound and bleak. This was a landscape that beat to the drum of Arthurian legend. The pounding heart of ancient Wales – a land of folklore and of myth.

A cold, damp and dismal morning and the lake of Llyn Llydaw was dark, deep and utterly still. Carved into the flanks of Mount Snowdon, Llyn Llydaw was long and thin and had formed in a cwm[1], a glaciated valley, about one third of the way up the mountain. The valley was believed to be the final resting place of Arthur, King of Britons. The site where a weary, dying King Arthur and Sir Bedevere threw Excalibur to the porcelain hand of the Lady of the Lake. An area of immeasurable power and myth.

A teenage girl ran carelessly down the uneven slopes of Crib Y Ddysgl. Her hair was dirty blonde, her left eyebrow pierced twice, and her eye make-up was heavy and black. She remembered from a school project that this place was where Merlin was supposed to have hidden the golden throne of Britain amongst the grey stone cliffs.

Letting gravity pull her down, she danced, leapt and jumped over the rocks until the ground evened out. She was glad she was wearing her blue parka coat. It was freezing. How stupid to be thinking that! What difference would it make? She winced as she felt her red face stinging from the cold.

She tried not to think or feel anything as she headed for the water.

---

1.   *https://en.wikipedia.org/wiki/Cirque*

CRYSTAL PALACE RAILWAY Station

Situated in the London Borough of Bromley, Crystal Palace station was originally built to serve the 1851 Crystal Palace Exhibition. Now, every year, it took two and a half million passengers north to Victoria, Wandsworth, West Norwood and Streatham Hill, or south to Beckenham and Norwood.

The wind whipped erratically across Platform 1 as commuters stood almost shoulder to shoulder waiting for the 08.05 to London Victoria.

An elfin-like woman, thirties, stood on the platform with the others. She was pretty, with high cheekbones and bright red lipstick. Her white-blonde hair was short, feathered and shaved a little at the back. Friends said she looked like Pixie Lott. She watched a crisp packet dance along in the strong breeze before it dived onto the leaf strewn tracks. She looked around as the train announcements burbled from tannoys, and people read papers and paperbacks, used phones, and avoided eye contact or, in fact, any human contact. It was like being in a crowd of robots, *she thought.*

She made herself oblivious to the chaos and uncomfortable nature of commuting to London by listening to loud music - The Electric Lady *by Janelle Monae – and scrolling through social media on her phone. Nodding to the beat and the electric funk bass, she checked text messages. She was in a buoyant mood. Today was going to be a good day, she could feel it.*

CHAPTER 6

RUTH COULD FEEL HER pulse thumping. She needed to make a good impression and convince the murder team they were in safe hands. But she was also keen not to come over as the 'big cop from the big city'.

Major Incident Room One was now buzzing with chatter, excitement and the odd boom of male laughter. Murders were very rare in Llancastell, so the anticipation was palpable. There were around a dozen Welsh CID officers, mostly male and middle-aged. Some were a little bleary-eyed at being called in after a long day but they didn't care. This was a murder case.

Gathering up her files, Ruth made her way to the front of the room. 'Good evening everyone. I think I met most of you briefly earlier today but if not, I'm Detective Inspector Ruth Hunter and I will be the senior investigating officer on this case initially. Detective Sergeant Evans, who lives in Dinas Padog, will be my deputy SIO. And yes, I have just arrived from the Met. And no, that doesn't mean that I think I know everything' – Ruth smiled – 'or that you can refer to me as "that cockney bitch" behind my back.'

There were some murmurs and laughter amongst some detectives, which she could see annoyed Nick.

CID had already set up a large investigation scene board, which surprised her. Everything in the Met worked like clockwork. She assumed that in North Wales things would be a little more ad hoc. She reprimanded herself for being so London-centric. It was a trait she disliked in others.

At the centre of the board was a holiday photo of Arabella Dixon, exotic cocktail in hand, looking directly at the camera, carefree and smiling. Her details were written in blue marker to one side - name and address, date of birth, plus the time and location of her death.

Ruth walked over to the whiteboard and pointed to the photograph of Arabella. 'Okay. I don't know if you've had a chance to see this photograph, but this is Arabella Dixon, our victim from tonight. I want you to look at this photo. This was an attack on a defenceless teacher as she made her way to her car. And I want you to look at the photo because it should be important to all of us that we get justice for her and her family. She had given her life to teaching and she deserves our best work. I want us to be meticulous in everything we do.' Ruth was calm but passionate. 'Okay, what have we got so far, Nick?'

'Boss. Arabella Dixon, aged fifty-one. Deputy head teacher at Ysgol Dinas Padog. She had worked there for six years. Prior to that, several schools in Cheshire and the Wirral. Divorced with one son, Alex, twenty. The family liaison officer has been with him since the news of Arabella's death came through. Alex's father, Jonathan Noakes, has also been there since then. He lives near Corwen with his current wife and daughter. Cause of death is suspicious but we're waiting for the pathologist's report. We believe that someone attacked her in the staff car park after a parents' evening.'

Ruth nodded. 'So, we need first statements from everyone that attended the parents' evening tonight. Did they see the victim? Where and when? Did they see anything when they left? Anyone around the school site who looked out of place? What about CCTV?'

A heavy-set officer with his balding hair shaved to a close crop stood up. Ruth had already seen him around the office and he was incredibly popular in CID. 'Detective Constable John 'Mac' Macdonald, boss. We've spoken to the school's IT people. Most of the main corridors are covered. Lots of coverage of the main car park. Far less of the crime scene. We should have it first thing in the morning.'

Ruth pointed to a photograph of the back of Arabella Dixon's right hand. There was something like a pattern that had been cut into the skin, but the blood and clotting had covered most of it. 'Any ideas what this is? Hopefully we'll get a better look at it when her body has been cleaned at the post-mortem, but they don't look like defensive wounds.'

Ruth knew it was time to bring the briefing to a close. 'At the moment, I want us to assume the killer targeted Arabella Dixon rather than this being a random crime. Let's see if we can build up a pattern of the victim's life. The answer will be somewhere in her lifestyle. Bank accounts or any money worries? Where is her mobile phone so we can access her mobile phone records? Did she speak to anyone around the time of the attack? Computer history. Social media. Any medical problems. It's unlikely, but is there a racial motive? Disputes with staff or students? What about the parents' evening? Did anything happen there or did anyone see anything? No one stay after one tonight. Can we reconvene here at six, please? Thank you everyone.'

Ruth closed her notes and headed for her office, feeling relieved.

First briefing as the new SIO and she had done an okay job. Now she needed a ciggie and some sleep.

CHAPTER 7

TESTICLES. WHY IS IT that alcoholic anxiety starts in the testicles? Is it a primeval reaction? Nick rolled over. He was angry and frustrated and thought maybe he would masturbate. Anything to change the feeling in his head, relieve the tension, and release endorphins. The sweats were starting and the back of his neck was damp. He turned the pillow over and could see the dark sweat patches on the cotton. But he knew the only thing that would relieve that feeling. *Booze.* That sensual, beautiful, warm feeling that the first drink of the day brings. Like a deep, warm bath. But, of course, then the guilt. Who drank vodka at four o'clock in the morning? Answer? He did.

Nick padded down to the kitchen. He worried about his balance in the semi-darkness. And part of him worried that he had merely imagined the new bottle of vodka he'd picked up from Bargain Booze six hours earlier. What if it wasn't there? What if he'd drunk it and forgotten? The panic that 'the illness' brings.

And then he opened the fridge door, the light came on and revealed it. Boom. The unopened bottle of vodka resting like a lazy hooker on the fridge shelf. Beautiful. What it promised. *I want you with passion. You will slip between my lips, into my gullet, warm my stomach, and then everything in my world will be right again. And when I'm done, everything will be okay. You're a beautiful sight.*

RUTH OPENED HER EYES and for a moment imagined she was still wrapped in a duvet in her flat in Crystal Palace. And then her heart dropped a little. Something was missing in the audio landscape. Airplanes. She had always found the sound of distant airplanes on their descent into Heathrow reassuring, even comforting. A rhythmic white noise. But there was a resounding silence.

And then, as Ruth saw the curtains and flat-screen television mounted on the wall, she remembered just how far from home she was.

The room was like any other hotel room in a reasonable hotel chain. Functional, comfortable, with some attempt at being stylish. The colour scheme of the curtains and the bedspread was dark plum and olive. There were two prints on the wall that showed stylised photographs of Snowdonia. Behind her there was an olive accent wall.

It was the early mornings when the agony and loneliness hit Ruth.

She looked over at the photo of Sarah that she had beside the bed. It had been four years since Sarah's 'departure' from their SE19 home. Theirs had been the idyllic set-up. Sarah was an occupational health nurse with a gift for seeing what was really going on in people's lives: co-dependent relationships, people-pleasing, guilt, and control. And that's what Ruth loved most about her. For seven years, until that blackest of all days, their lives were a joy. They fitted. They did jobs that made a difference and they shared the good and bad of every day. They were soul mates.

Ruth and Sarah were poster girls for their envious single or baby-weary heterosexual friends, wearing *The Future Is Female* t-shirts, dancing at festivals with day-glow face paint, and being the life and soul of everything.

Some sniped that they were 'just lipstick lesbians'. Men would approach them in a bar and not believe that they were a couple. And Sarah greeted those that persisted with drunken smirks and jokes with, 'Oh, excuse me, needle dick. I didn't realise that to be a lesbian I had to meet some ugly straight bloke's expectation of what a lesbian should look like. Now piss off!'

They also had to put up with straight women's admissions they were bi-curious because she and Sarah weren't butch or even 'proper gay'. Sarah would joke they needed to shave their hair, acquire piercings, no make-up, Doc Martens, cargo shorts and all the other clichés. And so they wouldn't have to come out on a daily basis.

And then, on 5 November 2013, Sarah Goddard vanished. Disappeared off the face of the planet.

She had not moved out. Not quit her job. Not gone travelling. Not met someone else. Not decided to cut ties with Ruth. Not had a terrible accident. She had inexplicably, gut-wrenchingly, gone missing. No note, no clues, no contact with friends or relatives. It was terrifying. The depth of pain Ruth had suffered, was still suffering, was inhuman.

Sarah had left their home, and boarded the 8.05am train from Crystal Palace to Victoria. The CCTV footage showed her getting on the train, as she always did. But she never got off that train. They examined CCTV at Victoria station millisecond by millisecond. They scoured every frame of CCTV on the line between Crystal Palace and Victoria. Every station scanned. Two passengers remembered seeing her chatting to a man as commuters were squeezed together in compartments. He was tall, handsome, late forties with glasses. There was nothing they thought looked sinister. No clues as to what they had talked about.

The efforts to find Sarah could not have been greater. With Ruth being one of their own, the Met Police were all over it, as was the charity Missing People, and the media. Sarah's face was on the web, on posters, and on twenty-five thousand leaflets that were distributed in London by family and friends. Her beautiful, flawless, smiling, thirty-five-year-old face stared out from a page on the Missing People website – a reminder of what she was. They handed leaflets out at a Disclosure gig, her favourite band. Nothing.

Back in Doncaster, where Sarah was born, her family kept her childhood things, clothes and toys, in the spare bedroom like a shrine. It took Ruth over a year to change anything in the flat. Another year before someone could persuade her to get rid of any of Sarah's possessions. Ruth still looked and hoped. What she could not do was grieve.

On the one-year anniversary of her disappearance, there were news bulletins, reconstructions, posters. And again, nothing. Since then whole hosts of crank sightings had come in from New Zealand to Norway. And Ruth became hypervigilant, seeing Sarah everywhere. She once stopped her car by Battersea Park because she thought she had seen Sarah crossing the road a minute earlier.

Now Ruth still felt broken when she thought of Sarah, but also felt guilty if she didn't think about her daily. She had become adept at putting the thought of her out of her head for fragments of time. They were only fragments, but they were a lovely reprieve.

Dragging herself out of bed, Ruth clicked on the kettle, looking forward to a cup of tea while watching the BBC News channel. Flicking the television on, a serious-faced male presenter appeared behind the news desk. Dressed in a grey suit and dark-blue patterned tie, he read from an autocue as dramatic news music played.

'A massive police hunt is underway in North Wales to find the killer of Arabella Dixon, the deputy head teacher at the Dinas Padog Secondary School in Denbighshire. Her body was found in the car park of the school, with police saying that Miss Dixon had been brutally attacked as she made her way to her car at around 8pm last night. They are appealing for witnesses who may have seen anything. Tributes, flowers, and cards have been arriving at the school overnight, for what many have called an "inspirational teacher".'

CHAPTER 8

THE KITCHEN AT ARABELLA Dixon's large farm-house, on the road towards Llandrillo, was bright with sun-light. Tasteful cabinets were painted in Farrow and Ball Cook's Blue. The first thing that Ruth had noticed about the kitchen, and the house in general, when she arrived was that it was clutter free. Not just tidy. Immaculate to the point of obsessive. The fridge door was barren, with no witty or retro fridge magnets, photos or paperwork. Key hooks were at-tached to the wall from which keys hung each with exactly the same fob – *Save Water – Drink Prosecco*. *At least she had some sense of humour*, Ruth thought. Even the cookbooks were in height order.

At the long, wooden kitchen table sat Alex Noakes, Ara-bella's twenty-year-old son. He had dark skin, and dark curly hair that was long and almost shoulder length and, Ruth thought, if she didn't know better, he looked Middle-East-ern.

His father, and the victim's ex-husband, Jonathan Noakes, was a handsome, silver-haired man in his late fifties. Ruth could see he was successful and had a physique that showed he took care of himself. She had also observed the new white Audi A5 Coupé, top spec, alloys, personalised number plate – JN 1000 – on the drive and assumed it was his. Next to that, Ruth had seen an older, dark blue Renault

Clio with a 2007 plate, which she assumed belonged to Alex Noakes.

Both Jonathan and Alex had the glazed look of shock as they sipped coffee. Moments of overwhelming grief followed by moments of sheer disbelief or denial. Ruth had seen it before, but people reacted in very different ways to death.

Sipping at her tea, she was glad she wasn't the one who had had to break the news. She had never been able to shake off the surreal feeling she'd experienced the first time she had to watch a family's life shatter. A small girl on her bike had gone under a bus at Clapham Junction and had been killed instantly. A pink bike with pink tassels and stabilisers crushed and twisted beyond recognition.

Ruth remembered knocking at the child's family's front door in her uniform, trying not to show her sickening anxiety. The parents refused to believe it. It was a mistake. Not their little girl. They wanted to see her and be with her.

Ruth indicated the family liaison officer who was keeping busy making more coffee, and said in a low, soft voice, 'I know that Sheila here has been through some things with you. And I can't imagine how difficult a time this must be. We're so sorry for your loss, but there are a few things we'd like to talk through.'

Jonathan nodded. 'Of course. Whatever you need.'

Ruth looked at Alex and asked, 'So, Alex, you were here all last night and you hadn't seen your mum since Wednesday night? Is that right?'

'Yeah,' Alex mumbled, not making eye contact.

'Did you notice any change in your mum's behaviour in recent days?'

Alex shook his head, 'No.'

'Did she seem agitated or nervous? Was she distracted about anything?'

'No, she was the same as always. There wasn't anything different,' Alex snapped.

Ruth's voice was gentle. 'Alex, I know this is really hard for you, but sometimes the smallest details can help.'

Alex ignored the question and Ruth watched as he then got up dramatically from his chair and headed for the patio door that was partially open. She could see that the garden outside was as pristine as the house. Lawn mown in symmetrical lines, decking, urns and perfect borders. Ruth concluded that a home like this revealed a lot about Arabella's need for control.

'I can't do this now ... I need a fag,' Alex mumbled as he walked out into the garden. Ruth watched him go. He was tall, with a skinny body that was still waiting to fill out. His skin-tight jeans hung too low, and he wore a baggy black *Walking Dead* t-shirt. It featured the character Negan holding a baseball bat covered in barbed wire, and the slogan *We're just getting started.* His clothes exaggerated his diminutive figure. Ruth could see that his hands shook a little as he lit a cigarette.

Outside, the sky was a flawless azure and dotted with clouds, although a dark awning seemed to be making its way towards them from the higher ground to the west.

'Must be very difficult,' Ruth said, commenting on Alex's exit.

Jonathan nodded and blinked tearily. 'It just ... doesn't feel real. That she's gone.'

After a moment, Nick looked down at his notebook. 'Mr Noakes, were you here with Alex last night?'

'No. Alex stays with me over in Corwen once in a while though. I'm remarried,' Jonathan explained.

'Does that mean Alex would have been here on his own then?' asked Ruth.

'Yes, I suppose so ... he didn't mention anyone else.' Jonathan's tone was a little hesitant.

Her voice was again gentle. 'Just so we can eliminate you from our enquiries Mr Noakes, where were you around eight o'clock last night?'

Jonathan seemed a little surprised. 'I was on my way home from a business meeting.'

'And where was that, sir?' Nick asked brusquely.

'Manchester.'

'So around eight o'clock last night you would have been where?' Ruth asked.

Jonathan thought for a moment.

'It's all right, Mr Noakes, take your time,' Ruth reassured him.

'Erm ... I guess somewhere between Chester and Llancastell. The A583, I don't know. I could have been past Llancastell.'

'Okay. Did you speak to anyone?' Nick enquired.

'No. Not that I can remember.' Jonathan shook his head. He was looking a little jittery, Ruth thought, as she watched his reactions.

'And how was your relationship with your ex-wife, Mr Noakes? Since the divorce? I imagine it can't have been easy for either of you,' Ruth asked.

Jonathan shrugged. 'It was fine. We got on okay. And we had Alex to talk about. She was my ex-wife, so we had the odd tiff but nothing horrible.'

'Can I ask why you got divorced?' Nick asked.

Ruth thought it was a good question. She had started to wonder if there was any lingering anger or resentment between Jonathan Noakes and his ex.

'To be honest, it was exhausting being married to someone who was always right and always perfect. Nothing more sinister than that. We didn't get on by the end.'

'Have you rowed with your ex-wife recently?' Nick asked, trying to get the full picture.

'No more than usual. There was always stuff we didn't agree on,' Jonathan said.

'Such as, Mr Noakes?' Ruth asked.

'Alex mainly. Arabella is ...' Ruth could see that Jonathan had hesitated as he realised he should now be using the past tense. 'Well ... she was very controlling, especially when it came to Alex. Alex was exceptional at art and he wanted to go away to art college, but she made him do a marketing and PR degree here in Llancastell, and that meant he could stay at home with her. She didn't like his friends. She certainly never liked any of his girlfriends. She picked his A-levels for him. Banned him from having his ear pierced even though he did it anyway.'

'Doesn't sound like they got on?' Nick said.

'Not recently. In fact, it was worse than ever, but that's kids for you.' Jonathan said.

His words hung in the air for a moment. Ruth wasn't convinced.

THE SCRUBS AREA OUTSIDE the mortuary at the university hospital had no windows, and the strip lights gave it a depressing vanilla glow. It smelt of detergents and bleach.

Home Office Forensic Pathologist Professor Norman Peters was washing his hands thoroughly having just conducted the initial post-mortem on Arabella Dixon. In his sixties, he was balding, with a sturdy build, and had the air of a man confident in his own ability. He put on his jacket to complete the expensive, tailor-made dark grey suit he wore with a waistcoat.

Nick took notes on his notepad while Ruth was holding some initial photographs that Peters had given her.

'What did you find?' Ruth asked.

'Cause of death is asphyxiation,' Professor Peters mumbled a little while looking at his notes. He then looked over at them and stated more clearly. 'She was strangled. There are contusions to the neck and windpipe, and to the back of the neck. We've swabbed the neck for DNA. We'll know more after the full post-mortem.'

'Anything else that could help us?' Ruth asked. The first forty-eight hours of a murder case were vital.

'Pattern handprints suggest small hands. Well, small-ish.'

'Female?' asked Ruth.

'Possibly, yes.'

Nick looked over at him. 'What about someone young? A teenager?'

Ruth was impressed. It was an astute question. Despite his lack of charm, Nick's ability as a detective wasn't in doubt.

Professor Peters nodded, 'Yes, that would fit too. And she had some bruising on the knuckles of her right hand, which suggests she struck her assailant at least once.'

Nick looked up, 'DNA?'

'No. She didn't break the skin, so we found nothing on her hand. Let me see ...' Professor Peters picked up a photo of Arabella Dixon's right hand. Ruth could see the clear reddish, purple bruising on her knuckles. She wore two silver rings on her fourth and little finger. 'However, the rings she was wearing would have left a distinctive shaped bruise on the attacker somewhere. And her knuckles would have left a row of round bruises. The size and spacing of the bruises could be used to at least show that the attacker had been punched by someone with the same sized hands as the deceased.'

Ruth held up the photo of the back of Arabella Dixon's left hand, which had now been washed. Someone had cut a neat and simple spiral shape into the skin, about three inches in diameter.

'What about this?' Ruth frowned. The image of the cut patterns was unnerving.

'The lack of clotting around the cuts suggests this was done post-mortem,' Professor Peters explained. 'Very strange. I remember an American killer, the Night Stalker.

Richard Ramirez I think his name was. He carved letters into his victims and left satanic symbols on the bodies. But I've never come across anything like this before. And I've been doing PMs for the police for thirty years.'

'Do you know what was used to cut the symbol?' Nick asked.

'At a guess, I would say a small, very sharp craft knife. Plus, it was done by someone skilled.'

'What do you mean by skilled?' Ruth asked. It seemed a strange choice of words.

'It was done freehand and it's almost symmetrical. So maybe someone who works as a designer. Possibly an architect or draughtsman.'

Nick shot Ruth a look and then asked, "What about a good art student?"

"Yes, that's a possibility." Professor Peters said.

'Any idea what it means?' Ruth asked.

Professor Peters shook his head. 'No, I'm sorry. No idea. You're looking for someone full of hatred for the victim. Strangulation, especially when the victim is facing you, is personal. Rather than a momentary loss of control that we see with a stabbing or a fight, it suggests a controlled, premeditated, hatred.'

CHAPTER 9

YSGOL DINAS PADOG WAS an ongoing crime scene, so it was closed for the day. Ruth and Nick followed the headteacher's secretary down the long corridor towards the headteacher's office. Her heeled shoes echoed on the wooden floor, which Ruth thought added to the strange, empty atmosphere. Schools were usually busy, noisy places, full of life. But not today.

The journeys to both the university hospital and the school had been frosty affairs, and Ruth had used the silence to make phone calls. She wanted the CCTV from the rear car park as quickly as possible. She also needed a detailed evidence log.

Ysgol Dinas Padog was a small rural high school. It catered to the local community, with various surnames repeating in the whole-school photos that dotted along the walls, dating back to the 1950s. There were also around half a dozen framed sports shirts – rugby, football, hockey – from students who had represented the county or country at sport. Along the corridor, Dylan Wilkins was on a step ladder, hammering and attaching a framed red Welsh Rugby shirt to the wall. Such was his intense concentration, Dylan didn't notice Ruth and Nick as they walked past.

Beside the headteacher's door was an ageing wooden trophy cabinet displaying shields and small silver awards. It seemed so parochial and old-fashioned, Ruth thought, compared to the ultra-modern academies of South East London.

Ruth and Nick were shown into the office of Neerav Banerjee. It was compact and functional; a desk and computer to one side, and then an oval meeting table and half a dozen high-backed dark blue chairs. It smelt clean and fresh, with a trace of coffee.

On the walls there were photos of sports teams, and of students taking part in canoeing and abseiling off Anglesey. Alongside were press clippings of the school's charity fundraising, all featuring Neerav shaking hands, grinning at the camera.

As they entered, Neerav moved his large, black, leatherette office chair back to face them and stood, coming over to greet them confidently. He had the presence of a headteacher, Ruth thought.

'Good afternoon.' His voice was suitably low and sombre as he shook her hand and then indicated two chairs. 'Please, come and sit down.'

'Thanks, I'm Detective Inspector Hunter. This is my colleague Detective Sergeant Evans.'

'Can I get you coffee or tea?' he asked.

'No thank you. We're fine,' Ruth replied.

'I'm sorry that we're meeting under such terrible circumstances,' Neerav said.

'Yes. There are a few things we'd like to clarify about Miss Dixon as part of our inquiry,' Ruth explained as she clicked the top of her pen.

'Of course, of course. Anything I can do to help. We're all in such a state of shock,' Neerav explained to Ruth, looking directly at her. There was something about him that she didn't like. He didn't fit right. Often, there were many people in positions of authority, however minor, that never truly believed that they belonged there. To compensate, they played the role with a mask, as if trying to prove something to themselves and everyone around them. But there always seemed something fake, a loud, false note to them and the way they acted that Ruth could detect within seconds. They were smug in their little fiefdoms.

Ruth looked up from her pad. 'Just to clarify, Miss Dixon was here last night because there had a been a parents' evening?'

'That's right. Year 11.'

'And when did you last see Miss Dixon?' Nick asked.

'Must have been about ten to eight. The parents' evening was due to finish at seven thirty. We even sound a bell so parents and staff are aware of the time and to hurry things along. But there are always a few stragglers. Arabella told me she was going home to have a glass of wine and watch *Bake Off* or something like that,' Neerav explained sadly.

'And what would her role have been during the evening? Would she have been in the sports hall all night?' Ruth asked.

Neerav took a moment, and a breath. She could see that her question had hit a nerve. She supposed that last night had seemed like any other school function. Now it had become a surreal nightmare. 'Yes, she was there all night. She spent most of the time talking to me and other members of the senior leadership team. There were a few parents and students she was keen to chat to. Nothing out of the ordinary.'

'How did she seem? Anything worrying her?' Ruth asked.

'No, she was fine. Just her usual self. Good at her job but with a sense of humour.' However hard Neerav tried to be professional, it was obvious to Ruth that he was caught up in his emotions.

'Anything else that might have been troubling her?'

'No ... not that I know of ...'

'Did you notice anything that might have indicated that she was having any problems either at work or at home?' Ruth asked.

'No. Work was going well. Privately she kept herself to herself, so I don't really know about that. But she'd told me that she had aspirations to get a headship. In fact, a couple of days ago we had talked about a headteacher's job that had been advertised in the TES on the Wirral. She was consider-ing it, and I told her that she would have my full backing and a strong reference. Professionally, things couldn't have been better for her,' Neerav explained.

Nick looked up and said, 'Any arguments recently with parents or students?

'No. Certainly nothing that could explain this.'

'What about the staff at the school? How did Miss Dixon get on with them?' Ruth asked.

Neerav hesitated and gave himself away. 'She was ...'

Now we're getting somewhere, Ruth thought as she gently pushed, sensing the hesitancy. 'Would you say that she was a popular member of staff here?'

Neerav sat back in his chair for a moment, and pursed his lips. 'I would say that she was tough on members of staff that she thought weren't doing their jobs properly. But that was her role.'

Ruth nodded. She knew the subtext of what he was saying. Arabella was a ball-breaking bitch. *But you don't go around strangling your line manager just because you don't get on,* thought Ruth.

'Any major conflicts or problems with staff recently?' Nick asked.

Neerav nodded. 'Yes. A couple of months ago, Arabella was in charge of an investigation into a teacher who is currently suspended. That teacher brought a case alleging workplace bullying against Arabella.'

'Workplace bullying? Is this the first allegation that's been made against Miss Dixon?' Ruth asked. The picture of Arabella Dixon was darkening.

Neerav's tone was now reluctant at the thought of sullying Arabella Dixon's name. 'It's the first formal allegation. But I've had to have informal conversations with both of the school union reps about her behaviour before.'

'Oh right. So she was a bully?' Nick asked.

Ruth bristled. She didn't want Nick to put Neerav on the back foot, and aggressive questioning would get them nowhere. She tried to get Nick's attention, but he deliberately avoided her gaze.

'I'd rather not comment on that. I mean ...' Neerav was looking emotional.

'What was the allegation against her?' Nick's tone was again verging on hostile.

'It's a child protection issue. I'm not sure it's appropriate for me ...' Neerav was trying to keep things professional.

Nick let out an audible sigh of frustration. He was really irritating Ruth. This was not how to get the best out of an interview. Even though Nick had shown that he had excellent investigative instincts, his people skills were woeful. Gone were the days when officers would bully or cajole. Every psychological test showed that individuals responded to a calm, friendly, and understanding approach. And she wasn't going to keep playing 'good cop' to his 'bad cop' like some terrible television cliché.

Ruth softened her voice to invite a more open response. 'Mr Banerjee, this is a murder enquiry. The more information we have, the more likely we are to make an arrest and quickly. Can you tell us what the allegation was?'

Neerav paused, as if contemplating what to do, before looking up at the detectives. 'The allegation was that the teacher, Bronwyn Wright, attacked a student.'

Ruth wasn't expecting that. 'And how serious was the attack?' she asked.

'Fairly serious. She didn't hit her, but the student alleged that Bronwyn Wright lost her temper and then pinned her against the wall by her throat.'

Ruth and Nick shared a look. It was the same MO as Arabella Dixon's murder.

'Any history of Bronwyn Wright acting like that before?' Nick asked.

'No, of course not. She wouldn't be working here otherwise. Bronwyn was a talented history teacher. In fact, she was a published historian, so it was a real shame that it came to that.'

'We'll need contact details for Bronwyn Wright,' Ruth said.

'Yes, of course. I know that she's not well at the moment, but my secretary can give you any information that you need.'

'Thank you, Mr Banerjee. I think that's all we need at the moment,' Ruth said, closing her notebook.

Neerav looked relieved that the interview had ended.

TEN MINUTES LATER, Ruth and Nick made their way out through the large steel gates that led out to the main school car park. A middle-aged man, slouching with what appeared to be the weight of the world on his shoulders, strode past them and gave them a solemn nod.

Nick and the man began to speak Welsh. Ruth couldn't begin to decipher what they were talking about, but they both looked at her and laughed. She was fairly certain that Nick had made a joke at her expense.

As the man went into the school, Ruth looked at Nick. "What was all that about?"

'Just catching up, you know?' Nick replied with a smirk. He was mugging her off and she knew it.

'Another relative? Ruth asked dryly.

'That's right, boss. We're all in-bred sheep shaggers in these parts,' Nick replied sarcastically. 'I'm surprised that anyone with your experience in the Met would want to work in a hillbilly hicksville dump like this?'

As Nick turned to go, Ruth watched him for a moment. To say that he had a monumental chip on his shoulder would be an understatement.

The wind picked up, and nearby hedges and bushes rattled noisily. Ruth pulled the sleeves of her coat down to cover the cold skin of her hands. She reached into her coat and got out a packet of cigarettes. Three left. She would have to get some more.

They passed a lowland beech tree that had been planted recently. Ruth noticed a plaque that read, *In Loving Memory of Megan Gardener 1999-2013*. The caretaker who had found Arabella, and was also Nick's uncle, was Mike Gardener. Was there a connection? Ruth saw that Nick looked at the tree too. Something imperceptible flickered across his face, but he said nothing. She wondered what he was thinking about.

Something drew her attention to the television camera crews, photographers, and vans that were lining the road outside the school. Behind the evidence tape, several uniformed officers policed the onlookers. Arabella Dixon's murder was a big story. It was a national story. Teachers don't get murdered, and certainly not in rural North Wales. A couple of reporters shouted over in Welsh to Ruth and Nick.

'What did they say?' Ruth asked as she lit her cigarette.

Nick didn't look at her and mumbled, 'Doesn't matter. Nothing.'

Ruth stopped walking, turned, and looked directly at him. She had had enough of him. 'What's the problem, Sergeant?'

'Problem?' Nick said innocently.

'Stop acting like the little boy that's been made to sit next to the teacher on the coach on the school trip,' Ruth reproached him. She rarely lost her temper with colleagues. 'We don't have to be friends. We don't have to even like each other. But the minute you act unprofessionally, Sergeant, you'll be off the case and back on whatever fascinating stuff you were doing before. Are we clear on that?'

Nick took a moment and then nodded resentfully. 'Yeah, very clear.'

Ruth composed herself and took a drag of her ciggie. She found that kind of confrontation difficult. Maybe that's why she had never pushed herself professionally?

Mike Gardener was attaching a sign at the school's entrance that read:

Dear Parents/Carers, the school will be closed today due to a police incident last night.

Mike looked over at Nick and gave him a quizzical frown.

Beside the sign there were flowers, cards, and even a soft toy. A young woman in her twenties, top-knot hair, denim jacket, patterned skirt, trainers with no socks, looked at the tributes solemnly and put her hand to her mouth. Ruth watched as two teenage girls wept as they laid down some daffodils and a homemade card. However Arabella Dixon had behaved, this was a tragedy that would shake the whole community.

Ruth watched Nick as he glanced down at the note he'd been given by the school secretary.

'Bronwyn Wright is in the Lighthouse Hospital, Welshpool,' he said. Then, after a brief Internet search on his phone, he added 'Looks like a private mental health and addiction unit.'

'How far is Welshpool from here?' Ruth asked, wondering if her previous words had helped or hindered the situation between herself and Nick.

'Twenty miles. Not far,' Nick answered.

'It doesn't sound like she's been sectioned. If it's a private place, I guess you can come and go when you want if you or your health insurance are paying. So, Nick, tomorrow can you go and see Bronwyn Wright and find out where she was last night?' Ruth's tone was lighter to signal she had now drawn a line under their disagreement.

Nick nodded and said, 'Yes, boss.'

Ruth could sense that his tone had changed. Her reprimand seemed to have cleared the air, and now they could get on with their job.

Ruth wondered how long it would be before Jones found a permanent SIO, and she could take more of a back seat. She also wondered if that's what she actually wanted.

CHAPTER 10

IT WAS SEVEN IN THE evening by the time Ruth held a debriefing of the day's developments. There were about a dozen CID officers sitting around Major Incident Room 1. To one side of the room, the large whiteboard now featured photos and maps of Dinas Padog, and diagrams and drawings of the layout of the school. In the centre of the board was a picture of Arabella Dixon, looking carefree with a cocktail in her hand. *Good teeth*, thought Ruth. It costs money to get teeth like that. Looked like veneers. Thousands of pounds.

Ruth's attention returned to Mac, who was giving feedback. She was leaning on a desk close to the whiteboard.

Mac hitched up his trousers over his sizeable waistline. 'Initial forensics has turned up little, boss, although the victim had what might be clothing fibres under the nails on her right hand. We're waiting for the forensic analysis of those. Also, Arabella Dixon's car had significant acid burns to the paintwork on the bonnet. They also think they've got two partial fingerprints that are embedded into the damage.'

Ruth nodded. 'Good, thank you.' She liked Mac already. Thorough, no-nonsense, old-fashioned, but a real sense of why they did 'the job'. He was also a paternal figure to lots of the younger male CID officers. She needed to keep him onside.

Detective Constable Luke Merringer, whose ginger hair and goatee beard made for a distinctive sight in the office, was next to feed back to CID. Again, Ruth thought Merringer was a good copper with the right instincts. 'The rain might have washed away some of the evidence, boss. I've asked Welsh Water if we can have access to the drain well where the rainwater would have washed away to. Then we can get Forensics to take a look,' he explained.

Ruth went over to the board and pointed to the image of the spiral that had been cut into the back of Arabella Dixon's hand.

'What about this? Any ideas on what it might be?' Ruth asked. She was concerned because carving symbols into the back of a victim's hand could be the sign they were dealing with someone with a darker purpose than they had considered so far. When a killer left their mark, it was always worrying. She didn't want to entertain the thought that there was a psychotic maniac out there.

Nick looked at it, thinking out loud, 'It's a symbol of something. Maybe a religious or Celtic symbol?'

'The killer is giving us a clue why Arabella Dixon was killed. It's a message. Can we find out what it means?' Ruth asked.

'I'll have a look,' Nick replied.

Ruth nodded and moved over to a detailed map of the school. She traced her finger over it. Start with the basics; what they knew to be true. 'So, the victim leaves the sports hall at around seven fifty-five, once the parents and students have gone. Says goodnight to Neerav Banerjee, who is the last person to see her alive. Miss Dixon then crosses the playground, cuts through the maths corridor, and heads out to the rear staff car park where she is killed. Mike Gardener, the school caretaker, comes out at around eight fifteen to lock up the school and the car park for the night, and finds the victim dead. That narrows down the murder to a tiny time frame. The victim still has her laptop and purse in her laptop case, so we can rule out robbery as a motive. No obvious sexual motive, but we'll see what the full post-mortem tells us. The killer takes the time to cut a symbol into the back of her hand. It's important to them. Why? What about CCTV, Mac?'

Mac walked over to a large computer screen where an image of the school's grainy CCTV of the car park was frozen. 'Not great news, boss. In the first instance, the CCTV camera only shows the doors that lead from the car park to the maths corridor and the first two rows of cars. However, the guttering above the CCTV camera was blocked, so there's a steady stream of rainwater that pours over the camera. I'll show you.'

Mac pressed play. The image from the CCTV camera was completely obscured by water gushing past the lens. It was impossible to see anything.

'A school jumper was blocking the guttering, if you can believe that? Some little bastard's idea of a joke, I guess,' Mac explained in a withering tone.

'Bet you did worse at school, Mac?' Merringer said with a grin.

'I put a sheep in the headmaster's car once. It shat all over the new leather upholstery,' Mac admitted. 'Took me a whole weekend to get it clean.'

Everyone laughed.

'Thanks, Mac. Can we get the video footage enhanced?' Ruth asked, still smiling at the anecdote.

'I've handed a copy to the forensic video team, but the system is pretty low grade in the first place so I'm not holding out a lot of hope,' Mac said.

'Great! What about the maths corridor?' Nick asked. Ruth noticed that he seemed annoyed and unsettled. He also seemed to have a sweaty sheen over his forehead. She wondered if he drank. She had seen it lots of times before in the Met. Bottles of Scotch in the desk drawer were virtually a requirement of senior detectives when she first started in CID. She needed to keep an eye on Nick. A drinking problem would explain a lot.

'The footage of the maths corridor is good.' Mac played the CCTV, which showed Arabella Dixon striding along the school corridor and then using her security pass on the lanyard around her neck to open the doors out to the car park. The time code read: *19.58.*

'Okay. And that fits with the time frame we've got. I assume that no one else comes along that corridor either before or after?' Ruth asked.

'No. No one until Mike Gardener comes to lock up the school. And before, the corridor is empty except for two members of staff, Graham Williams and Chris Roberts, going to the car park together at seven thirty-four. They shared a lift and saw nothing suspicious,' Mac clarified.

'Right, I want statements from those two teachers. And I want detailed statements from Mike Gardener and Dylan

Wilkins about the exact series of events when they found Arabella Dixon. Then I want them compared.'

Ruth looked over at a female detective constable, early forties, dark auburn hair, freckled face, and attractive bone structure.

'I'm sorry, I'm still learning who everyone is,' Ruth admitted as she looked at her.

'DC Sian Hockney, boss,' Sian explained.

'Okay. So, Sian, what have we got?'

'We've contacted nearly all the parents and staff that were there that night. We've taken preliminary statements, but no one saw anything out of the ordinary. We're also trying to match the number plates of the cars we can see in the main car park on the CCTV with the PNC and number plate recognition software, to see if anyone was there that wasn't on the list of parents that the school gave us.'

'Good work.' Ruth looked at Sian for a moment, taking in her green eyes and cheekbones. *She is pretty*, Ruth thought, before catching herself getting distracted as she walked back over to the screen showing the CCTV.

'Arabella Dixon was on her way to her car, correct?' Ruth asked.

Mac nodded.

'Luke, you've seen the evidence log we got from SOCO?' Ruth asked.

'Yes, boss.'

'Do you remember seeing any mention of Arabella Dixon's car or house keys in any of the evidence that was logged?' Ruth was thinking aloud. Had they been taken on purpose? Did the killer want access to Arabella's home?

'No. There were no keys, phone, or her security pass found on or around the victim at the crime scene, boss.' Luke confirmed.

'Arabella Dixon is wearing her security pass in the CCTV. She uses it to get out into the car park. Where is it? And why aren't her keys, phone, or pass on her person, or near where she was killed?' Ruth asked.

'Maybe the killer took them?' Mac suggested.

'What for?' Ruth asked. It was troubling that Arabella's purse and cards weren't taken, but the phone and keys were.

'Ebay?' quipped Mac.

Ruth rolled her eyes and continued, 'Why? What does the killer gain from taking her phone, keys, and security pass?'

'They planned to use her car to get away?' Mac suggested.

'But they didn't. And why take the phone?'

The phone in the corner started ringing, and Sian went to answer it.

'It's someone she knows and they'd been in contact recently?' Mac said.

'Sounds about right,' Ruth agreed.

Sian pointed at the phone, 'Boss, SOCO have done their initial search of Arabella Dixon's home. They found a used condom in tissue paper in the bin of her en suite bathroom. Given the cleanliness of the house, they're assuming it could only have been in there for a couple of days. They're sending it for DNA testing.'

'Thank you, Sian,' Ruth said, and then glanced at her watch. 'Okay, people, go and get some sleep. Back here at six please.'

Ruth was beginning to like being an SIO in Wales.

DAYLIGHT HAD FADED as Ruth dragged on a cigarette while she sat on the patio to the rear of her hotel. She was running things through her head. Being the SIO on a murder case was not the plan for week one in Snowdonia – or any week as a matter of fact. But she was enjoying it more than she cared to admit.

Ruth's gut instinct told her that someone had targeted Arabella Dixon. That strange symbol on her hand was creepy, and it had to be something to do with her murder. However, the first thing to do was to apply the basics of police work: motive, means, and opportunity. Alex had a tempestuous relationship with his mother. The ex-husband had a loose alibi but little motive. He was happily married with a new family. Bronwyn Wright had motive, but opportunity needed to be established. Where were Arabella Dixon's pass, phone, and car keys? What had she done that made someone want to kill her? Ruth sensed that something else would show up. *Keep digging away and be methodical,* she told herself.

She felt the vibration of a text message on the phone inside her jacket, but didn't even look. Even after four years, her instinctive reaction was to think it might be Sarah. That hope was so destructive, so painful.

She stubbed out her cigarette and went inside, past reception and into the small bar where a middle-aged couple were sitting drinking and talking in hushed tones.

A teenage girl, looking lost in thought, stood behind the bar. She wore a white blouse with a small, navy-coloured name badge. *Rhiannon*. She was pretty, with dark eye make-up and dip-dyed hair pulled up in a ponytail.

'Sparkling mineral water, please,' Ruth said, without making eye contact. She was looking at the *Llancastell Leader* and the headline: *Murder victim was an inspirational teacher.* Below was a photo of the floral tributes outside Ysgol Dinas Padog.

Rhiannon poured the final drips of the sparkling water into the glass and placed it beside Ruth.

'Shall I put that on your room bill?' Rhiannon asked with a nice smile.

Ruth nodded and smiled. 'Good idea. Room 6. Thanks.' Ruth saw that Rhiannon was looking at the newspaper headline.

'Horrible, isn't it?' Ruth indicated the paper.

'Can't believe it. She was all right, Miss Dixon was.' Rhiannon shook her head.

'She taught you, did she?'

Rhiannon nodded. 'She's the only reason I got a C in my history GCSE. We used to go for revision with her at lunchtimes. She didn't have to do that.'

Ruth looked up at Rhiannon with empathy, and noticed that her left eye was bruised and slightly swollen even though she'd done a good job of covering it with make-up.

Ruth indicated her eye. 'Looks nasty. How did you manage to do that?'

'Got drunk at the weekend. Fell over, like. Don't really remember,' Rhiannon mumbled with an embarrassed half laugh, but Ruth's copper instincts didn't believe her.

Ruth took her drink, 'We've all done that. I'm heading up to my room, so, goodnight.'

'Yeah, goodnight,' Rhiannon said, sounding awkward.

NICK TOOK THE B239 out of Padog and headed west to a small hamlet, Pen y Bryn, where his uncle and aunt, Mike and Pat Gardener, lived. As he drove, Nick squinted into the distance. He could just make out the uneven tip of Cadair Idris, the literal translation being 'the giant's chair', in the moonlight. His *nain* – Welsh for 'grandmother' – used to tell him the legend of the giant Idris, who once used the mountain as his throne, and of how the huge boulders at the bottom of the mountain were supposedly the stones that Idris shook out of his shoe. Then Nain would say, in as spooky a voice as she could muster, that the legend warns that those who sleep on the mountain will awaken either as a madman, a murderer, or never wake again.

Nick's mum, Mike's sister Mel, died from ovarian cancer when he was twelve. It was vicious and quick, and only three months from diagnosis to death. People thought that was a blessing. *At least she didn't have to suffer.* Nick hated them for that. What the hell did they know? He wanted to know why her? He would look at his classmates and wonder why it had happened to him? It made him feel isolated and full of self-pity. He wanted more time with her. After she had died, there were things he wanted to ask her. Details about her childhood that were lost forever, and advice that could never be given.

Nick's dad, Rhys, got compassionate leave and returned from West Germany where he was a sergeant in the Royal Welsh Fusiliers. But Rhys Evans was a hard man, and barely shed a tear at his own wife's funeral. He was the son of a tough copper miner, Taid Evans. Not only did they not show their emotions, they actively beat those that showed weakness. When Nick wet the bed, his father's solution was to rub his face in it and make him sleep in the wet patch until his body heat dried it. He hit Nick's mum if food wasn't ready on time, if his clothes weren't ironed properly, or if she ever dared to question him.

A few years ago, Nick had walked across a local pub and knocked his father clean out with a punch, breaking a metacarpal in his knuckle in the process. Nick thought it was definitely worth it. He was a big believer in revenge, however wrong that might be.

After his mother's death, Nick went to live with Uncle Mike and Auntie Pat, while Rhys Evans returned to active duty. During the Bosnian War, Rhys' regiment came under attack in 1995. Rhys and thirty other Welsh Fusiliers, part of the UN Peacekeeping Force, were in a fierce firefight with Bosnian Serbs, and then taken hostage and tortured. Rhys didn't recover from the experience. He got what Nick now knew to be PTSD, but he had no sympathy. His dad was a nasty bastard, and although he now lived behind closed curtains, in shitty squalor, as a raging alcoholic only ten miles from Dinas Padog, Nick rarely visited.

Clouds had covered the moon and it was ink black by the time Nick took the turning to Pen y Bryn. The road climbed steeply, and as the wind picked up he felt the car sway. Even though it was early spring, the car thermometer showed that it was down to just three degrees. To the left, there was a steep mountain bank covered in an impenetrable canopy of pine and Welsh oak trees that had remained untouched since the last ice age ten thousand years ago. It was the setting for many of the medieval tales and fables collectively known as the *Mabinogion*. Nick knew that the forest rose high above him towards the sky, but it was invisible in the darkness, and that felt unsettling.

Nick and his cousins had hung out close to the forest when they were teenagers, and he had had his first fag with Cerys there. She was only twelve. Dunhill Menthol. It made him feel giddy and sick, but he laughed his head off. He and his cousin passed the fag back and forth, sucking deep on the smoke and getting a 'nico-spin'.

A few miles away was the Coed y Brenin Forest. There was an old footbridge over a dramatic gorge which used to give Nick vertigo, although he always bragged that he felt no fear. The bridge was also the supposed setting of the legend of Susie Dol Y Clochyd, who was a local witch in the eighteenth century. The local lord claimed Susie's beloved black cat was hunting on his land, so he killed it and beheaded it. It filled Susie with rage. She transformed herself into a hare, and lured the lord's prized hunting hounds to chase her towards the gorge. She jumped out of the way at the last minute, but the snapping hounds fell to their death into the roaring water below. Apparently, when the river was high, you could still hear the drowning yelps of the dogs.

Nick, Cerys, and Megan had spent afternoons sitting on the edge of the gorge, before one of them would give a loud echoing dog-like howl, and the others would follow suit in between fits of laughter. He really missed Megan, and it was painful to think about her.

Nick felt the road surface deteriorate. He hit a small pot-hole with a bang and slowed the car. Tractors and farm machinery ruined these roads. Bloody farmers. His headlights lit up his uncle and aunt's small worker's cottage set back from the road.

Nick parked by the hedge and sat for a moment. He clicked open the glovebox, took out the new half bottle of vodka, and knocked back a good two mouthfuls. Nice and warm. He already felt calmer even though the vodka had been in his body for no more than thirty seconds, and he knew alcohol took a good twenty minutes to get going. It must be psychological, Nick thought. He popped the bottle into the large inside pocket of his jacket.

Part of him could do with a big night out. He had mates in Chester if he ever fancied a blowout and they weren't coppers. But he knew how that would go. Booze, cocaine, lap-dancing, hookers or a one-night stand, blackouts, maybe a fight, vomit. Wake on a mate's sofa feeling like he was going to die. Kids or wife circling around, waiting for him to leave, while he would check that he hadn't wet the sofa, which had been known. Drive home, while collecting enough booze to drink off the hangover, and more for good measure. Close the curtains, and more than likely call in sick to work. His heart sank at the idea, and he put the thought out of his head.

Nick looked out at the scruffy paving and weeds that led up to the side door, and smiled. The booze, and being here, calmed him.

Home sweet home.

RUTH KICKED OFF HER shoes and lay back on the hotel bed. Turning to one side, she adjusted the framed photo of Sarah beside her bed. A tear came into her eye. How did Sarah vanish from her life? Four years later and it still really hurt. She pursed her lips to stop the tears from coming. Then, images from her memory tumbled over each other; Sarah's mouth, her chestnut eyes, her platinum-blonde hair, her raucous laugh. And the silent tears rolled and dripped off her face onto the duvet cover.

'Jesus!' Ruth cried under her breath in frustration. She could numb herself with codeine or alcohol.

The irrational part of her brain latched onto the possibility that Sarah was one day going to turn up on her doorstep. Then she tried to quieten the other thoughts, but sometimes they would surface unexpectedly, throwing her off kilter. Sarah was with someone else; Sarah was just taking a long time-out.

Ruth tried to put the other darker possibilities out of her head. Sarah had been raped, tortured, and died in great pain. Her body was lying rotting in some remote shallow grave. Or it had been dismembered and disposed of. Being a police officer didn't help Ruth's imagination.

Her thoughts now changed direction. She let herself believe that Sarah would come back, that it was possible. Remote, but possible. She ached inside. Just to kiss and hold her. For a moment. Ruth surrendered, and let the feelings she had avoided and guarded against all day get the better of her and sweep through. *Idiot! I'm such an idiot. My life wasn't meant to be like this.* Her body shook as she wept and struggled to breathe.

She rolled over on the bed, wiped another tear away. Blowing out her cheeks, she took a long deep breath. Taking her phone, she read the text message.

How you doing, Ma? Googled where you're staying. Looks all right. Or 'tidy' as they say. Let me know you're okay xx.

Ruth smiled. Ella was the best thing she had ever done with her life. Seeing her text gave her a bit of a lift as she turned on the television. The BBC News was on.

Walking over to the window, she opened it, took a ciggie from the packet, lit it, sat down beside the window, and smoked. She hoped the smoke alarms didn't go off.

After about ten minutes, the female newsreader looked at the camera. *'The family of a teacher who was attacked and killed at a school on Thursday evening have paid tribute to her, saying they are devastated. North Wales Police are searching for the attacker, following the death of Arabella Dixon, a deputy head teacher, saying they believe it was a targeted attack at a rural high school close to the Snowdonia region of Wales. Ian Clinton reports.'*

Ruth watched the aerial shot of Ysgol Dinas Padog as a male reporter took over. *'The centre of the police operation remains the car park at the rear of the Padog Dinas High School where detectives say that Arabella Dixon was attacked and killed after a school parents' evening yesterday. Miss Dixon was fifty-three and a deputy head teacher at the Padog Dinas High School. In a statement today, the school said that Arabella was a caring and compassionate teacher whose work enriched the lives of thousands of students. "We are devastated that Arabella's life has been cut short in this way, and she will be in our hearts forever".'*

NICK WAS SITTING ON an enormous patterned settee next to his twenty-six-year-old cousin Cerys, who was more like a little sister to him. Cerys had purple-and-black dyed hair, piercings in her nose and around both ears, and tight clothes that showed every bulge, of which there were plenty. Nick loved her because she was loud, opinionated, and argumentative, which made up for a lack of intelligence and common sense.

Cerys still lived with her parents and had been a great support when her sister Megan had died four years ago. Auntie Pat had never been the same since his cousin's death.

Uncle Mike was sitting in a large armchair, and all the furniture faced the television from which blared a noisy talent show. Mike had a huge mug of tea, which he sipped. Nick knew that Mike's stillness and blank expression were unusual, and the events of the previous evening weighed heavily on his mind. Finding Arabella Dixon, administering CPR, and getting Dylan Wilkins to call for an ambulance would have been a great shock.

Auntie Pat walked in with plates of fish and chips. On a low-level table, there were bottles of ketchup, pickled onions, and cutlery.

'Chippy tea all round.' Pat's voice was upbeat and sing-song as she handed plates to Nick and Cerys.

'Pass us the red sauce, Nick, before you use it all, you greedy git!' Cerys blurted with a mouth full of food.

'What's the magic word?' Nick asked, in a well-rehearsed routine.

Cerys rolled her eyes, 'Sorry. *Twat*. Could you pass the red sauce, Nick, you twat!'.

They both laughed as Nick passed her the ketchup, 'That's more like it, Morwenna.' Nick winked, taking the piss out of the Cerys' goth style. She gave him the finger before looking over at Mike, who was eating and watching the TV quietly.

'Bit quiet, Dad, you all right? Cerys asked.

'Yeah, fine.' There was an awkward silence. Mike didn't appear to be a man who was fine. Nick knew Mike would be struggling with what he had seen.

'Can't imagine finding a dead body,' Cerys said to Nick in a quiet, slightly melodramatic tone. 'I mean I know you do in your job, PC Pig, but ...' Cerys realised that humour was inappropriate and that she might be talking too much.

Mike looked over at them, 'Just a bit of shock, you know? I'll be fine.'

Nick glanced at Mike. He was the most centred, grounded, man he knew. Gentle, thoughtful and comfortable in his own skin. He also had a dry sense of humour that would disguise a joke for seconds before the penny dropped.

'You gonna be on the telly, Dad?' Cerys asked.

'Yeah, camera crew's on its way. Then I'm on Graham Norton tomorrow night with Gary Barlow.'

'What?' Cerys exclaimed, not quite getting it.

'Don't be soft.'

Pat came in, handed a plate to Mike, and sat down on the settee. 'Room for a little one?'

They watched the television talent show for a moment.

'She was a bitch anyway,' Cerys mumbled through half-munched food.

'Who was?' asked Auntie Pat.

'Miss Dixon. Right bloody snob.'

Nick winced at Cerys' bluntness, even though this was the picture they were getting.

'Cerys! Someone's killed her. Poor woman,' Pat spoke in a soft but reprimanding tone.

'Still was a bitch to me and my friends. And her son Alex. Thought they owned the world. Stuck-up, they was. But Alex was a right weirdo.'

'Weirdo? Why d'you say that?' Nick asked.

'Just all that emo, goth stuff. Horror films. He was just strange. Probably genetic,' Cerys continued.

Mike turned and looked at Cerys, 'I think that's enough now, Cerys. Please. Someone died.'

'Well, I was only saying what everyone thought,' Cerys mumbled, and then, after a slightly awkward break in the conversation, produced a very pronounced fake smile, 'Well, I've got some news.' They looked at her and Cerys' smile turned into a grimace. Nick knew there was bad news coming. 'I'm pregnant!'

'What?' Auntie Pat was confused.

'Bit of a surprise, actually,' Cerys explained in an upbeat voice, continuing the fake smile.

'How?' Pat exclaimed without thinking.

'Mam, how do you think?'

'Hold on. I thought you and Aled split up?' Uncle Mike was surprisingly calm. 'Didn't you?'

'Yes, Dad, we did. He was a dickhead. I told you that,' Cerys said, exasperated.

'So, who's the father, Cerys?' Auntie Pat asked, perplexed.

'Yeah, you see that's the thing, Mam, I'm not sure.' Cerys winced.

Nick looked at her. 'Cerys!'

'Oh, now I've heard it all.' Mike shook his head.

HALF AN HOUR LATER, Nick and Mike were playing pool in the garage; Mike needed a moment after Cerys' bombshell. The garage was lit with neon strips. It was cluttered with messy paint pots, a rusty step ladder, tools, old bikes, and general clutter. There were also three motorbikes, which were Mike's passion. There was a silver BMW 1200RT touring bike, a dark blue Suzuki GSX-R sport bike, and a red Honda dirt bike.

'Top left.' Nick predicted, as he potted a green striped ball, 'Get in!' As he went to play the next shot, his left hand, with which he was creating a bridge, shook. Mike noticed.

'Back on the pop again, are you, lad?' Mike asked him.

'A bit.' Nick lied, and wondered why he had bothered as his uncle saw straight through him.

'That's bollocks. When are you going to stay stopped?' Mike asked, getting frustrated.

'I'm sorry. I stay sober for a bit and then I think it'll be different this time,' Nick explained. It was the excuse of every relapsing alcoholic.

'Is it ever different?' Mike barked at him.

'No.' That was the agony. His head told him that he needed to drink. Life was boring and pointless without it. And this time he'd be able to control it. And every time, Nick went back to drinking all day, every day, often to the point of blackout.

'Have you ever heard of any alcoholic miraculously controlling their drinking?'

Nick shook his head. He felt ashamed. They had had this type of conversation a thousand times.

'You're an idiot. And you're gonna kill yourself,' Mike said. 'I've been to enough funerals.'

Mike had been in AA for over twenty-five years, and still attended two or three meetings a week. He chaired the meeting in Corwen. Before that, he had been a hellraiser, and in the 1970s and 1980s was no stranger to blackouts, fights, and police cells. By the time Nick had arrived at their house, Mike was in recovery, and Nick can't remember ever seeing him drink alcohol since then.

'Get yourself to a meeting. If needs be, every day,' Mike told him sternly.

'I did. But I'd picked up just before and ...'

'Stop the excuses! You're not gonna beat it on your own. And if you carry on, it'll have you in the ground. It wants you dead, lad.' Mike warned him. 'Where is it?'

Nick pointed at his jacket that hung on a hook. 'In there.'

'Go and get it. I don't want you shaking like a prick with Parkinson's and blaming that for me murdering you at pool.' Mike said darkly. 'What about a detox or rehab?'

Nick shook his head as he took the vodka from his pocket and took a swig, 'No. I'm not doing that again.' Within seconds his stomach was glowing nicely.

'You need to sort it out lad. Okay? And taper it off slow so's you don't fit.' Mike advised him as he took a shot and then looked up at Nick.

Nick didn't reply as he looked at the balls on the table, trying to calculate his next shot. He wanted to change the subject. 'You okay after last night?'

Mike thought and then nodded. 'Horrible. I can't seem to get it out of my head, you know, her lying there like that. If I close my eyes ...'

Nick knew that feeling. He'd seen a handful of dead bodies over the years. The images of them all took time to fade and never truly left your mind.

'Did you know her, Arabella Dixon?'

Mike seemed unsettled. 'Yeah, not well. I pitied her, see.'

'Pitied her, why?'

'Anyone who acts like that, and treats people like that, must be very unhappy. The "Nazi in nylons", the girls in the office called her. A perfect case of Schadenfreude, if I ever saw one.'

'Schadenfreude?'

'Aye, German phrase. Taking pleasure in others' misery. That was Arabella Dixon to a tee.'

CHAPTER 11

BY THE TIME RUTH ARRIVED at Ysgol Padog Dinas, she had already been for a three-mile run and had breakfast. She had also shaken off the emotional hangover from the previous night. Now she had snippets of *Get Up Everybody* by Byron Stingily replaying in her head from her morning's exercise. She always ran to music, especially nineties' dance music – Ministry of Sound's *Funky House Classics* was the mix of the moment.

Uniformed officers on the early shift were conducting a thorough and protracted fingertip search of the woods that backed onto the car park and school, so the main car park was full of police vehicles. In the distance, someone was cutting wood with a chainsaw and the fluctuating noise grated on her teeth.

Ruth ducked under the scene of crime tape. A private plane buzzed overhead, banked, and turned east towards England. The sun was trying to burn away the thick early-morning cloud cover, and Ruth couldn't believe how cold it was for late March. Maybe they only had two seasons in Snowdonia? Winter and summer.

Ruth paced purposefully over to the glass double doors that led from the rear car park to the maths corridor. There were still fingerprinting chemicals and dust on the glass from where SOCO had done their second walkthrough yesterday.

She expected more sketches and photographs of the crime scene to arrive on her desk by the time she got in.

She filled her lungs with crisp air and let it out slowly. She wanted to clear her head, let the tension go, and do her own walkthrough of Arabella Dixon's last moments in the stillness of early morning. It was the best time of the day to think, and even feel, what might have happened on Thursday night.

Ruth imagined that the car park was now full. She turned and scanned its full length. It was dark, and the rain was heavy and noisy. At some point, it seemed likely that someone put acid on Arabella's car, but she didn't know if that was the killer or not. Someone was clearly furious with her, so it was possible. Did she catch them in the act, and an argument or struggle ensued that led to her being murdered? They had two partial prints, but they always took Forensics a long time to analyse.

Arabella came out at around 7.55pm and saw it was raining. She had put up an umbrella and headed for her car, which had been parked in the far-left corner. Apparently, this is where she always parked. Like clockwork. Staff had mentioned it in preliminary statements that no one dared park in that space. Maybe Arabella jogged towards her car to escape the rain? And then halfway across the car park, Ruth guessed the killer had intercepted her and she had tried to escape through the parked cars. Ruth didn't know if Arabella recognised her killer. Either way, she would have been startled. At what point did she realise that she was in danger? Or did she see someone vandalising her car, go to confront them, and it got out of hand?

Ruth walked over to where a Gucci shoe heel had been found, the place now marked with a yellow plastic-numbered evidence tag No 3. Both shoes had been discovered by the green wired back fence, tag No 5.

As Ruth walked the crime scene, she imagined the terror and fear that Arabella would have felt, and it hit her. Arabella must have kicked her shoes off so she could run as fast as she could to get away. They had found an umbrella towards the back of the car park, but it was still at least fifty yards from Arabella's body. This is where Arabella realised that she was in danger and dropped the umbrella. Or where she had first been punched?

Ruth looked around at the high wire fences and tall buildings. Arabella's mistake had been to head through the parked cars. Once she had decided to run to the back of the car park she was trapped, like an animal in a cage. There was no escape, except back towards the killer. If she had headed the other way, down the side of the school, she may have escaped and lived.

Ruth remembered where the body had been found and how Arabella's corpse had lain, rain-sodden, lifeless, legs splayed at an awkward angle.

The hairs on Ruth's neck stood on end as they often did at a murder scene. Almost as if the dead victim was still present and the toxic, black atmosphere of murder lingering.

Above her, a deeper croak joined the high chatter of robins and chaffinches. It broke Ruth's train of thought as she looked up to see a dark black crow overhead, before it soared away. Ruth thought it looked enormous, like a bird of prey.

Her eyes trailed back to the rear car park, and then in the distance the red steel gates that led out to the main school car park.

She cut down the side of the school site, past the art department, and then into the main school car park. As she scanned the area, she spotted an old, innocuous, wooden hut-like building that sat in the far-left-hand corner on a patch of grass.

Ruth approached, and saw it had half a dozen steps leading up to a door and a wooden railing. At first, there was little to identify the hut-like building. Maybe it was used for storage? The weather-beaten wooden door was locked, so she cupped her hands on the dirty glass to get a better look inside. If she squinted, she could just make out a cork notice board on the wall. Someone had pinned a notice across the top of the board: *Be Better Prepared – 1ˢᵗ Denbighshire Scouts.*

NICK HAD TAKEN THE A498 out of Denbighshire and headed for the town of Welshpool, Y Trallwng. Welshpool was in the county of Montgomeryshire but fell under the jurisdiction of the county of Powys. It was only four miles from the Wales-England border, and lay on the low banks of the River Severn. Its name meant the marshy or sinking land.

Sitting in the car park of the Lighthouse Treatment Centre, Nick gave himself a moment. A mist hung low over the neat lawns and tidy flowerbeds. Across the gardens, he could see the huge Georgian manor house which housed the treatment rooms and dining facilities. It was built from a distinctive honey-coloured limestone and featured long, twelve-paned sash windows.

Nick held out his right hand and rested it on top of the steering wheel. It shook a little and the first signs of anxiety were rumbling in his lower belly. He reached for the bottle resting on the passenger seat, pinged some vodka – only a fifth of the litre bottle he had with him – and then his brain fogged and his body relaxed. He popped chewing gum into his mouth, got out of the car, and headed for the reception.

The long corridor at the Lighthouse Treatment Centre was softly lit and tastefully decorated in muted taupe and cream. *It looks more like an expensive hotel and spa than a medical facility*, Nick thought, as he was shown into one of the counselling rooms. There were four comfortable armchairs around a low-level table. There were no windows, and the walls carried tranquil photos of Snowdonia's lakes and countryside. *This is what money gets you,* Nick thought enviously. *Maybe I would have overcome my 'illness' by now if I'd had a month here*, he thought, knowing that this was the delusional thinking of an alcoholic, but not caring.

Nick had been into rehab and detox three times, courtesy of the NHS. The last time was a horrific place called Temple Villas in Llandudno. It was full of skagheads, junkies, and other general lowlifes. He had to share a bedroom with a one-legged heroin user from Shrewsbury called Kev who had had his false leg stolen weeks earlier when he was off his head. Nick kept the fact he was a copper to himself, and said he worked for the NHS. There were two squaddies, who had served in the Middle East and now drank themselves to sleep with two litres of rum a day. They were the only two 'inmates' that Nick liked and spoke to.

The regime at Temple Villas was strict; up at seven every morning, making beds, cleaning, writing daily diaries for the counsellors. No phones, no money, and television only for an hour between nine and ten. They were trying to teach the junkies how to live normally and not in smack squalor. Well, as normal as having to be breathalysed daily and have urine samples taken from the druggies twice a week.

Nick felt he was in a halfway home for offenders, or a bail hostel. They spent every evening at an AA or NA meeting where they would be greeted with tea, biscuits, and even a hug from a stranger, which Nick thought was bollocks. *Get off me, you druggie moron. I don't know where you've been.*

The worst were the Christians who would try to have 'a quiet word' with him before the meeting, trotting out the usual shit. They based the twelve steps on the Bible. He needed to say his prayers every morning. Fire and brimstone. Nothing worse than a converted alcoholic who then becomes a bullying AA zealot.

The door opened, and a nurse showed Bronwyn Wright into the room.

Nick stood and showed her his warrant card. 'I'm DS Nick Evans from the North Wales Police Major Incident Team. Would you like to take a seat, Mrs Wright?'

Bronwyn Wright sat down. She was in her fifties with short brown-blonde hair. She was far-sighted, so her thick glasses made her dark eyes appear bigger than they were. Her face was colourless and expressionless and she was, as far as Nick was concerned, asexual. Probably drugged up on diazepam, zopiclone, or something stronger. Nick loved diazepam, and if he ever nicked any dealers who had some, the evidence bag would often come back a little lighter, having kept some aside for himself. He loved the warm, dozy feeling it gave him. If only it wasn't addictive. If only he wasn't an addict.

He sat forwards with his notepad and pen. 'I'm investigating the murder of Arabella Dixon.' He hoped the chewing gum was masking the smell of booze on his breath.

Bronwyn nodded. Everything about her was at half speed as though there was a two-second delay, like they get on a foreign news feed.

'Yes. I saw that on the news. Tragedy. Horrible,' Bronwyn said.

'You knew Arabella Dixon, didn't you, Mrs Wright?'

'Yes. We worked together. It was such a shock when I saw what had happened to her,' Bronwyn explained in a tone that showed her broken state.

'How would you describe your relationship with Arabella Dixon?'

Bronwyn shook her head. 'Fine. We weren't great friends, but what happened was horrible.'

Nick looked down at his notepad. 'Arabella Dixon conducted an investigation that led to your suspension from work, didn't she?'

Bronwyn nodded, uncrossed her legs and looked down at the floor, almost as if she was embarrassed by the question.

'I'm just trying to eliminate you from our enquiries, Mrs Wright. Why were you suspended from school?' Nick asked, his tone business-like as always.

'I was provoked. I restrained a student … Very regrettable,' Bronwyn explained quietly, almost as though she was speaking to herself. There was definitely something distinctly strange about her.

'But you must have hated Arabella Dixon? It was her investigation that led to your suspension,' Nick suggested.

'Hate is a very strong word. She was an unpleasant woman but I don't go around killing people because they're unpleasant. That's ridiculous. I was shocked when I heard about her death,' Bronwyn explained, shaking her head at him.

'She's ruined your career. You've had a nervous breakdown. The school had a duty of care towards you, didn't they?' Nick asked.

'Yes, they did. And they treated me very badly. But that doesn't make me a murderer.'

Nick then looked up from scribbling in his notebook, 'Mrs Wright, can you tell me where you were on Thursday night?'

Bronwyn gave an ironic smile. 'I've been in here for two weeks, Sergeant.'

'So, you were in this building all evening on Thursday?' Nick asked.

'Apart from going for my little walk, yes.'

'And when do you go for your "little" walk?'

'Depends. Seven-ish normally. I didn't walk from here to Dinas Padog and back, before you ask.' Bronwyn snorted sarcastically.

Nick was now annoyed. *Smug cow.* 'Do you have to sign out and sign in here?'

'Technically. They're a bit lax unless you're on the addiction programme. Sometimes I forget to sign back in, or do it later,' Bronwyn explained.

'What about on Thursday?'

'I've no idea. I'm sorry but every day is the same here.' Bronwyn huffed.

'How long do you walk for, on average?'

'Thirty or forty minutes. Depends.'

Nick looked down at his notes to clarify. 'So you would have signed out on Thursday at around seven o'clock. Walked for up to forty minutes and then you "might" have signed back in, but you can't remember. Do you have a car here at the Lighthouse, Mrs Wright?'

'Yes. But the keys are taken from us and locked away until we leave.'

'Spare car keys?' Nick asked.

Bronwyn rolled her eyes impatiently. 'At home, I guess. I can't remember where exactly. I haven't seen them in years. Look, I went for a walk. I didn't drive anywhere. I'm afraid you're wasting your time talking to me.'

'Thank you for your cooperation. I will need to take a DNA sample and fingerprints before I leave, unless that's a problem?' Nick had taken a distinct dislike to Mrs Bronwyn Wright.

Bronwyn shook her head. 'That is a problem. I have nothing to hide, but you're not getting my DNA or my fingerprints.'

RUTH SAT TAPPING ENERGETICALLY away at her computer. On her screen was a crudely constructed website.

BE PREPARED – Byddwch yn barod – 1ˢᵗ Denbighshire Scout Group.

We are a Welsh rural village Scout Group based at Ysgol Dinas Padog. Home to Beavers, Cubs, Scouts and Explorer Scouts.

Ruth clicked her mouse again and her eyes ran down the screen. There it was – *1ˢᵗ Denbighshire Scouts – Thursdays, 7pm to 9pm*. Why hadn't anyone noticed this on the night? Was there a meeting that night? There could be valuable witnesses; Scouts, parents, the Scout master.

DC Sian Hockney tapped on the open door to the office.

'Boss?'

Ruth was lost in thought. 'How can I help?'

'I checked Arabella Dixon's current account and there's nothing suspicious. However, she has a savings account and there are six incoming payments of a thousand pounds each over the last six months,' Sian explained.

For a moment Ruth was lost in Sian's eyes. She glanced at Sian's left hand – no ring. However, she was more than likely straight.

'Could you trace where they came from?' Ruth asked.

'Jonathan Noakes pays her maintenance into her current account by standing order. But these payments were paid in cash, so there's no way of tracing the source. Seems strange.'

'It does. Thanks, Sian. Could you ring the bank and see if they remember who made the payments? You never know.'

Sian nodded and Ruth followed her out, watching her as she went.

Back in the incident room, Nick had already fed back regarding his interview with Bronwyn Wright. Despite what she said, both Ruth and Nick thought she had motive. If she had the spare keys to her car, she also had the means. She had also refused a DNA test. Ruth thought it was also a good idea to talk to Graham Williams and Chris Roberts. They were the last two people in the rear car park before someone murdered Arabella Dixon, even though there was a half-an-hour gap before her murder.

Moving further out into the main office area, Ruth approached Mac and Nick, who were sitting at their desks facing away from her. They hadn't noticed her presence.

'What's the new plonk DI like?' Mac asked Nick.

'Plonk? Do you mean *plonker*?' Nick frowned.

'No, it's old school. Person of little or no knowledge. Female copper,' Mac explained.

'Don't worry, Nick. When I first joined, I was a plonk, a Doris, and if I was lucky, a luv or a darlin'. That's until I did some good work and they realised I wasn't just a walking pair of tits,' Ruth said, causing the two men to jump.

Mac squirmed. 'Sorry, boss.'

Ruth turned back towards her office and without breaking stride. 'Don't worry, Mac. I've been called far worse.'

Mac looked at Nick. 'Shit! I hope she doesn't think I'm some sexist wanker still stuck in the eighties.'

Nick patted his shoulder with a grin. 'I think that ship has sailed, mate.' He might have still been annoyed at the bollocking he'd got the day before, but he wanted to stay on the case and that meant toeing the line. He could also see she had hit the ground running and knew what she was doing.

Ruth could hear Nick hurrying after her as she went back into her office, knocking on the half-open door when he reached it. 'Sorry about Mac. Too many *Sweeney* repeats on Sky. I've spoken to a Gareth Thomas who was working on reception at the Lighthouse on Thursday. Bronwyn Wright signed out at seven ten in the evening but when she signed back in, there is no recorded time. He wouldn't admit that they were relaxed in their signing in and out procedure. But he was lying, I could tell.'

'Bronwyn Wright left the Lighthouse at seven o'clock but we have no idea what time she returned. And if she had the spare keys to her car, she could have driven to Dinas Padog by seven forty-five, killed Arabella Dixon, and been back at the Lighthouse before nine?' Ruth was thinking out loud. 'Get onto traffic. Check ANPR and see if we can find out if Bronwyn Wright's car was anywhere between Welshpool and Dinas Padog between seven and nine.' ANPR stood for Automatic Number Plate Recognition – it was only used on major roads.

Nick nodded. 'Yes, boss.'

Ruth was surprised at Nick's less hostile attitude. She pointed to the computer screen. 'There is a Scout hut in the grounds of the school. In fact, it's on the far-left of the main car park. Can you find out if the scheduled Scout meeting on Thursday took place? I'm not sure how we missed it.'

Ruth rose out of her seat, and the two officers walked into the main body of Incident Room 1. Most of CID were out following up first statements, house-to-house enquiries, and any witnesses who had seen Arabella Dixon that night.

Luke walked over and opened his notebook. 'Boss, I might have got something. One of our neighbours, Jo Foreshaw, says she remembers seeing Arabella Dixon arguing with someone in the main school car park around seven o'clock when she and her husband were leaving the parents' evening. She thought it was something to do with a car. She was vague.'

'Who was she arguing with?' Nick asked.

'Male, thirties, IC1. She told us he looked "normal" except he was wearing a uniform,' Luke explained.

'A uniform?' Nick frowned.

'She thought it might have had something to do with the Scouts that meet there.'

'Dan Hughes runs the Scouts, boss,' Nick said.

'I need an address for him.'

'I know where Dan lives. I can take you there.' Nick shrugged.

'You know him?' Ruth asked.

Nick nodded. 'He's an old mate. Went to school with him. Long time ago, mind. But I see him around.'

'What's he like?'

'Good bloke. Not the sharpest tool in the box but he's an all right bloke. I see him down the pub and we talk about the rugby, you know? I'll take you there now, boss.'

Ruth couldn't believe how everyone really did know everyone. It was such a stark contrast to London. This was starting to feel like an episode of *Midsomer Murders*.

DANIEL HUGHES LIVED on a small housing estate called Abbots Way, or *Rhodfa'r Abad*. There was a scruffy rectangular piece of grass at the centre of a covered road, on which sat a bright blue Volkswagen GTI that was jacked up and had no front tyres. The grass was bordered by identical block houses, made from red brick, that looked cramped and slightly run down. Each had a white front door with different shapes of glass. The plain brick frontage of each house was adorned with some kind of satellite dish, and the house at the end still had a fringe of cheap white Christmas lights hanging at an angle from the grey plastic guttering. *Not the traditional face of rural North Wales or Snowdonia,* Ruth thought to herself as they drove into the estate and parked outside number twenty-two.

There were some old pots of paint in the front garden, and an empty hanging basket beside the front door, which had diamonds of glass cut into the white UPVC in a vertical line.

Ruth knocked on the door and a tall man in his thirties answered, holding a toddler with a pink dummy, top-knot hair, and dirty yellow tights.

She showed her warrant card. 'Mr Hughes?'

'Yeah,' Hughes said, and then he looked at Nick. 'Hi, Nick. Everything all right, is it?' Hughes asked in a friendly tone.

'Just a few questions about Thursday night, Dan. That's all. Routine, mate,' Nick said, and winked reassuringly.

Ruth clocked this. What the hell was Nick doing? He couldn't have been more unprofessional.

'Oh, that teacher that got murdered. Horrible, weren't it? I was shocked, you know?' Hughes said with a frown.

Hughes was over six feet tall, skinny, round shouldered, and looked tired. He had a strong jaw, straight nose, and his receding hair had been given a Grade 1 all over. As he ushered them in, a small boy appeared by his calf and peered up at Ruth and Nick.

They got to the kitchen, and Ruth was surprised how clean and tidy it was, having already decided it would be a mess.

'We wanted to check your whereabouts at around eight o'clock on Thursday, Mr Hughes,' Ruth explained.

'I run the Scouts so I would have been in the middle of doing the meeting, like,' Daniel said.

'Dan, did you know Arabella Dixon?' Nick's tone was friendly. Too friendly for Ruth's liking.

'Not really. I knew who she was.'

'And what did you think of her, as a person?' asked Ruth.

Hughes frowned a little nervously. 'I don't know. I didn't really know her. She wasn't at the school when I was there.'

'Dan, we have a witness that saw you arguing with Arabella Dixon at around seven o'clock on Thursday night. Is that right?' Nick asked.

Hughes put his daughter down. 'Go and play upstairs, darling.' He turned to them, full of anxiety. 'Yeah, okay, we had a bit of a row like. But I haven't got nothing to do with what happened to her. You don't think I did, do you?'

'You've just lied about knowing her,' Ruth said.

Nick gave him a reassuring smile. 'Mate, we're just eliminating you from our enquiries. If you just tell us the truth, you'll have nothing to worry about, okay?'

Ruth glared at Nick, who ignored her. What was he doing? She wasn't impressed.

'Okay, yeah, course. She came over to complain about the parents dropping off the boys for Scouts, see. She says it causes chaos in the car park for parents' evenings. Does this every time, like clockwork. Couple of years ago, she told me to cancel Scouts if there was a clash. I didn't, 'cos I thought it was a bloody cheek, you know what I mean?' Hughes explained.

'So, you didn't like Arabella Dixon then?' Ruth asked.

'If I'm honest, not really. Thought she was bloody full of herself. Stuck-up. We fell out when I kicked her son out of our Scout group.'

Ruth and Nick shared a look. 'Alex Noakes?'

'Yeah.'

'And why was that?'

'I caught him smoking weed out the back. I knew he'd done it before, but this time I got him red-handed. Think he was dealing too but couldn't prove it, like. The dad apologised to me. But she didn't believe me, stupid cow. She said it was 'cos they was both half-caste. Thought her son was perfect, you know what they're like?' Daniel explained.

Ruth glared at him. 'Know what *who* are like?'

'You know. Blacks. Chips on their shoulders because the whole world is against them. Made me laugh 'cos they wasn't even proper black.' Daniel snorted.

Ruth shot Nick a glance at the blatant racism. He wasn't impressed either. 'I saw him on Thursday actually,' Daniel added.

'Alex Noakes?' Nick asked.

'Yeah, here at the school. Heading through the car park towards the back of the school. I suppose he was there to see her, was he?' Daniel shrugged nonchalantly.

'And what time would this have been, Mr Hughes?' Ruth probed.

'I dunno. I get here about six thirty to set things up, so about then.'

'Okay. Thank you for your help, Mr Hughes,' Ruth said.

THE MIDDAY SUN WAS out, bathing the passing fields and hedgerows in light but the temperature was still low, and as Ruth looked over to see the car's gauge she saw it was recording a measly five degrees centigrade. *Is it ever warm here?*

There was silence between Ruth and Nick, who was driving slowly behind a tractor and uttering the odd swear word at having to travel at 25 mph.

She wasn't happy with his 'matey' approach to their questioning of Hughes. Her 'softly, softly' approach was based on experience and current research by psychologists. Despite what they showed on the telly, Ruth knew that a tough questioning technique often made a suspect clam up and go to 'No comment' quicker than she could open her notebook. Empathy, compliments, and finding things in common got much better results. Nick's questioning of Hughes was simply unprofessional.

'Can I suggest that you take a more professional approach next time you interview someone you know?' Ruth said.

'What's that meant to mean?' Nick growled.

'It means that if your friend Dan is involved in Arabella Dixon's murder in any way, winking and calling him "mate" is going to make you look, at best, a moron. At worst, it can open up an accusation of colluding with a suspect.'

There was silence and Ruth could feel the tension.

'I'm not undermining you, Nick. I'm trying to protect you,' Ruth explained.

'This isn't London. We do things differently up here. People talk to us because they know and trust us. I guarantee it's not like that in the Met, is it?' Nick said.

Ruth waited a moment. He had a point, but he had crossed the line earlier. Getting out a cigarette, she looked over at Nick. 'Do you mind if I smoke?'

'Do I have a choice?' Nick said.

Ruth took that as a yes but lit the cigarette anyway and buzzed the window down a couple of inches to let the smoke escape. He could sod off.

As she looked out at the passing landscape, Ruth had an empty feeling of being a long, long way from anywhere. In a place reserved for the resilient. And then a feeling, part loneliness and part freedom, swept over her. She breathed a deep sigh. As much as this new environment was testing her, it was good to get out of the office, especially in a place that looked like this. It beat Peckham High Street.

Ruth's phone rang. 'DI Hunter?'

It was DC Sian Hockney. 'Boss, I've just had a uniformed officer in here with some information that might be useful. Someone called them out to a domestic disturbance at Willow Cottage – Arabella Dixon's place – last Tuesday.'

'What happened?'

'Neighbours – a Mr and Mrs Lincoln – heard shouting and then glass breaking so they called the emergency services. When a uniformed patrol got there, Miss Dixon said it was just a row with her son, and the wine glass breaking was accidental. She made a fuss and asked them why they weren't out doing proper police work. The officer described her as a "real piece of work".'

'Thank you, Sian. Anything else?' Ruth asked.

'Uniform recorded that there was someone else at the house at the time of the incident. A Rhiannon Baker was leaving when the patrol got there,' Sian explained.

For a moment, Ruth ran the name through her brain. She knew that name. Of course, it was the girl who had served her at the bar in her hotel.

'And, last thing, boss. Forensics have come back with analysis on the acid damage on Arabella Dixon's car. It was sulphuric acid drain cleaner, which is available in supermarkets. Virtually no oxidisation on the primer or metal underneath, so the car was damaged within the last twenty-four hours. The partial prints are on the primer and metal, which means they belong to the person who damaged the car.'

'Thanks, Sian. That's great work.'

Although Ruth thought DC Hockney was gorgeous, it was also clear that she was smart and intuitive, which made her even more attractive.

As Sian left the office, Ruth activated her phone, where one headline, which had automatically appeared on her phone, caught her eye and made her stomach lurch. *Old Bailey trial hears how baby was splattered in blood at christening robbery.* The story referred back to a crime that had scared Ruth to her very being, her very soul, and finally made her mind up to leave the Met.

Last summer, she and another CID officer were out on response when they had a shout to go to the Ledbury Estate in Peckham. An emergency call had come in, reporting that masked gunmen had attacked a christening. There were around forty guests, mainly of Sierra Leonean descent.

By the time Ruth and her partner, DC Cooper, arrived, many of the guests had fled in terror. However, Binta Mali, the thirty-one-year-old aunt of the christened baby, had been shot in the head and killed. She had crumpled to the floor still holding her eight-month-old niece Jenneh, who was covered in her aunt's blood and brains.

Ruth remembered the sound of Jenneh's screaming, as her parents, still shaking uncontrollably, wiped the blood from their unharmed daughter with baby wipes. A relative told Ruth how the four teenaged gang members had calmly walked around with bin bags telling guests to hand over any valuables, wallets, and jewellery, as Binta Mali lay dying.

Ruth later learned that Binta and her family had come to Britain because Sierra Leone was too dangerous. She claimed that living in London was a dream come true.

A week later, four teenagers from the notorious Dem Africans gang were arrested and charged. Ruth watched as they laughed as they were cuffed, and the fifteen-year-old gunman wondered why that 'bitch's head not explode' when he shot her. At that moment, Ruth thought enough was enough, and felt more disillusioned than ever before.

For a moment, Arabella Dixon's face came into her mind. Was there a racial element to the attack? She hadn't seen a black face since she arrived in Wales, and she knew that racism flourished in predominantly white demographics. And what Daniel Hughes had said earlier played again in her head, '... *you know what they're like? Blacks. Chips on their shoulders because the entire world is against them. Made me laugh 'cos they wasn't even proper black.'* Was Daniel Hughes worth another look, given his views on race?

CHAPTER 12

IT WAS GONE TWO BY the time Ruth and Nick turned off the A235 towards Llandrillo.

'Why do you think Alex Noakes lied about being at Dinas Padog school?' Ruth asked.

'Maybe he was just scared?' Nick suggested. 'He could have been there to confront his mother?'

'That would make sense if they'd had a blazing row,' Ruth said.

'Maybe he was there to damage her car?' Nick said.

'If she caught him doing it, they could have argued and then things got out of hand?' Ruth said, thinking out loud.

'In terms of motive, means, and opportunity, that would put Alex Noakes as a frontrunner,' Nick said.

It was moments like this that Ruth could see Nick's potential for becoming an excellent copper. He just needed to stop being so defensive.

'Let's see what the neighbours have to say,' Ruth said, as they pulled over and parked.

Mr and Mrs Lincoln lived in a large bungalow to the left of Willow Cottage. As they approached, Nick told Ruth that the surname *Lincoln* rang a bell somewhere. They knocked at the glass-patterned front door and noticed a poster in the window: *Yr Eglwys Fethodistaidd Yng Nghymru – The Methodist Church In Wales.*

A grey, bearded man in glasses answered the door. Ruth explained who they were and that they would like to ask him some questions about Arabella Dixon. The man – Mr Arlo Lincoln – welcomed them inside.

The house was tidy but a little sparse and basic. Ruth immediately noticed that some of the paintings on the wall had religious themes. There were also posters including one that read, *Connecting with God - Welsh Methodist Youth*, which featured the Methodist symbol of a black cross and a red flame. Beside that, a poster that had in large black writing, *Not Today, Satan!*

Arlo Lincoln explained that he was a reverend at the local Methodist chapel.

Ruth noticed a photograph of around twenty teenagers posing. Reverend Lincoln was in the middle, and to one side were two men that she recognised from the school's CCTV – Graham Williams and Chris Roberts, teachers from Ysgol Dinas Padog. The photo had a printed caption: *Methodist Youth Camp in Aberystwyth, 2015.*

'Mr Lincoln - or do I call you *Reverend*?' Ruth asked.

'I'd prefer Arlo, actually. Can I get you tea or coffee?'

'We're fine, but thank you.' Ruth gave him a smile and looked back at her notes.

'How long have you lived next door to Arabella Dixon?'

Arlo thought for a moment. 'Must be six or seven years.'

'And what opinion did you form of Miss Dixon over that time?' Nick said.

Arlo paused, thinking of a diplomatic way of responding. 'She wasn't our sort of person. And to be honest, she seemed like a troubled soul. My wife and I both prayed for her.'

Ruth frowned. 'A troubled soul? Could you explain what you mean by that?'

'There was a lot of screaming. We felt sorry for her son – Alex, I think it is. He seemed to bear the brunt of her anger a lot of the time. And in recent years there seemed to be a lot of coming and going. Different cars, usually men, in the middle of the night.'

Ruth shot Nick a look. No wonder Alex argued with his mother – it sounded like she was the village bike.

Ruth glanced over at Arlo. 'Different men in the middle of the night? Do you know who they were?'

'We tried to keep ourselves to ourselves. But we couldn't help noticing the different cars. The headlights would sometimes wake us up at all times of the night.' Arlo seemed annoyed.

'Do you know what they were doing there?' Ruth said. *They weren't playing chess,* she thought to herself, but she needed to ask.

Arlo snorted and said, 'I've got a pretty good idea. "The works of the flesh are evident. I warn you, as I warned you before, that those who do such things will not inherit the Kingdom of God." And that's why we prayed for her.'

Nick looked at his notes. 'You called the police last Tuesday evening due a disturbance next door, is that correct?'

'Yes. It was the usual story. She was screaming, and then we heard the sound of breaking glass. We didn't know what else to do.'

'Did you notice whether anyone was next door between seven and eight o'clock last Thursday?' Ruth enquired.

'I'm sorry. I was out at a Bible meeting until ten.'

'What about your wife?' Nick said.

'She was with me I'm afraid,' Arlo explained.

Ruth and Nick finished up and asked Arlo Lincoln to get in touch if he remembered anything else.

Ruth was amused by the encounter, although it was frustrating that Arlo couldn't shed any light on who had been in the house last Thursday. Nick said he thought he was a self-righteous twat, until he remembered why the name rang a bell.

'Boss, I thought the name *Lincoln* was familiar. CID have looked at Arlo Lincoln before, I'm sure of it,' Nick said with a frown as they walked out onto the street and towards the neighbouring house.

'What for?' Ruth asked.

'I was still in uniform then. I think it was allegations of child sex abuse. I can't be sure,' Nick said.

'Right. Have a look back at the files,' Ruth said, taking the information in. 'I'm not sure if there's any connection, but there was a photo in the living room of some Methodist Youth Camp. I noticed that Graham Williams and Chris Roberts were also in the photo. And Graham Williams' name seems to crop up a lot. I've read his statement and there doesn't seem to be anything untoward, but I think I might pop in for a chat when I've got a moment,' Ruth said.

They walked next door, went to Arabella Dixon's house and knocked on the door. After a bit of a delay a reluctant Alex Noakes showed them into the house, which stank of weed. Ruth looked at the young man's eyes, which were puffy and bloodshot. The kitchen was now a mess, with a sink full of washing up, surfaces covered in empty cereal boxes, cans of beer, and an ash tray full of the remnants of spliffs.

Alex sat at the kitchen table but looked down at the floor. He looked tired and broken. His white Uzumaki manga horror t-shirt was stained with food.

Ruth waited a moment. 'Alex, there are a few things we need to go through with you.' He nodded, but continued staring at the floor.

'Do you know why Mum was killed yet?' Alex asked.

'I'm afraid not. But we will find the person who killed your mother and bring them to justice. I promise you that. You told us that on Thursday evening you were here all night? Is that right?' Ruth asked.

'Yeah, I was.'

'You see, we have an eyewitness that saw you at the school at around six thirty. Is that possible?' Ruth enquired.

Alex looked up at her, pushed his hair off his face, and wiped his hand across his mouth nervously. 'Who the hell said that?'

'We're not at liberty to tell you that information.' Nick looked over as he took notes.

Alex took a deep breath as he weighed up what to say next.

'Alex, is it possible that you were at the school on Thursday at some point?' Ruth asked calmly.

'Yeah, maybe I was,' Alex shrugged.

'Okay. Can you tell us why you went to the school?'

'To talk to my mum,' Alex mumbled.

'Couldn't it have waited until she got home?' Nick frowned.

Alex shook his head. 'No. It couldn't wait. It was urgent.'

'Can you tell us what was so urgent that you had to go to school to see your mum, Alex?' Ruth asked.

'Do I have to tell you? I mean, can you make me tell you?'

'No, but you've lied to us about being at the school, which is the scene of a very serious crime. We need to understand why,' Ruth said.

'I was moving out of the house and going to live with my girlfriend.' Alex was reluctant.

'And why did you feel the need to move out?'

'I couldn't live with her anymore. She was suffocating me. Sometimes she scared me,' Alex admitted.

'Is Rhiannon Baker your girlfriend?' Ruth asked.

'Yeah,' Alex said, as he looked down and let out a breath.

'Did you see your mum on Thursday night?' Ruth asked.

'No. Well, I saw her in the hall talking to parents and that. I waited for ages. She didn't see me, or if she did, she ignored me. Rhiannon texted me to ask where I was. So, I went back out and drove home. I thought I could wait until Mum got home and talk to her properly,' Alex explained.

'Would it be fair to say you were very angry with your mum?'

'Not really. A bit, maybe.'

'Has this anything to do with what happened on Tuesday night? We heard there was some kind of disturbance?' Ruth asked.

'Disturbance? No ...' Alex said with a frown.

'Alex, we know there was a row here on Tuesday. Why was that?' Ruth asked.

Alex looked at the floor and said nothing. He was lying.

'Alex?' Ruth said, almost as if she was talking to a child.

'It was nothing,' Alex mumbled.

Ruth coaxed him softly. 'There were police officers here, Alex. Come on.'

'She came home and ... caught us in bed together. Only watching TV. She went mental.'

'Can you tell us exactly what happened?' Nick said, as he looked over at him.

'We got dressed and came downstairs. Mum screamed that Rhiannon was a chav and I was to have nothing to do with her. She wasn't good enough for me. I'd heard it all before. We carried on rowing. Eventually, Rhiannon told Mum that I was going to move out and live with her. My mum hit her in the face. I told her to calm down and then she threw a glass at me. Rhiannon drove home and then the police came.'

There is motive right there, Ruth thought.

Ruth gave Alex an understanding nod. 'Thank you for being so honest, Alex.'

'Do you know how your mum's car got damaged?' Nick asked.

Alex shrugged. 'No. I didn't know it was damaged.'

'Someone poured sulphuric acid on the bonnet. Do you know anything about that?'

'No ...' Alex said. He seemed genuinely surprised.

'Did anyone see you leave the school, or did you speak to anyone when you got home?' Ruth asked.

Alex was getting emotional. 'No. This is ridiculous. Why aren't you out there looking for the person who killed my mum? I didn't kill her, did I? I'm not some kind of weird psychopath!'

Ruth looked at Alex. She wasn't sure. Maybe he had just been a confused teenager trying to escape a controlling and emotionally manipulative mother. But maybe, for a split second, his rage had got the better of him?

CHAPTER 13

IT HAD TAKEN RUTH FORTY minutes to drive over to Liverpool to see her daughter, Ella. It was nearer than she thought. The wind from the Mersey cut right through her as she made her way out of the NCP car park and headed for the Liverpool ONE shopping centre. She had spent most of the journey playing out scenarios and hypotheses in her head about Arabella Dixon's murder. Bronwyn Wright's motive seemed a little weak, and unless they could find evidence she had left the Lighthouse, her alibi was fairly tight too. They were still trawling traffic cameras to see if Jonathan Noakes was travelling at the time of the murder. Daniel Hughes had an alibi and, although he was racist, arguments over parking problems rarely led to murder.

Then there was Alex Noakes. His relationship with his mother was volatile and at breaking point. Arabella was clearly controlling, and forty-eight hours earlier had punched his girlfriend and thrown a glass at him. A witness put Alex at the school, and he had no alibi. If he had confronted her, then it could have escalated out of control. There was a lot of anger and resentment between them. But it didn't explain the carved symbols. Was Alex calculating enough to try to throw the police off the scent? That would imply planning and premeditation.

Seagulls screeched noisily overhead, breaking her train of thought. It was now dark, and Ruth crossed the busy road that split the Albert Docks from the rest of the city. She was meeting her daughter, Ella, who was doing a postgraduate Master's in child psychology at Liverpool University. With the rocky childhood she had been subjected to, it wasn't entirely surprising. Mixed with her guilt, Ruth was just grateful her daughter had emerged a relatively unscathed adult. The very thought of Ella made Ruth smile. That beautiful, perfect face, her smiling eyes. That was what unconditional love felt like. Powerful, overwhelming, beautiful.

They hadn't seen each other since Ella's visit to London at Christmas. Back then, Ruth had been an emotional wreck, full of self-pity and totally absorbed with Sarah. Ruth was also getting nightmares and flashbacks from Binta Mali's murder, and self-medicating with gin and codeine. Basically, Ruth hadn't been 'present' for much of the holidays, and Ella had made her excuses and returned to Liverpool early. Ruth felt she had some making up to do.

Ella's father, Dan, had moved to Australia ten years ago with his new family and, apart from the odd phone call, Ella had virtually no contact with him. Ella was the best thing that Ruth and Dan did in their brief, explosive, and messed-up marriage in the 1990s.

Ruth walked through the crowded shopping centre, wondering when and why people had the time to go shopping. She hated it. Sarah used to love to shop, and Ruth would trawl around after her along the King's Road, Notting Hill, or Camden. It didn't matter that she found it tedious, because she was with Sarah. And she lived for those moments when she and Sarah would pop into a pub, bar, or café for some food and a quick drink. She remembered the laughter, and the pure joy of those moments, and her stomach turned.

Then Ruth saw a figure waving at her from a small café table. A tall, slim, blonde woman in her early twenties. Her baby. She was wearing ballet pumps, white jeans, and a baggy, navy, cross-knit jumper and a long scarf. Ruth looked at Ella's skin that was porcelain perfect and made her look younger than she actually was.

They hugged, and then Ruth squeezed a little tighter. 'You got here before me, you sod!'

'I did some retail therapy.' Ella lifted up shopping bags to show her mum.

Ruth looked down at the table to see two large mugs; flat white for her, Americano for Ella.

'And I was going to treat you.'

'Just sit down, Mum.'

'I could do with a ciggie. I used to love smoking in cafés. Blowing a great big lungful up into the air,' Ruth reminisced, not sure where to start and feeling a little nervous as Christmas had been so awful. Since then there had only been a few short phone calls and brief weekly texts.

'Yeah, and killing yourself and everyone around you.' Ella snorted.

'Oh God, live and let live.' There was an awkward beat as Ruth sipped her coffee and looked up at Ella. 'So ... how are you?'

'Good. I'm fine,' Ella said unconvincingly.

'Not buying it. Something wrong?'

A moment, as Ella looked down at the bags of shopping.

'No ... Want to see what I bought?' Ella was trying to be bright and breezy.

'Of course. But first, what's this Andy like?'

Ella had briefly mentioned an Andy at Christmas, but Ruth was so befuddled by gin and codeine that she hadn't taken too much of an interest. But in the short phone call catch-ups since, his name had kept popping up. He was a fellow student and they had now been on several dates, but that's as much as Ruth knew.

'I don't know. He's nice. Intelligent. Bit intense.' Ella was being guarded.

'Intense? Where's he from?'

'North Wales, funnily enough. He lives with his mum, who he says is a nightmare.'

'Did you tell him that your mother was also a night-mare?' Ruth said, with a teasing smile. It was such a relief that Ella still felt able to tell her what was going on in her life.

'No. I said you were great.'

Ruth felt a little tingle of warmth. She didn't deserve a daughter like Ella and it made her feel guilty.

'Did you tell him I was gay?' Ruth asked.

'Yes.' Ella said, as if to say, 'Why wouldn't I?'

'What did he say to that?' Ruth asked. She wasn't surprised at Ella's openness. She had been brought up by two lesbian mothers and she was proud of that fact.

'"*Cool. That's very progressive*" were his exact words, I think.'

'Good ...' Ruth smiled at her. She held on to the moment as she watched her daughter smile. She lived for these glimmers, and realised that it was partly her fault they were so rare. She sighed. 'I'm sorry about Christmas. I really am. But I've moved on and I'm fine. I'm really fine. So, you must tell me if you need to talk about anything. I mean it. We used to tell each other everything.' Ruth's tone was urgent.

'Of course.' Ella swept the hair from her face.

Ella gave her a reassuring smile, but Ruth knew there was a lot of work to do.

IT WAS NIGHT-TIME AND a rolled ten-pound note was placed down to a four-inch line of coke that snaked over a woman's naked buttock. Nick leant down, put the note up his nostril, and snorted the white powder up in one swift motion. He licked his finger, wiped it over the residue and then rubbed his gums. *Bloody lovely.* He then sniffed loudly, making sure that all the coke was out of his nose and that it had trickled down his throat that was now numb. It was a feeling that excited, and promised so much.

Nick nodded to himself as he took a glass of Jameson whiskey and swigged it down. 'That is good, man,' he said to himself. He clenched his fist as the euphoria swept through him. The rush was overwhelming and caught his breath.

Becci – or SexyBex33 as she was known on Noquestion-sasked.co.uk – rolled over. She was pretty, in a cheap sort of way, with dyed-blonde hair in a ponytail, and a nose ring. She was wearing a cheap black bra, stockings, and heels.

'Do you want another line?' Nick asked her.

'No. Just fuck me, will ya.' Her voice was pure North Wales.

Nick lay on top of her, holding his weight on his elbows as he entered her. 'You want to be fucked, do you?' He looked into her eyes and smirked, which he knew made his eyes twinkle.

'Yes. Yes.' She was so into it, and nodded.

'Yes? Are you sure?' Nick asked teasingly.

'Yes. Just do it, you nob!'

Nick thrust into her hard and fast and she came in a matter of seconds. Job done.

'Come on. Don't stop!' Her voice was now frustrated. She wanted to cum again, greedy bitch. No chance.

Nick stood up, looked down at her, and gave the cheeky grin that he could only seem to muster when he was off his head.

'Stand up.' Nick's voice was commanding.

Becci stood up and Nick pulled her waist close to him and kissed her hard on the mouth. Their tongues fought for a moment before she relented. They both groaned as the kiss became deeper and more passionate. It was too much for Nick. It was too intimate, and this wasn't about feeling anything other than sexual power. He knew kissing on the mouth was his undoing and messed his head up. Don't feel anything or get involved.

'Bend over,' Nick said in a deep, confident voice as he spun Becci around, hands on her hips, and pushed her over the end of the bed. Her arse in suspenders looked amazing. The stuff of great porn.

'Kinky. What are you going to do to me now, Sergeant?'

'If you don't shut up, I'm going to spank you so hard you're not gonna believe it!' Nick warned her, pushing himself against her.

'Oh, really? Show me,' she gasped.

Nick hit her hard with his hand, which thwacked against her skin with an erotic smack. She panted again.

'You like that, yes? Have you been naughty?'

'Fuck yes, just make it harder, will you?'

Nick obliged, suddenly losing total control and hitting her with all his might. And then again and again. This was now about control and violence, but Nick was lost in the feeling. It felt amazing.

'Ow! That hurts, you twat!' Becci complained.

'Make your mind up, bint!'

Nick pushed her lower back down and now she couldn't move. He could feel her pushing back, trying to get up.

'Just stop!' Becci shouted.

Nick hit her again and felt he was totally out of control. His hand was numb from hitting her. And then tears formed in his eyes as he continued.

He stopped, turned and walked away, full of self-loathing, hoping she would get dressed and go and he would never see her again.

Becci grabbed her clothes off the floor, walked over and hit him hard with the flat of her hand. He could feel the outline of her rings against his skull.

'You're a pathetic prick, you know that?'

She ran to the bedroom door and then slammed it behind her angrily.

Nick let out a breath of relief and sat on the bed. He looked out of the window and wept.

He was so broken and so lost.

CHAPTER 14

RUTH WAS DESPERATE for a ciggie. She had been sitting in Chief Superintendent John Jones' office, filling him in on the developments in the case for nearly an hour. Jones loved the sound of his own voice. He talked in platitudes as if he was overcompensating for something.

'We're taking a hammering on social media on this,' Jones said.

'It's early days, sir. We're waiting on a lot of forensics, and since the cuts, it's taking longer than ever,' Ruth explained.

'I can lean on Forensics for you, if that'll help,' Jones said in his usual supercilious tone.

That wouldn't work. The worst anyone could do was throw their weight around with the Forensics team. They could react badly and even drag their heels. It was another sign that Jones' man management skills were woeful.

'Thank you, sir, but I've been over this morning with biscuits and a big, pleading smile. I find Forensics react better to that than a bollocking,' Ruth said.

Jones looked at her for a moment with a furrowed brow. 'You know, Ruth, I've been really impressed with how you've hit the ground running up here. When I got the transfer papers from the Met, I feared you were up here to see out your pension. And I thought you'd be looking down on us all as small-town yokels. But from what I hear, there's been none of that,' Jones said.

That was the thing about being a CID Detective, thought Ruth. You couldn't just coast and settle for an easy life. Her instinct was that the victims and their families deserved justice, and that made it impossible to do anything but your best work.

'I can't see any point in replacing you as the SIO on this case. In fact, I'm glad that you are the SIO,' Jones said.

'Thank you, sir.' It was nice to get a compliment, even if was from Jones.

'I suggest you do a press conference. And I really need to go to the commander with a decent lead in the next forty-eight hours.'

'Yes, sir. I'll do my best. We've got a good team in CID,' Ruth said, as she got up and left Jones' office to head back downstairs.

Ruth didn't like Jones. She knew exactly what he was. On the surface, he was a politician. Every word and phrase he spoke, in his considered voice, felt calculated and premeditated. He had the fondness of starting sentences with 'Let's just say ...', as if making comments hypothetical would be less annoying. Obviously not. She knew that underneath the mask, he was ruthless, controlling, and maybe even vindictive if he didn't get his way.

Arriving at her desk with fresh coffee, Ruth stood and looked out the window of her office, which was on the sixth floor of the concrete tower block that housed North Wales Police Eastern Divisional Headquarters. It was a grey, dismal day in the town, and the wind was pushing and pulling the

trees below. She could see the newly-built law-courts building, and the modern glass sides and parabolic, symmetri-
cally-curved roof of the leisure centre. Behind that, the
140-foot tower of St Mark's, which had been there since the
seventeenth century, jutted into the sky with its blackened
hexagonal turrets. It was a depressing view, Ruth thought to
herself, especially on a drizzly day like today. Maybe it was
because it reminded her of London.

Ruth glanced back at her desk where the SOCOs' photos of Arabella Dixon's body and the crime scene were
arranged. She wasn't satisfied with what they had at the moment. This wouldn't do. Nothing was leaping out at her.
Nothing compelling, and that was unusual. Had they missed
something? That's why she had essentially started again.
Sometimes police work was about going back to basics, pa-
tiently returning to the evidence. She sat for a while looking
at the photos, waiting to see if something clicked. Until it
did, she knew it was just a matter of meticulously working
through what they had.

Beside her computer were printed A4 sheets where she
had been doing some digging on Alex Noakes. According to
the school, he had left Dinas Padog High School in 2013 to
go to the sixth form at St Gerard's Hall, a public boarding
school that was nearly seventy miles away. Given what she
knew about Arabella Dixon, that didn't surprise Ruth. She
was pushy, controlling and unemotional. She also imagined
that Alex would have been thrilled about moving away from
her. Maybe that was when their relationship broke down?

Ruth took some files and wandered out into the office.
On one side, Sian was on the phone and scribbling notes.

Luke was busy trawling through CCTV footage of the road outside Ysgol Dinas Padog on Thursday night. Something about the intensity with which Luke was looking at the footage, and then replaying it, stirred her interest.

'Got something, Luke?' Ruth asked heading over.

'Not sure, boss. This white Audi is parked on the road and stays there for about ten minutes. At first, you can't see the plate because of the car parked behind.' Luke explained, showing Ruth the grainy footage of a white car. 'Then at six-fifteen these two figures get out the back of the car. This one smokes a cigarette. They've got hoods up and they're talking to someone in the driver's seat.'

Luke paused the image as Ruth gazed at it and thought. The image seemed out of place at a parents' evening.

'Definitely not parents, but not pupils either because they're not in uniform.' Ruth was thinking out loud.

Luke continued playing the CCTV footage and Ruth watched as the two hooded figures hugged for a while.

'Then around six thirty both these figures go through this gate into the school.'

Ruth looked at her notes. 'Daniel Hughes saw Alex Noakes walking across the school site at six thirty. And we're assuming' – she pointed at the figure on the frozen CCTV image – 'that this could be Rhiannon Baker, but Daniel Hughes made no mention of her, so where did she go? And whose car is that?'

'Boss, ten minutes later, this happens,' Luke replied as he played the CCTV footage again. The car behind pulls out and away, revealing the number plate of the white Audi – JN 1000.

'I haven't run the plate through the PNC yet—'

'No need. That's Jonathan Noakes' car. So, Alex lied to us when he said that he drove himself to school to talk to his mother. Looks like Jonathan Noakes drove Alex and possibly Rhiannon Baker to the school.' *Lying bastards.* But why lie to her? Something didn't feel right. 'How long does the car stay there?' Ruth asked.

'Another ten minutes. Then at 6.42 pm the car drives up the road and turns left into the school,' Luke explained.

'And when does the car come back out?' Ruth asked.

'It doesn't. That's the problem.' Luke walked over to the plan of the school that was on the whiteboard. 'You see, boss, this road goes right across the school site, past the playing fields, the back of the sports hall, and comes out here on Ash Lane.'

'Do we have CCTV?' Ruth asked, already fearing the answer.

'No, boss.'

'Shit! We're assuming that Jonathan Noakes is driving his car. But we've no idea what time Alex Noakes or Rhiannon Baker left the school or how they left?'

The evidence was stacking up against Alex Noakes, and Ruth wondered how Jonathan Noakes and Rhiannon Baker were involved? They had all lied about their whereabouts on the night of Arabella Dixon's murder.

'Good work, Luke.' Ruth stayed by the whiteboard and gazed at the image of Arabella Dixon at its centre. She then looked over at Sian, who had finished her phone call. 'Sian, where are we at with Bronwyn Wright at the moment?'

'Traffic gave us a county-wide traffic camera survey for Denbighshire.' Sian explained, coming over from her desk. 'Most were with ANPR technology but not all. Bronwyn Wright's number plate doesn't show up anywhere in the twenty-four hours around Arabella Dixon's death, ma'am.'

'Okay. Thanks.' Ruth looked up at her and their eyes locked for longer than was comfortable. Sian smiled, turned to go, and Ruth couldn't help but feel a little tingle of excitement. She hadn't even thought of a relationship since Sarah's disappearance.

Nick came into the office, coffee in hand. His complexion was grey, eyes sunken.

'Sorry I'm late, boss.' Nick was a little out of breath.

Ruth pulled a face. 'You look like shit, Nick.' She wasn't impressed, and that was reflected in her tone of voice.

'Mate's stag do. Sorry, boss.'

'We'll talk about this later,' Ruth warned him.

'Yes, boss.'

Now irritated, Ruth snapped, raising her voice almost to a bark. 'Right! I want contact made with Alex Noakes, Jonathan Noakes, and Rhiannon Baker. I want them in first thing tomorrow for voluntary questioning. Rhiannon Baker will need an appropriate adult as she's seventeen. They've all lied about their whereabouts on Thursday evening and we need to find out why they are dicking us about.'

The room fell silent. They'd become accustomed to Ruth's gentle manner and were surprised. Outside in the corridor, two men were laughing, which added to the tension in the room. Ruth looked around. She didn't really know any of them, and they weren't friends or colleagues yet. But she was impressed with what she had found, and they were beginning to feel like a team. At least she hoped the others felt the same way.

Ruth walked over to Arabella Dixon's photo and pointed to it. 'Three days ago, Arabella Dixon was murdered brutally. She was a teacher for God's sake. I want the bastard or bastards that did it.'

THE PRESS CONFERENCE started at 4pm and the room was bustling with local and national journalists from newspapers, radio, and television. Ruth could feel the nerves in her stomach, and had popped a couple of painkillers so the codeine could take the edge off. She looked for Superintendent Jones and saw him talking intensely with the North Wales Police press officer. He clocked Ruth's gaze and gave her a supportive nod. *Piss off,* she thought as she looked at him.

Nick sat beside her, looking a good deal healthier than he had done five hours earlier. She was now convinced that he had some kind of drink problem.

Behind them was a banner on the wall, *Heddlu Gogledd Cymru – North Wales Police. Gogledd Cymru diogelach – A Safer North Wales,* and beside this the North Wales Police badge. There was also a large map of North Wales with various locations marked with red plastic pins.

On the table in front of Ruth was a jug and glasses of water, and several small tape recorders and microphones that journalists had placed there.

'Good afternoon, I'm Detective Inspector Ruth Hunter and I am the Senior Investigating Officer for the investigation into Arabella Dixon's murder. Beside me is Detective Sergeant Nick Evans, who is also working on this investigation.

'This press conference is to update you on the case and to appeal to the public for any information regarding the murder of Arabella Dixon at Dinas Padog High School last Thursday, 13 March. This is a dreadful tragedy and the Dixon family, Dinas Padog High School, and the whole community are devastated by this loss.

'At this stage in the investigation, we know that Miss Dixon was making her way to her car at around eight, after a parents' evening at the school, when she was attacked. The school was very busy that night and my appeal is that if you were there that evening and you saw anything out of the ordinary, however insignificant you think it might be, that you contact us as soon as you can so we can come and talk to you.'

Ruth spent the next fifteen minutes fielding questions about the investigation. She had clarified they were sure someone had targeted Arabella Dixon, that the attack was not random, and that there was no immediate danger to the local community. She reiterated their need for information about anything suspicious that had been seen that night.

Afterwards, Ruth and Nick made their way along the corridor that led back to Incident Room 1.

'If you're ever late again, I'll put you on a charge,' Ruth warned him.

'Yes, sorry, boss. Won't happen again.'

CHAPTER 15

ON HER WAY BACK TO her hotel, Ruth thought she would pay Graham Williams a visit. She parked outside the detached farmhouse that had the sign *Bryn Haul* on the wooden gate.

The house was large and sat high on the hill, so the walk from Ruth's car and up the stoned path to the front door was steep. She noticed the immaculate garden with herbaceous borders and an ornamental pond.

Ruth rang the doorbell and a moment later a man opened the door.

'Mr Williams?' she asked.

'Yes?' Williams asked with a bemused smile.

Ruth showed her warrant card, 'DI Hunter. If you've got a moment, there are a couple of things I'd like to go through with you about the murder of Arabella Dixon.'

'Of course. Come in, come in.' Williams opened the door wide and beckoned Ruth in with a warm smile.

Ruth walked into the hallway. Mahler's Fifth Symphony was playing somewhere in the house. It had been one of Ruth and Sarah's favourite classical pieces ever since they saw Visconti's film *Death in Venice* starring Dirk Bogarde.

'Coffee?' Williams asked.

'No, no, I'm fine,' Ruth said as she followed him into the living room.

The house was warm, tidy and immaculate. The decor was tasteful and modern, with thick fawn carpet and rust-coloured sofas with cushions. Two of the walls had floor-to-ceiling shelves full of neatly arranged books.

Ruth was making no assumptions about his sexuality, but he was a man with refined taste who lived on his own.

She sat down and pointed to nowhere in particular. 'Mahler?'

'Ah, a connoisseur of music,' Williams said in a loud, affected voice.

'Not really. It's one of the few classical pieces I know,' Ruth replied.

'Ahh, but certainly a good one. Anyway, how can I help, Detective?' Williams asked.

'Mr Williams—' Ruth began.

'Graham, please,' he said with a polite nod, but a stare that was a little unnerving.

Ruth was a little thrown. 'Graham, could you just run through what you were doing on the night of Thursday the thirteenth of March for me?' Ruth asked.

'Of course. Chris Roberts and I were at the Year 11's parents' evening. We left the hall at around seven thirty. We made our way to my car and left. I dropped Chris home. I'm afraid we didn't see anything or anyone suspicious that night,' Williams explained in a friendly tone.

Ruth watched Williams as he spoke. There was definitely something peculiar about him. Something artificial. It wasn't just the affected way he spoke. His hair was curly and fell between his ear lobes and shoulder. It had been coloured with highlights to hide the grey. His facial muscles didn't seem to move naturally, and Ruth guessed that he had had fillers or even Botox injections.

'Did you see Arabella Dixon that evening?' Ruth asked.

'Yes. She was still in the hall when we left,' Graham explained.

'Did you speak to her at all?' Ruth said.

'No. No, I'm sure I didn't speak to her. Only to say hello or goodbye, possibly.'

'And what was your relationship with Arabella Dixon like?' Ruth asked.

'We were colleagues. We weren't close.'

'What did you think of her?'

'Think? Right, well that's a tricky one. I suppose we came from two very different pedagogical schools of thought,' Graham said.

Ruth gave a half laugh. 'I'm sorry, Graham, but now I'm lost. Did you like Arabella Dixon as a person?'

'I'm not sure "like" comes into it. I thought a child's education should be wide-ranging, inspiring, challenging and exciting. I'm afraid she didn't,' Williams explained.

'She was only interested in league tables, data and exam results?' Ruth asked.

'Now you're putting words in my mouth. We didn't see eye to eye on an intellectual level, nothing more sinister than that,' Graham said with a wry laugh.

Ruth could see that Williams wasn't going to freely admit to any ill-feeling between him and Arabella Dixon.

'Graham, do you know a Reverend Arlo Lincoln?' Ruth asked.

Williams was a little disconcerted by the sudden change of direction of Ruth's questioning. 'Erm, yes, I know Arlo.'

'How long have you known Reverend Lincoln?' Ruth asked.

Williams frowned and said, 'I've known him for a long time. If you don't mind me asking, how is this relevant?'

'It's just part of our investigation.'

'I knew him when he was at St Mark's College in Ruthin. I was a house master there for quite some time,' Graham explained, but his manner suggested that he had been thrown by the question.

Ruth took in this information and the link. 'Okay, Graham. That's all I need at the moment. Thank you for your time.' Ruth got up to go.

AS NICK TURNED LEFT off the A463 and took the B234 towards Padog, he caught his reflection in the rearview mirror and took stock. He looked like shit and he was killing himself. He needed to get off the booze and sort himself before he was out of a job.

There was no way he was going to another treatment centre. He was done with those hellholes. He would do his sums, write an alcohol plan and slowly taper off the units. He had done it before but it was hard work. Days were spent clock watching and unit counting. The danger was always that the cravings for booze, and his restricted drunkenness, would override his desire to stop and he would end up pressing the oh-fuck-it button.

He looked into his own eyes. He gave himself a look. *Have a word with yourself, you twat!* He clicked on the stereo. *Do I Wanna Know* by the Arctic Monkeys boomed, the bass rattling the speakers, as Nick pushed the accelerator and picked up to 60 mph.

It was six by the time he pulled the car up outside Uncle Mike and Auntie Pat's house. He pinged some vodka before going in. Once inside and up to her usual fussing, Pat said it was a shame he couldn't have made it for Sunday lunch. They'd had lamb with roasties but Nick hadn't been hungry. Drinking killed his appetite and he was never sober enough to get that craving for fried, greasy food that a 'normal' hangover brings.

Pat said he looked tired and needed feeding up. Nick and Mike shared a look; he knew how his nephew was feeling. You never forgot withdrawals.

Nick had brought the drawing of the spiral found on Arabella Dixon's hand with him, and he sat with Mike at the dinner table that adjoined the living room. Cerys was out, and Mike confessed that they had seen little of her since she dropped the pregnancy bombshell.

Nick placed the spiral in front of his uncle. 'What do you make of this?'

'It's a spiral, lad.'

'No shit, Sherlock. Does it mean anything to you? Does it have some weird Welsh meaning? You're into all that mythological stuff,' Nick said mockingly.

'Something to do with this case?' Mike asked, looking again at the symbol in more detail.

'I can't tell you that. But I thought you might know or have some idea.'

Mike got up from the table, went to the bookshelf and pulled two thick hardback books out.

'Aye, I got a feeling I've seen it before,' Mike said, half talking to himself while thumbing through *Welsh Myths and Legends*. He stopped at a page and showed Nick a picture of a spiral.

Mike began to read aloud. 'Well, it says here, "Spirals are some of the oldest geometric shapes in the ancient world and date back at least to the Neolithic period. They are the product of people thousands of years away from the invention of writing. The spirals represent the cycle of rebirth, as indicated by their presence at tombs and burial grounds. Sometimes they are a symbol of a mother goddess and could be symbolic of wombs"'.

Nick shrugged. 'Anything else?' *Because none of that really helped.*

Mike turned the page, read, and then handed the book to Nick, pointing at a passage.

Nick's attention heightened as he saw the intriguing text.

The Revenge Spiral. The revenge spiral is a simple spiral consisting of any number of revolutions. It signifies there is a blood debt to be paid. Its earliest mention comes from Welsh Druids during the first century BC. It is also the symbol of Arawn who was the king of the Welsh underworld. Arawn was a warrior and associated with revenge and terror. He was known to ride to the hunt with his hounds. A verse about Arawn goes as follows: 'Hir yw'r dude a hir yw'r now a hir yw aros am Arwawn'. *This roughly translates to: 'Long is the day and long is the night, and long is the wait for Arawn'.*

That was more like it, Nick thought. Revenge would make perfect sense. Arabella Dixon seemed to have made a habit of making enemies.

Mike looked at Nick. 'Helpful?'

Nick, indicating the book, asked, 'Can I borrow this and anything else you've got?'

Mike went over to the shelf, pulled out two more folklore books and handed the pile of books to Nick. 'Knock yourself out, boyo.'

'Ta la,' Nick replied as he sifted through the books in his hands. Something caught his eye as he got to the last book in the pile. *Wales in the Iron Age – Celts and Druids* by Bronwyn Wright. *Could it be?* He opened the pages, and on the dust jacket was a picture of Bronwyn Wright, the teacher he had interviewed at the Lighthouse. Was that a coincidence? Nick didn't like coincidences in investigations.

That evening, Nick returned home. He read through Bronwyn Wright's history of Iron Age Wales while knocking back vodka and coke. He looked at the close-up of Arabella Dixon's hand and the blackened, congealed blood in a spiral shape. At this time of night, it felt more macabre and unnerving than before.

Nick read about the spiral and how it had been used for over four thousand years. Wright's book explained that symbols mean different things to different cultures at different times. The phrase 'pagan religious symbol' had become a byword for devil worshipping, especially since its corruption in twentieth-century culture. Wright blamed things such as modern American horror films or literature for this. In fact, the word *pagan* was Latin and merely meant those less-educated people who clung to ancient customs and rituals.

The ten milligrams of diazepam soon kicked in and Nick fell asleep with the book open beside him.

CHAPTER 16

RUTH WOKE WITH HER pulse racing, yet felt exhausted after another anxiety dream. She drank her first coffee – knowing it would be the first of many – as she watched the breakfast news. Arabella Dixon's murder wasn't mentioned and was slipping down the news agenda. From experience, she knew it wouldn't resurface until they made a collar, and Ruth could feel the pressure growing. Jones had already flagged up that North Wales Police were taking a hammering on social media for their inability to find a suspect. She not only had her immediate superior on her back, but also the angriest of Twitter trolls. Oh great.

Fed up with the depressing media coverage, Ruth switched to the radio channel which was playing some upbeat pop music. It immediately annoyed her, so she turned it off.

Feeling the pressure of the case, she ran through the voluntary interviews that would take place that morning of Alex and Jonathan Noakes, and Rhiannon Baker. She could predict what they would say. Jonathan Noakes was helping Alex to move his stuff over to Rhiannon Baker's house on her family farm in Llandderfel. Alex and Rhiannon had gone into the school so that Alex could tell Arabella that he was moving out that night.

What Ruth didn't know was if there was some kind of confrontation later in the evening. Had Alex and Rhiannon gone to the car park to vandalise his mother's car as a parting act of revenge? Was Rhiannon's bruised face a result of being attacked by Arabella Dixon that night? They could do with photographing Rhiannon's face without make-up to see if there were knuckle or ring marks. Marks that matched Arabella Dixon's hand.

Ruth finished her coffee and grabbed her car keys, slamming the room door behind her.

BY TEN O'CLOCK, RUTH had briefed everyone on how the investigation was progressing. They were still waiting for Forensics to process the two partial prints on Arabella Dixon's car. She knew that partial prints took an eternity to come back, and sometimes Forensics drew a blank.

The CCTV footage of the rear car park was unusable, although the Tech boys downstairs said they would have a go, or send it away, to see if anything could be salvaged. Nothing on the clothing fibres found under the deceased's nails yet either. There was still no sign of Arabella Dixon's mobile phone, car keys, or security pass, and the search of the nearby drains had revealed nothing of note.

Nick had reported his findings about the spiral symbol being one of revenge. He also showed them the book that Bronwyn Wright had written, which proved that she had a thorough knowledge of ancient Druid and Celtic history. Wright also hated Arabella Dixon for what she had done to her. However, in terms of opportunity, she was in Welshpool at the time with her main set of car keys locked away. It seemed a bit of a stretch.

A phone call informed Ruth that Alex, Jonathan, and Rhiannon were waiting to be interviewed. 'We've still got a lot of work to do, team, so let's jump to it.' Ruth closed the meeting.

As everyone in CID got going, she beckoned Nick over for a moment. 'Hold on a sec, DS Evans. I want a quick chat with you.'

'Sorry about yesterday, boss. Won't happen again,' Nick said.

'Are you okay?' Ruth asked. She wasn't expecting Nick to come clean about the inner demons that he was battling. She did, however, want him to know that she could tell that there was something wrong and that he might be struggling.

'Fine. Honest, boss. It was a stupid mistake.'

Ruth gestured to the door. 'Come on, we need to go down and get these interviews done.'

Ruth worried that Nick wasn't up to being deputy SIO on the case. When he was focussed, she could see he was a fantastic copper with great instincts. However, he seemed to swing between anger and a withdrawn blankness, and there was clearly something troubling him.

After Nick had reassured Ruth that he was fine, they headed down two floors to Interview Room 3 where Alex Noakes was waiting. In terms of interview technique, Ruth wanted to get Alex as relaxed as they could and allow him to talk.

'Nick, I have no intention of telling you how to do your job. I can tell you're an experienced officer,' Ruth said. 'But for what it's worth, I'd like us to go in gently at first. Get Alex to give us details, that's when we can find the provable lies.'

'Yes, boss.'

Ruth entered and sat down. Alex looked tired and unshaven, and his bloodshot eyes were a sure sign he had been smoking weed that morning. He was wearing a black Horror Clown t-shirt and skinny jeans.

'Alex, although this is a voluntary interview, I need to caution you. So, you do not have to say anything, but it may harm your defence if you do not mention when questioned something which you later rely on in court. Anything you do say may be given in evidence,' Ruth said calmly.

'Don't I need a solicitor or something?' Alex asked grumpily, his feet fidgeting.

'Not necessarily. You can have one, but it could take time to get one here. You could end up being here all day.' Nick's voice was friendly.

'Alex, we just want to hear your side of what happened last Thursday night. And we want you to tell us the truth this time,' Ruth explained in a soft parental tone.

'I told you the truth!' Alex snapped, pushing back his hair with his hand.

'Come on, Alex, we know you were with your dad and Rhiannon at the school. We can see it on the CCTV,' Nick said, genially.

Alex paused, taking in what he had just been told. 'I didn't want them to get into trouble.'

'They won't be in trouble if you tell the truth,' Ruth told him.

'Why aren't you out there finding the person who killed my mum? This has nothing to do with any of us.' Alex was emotional and rarely looked up from staring at his twitching feet.

'Okay, what did you and Rhiannon do once you were on the school site?'

'I went to talk to Mum to tell her I was moving out, and Rhiannon waited for me by the sports hall. My mum was busy, so I didn't get to talk to her. Rhiannon texted me, told me to hurry up, so then we left.' Ruth knew this was progress. Alex had now put himself on the school site on that evening.

'What time was this?'

'About seven o'clock.'

'But you saw your mum, Alex?' Ruth asked.

'Yeah, I told you that. I went to see her, but she was all over that prick of a head, which wasn't a big surprise. That pissed me off. So, I thought sod her, and left her to it,' Alex snorted, but then thought he had given too much away.

'You're talking about Neerav Banerjee, Alex?' asked Ruth with a frown. Was Alex suggesting there was more to Arabella Dixon and Neerav Banerjee's relationship?

'Yeah, of course.'

'You said she was "all over him". Why wasn't that a surprise?' Nick asked, taking notes.

'How do you think my mum got promoted to deputy head?' Alex pulled a face as though this was common knowledge. He mimicked a blow job with his hand, pushing his tongue into his cheek.

'Are you suggesting they had an affair?' Nick asked.

'Not suggesting. It's been going on for years. And the prick spent a lot of time at our house last summer holidays "helping Mum with her garden". Sometimes he would "pop" round for brunch but I knew that he had stayed over. They must have thought I was an idiot,' Alex explained. 'I saw his car on the drive in the middle of the night a few times. Deserved each other, they did.'

'Were they still seeing each other?' Ruth asked.

'You're joking? After her promotion, she dropped him just like that. He was gutted but what could he say. Wanker was married with two kids. That's what she was like. Got off on it.'

'How do you know Neerav Banerjee was gutted?' Ruth asked.

'He came around a few times and I heard my mum telling him he needed to "get over it". Then he rang late at night and my mum told him to leave her alone. She said she would call the police if he didn't stop hassling her. Sad little dickhead.'

'But if I've understood what you've told us, your mum still flirted with Neerav Banerjee?' Ruth asked with a slight frown.

'Oh yeah. He was totally under her spell. She loved all those mind games. Must have done his head in though.'

BY LUNCHTIME, THE INTERVIEWS with Alex and Rhiannon were both over but Ruth was frustrated at the lack of progress in the case.

Mac and Sian had fed their findings back to Ruth. They had interviewed Rhiannon, with her father acting as the appropriate adult. Rhiannon was a little teary and explained that Arabella Dixon had often been verbally, and a couple of times physically, abusive to Alex when he didn't do what she wanted. Sian looked at Rhiannon's bruised face that now had little make-up. There seemed to be one point of impact and nothing like knuckle or ring indentations. It didn't come from an altercation with Arabella Dixon.

Rhiannon had cried when confronted about her deception regarding her whereabouts on Thursday night. She was upset and scared, and claimed that it was Jonathan Noakes' idea to fabricate their stories. When news of Arabella Dixon's murder surfaced, he had called and told her if the police questioned her, she needed to say she was at home that night. Jonathan had said that it wouldn't look good they had all been at the school and that Alex had gone to confront his mother and tell her he was leaving home. Jonathan had reassured her it was very unlikely that Rhiannon would have to talk to the police, but it was best they all said they were elsewhere.

Rhiannon then confirmed Alex's version of events that they went back to Rhiannon's house where Alex unpacked his stuff into the spare room. Rhiannon's father confirmed they were both at home on Thursday night, although he was a little vague on timings as he had been out on the farm for part of the evening.

JONATHAN NOAKES LOOKED like a man who hadn't slept properly in days. His eyes were rimmed by dark circles, his skin sallow and, as he brought a glass of water to his lips, he was visibly shaking. Ruth looked around the room, which was painted in a nondescript blue, and a white plastic socket strip dissected the wall beside them. There were four matching plastic chairs that were uncomfortable when interviews dragged on. The light was dim and artificial as there were no windows. She felt that she could do with some sleep too.

'Mr Noakes, why did you lie about your whereabouts last Thursday night?' Ruth asked in her usual controlled, soft tone.

'I wanted to protect Alex. Well, all of us,' Jonathan explained.

'You could be looking at a charge for perverting the course of justice. The maximum charge for that offence is life imprisonment,' Nick warned him. Jonathan's face dropped as he took an anxious breath.

'Yeah, I'm sorry ... I-I-I panicked. It just didn't look good. Alex was going to see his mum to tell her he was moving out. The fight with Rhiannon the other day. When I heard Arabella had been attacked and murdered, I was in total shock.'

'And so you lied to us and told your son and his girlfriend to lie too?' Ruth said sternly.

'Look, I couldn't think straight. I just thought it was better that none of us admitted we had been at the school around that time,' Jonathan blurted.

'You're happily married aren't you Mr Noakes?' Nick asked.

'Yes, of course.' Noakes was now on the defensive.

'And you and Arabella Dixon were on speaking terms and were civil to each other?' Ruth asked.

'Yes. I told you that the other day,' Noakes said, sounding worried.

'But you lied to us the other day, Mr Noakes. And now we have you down as a liar, we're not sure we can believe anything you tell us, I'm afraid,' Nick said.

'Please believe me. I would never harm Arabella. We were still close. We had a child together.' Noakes sounded desperate but genuine.

'Did you murder your ex-wife, Mr Noakes?' Ruth asked.

'No. No. I didn't.' Noakes put his head in his hands.

'Just talk us through where you went the other night, will you?' Nick asked.

'I took Alex and Rhiannon to the school at around six. Alex went to speak to his mother. He said he hung around for a while but she was too busy. I drove up to the Astroturf pitches and picked him and Rhiannon up. I took them over to the farm and Alex unpacked his stuff. I then drove home,' Noakes explained.

'And your wife will confirm this, will she?' Nick asked.

'No. She's away in Spain with my daughter, seeing her parents.'

Ruth frowned and said, 'So there is no one who can confirm that you went straight home from the farm in Llandderfelm?'

Noakes shook his head. 'I'm afraid not. No.'

AN HOUR AND A HALF later and Ruth was in her office trying to sort interminable paperwork. She needed to collate the results of the investigation into a format both senior officers and the Crown Prosecution Service could work with.

She was creating charts, spreadsheets, timelines, and gathering all the information from witnesses and interviews. It was the worst part of the job, but she reminded herself that she was the SIO now.

Ruth took a chewed pencil and scribbled the formula on some paper. *WHAT* + *WHY* + *WHEN* + *WHERE* + *HOW* + *WHO*. She sighed, picked up her coffee and went out and over to the map on the whiteboard. She looked at the detailed plans of the school site.

Nick came in holding some computer printouts and a folder. Ruth still had doubts about his attitude. However, Nick seemed to be trying to redress the situation, which was an improvement.

'Boss, Tech got some interesting stuff off Arabella Dixon's personal laptop.' Nick waved the printouts purposefully.

Ruth pointed at the map as Nick came over. 'Okay. Let me run this past you first. Arabella Dixon and Neerav Banerjee have an affair. Possibly last summer. Arabella Dixon dumps him as soon as she gets promoted. Neerav can't say too much as he's married with two kids. However, he's now besotted with her. And although she says it's over, she continues to flirt with him. We have the used condom in the bathroom. So, let's say they have sex again in the last forty-eight hours, only for Arabella to tell Neerav it's a one-off. She flirts with him again at the parents' evening, by which time Neerav's head is completely twisted. She leaves at seven fifty. He leaves a couple of minutes later. She heads for the rear car park via the maths corridor. Meanwhile, Neerav goes out this door here and cuts down to the rear car park through this alleyway.'

Nick nodded and said, 'He confronts her. Why is she treating him like this? He can't cope, he can't sleep, his work is suffering. Something like that? Things get out of hand. Because she's a bitch, she says something horrible. He flips and kills her. He comes back up this alleyway, along past the main school office and out through the main entrance at eight ten, which is what we see on the CCTV.'

Ruth nods in agreement. 'Sounds feasible, doesn't it?'

'It does, especially when you read these. Tech boys found a series of deleted emails on Arabella Dixon's laptop. They're clearly from a man who she has been having an affair with. He wants more, but she doesn't. In the last few emails it escalates. He's becoming aggressive and she is threatening to call the police,' Nick explained, gesturing to the email printouts in his hand.

Ruth took this in for a moment. If the emails were from Neerav Banerjee, then they had a suspect. Was this the break they'd been waiting for?

Ruth read them out loud. 'Twenty-seventh of January ... "I was thinking about the time we shagged on that beach in Abersoch under the stars. One of the best nights of my life. Shall I take you there again?" followed by two kisses.'

'There's no reply from her for a few days, so he tries again.' Nick pointed to an email. 'Here. She says on the third of February, "We need to be careful. Lots of people could get hurt. I'm just not sure this is a good idea."'

Ruth flicked through the printout. 'He writes: "I keep emailing you and you don't reply. I thought we felt the same. It's making it really hard to act normally when I see you."' Ruth kept reading, '"You need to stop emailing me. You've got a family and you need to get on with your life. If you don't stop, I'll have to take it further!"'

Nick pointed to the emails and said, 'That's two weeks ago. And then here, she says, "If you don't stop contacting me, I will have to go to the police. Pull yourself together and move on. I have." His last email is the fifth of March. "You really are a cold, narcissistic bitch. I hope you die a slow and painful death and I'm there to witness it!" She writes the next day: "Email me again and I will go to the police."'

'How quickly can we get the IP address of the sender?' Ruth asked.

'It's unlikely to be less than forty-eight hours, boss.'

'If those emails are from Neerav Banerjee, then we definitely have motive. We need the DNA from that condom to see if it's a match. Right, I don't want to wait on this. And I don't want him doing a runner or doing something stupid if his head is all over the place.' Ruth glanced up at the clock on the wall and then looked at Nick. 'He should be home by now. We take him by surprise and see what he says. You drive, I'll smoke.'

Four years earlier...

With white headphones in her ears, the girl by the lake could drown out the silence all around her. Sam Smith's Stay with Me *was as a poignant hymn to the scene.*

As she arrived at the water's edge, she gazed across its length – the water a dark, green-copper colour – and then away into the distance. She was feeling frightened and her make-up had smudged a little.

She took the bottle of vodka and gulped, hoping it would make her feel numb and anaesthetised. She took a silver cross that hung around her neck, kissed it, and then looked up at the sky. She hoped that if there was a God, he would understand. He would forgive her. The pain of what had happened was too much to bear and she was certain that this was the only answer.

Wading a little into the water, she could feel it was icy. She reached again for the litre bottle of supermarket vodka that was in her coat. She swigged the last two inches and then launched the empty bottle high into the air with defiance. It landed and splashed quietly, disappearing below the glistening surface. There was silence again.

She looked up at the sky that was leaden and colourless. Wishing it had been a beautiful sunny day, she nodded her head to the beat of the song, mouthing the lyrics, as she waded further into the water, which was now at knee height. Tears fell down her face and rolled off her cheeks, streaking them black. This didn't feel real. Nothing had felt real for a long time.

She waded further in until the water came to her waist. She shivered and then clenched her fists as she fought the intense pain of the cold. Her legs were becoming deadened and weak. She pushed on, and water came over her shoulders and darkened her hair. Her feet lost their footing on the slippery rocks below and she was forced to swim forwards, then she turned and swam on her back gazing up at the sky. She gasped. It was so unbearably cold.

She closed her eyes and the icy water dulled all her senses, dulled her brain stem as she floated and waited to die.

THE ELFIN-LIKE WOMAN didn't even look up from her phone as the 08.05 to Victoria pulled into Platform 1 of Crystal Palace station. It was Groundhog Day for her, as it was for every other commuter waiting there. Routine. She knew that most of them even stood at the same place on the platform, got on the same carriage, and stood or sat in their favoured place. Making more exciting choices required effort, and they had a long, interminable day in the capital city ahead of them where many more difficult decisions had to be made. Best to keep this part of the day nice and simple.

The train doors opened with a hiss. Sarah's carriage of choice was already busy and there were no seats. Nothing different there, she thought. She stepped on, still checking her phone. A text from her girlfriend.

Meeting Jess and Andy for the fireworks display on Clapham Common outside the Windmill Pub at 7.30pm. See you there. Love you sooooo much xx.

She smiled at the message, then looked up and saw a friendly face. Someone she half recognised maybe? A tall man, blonde hair, well-groomed, preppy glasses, and an expensive charcoal-coloured suit and navy Crombie coat with its red lining and distinctive velvet collar. Maybe she had seen him on the carriage before? Or was it at work? If she had been straight, she would have definitely thought he was fit. He nodded a confident hello. She already had him down as a public-school type. You could smell the privilege. She smiled back. There was no harm in that, was there?

The train doors closed and then the 08.05 to Victoria pulled out of Crystal Palace station.

'It's Sarah, isn't it?' the man asked. He had an accent. European, but she couldn't place it.

'Yes. Have we met?' she asked with a frown. She didn't think they had. She was normally pretty good at names and faces.

'Don't you remember?' the man answered with a confident, but unnerving smile.

CHAPTER 17

LLANFIHANGEL GLYN MYFYR was a picturesque village in Conwy County Borough, set beside the Afon Alwen river, at the south-western edge of the Clocaenog Forest. Wordsworth visited the village in 1824 and it inspired him to write the poem *Vale of Meditation*. Llanfihangel Glyn Myfyr was also where Neerav Banerjee and his family lived.

As they came over the brow of the hill, Nick and Ruth saw the sweep of fields away to their left and the dark forest rising up to the right.

'I can't believe that you didn't know female officers used to be called *plonks*, Nick,' Ruth said as she pulled down the visor against the low sun. 'Didn't you watch *Life On Mars*?'

'I've only been in the job for ten years. I wasn't an officer in the dark ages,' Nick said with a grin.

'Oi. You cheeky sod. The nineties was not the dark ages. Although now I think about it, we still had to wear a skirt, tights, handbag, and a hat. And I was meant to chase criminals dressed like that! It took nearly a decade for that crap to be phased out,' Ruth explained.

As she said it, she realised she had been a police officer for nearly twenty-five years! *How the hell did that happen?* she thought.

'For the first couple of years, it still felt like the seventies. Being called *love* and *darling*, and making senior male officers cups of tea and sandwiches.'

'Christ, if you tried to tell a female officer to make you a cup of tea now, you'd be wearing it,' Nick quipped.

'Too right!' Ruth said.

Nick clenched his fist in the air, 'Hey, I'm with you, sister.'

'Actually, I refused to wear the skirt after six months. I made them get some male police uniform trousers to fit me. When the trousers arrived, my prick of a super made me put them on and twirl around in front of male officers.'

'What a wanker,' Nick said.

'That's all right. I waited until he was hammered one night. When he went to drive home I got him nicked and banned from driving.'

'Nice. Sweet bit of revenge?'

'Oh yes. Don't ever cross me, Nick,' Ruth said laughing. 'They deployed me to guard 10 Downing Street in 1992 as cover at the last minute. When I arrived, the police officer in charge asked me where my gun was. Of course, I didn't have one. So he asked if I was intending to guard Mr Major with my "sodding handbag"? So actually you were right, Nick. The nineties were the dark ages,' Ruth said.

Driving along the A497, Ruth looked out at the sky. The sun had been replaced by a sombre canopy of different greys and white. The lower clouds were a deep steel-blue-grey that matched the hues of the tarmac road that stretched before them. Above that were clouds that looked more like smudges from a child's pencil drawings. The sky seemed alive, changing and growing before her eyes. There was every shade of grey, Ruth thought to herself. *Fifty Shades of Grey!* she joked to herself and snorted out loud.

Nick put on the wipers as the first few splats of rain landed on the windscreen. He pointed at a sign to Llanfihangel Glyn Myfyr and they turned right onto a narrow country road lined by high hedgerows. Beyond that the spectacular countryside and trees stretched away and then rose high to a stunning ridge. Houses and farms were dotted intermittently across the landscape. Up ahead of them were the dark edges of Clocaenog Forest.

As they pulled slowly into the small village, the rain fell heavily. The houses were built from dressed blocks of local dark grey stone, with shallow-pitched slate roofs. An eighteenth-century pub, the Old Crown, whose stone exterior had been painted white, stood nearby, overlooking the river.

'Long way from Bradford,' Ruth said, referring to Neerav Banerjee's hometown.

'Long way from anywhere,' Nick replied.

They found the Banerjee house, a large five-bedroomed farmhouse, Brotegir, at the far end of the village, and parked next to it was a navy Volvo XC-90 4x4. It looked like Neerav would be home. But if his family were home, things might be difficult. Nick stated that he thought Neerav might admit to writing the emails if they hinted they'd been found, even before they had confirmation of the IP address.

Nick and Ruth approached, boots crunching on the gravel drive. Noticing that the wooden front door was open slightly, Ruth looked up at Nick with concern. Nick only grinned and smiled back.

'It's all right. I don't lock my car or my house at night. It's not South London,' Nick reassured her.

'No, it's definitely not that.'

Nick knocked on the door, waited, and then pushed the door open. On the left, coats on hooks, wellies and an umbrella. The hall had a dark burgundy stone floor, and to the right a wide oak staircase with olive carpeting led up to the first floor.

'Mr Banerjee?' Nick said.

'It's Detective Inspector Hunter,' Ruth called in a raised voice.

There was silence. The house smelt of polish and freshly made coffee.

'Mr Banerjee?' Nick shouted.

The ticking of a tall, antique grandfather clock added to the stillness. Nick made his way past the staircase towards the back of the house while Ruth checked the dining room and then the living room.

Nick opened a door to see a large modern kitchen and breakfast area with floor-to-ceiling windows and a magnificent view towards Snowdonia. However, he wasn't looking at the view. He was staring at a large pool of spilt milk and a smashed mug on the tiled kitchen floor. The coffee machine was bubbling quietly in the corner.

'Boss?' Nick shouted as he went in, looking around, his pulse quickening. A moment later, Ruth appeared and saw the mess on the floor for herself.

Nick looked left and saw a door that led to a utility room. He shot Ruth a look and pushed the door but something was stopping it moving, so he eased himself through the small gap. His blood went cold as his eyes scanned the floor – a body was lying there. Grey-socked feet, bare legs, boxer shorts and a smart blue shirt. He saw a hand with cuts and blood. The nose and top lip also had blood on them, possibly from some kind of struggle. Neerav Banerjee was lying on his back, eyes staring up, blank and dead.

'Jesus!' Nick bent down and felt for a pulse on his neck. There wasn't one. 'He's dead.'

'I'll call it in. Have a look around,' Ruth said urgently. 'Shit!'

Then a sudden noise seemed to come from just outside, by the side of the house. Nick tried the side door that led out to the garden. It was open.

The rain was now lashing down loudly as Nick walked out onto a patio. It battered rhythmically on the decking and a bottle-green sun umbrella that was still open over wicker garden table and chairs.

About fifty yards away, a figure in a black raincoat and hood was climbing over the slatted garden fence. The figure looked back. It was wearing a latex pig horror mask. It startled Nick for a moment.

'Shit! Boss!' Nick shouted as he sprinted across the lawn towards the figure who had reached the top of the fence and dropped down the other side. 'Stop! Police!' he shouted.

Nick arrived at the fence and vaulted over. Ruth followed and jumped down the other side.

A muddy pathway led right, and down past a field. The figure was running and already two hundred yards ahead of them. A dark green sign read: *Public Footpath – Llwybr Cyhoeddus*. Nick gave chase as rainwater filled the shallow potholes. A fence of wooden poles and barbed wire to the left marked out a field where cows laid in the long grass, oblivious.

Nick was running flat out and panting. Behind him, Ruth had got into her stride. The hooded figure disappeared around the bend and out of sight. Nick was trying to calculate who the figure could be as they sprinted. The large, ill-fitting weatherproof coat with a hood meant that from this distance it was impossible to tell height or build with any accuracy. It wasn't even clear what gender they were.

Nick splashed through the deepening puddles and felt the water flood into his boots and soak his socks. He wiped the rain and sweat from his stinging eyes. As he rounded the corner, he came to a ramshackle farm and outbuildings. It was a dead end, and the thick smell of slurry took him by surprise.

Rusty steel-pipe fencing enclosed the pens where dairy cows were kept at night. Hay bales and an enormous feed shed towered over a weathered red tractor. The figure was nowhere to be seen.

Ruth arrived beside him and stopped. They both sucked in air as their lungs burnt.

'Where did they go?' Nick panted, his pulse thundering. His eyes scanned around, looking for the smallest movement but the incessant rain wasn't helping.

Then the distant sound of rustling, and a twig cracked as the figure emerged from the back of the farm. Even at that distance, the pig mask was unnerving. The figure turned and headed up the slope into the dense eastern edge of the Clocaenog Forest.

'Come on!' Nick beckoned Ruth as they broke into a run again. His legs felt heavy as they slipped and lost their footing on the muddy bank that led up to the forest's edge.

When they reached the forest, Nick stared deeply into the darkness created by the tightly knit rows of Welsh oak, pines and birch. The trunks reached over a hundred feet above their heads. The whole atmosphere had suddenly changed. The forest's canopy stopped much of the rain and so a tense, still darkness replaced the lashing rain.

There was movement in the undergrowth about two hundred yards straight ahead and Nick navigated through the trees. It smelt of dampness and the decay of fallen leaves. But the rain had also made it fresh and light.

They came to a clear path and both sprinted.

Suddenly there was a cry behind him, and Nick turned to see Ruth with her foot jammed under a thick root, and what looked like a twisted ankle. Standing again, she limped, cursing the fact she was now having to hobble.

'For God's sake!' she yelled in frustration.

Nick was caught in two minds; go back or continue the chase.

Ruth waved him away. 'Go after them! I'm fine.'

Nick turned and ran, ducking and weaving through the branches. He pumped his fists as soon as he got a clear run. He was gaining on the figure who had now slowed down. Maybe they were tiring.

For a moment, Nick thought of the Welsh rugby star Dan Biggar crashing through the English centres in the 2015 World Cup. One of the best fly halves in the world. Nick's feet pounded on the soft forest ground as the adrenaline kicked in and his body felt the rush. He looked to his left. The figure was now only fifty yards away. *I'm taking you down,* thought Nick.

Suddenly there was a thunderous boom and the air around Nick shattered. He instinctively dived to the forest floor, his face and hands hitting the soil, bark and decomposing leaves. Undergrowth and branches nearby were ripped to pieces by metal pellets. The figure had fired a sawn-off shotgun at him. Jesus Christ!

Nick got to his knees and glanced back the way he had come. Ruth was limping towards him but was still a few hundred yards away. Now shaken, he peered around a tree gingerly and saw the figure was again running through the trees heading north. Nick knew he had to keep chasing. He sprang to his feet and sprinted up the incline again, wondering if the killer had only one cartridge left or had more ammunition.

Up ahead, he could see light where the edge of the forest thinned out into a clearing, but he had lost sight of the killer. His eyes zipped right and left across the greenery.

The sudden noise of twigs snapping two hundred yards away brought his attention hard left. There he was. Nick could see undergrowth moving as the killer headed for the clearing. He zig-zagged quickly through branches and brambles until he found a pathway and picked up speed. His boots were rubbing painfully, and he could feel the sweat running down his back.

Nick reached the clearing and glanced around. *Shit! Lost him again.* But then he heard a metallic spring-like sound that he didn't recognise.

Up ahead were steep walls of damp, moss-covered slate, which were partly hidden by wild undergrowth. Then an old Victorian brick archway which was about twelve feet tall at its highest. Across the archway was a rusted metal-mesh gate. However, there was a small gap in the mesh at the far-right-hand end which, if crawled through, would make the metallic sound that Nick had just heard.

He knew this was Capel Celyn, an abandoned nineteenth-century slate mine, whose terrible working conditions meant it became known as 'the slaughterhouse'. Sixty-three mine workers had died here in the last two decades of the 1800s.

Fastened to the brickwork was a yellow sign with a black triangle and black exclamation mark: *PERYGL – Adeileith Amniogel! DANGER – Unsafe Structures!* Then a less vague sign: *CADWCH ALLAN! – KEEP OUT!*

Nick followed, easing through the gap in the fence and then along the entrance to the slate mine. The wide entrance soon narrowed as the pathway descended into darkness, and Nick navigated the narrow-gauge rail tracks, now covered in orange rust, that used to ferry back the miners' slate by the tonne.

Fifty yards down the mine, the tracks disappeared under ankle-high water. The sound of running footsteps splashing echoed up the passageway and Nick gave chase. He slowed as the mine became increasingly dark, and flicked on the torch on his phone. *Where was he?* It was getting impossible to see anything.

Up ahead, the mine split into two tunnels going left and right. As the terrain rose again it revealed a huge, corroded iron turntable where the slate trucks could be turned to any direction.

Nick stared and peered into the darkness. His heart was pounding. He was half expecting the masked man to appear with the shotgun and blow his head off. Holding his breath for a second, he listened intently. Nothing. Which way should he go?

He shone his torch up and it caught a seam of metal ore that had pushed itself into the green slate and glinted like jewellery in the phone's bright beam. The mine was cavernous like a church, its roof thirty or forty feet high.

As Nick moved slowly to take the tunnel to the left, the sound of the water that he was wading through echoed loudly. He stopped again. His pulse was banging in his ear.

Boom!

An explosive shot that seemed ten times louder in the echo chamber of the mine. Nick saw the orange flash of the shotgun out of the corner of his eye. Shit! He spun and tried to crouch but it was too late. A searing hot pain in his right thigh. A pellet had hit him. He stumbled backwards, slipped on the wet rock, and his head cracked on a jagged slab of slate. He felt warm blood trickling down his forehead before he was swallowed by the darkness.

CHAPTER 18

MONITORS BEEPED RHYTHMICALLY as Nick waited on a hospital trolley in a small, curtained-off bay in Accident and Emergency. He was relieved that he would be discharged. The sound of nurses walking back and forth, chatting and talking to patients, could be heard through the clinical-blue curtains. And the redolent smell of disinfectant and medication transported him back twenty-five years. It was almost like being back there by his mum's bedside, watching her disintegrate before his eyes on the Enfys women's oncology ward. The chemo had aged her so quickly. She wore a sad smile and tried to hide the pain from him as he held her bony hand. Now, Nick felt that overwhelming sensation of loss rise from his stomach and up to his chest, and his eyes watered for a moment. Grief. It never left you. He tried to bury it, concentrating on the present and all that had happened as a way of distraction.

A young female doctor, who Nick thought looked fit but also young enough to be a sixth-former, had removed his trousers and pulled out the shotgun pellet with medical tweezers an hour earlier. *Don't get an erection,* he told himself, but the pain held that embarrassment at bay. He told her it needed to be kept for Forensics, playing up the whole brave 'shot copper' routine. She didn't seem to notice.

The pellet had been close to the skin's surface and had done no major damage. Nick had a concussion, and seven stitches in the back of his head, but that wasn't a big deal; he could sleep that off. In fact, he couldn't wait to get home, get some booze and diazepam in his system, and forget the day had ever happened.

After he'd been shot, fallen and become unconscious, Nick had come to as Ruth arrived in the mine and called his name. He had heard it as if he were in a dream at first. As he came back into consciousness, he saw he was up to his armpits in water and was shivering. Ruth had called for back-up, and paramedics had stretchered him to an ambulance once they had emerged from the mine.

Nick's train of thought was broken by the patient in the next curtained bay who was roaring with laughter with his friends. They were all hammered and thought a trip to A&E was hilarious. A war story. *Wankers,* he thought. Probably students.

Nick lay back and gazed up at the ceiling. It was hard to take in what had happened in recent hours. Two murders in a week, which were clearly by the same killer. The same MO and the victims were lovers and colleagues.

The curtain swished and Ruth came in, hobbling a little, and handed him an insipid-looking tea from the machine.

'Thought you might need this.'

Nick took a sip and pulled a face. 'Jesus, are you trying to kill me? That's twice in one day.'

'I saved your life, dickhead.' Ruth hit him softly on the shoulder.

'Oh yeah. Thanks, boss. What's going on?' Nick asked.

'I left SOCO at the Banerjee house. Exactly the same as Arabella Dixon. Looks like strangulation. Someone has cut something into the back of his hand,' Ruth informed him.

'How's the ankle?'

'Fine. Sore ... How are you feeling?' Ruth asked.

'Okay. Good.' Nick sipped his tea again, but it was too hot and watery. And it didn't have booze in it. He was feeling fidgety and anxious, and booze and benzos were the only thing for it.

Ruth sat down and leaned forwards. 'How long have you had a drink problem, Nick?' she whispered.

Nick frowned. 'Sorry, boss? What?'

'Come on, Nick. I'm a copper and I used to work in the Met where it was a badge of honour. And by the way, only alcoholics think vodka doesn't smell on their breath.' Ruth gave a knowing nod of the head as she looked at him with genuine concern.

'I'm getting it under control, boss.'

Ruth wasn't buying it. 'Are you? Coppers think a big night out is a substitute for counselling. But it's not. We've seen all kinds of shit and if we didn't feel shocked, upset or depressed, we wouldn't be human. And not asking for help is stupid, Nick.' Ruth knew that coppers were twice as likely to suffer from alcoholism than civvies, and she had seen too many coppers drink or drug themselves out of job or into a grave. The job was relentless and unforgiving.

'I know. I'm on it and I will sort it, boss.' Nick meant it, but knew that tonight he had to get alcohol in his system or he could fit, blackout and die. Coming off booze was more dangerous than coming off coke or heroin.

'If you don't, I'll end up having to flag it up with your superiors. You can't work if you're struggling with alcohol.' Ruth glanced at her watch. 'The super is going mental. Now it's a double-murder investigation, he's gonna bring in some big guns from Liverpool CID. And I know what that means.'

'A dick-swinging competition?'

'Could be. Depends on what kind of coppers they are. I have a theory that there are only four types of detective.'

'Enlighten me, boss.'

'There's the bully who tries to put the frighteners on a suspect. The quiet charmer who makes everything appear like it's gonna be all right. The surrogate parent. They're getting a little bit of a telling off but there's a lot of love so tell Mummy everything. Then there's the naughty best mate. Come on, we've all done bad things, mate, a wink of an eye. I ain't gonna judge you. Me and you, we're the same, really.'

Nick nodded and smiled. 'Yeah, that does pretty much sum it up. So, what are you?

'Mummy, of course. Always "Mummy will make it better".'

'What about me, boss?'

'Not sure yet, Nick.'

'No one's arriving from Liverpool CID for at least forty-eight hours so it just needs to be business as usual until they descend ...'

Nick hopped off the bed and put on his trousers.

'What are you doing?' Ruth asked.

'Getting out of here. I'm not waiting another four hours for them to tell me I'm okay and can go home,' Nick replied.

'All right, but you don't come in tomorrow. You take a day to rest,' Ruth said.

Nick said nothing for a moment. 'Quick drink before we go home? Don't worry, I'll have a soft drink. I could do with winding down for half an hour before going home to an empty house.'

Ruth thought for a moment. 'Yeah. After today, I could do with a drink. Take me to the most Welsh pub you know,' Ruth said.

NICK WAS AT THE BAR in the Horse and Jockey. He had ordered himself a treble Jameson's which, in true alcoholic style, he had sunk in one go, making sure Ruth wasn't looking. He got that nice, warm burning at the back of his throat and the sweet, oaky grain smell in his nostrils. Nice one. He turned back and sat down at the snug, corner table where Ruth was sifting through some papers.

'This used to be our local for CID. No one seems to bother anymore.' Nick sat back for a moment. 'Bet you've got some stories from the Met?'

'The Met,' Ruth said sipping her drink and shaking her head. 'Don't get me started. This is what it's like. Donkeys' years ago and it's Sunday afternoon. I'm still uniform and we get a shout that some toe-rag on an estate is smashing up a car with a baseball bat. When we get there, there's this bloke dressed as Ronald Macdonald taking out the windscreen with a bat. Not joking, and I mean red hair, blue nose, make-up, size fifty shoes, the lot. We go over and he is off his head on something and decides to have it on his toes. So we're running around the estate chasing Ronald Macdonald, and he's running in circles, so it's like the Keystone bloody cops.' Ruth and Nick are now both laughing. 'And the kids on the estate, and some of the adults, are watching and they're only cheering him on. The more he runs, the more they cheer. Big joke. And we're going around and around in circles. Eventually he's out of puff, puts his hands up, and we cuff him. And now the whole estate is booing us, and I mean forty or fifty people now, as we lead Ronald away. And he's jabbering to himself about beef patties. It's bonkers. You never know what you're walking into.' Ruth was laughing at the thought of it and Nick smiled at the story.

'Oi, that doesn't look like a soft drink,' Ruth said pointing at his pint of cider.

Nick forced a smile. 'Fermented apple juice. That's all it is. Tonight's not the night to stop. But from tomorrow ...'

'Okay. I can borrow a breathalyser if you lie to me, Nick,' Ruth joked.

'You're all right, you know, boss?' Nick sucked the first two inches off his pint.

'Thanks. Almost sounds like a compliment.'

'Not a big fan of the English if I'm honest. And Londoners, Christ!' Nick confessed.

'Right. That's very enlightened of you, Nick,' Ruth said. 'So, no wife or girlfriend to go home to, then?'

'Nah. Taking it nice and steady. No Mr Right back in London then?' Nick asked, feeling that he needed to reciprocate.

'Miss Right,' Ruth corrected him.

'Oh, okay.' Nick was embarrassed but trying to cover it.
'And don't say it ...'

'Say what?'

'DI Dyke, Detective Dyke, Constable Carpet Muncher ... and so on. Heard it all before.' Ruth gave a little laugh. 'But yeah there was someone. But not anymore ... I wish I wasn't driving. I could go on the piss and go to a club. I could do with a big night out. Does Llancastell have clubs?'

'Yes, sort of. Central, Clubland ... Anyway, I don't dance. Well, I can't dance,' Nick confessed.

Ruth was smiling, running away with herself, 'Shots, disco or vocal house music. That's what I need.'

'Vocal house?'

'Don't worry. I'll make you a CD sometime.' A moment passed as Ruth's face turned into a beaming smile. 'Karaoke. I love karaoke. *I will Survive* by Gloria Gaynor. What's your song?'

Nick shook his head. 'I can't sing either.'

'Piss off, you're Welsh. Can't sing? Twat.' Ruth pulled a face.

'Not everyone in Wales can sing, racist!'

'Come on, Tom Jones, Shirley Bassey, Kelly Jones ...'

'He's from Cardiff.'

'So?'

'South Wales. All wankers.' Nick grinned.

'Oh, and I'm prejudiced?' Ruth said playfully.

'Don't forget Shakin' Stevens.'

'Shaky? *Green Door, Oh Julie.*' Ruth starts to half sing the lyrics. 'Come on, you're meant to be helping me out with this,' she said when Nick didn't join in.

'Sod off. You'll get us barred.'

'One for the road?' Ruth asked, seeing that Nick had finished his pint. 'Is that a good idea?'

'Go on.' Nick handed her the empty pint glass.

Ruth's phone rang as she approached the bar; it was Ella. Ruth indicated to the barman they wanted the same drinks again.

'Hello, sweetheart. Everything all right?' she asked in a concerned voice. Ella rarely called, so Ruth was worried.

Ella voice was faint. 'I split up with Andy. He told me I was paranoid and needy.'

'Dickhead! I'm sorry, sweetie. Do you want to come here tonight?' Ruth asked. She immediately felt angry and protective. She hadn't always been there for her daughter, so she was keen to make amends whenever she could.

'No, no. Steph's coming over. We're going to drink wine and watch Netflix,' Ella reassured her.

'Okay. Ring me tomorrow and we'll talk it through.' Ruth comforted her gently. 'You're going to be okay, you know that?'

'Yeah, thanks, Mum. Love you.'

'Love you too.'

Ruth hung up, picked up the drinks and headed back to the table. She indicated her phone. The drink had made her warm, fuzzy and relaxed.

'Kids. It never stops and you never stop worrying,' she explained.

'Kids?' Nick pulled a confused face.

'My daughter Ella. She's grown up now. Well, twenty-one, if that's grown up. She's more grown up than me, that's for sure.' Ruth looked at Nick's expression and then realised why he was confused. 'Oh right, yes. I was straight, I think, and married, in the nineties. Came out at the millennium.'

'And now?'

'God knows. I don't care. Nothing. Gender fluid, bi-sexual, gender neutral. All the above.' Ruth took her glass and clinked Nick's glass. '*Iechyd da!*'

'*Iechyd da.*' Nick smiled to himself. DI Hunter wasn't what he was expecting when he had first met her. Now they were getting to know each other, he was warming to 'the cockney plonk'.

CHAPTER 19

UNIFORMED OFFICERS were either glaring or laughing as Nick ran as quickly as he could through Llancastell Police HQ. He was wearing a shirt and tie but no pants or trousers. What the hell was he doing? He was covering himself but there was a lot of giggling. He fell over a chair and ended up on the floor. And there was his dad sitting with another group of officers in the canteen. His dad shook his head and laughed as he shovelled food into his mouth. That was his son, all right. Total embarrassment.

Nick ran across a school playground and the kids ignored him. As he reached the car park, there was a gang of teenagers smoking weed – baseball caps, trackies and trainers. They blocked his way and confronted him. Where was he going? Who did he think he was?

Sucking in air, Nick woke with a start. Today was the day, he told himself. He had taken on board Ruth's concerns about his drinking. It was nothing new, but she had struck a chord.

Looking at his watch, he saw it was 6am. He had managed six hours with no alcohol, although the diazepam was starting to wear off and he could feel the anxiety worming away. He took his notepad and looked at the calculations for his detox. He could have five units of alcohol now, which was to last him until ten o'clock. He could do this. He went over and grabbed the bottle of white wine from the floor. It was ten units dead on. He could have a quarter of the bottle now, which would be two and half units, and then the other two and a half units at eight. It was going to be tough to keep to the schedule, especially with the whole ten units just sitting in that bottle, waiting for him. But he had to be strong. He could take two milligrams of diazepam if the withdrawals got too much for him to bear. Today was a twenty-five unit day.

After showering in tepid water, Nick went to clean his teeth at the sink. He met his eyes in the mirror and could hold his own gaze. It had been a long time since he'd been able to do that. Self-loathing and self-destruction were his speciality. Alcohol wasn't the problem. *He* was the problem. The pain, anguish and anxiety he felt needed to be masked, and alcohol was his medicine of choice. It did the trick. Or at least it used to.

However, he was doing something about his alcoholism and that allowed him a modicum of self-respect. There was light at the end of the tunnel. He spat the water into the sink and dabbed his face dry with a towel.

He inspected the pellet wound, which was still sore, and changed the bloody dressing. As he came out of the bathroom, he stopped as a wave of dizziness and fogginess swept through his head. He was still concussed. He took a sharp intake of breath, steadied himself, and got dressed. He knew he probably shouldn't go to work, but he was determined to carry on and find Arabella and Neerav's killer.

RUTH SAT DRINKING COFFEE and smoking a cigarette, being careful to blow the smoke out of the open hotel-room window. As she ran the various theories about Arabella Dixon and now Neerav Banerjee's murders through her head, she felt her anxiety climb. She could feel herself becoming possessive of this case. It had been a while since she felt like this about being an SIO. Maybe it was the connection she was making with the CID team at Llancastell. Despite all her preconceptions, they were committed and talented police officers, and she was impressed.

Up on the television screen, a female news anchor was sitting behind a desk. She was wearing a dark burgundy top under a black suit jacket. Behind her there was a large graphic of police evidence tape with the words *Police Line* written on it in dark blue. She looked at the camera: '*Neerav Banerjee, the headteacher at the Dinas Padog High School and father of three, was found dead in his home in Snowdonia. Peter Lowe has been following developments.*'

The camera moved to live shots of outside the Banerjees' home. '*The forty-two-year-old was found in the kitchen of his five-bedroomed house in the idyllic village of Llanfihangel Glyn Myfyr. Police are describing the attack as calculated and vicious. Detectives say they are very keen to speak to anyone who was in that area at around five o'clock last night and saw anything out of the ordinary, however small. The murder comes only days after Arabella Dixon, the deputy headteacher at the same school, was discovered murdered in a nearby car park.*'

THERE WAS A STRANGE hush in Incident Room 1, and Ruth could sense that the detectives were processing the events of the last twenty-four hours. Murder was a rarity. There were around twenty murders a year in Wales, and they were mainly in the major cities in the south. Two murders in a week had floored some officers, who were wondering if they were out of their depth. Many had heard the rumours it wouldn't be long before big guns from Liverpool and Manchester were drafted in to take over. There was a murder a week in those two metropolitan areas. Ruth knew that for some, having the support of a team of experienced homicide officers was a relief. For others, it would be a frustration.

Striding out of her office, Ruth went over to the second whiteboard that had been set up in the incident room. A photo of Neerav Banerjee was at its centre. Wearing a traditional grey jubbah, he had his arm around his wife Raeleah's shoulder. They were beaming and Neerav was squeezing her close to him. His name was written in blue board-marker alongside his date of birth, and the details of the murder.

Ruth had spoken at length to Raeleah Banerjee the previous evening at a neighbour's house. She was in a state of shock and couldn't comprehend what had happened to her husband. She wore a simple pink hijab. Behind her glasses, her big brown eyes welled to tears every few minutes.

Raeleah shook her head a lot and told Ruth that she did not understand why anyone would want to harm her husband. They were Muslim. Was that it? Both she and Neerav had been active in the Muslim Council of Wales for over fifteen years. Perhaps someone didn't like that?

Originating from Tamil Nadu in India, Raeleah said her grandparents had arrived in the Midlands in the 1960s. They had settled for a time in Leicester before moving north to Leeds and then finally Bradford. She had met Banerjee at a school in Bradford when she was working as a teaching assistant. There was nothing she could tell Ruth about Neerav's life that gave her any clue as to why someone had targeted him. As she left, Ruth glimpsed the Banerjee children sitting motionless on a sofa, watching television. The emotion of their loss caught her by surprise as she got into her car and drove back to the hotel.

Ruth had spent the previous evening in her hotel room, running the case through her head and making notes to see if anything clicked. It didn't. She ran a bath, lit candles and played classical music – Vaughn Williams, Mahler's Fifth, Peer Gynt. And if Ruth lay there and closed her eyes, she could almost sense Sarah's presence. The touch of her foot against her thigh. It's what they used to do together. Lie in a hot bubble-bath, sipping prosecco and putting the world to rights.

Ruth took her notes and walked to the front of the incident room. 'Okay, everyone, listen up.' Ruth pointed at Neerav's photo. 'Neerav Banerjee, headteacher at Dinas Padog High School, was murdered at his home yesterday at around 4pm. Same MO as Arabella Dixon's murder so it is likely that we are looking for the same killer. He was strangled and there was something cut into the back of his hand. SOCO are still working the scene and I don't expect anything from Forensics until tomorrow. Post-mortem is this afternoon. The killer was wearing some kind of Halloween pig mask.'

'Like in the *Saw* movies?' asked Merringer.

Ruth shrugged. She had no idea. 'If you say so. Anyway, where can you buy a pig mask like that, have they sold any recently, and to whom? Can someone chase Forensics on the condom in Arabella Dixon's bathroom? That way we can know either way if she was sleeping with Neerav Banerjee. Uniform are checking the area where myself and DS Evans pursued the suspect. At that distance, it was impossible to tell the height or build of the killer except that they seemed average.' Ruth glanced up to see Nick arriving. He had a coffee in hand and perched himself on a table at the back of the room. Ruth could see his hand was shaking as he brought the mug to his lips. 'You're meant to be recovering at home, DS Evans.'

'I'd rather be here, boss. Not a problem. I'm fine, honest,' Nick said.

Ruth could tell from where she was that Nick wasn't fine. He was three hours into his 'home detox'. That meant combining a slow taper from his alcohol consumption – five to ten units a day – with taking small doses of diazepam. Done wrong, it could lead to a lethal overdose. But Nick had reassured her last night, over what he called his 'final cider as an alcoholic', that he had been through enough medical detoxes and on enough helpful websites to know the right quantities. It would stop him feeling the anxiety, shakes and sweats of a sudden detox, but she feared that too much and he would fall asleep, become unconscious or worse.

'Okay. Take a seat. And the first sign of concussion or anything else, someone takes you to hospital.' Nick gave a short nod and Ruth turned back to the whiteboard. 'So what links our two victims?' She pointed at the photograph of Arabella Dixon and then to Neerav Banerjee on the other board. A nearby phone rang, and Merringer answered it. 'We know that they worked together. It is possible they had had an affair. Any news on the IP address for those emails anyone?'

'I've pushed the Hi-Tech Crime Unit and they're trying to do it by the end of the day, boss,' Mac replied.

'Good. Sian, house call to Alex Noakes. Where was he yesterday afternoon? His whereabouts on the night of his mother's death are still very vague. He hated her enough to move out. Maybe he didn't like her sleeping with Neerav Banerjee?'

Sian nodded, stood, and took her jacket off the back of her chair. For a moment, she looked back and they made eye contact. Ruth gave her a smile and they held each other's gaze for a second. Was it a little moment between them, Ruth wondered?

Luke put the phone down and shot Ruth a glance. 'Boss, Bronwyn Wright was released from the Lighthouse two days ago.'

'Right. Nothing to link her to Arabella Dixon's murder but she has motive. She hated them both. Luke, pay Bronwyn Wright a visit. Take Mac. I need house-to-house in ...' Ruth looked searchingly at Nick.

'Llanfihangel Glyn Myfyr,' Nick prompted her.

'Yeah, what he said. Then we need to look at teachers and parents. Get onto Traffic and see where there are cameras between Dinas Padog and the Banerjee house. Our killer had access to a shotgun. Right, we need to think. What links Arabella and Neerav? What did they do to make someone want to murder them both?'

An hour later, Ruth and Nick drove through the bustling town of Llangollen, heading from Llancastell to Dinas Padog. Nick, Ruth could see, was feeling jittery due to his detox.

As they approached, Ruth had gazed up to see the remains of *Castell Dinas Bran,* Crow Castle, which could be seen high on an isolated hill above the town.

According to legend, this was the burial site of the Holy Grail of the Arthurian legend.

For the first time since she had arrived, the bank of leaden clouds had been replaced by irregular white ones in front of a solid blue sky. Spring seemed like a season that washed in and out like an interminable tide. The cold, windy and grey days were broken up by bursts of promising warmth, only to be dragged away as spring retreated again. Yet trees had started to bud with blossom, and as they made their way along the A5, the landscape that stretched either side seemed to be changing.

Ruth decided to run the various hypotheses around the two murders past Nick.

'Do we think that Alex Noakes had confronted his mother and things got out of hand?' Ruth asked.

'Maybe. But can you see Alex Noakes killing Neerav Banerjee in cold blood at his home?' Nick asked.

'He's a bit grumpy, but that doesn't make him a cold-blooded killer,' Ruth said sardonically.

'Bronwyn Wright had a grudge against them both. Even though she gives me the willies, opportunity and means are going to be hard to prove,' Nick said.

'The willies?' Ruth said with a smile.

'Yeah, she's a bit Rose West. Dead eyes behind those bottle-bottom glasses. Creeps me out.'

'I know what you mean ... And Jonathan Noakes seems to be happily married with a new family. Maybe our killer is someone who we haven't even come across yet?' Ruth suggested.

By the time they arrived at Dinas Padog High School, they were both frustrated at not making any headway on the case. Ruth could see the school was now up and running again. The main staff car park was full, and small groups of sixth formers came through the gates with bags of food from the nearby chip shop.

'Glad the healthy eating initiative is getting through to teenagers,' Nick said sarcastically.

'Don't. I'm living off fast food. Living in a hotel is not good for my health,' Ruth said.

'What are you doing tonight?' Nick asked.

'If you're asking me out, Nick, remember that I'm gay,' Ruth said with a grin.

'It's my Auntie Pat's birthday today. I'm going over for some dinner, why don't you come along?'

'Thanks, but I'll be okay,' Ruth said.

'Seriously. They would love to have you there.'

'I don't want to impose.'

'Come on. It's just my uncle, aunt and cousin. Nothing fancy. And they're always complaining that I never bring a woman with me.'

'I'm not sure that I'm quite what they had in mind,' Ruth said with a smile.

'I'll take that as a yes, then,' Nick said.

There was still a large police sign by the main school gates with the North Wales Police badge, the time and date of Arabella Dixon's murder, and *Fearwch Chi Helpu? Can you help? Ffoniwch Tel: 01978 897997.*

As they parked, Ruth looked over to see a marked Police/*Heddlu* patrol car parked over by the Scout hut. A female uniformed officer was talking to a woman of a similar age.

'What are they doing here?' Ruth said out loud.

Ruth and Nick got out of the car and approached. The uniformed officer, slim, blonde hair in a ponytail, spotted them and walked towards them.

'Everything all right?' Ruth asked.

'Ma'am, the Scout hut doubles for a nursery three times a week. They were playing outside and a three-year-old boy crawled under the hut. Below the middle of the hut, he found a Stanley knife.'

Ruth shot Nick a look. Arabella Dixon's cut hand had been caused by something like a Stanley knife. Their pulses quickened a little.

'Thank you, officer. Nick, get gloves and an evidence bag from the car.'

A plump, short woman, presumably the nursery manager, came over. She was holding the dark blue Stanley knife.

Ruth's heart sank. She was contaminating the evidence with every step.

The woman smiled, not understanding the implication of what had been found. She gave a self-effacing laugh. 'I don't make a habit of leaving the little ones outside unsupervised. I was only gone a second. Little monkeys, aren't they?' She was clearly worried that she had breached the nursery's health and safety policy.

Nick arrived just in time, opened the evidence bag, and with his blue-gloved hands carefully placed the item into it. It was now that Ruth noticed that the handle of the knife had a dark stain on it.

'Thank you. We'll take it from here,' Ruth said. 'Officer, can you get a statement from the boy as well as the nursery manager?'

The officer nodded and said, 'Ma'am.'

Nick and Ruth turned and headed for the car. They said nothing for a moment as their brains processed the find. Nick took off his blue latex gloves and put them and the evidence bag into the boot.

'If you murder her, why do you decide to throw the knife under a Scout hut? Doesn't make any sense, does it?' Nick said.

'It does if you've murdered her but you've got to go back into the hut and act as if nothing has happened.'

'Daniel Hughes?'

'He makes an excuse to go outside during the Scout meeting. He goes to the car park where he attacks and kills Arabella Dixon?' Ruth said, thinking out loud.

'Why not leave the knife where it was then? And why haven't we found the phone or car keys yet?' asked Nick.

'Someone is attacking you. You stop and need to protect yourself. What do you use?' Ruth asked rhetorically.

'Car keys and maybe a phone,' Nick said with a nod.

'Arabella Dixon defends herself with her car keys and phone. She hits her attacker with them and they worry that their DNA is now on the keys and phone? They take them to destroy, throw the knife, which you're confident only has her blood on it, under the hut.'

'Why not destroy everything? Maybe Daniel Hughes went into the car park to pour acid on Arabella Dixon's car to get her back for the earlier argument. She comes out and catches him doing it. They fight, he panics and kills her,' Nick suggested.

RUTH TAPPED AT HER computer, digging around for what she could find about Daniel Hughes on the Police National Computer, PNC. Nick was contacting everyone who had attended the Scout meeting the night of Arabella Dixon's murder. Had Daniel Hughes left there and found enough time to murder Arabella Dixon? And what linked him to Neerav Banerjee? Race? Daniel Hughes had made his hateful views on race very clear.

And then, there it was on the screen. *Daniel Hughes – Date of birth: 23 November 1976.* The address matched. And then a note on Daniel Hughes that he had changed his name by deed poll nine years ago from Daniel Holmes. As a Scout leader, he would have been subject to a DBS check (Disclosure and Barring Service), or, more likely, the old CRB check (Criminal Records Bureau) that only changed in 2012.

Ruth then searched for more detailed background checks. There was intel on Daniel Hughes that showed that he was a member of the North Wales British Movement, which was a Neo-Nazi group. Hughes had sent out a newsletter in 2014 with the image of Lee Rigby, in the red dress uniform of the Royal Fusiliers, on the front. The more Ruth checked, the more disgusted she became with what she found. A newspaper article described the North Wales British Movement as a 'poisonous' far-right group operating in North Wales that 'had come under fire after setting up a wing to recruit children'. She read how, under the banner of Young Dragons, the North Wales British Movement had been taking youngsters to the seaside in places such as Barmouth, Abersoch, and up onto Anglesey to add to what they claim is their 'ever-growing white family'. Another article showed the members, dressed in the white robes of the Klu Klux Klan, re-enacting a lynching with a golliwog doll. Then there was footage on YouTube of members of the North Wales British Movement attacking Muslims outside the Islamic Cultural Centre in Rhyl. It seemed that Daniel 'Hughes' was using the Scouts as a way of recruiting teenagers into the British Movement, and that was despicable.

In terms of a criminal record, Daniel 'Holmes' had his own past, including some offences for affray and assault as a teenager and in his twenties. Most of these seemed to have happened at BNP or National Front marches, or at football games.

Daniel Holmes also had a conviction – a suspended sentence for affray and assault during the notorious race riots in Reeds Park, Llancastell. Ruth thought she remembered the story and soon found a news report online. She read how fifty-one people were charged in connection with the disturbances in June 2003, which involved teens as young as thirteen. Trouble had flared a day after an Iraqi Kurd was set upon by local residents, suffering a fractured skull. The next night a group of around twenty Iraqi Kurds armed themselves with baseball bats and clubs and confronted men inside a pub on the notorious Reeds Park estate, whom they blamed for the attack. The mass brawl that ensued spilled out onto the street. The following night Daniel Holmes was involved in the violence that erupted when police in riot gear were bombarded by a mob with stones and petrol bombs. A lot of the Iraqi Kurds had already fled their homes on the estate having taken refuge in a church hall. Ruth could see that Daniel had been fuelled by racial hatred from a young age. No doubt from what he had seen and heard at home. That's how that kind of bigotry works. You get your parents' genes, resentment, bitterness and moral code.

There seemed to be nothing in the last twelve years since the riots. That would explain how Daniel 'Hughes' got his CRB check – non-custodial sentences were wiped off a criminal record after eleven years.

Ruth sat back, took a breath, and thought for a moment. The two victims were mixed race and Asian. Hughes already had an ongoing feud with Arabella Dixon. He was a racist with a history of violence. They had found a knife under the hut where he was a Scout leader. She just prayed that his DNA showed up on the knife. How would he explain that?

It was at that moment that Nick came in with a bright look on his face. 'Boss?'

'Nicholas?' Ruth said brightly.

'I've got half a dozen Scouts who will testify that Daniel Hughes went out of the Scout hut for a ciggie before eight o'clock on the night of Arabella Dixon's murder. They all say independently that he was gone for fifteen minutes or more. One of them said he was certain it was more like twenty-five minutes.'

Everything was pointing towards Daniel Hughes.

CHAPTER 20

RUTH WAS IN FULL FLOW now that the case had blown wide open in the last few hours. The High-Tech Crime Unit had downloaded texts from Arabella Dixon's mobile server and found that the abusive, racist texts to her had come from Daniel Hughes' phone number. There were also two similar texts to Neerav Banerjee, referring to him as a 'Paki Islamic bastard'.

Hughes had been arrested and brought in for questioning as the CPS agreed that there were now sufficient grounds for suspicion of his involvement in Arabella Dixon's murder, and possibly Neerav Banerjee's. They had handed his phone and laptop to the Hi-Tech Crime Unit and a swab was done for his DNA.

At last Ruth and Nick thought they were getting somewhere. As they walked down to Interview Room 3 they discussed how they thought they had their man. At least he was a frontrunner with motive, means, and opportunity for Arabella Dixon's murder. And given that Neerav Banerjee was an Indian Muslim, and that there was an identical MO, it was likely that these were racially motivated hate crimes.

As they entered the interview room, Ruth could see that Daniel Hughes was nervous. His eyes flicked around the room and he was fidgeting. Beside him was his legal aid solicitor, a skinny, grey-haired man in an ill-fitting suit.

Ruth clicked on the recording device, cautioned Hughes and told him why they were questioning him.

'Is this about the car?' Hughes asked frowning anxiously.

'What car would that be, Mr Hughes?' Nick asked.

'Arabella Dixon's car. Is that why I'm here?'

'Why do you think you're here, Daniel?' Ruth asked in her gentle, confiding tone.

'I'm not sure.'

'Is there something you want to tell us about Arabella Dixon's car, Mr Hughes?' Nick said.

Hughes paused for a moment. 'No. I have no idea what you're talking about.'

'We have abusive, racist texts you sent to Arabella Dixon and Neerav Banerjee. We have your record of racist violence and membership of the British Movement stretching back twenty years,' Nick said.

'Being in the British Movement is not illegal. I know my rights. What's this all about, like?' Hughes' face reflected his panicked tone.

'Daniel, a Stanley knife was found under the hut where you are a Scout leader. You were seen rowing with Miss Dixon the night she was killed. You sent her threatening texts. We have witnesses that say you were out of the Scout hut for up to twenty-five minutes at the time of Arabella Dixon's murder.'

'I went for a smoke. I always go for a ciggie halfway through.' Hughes shook his head as the severity of what was being said dawned on him. 'This is crazy. Jesus Christ, I didn't kill anyone.'

'But you left the Scout hut to damage Arabella Dixon's car?' Nick said sternly.

Hughes was now wide-eyed with fear. 'I wish I had. The bitch had it coming. But I didn't kill her for God's sake!'

'Didn't you?' Nick barked. 'You went to put acid on Miss Dixon's car out of revenge after your row about the car park. But she caught you doing it. Threatened you. You argued and then in a panic you killed her, didn't you?' Nick thundered.

'No! That's not what happened. I was shocked when I heard someone had murdered her.'

'Christ, like hell you were. You threw a party,' Nick shouted at Hughes.

There was a moment's silence as the comment hung in the air. Hughes' anxiety was palpable and he looked at the floor for a moment.

Ruth cleared her throat, and then said softly, 'When did you last see Neerav Banerjee, Daniel?'

'I don't know. Erm ... months ago. I can't remember.'

'You think that he is a "Paki Islamic bastard" though?' Nick said reading from the transcripts of Neerav Banerjee's texts, as though he was trying to clarify something.

There was silence again and Hughes took a sharp intake of breath and leant forwards on his chair, arms and elbows on his thighs. He then ran his hands through his hair.

'Daniel, or is it Dan?' Ruth asked quietly.

'Dan. It's Dan.'

'Dan, right. Okay. Can you tell us where you were yesterday around five in the afternoon?' Ruth asked.

'At home, asleep. I work shifts at the dairy. I'm on nights, so I sleep until five or six during the day,' Dan explained.

'Can anyone vouch for that?' Nick growled.

Dan's tone was now one of desperation and disbelief. 'No. My wife was at her mum's with the kids.'

'Well, that is convenient, isn't it?' Nick snorted.

'Dan, do you own a shotgun?' Ruth asked.

'Of course. Everyone does round here. Me and the lads go lamping in the winter. I do some beating in the autumn. That's all.' Hughes frowned and looked at the floor again.

'And if I wanted to look at your shotgun, that would be okay, would it?' Nick said steadily.

'My father-in-law's had it for a while. You'll have to ask him,' Hughes said with a shrug.

'Violation of your shotgun licence, isn't it?' Nick asked.

'No, copper. You check the 1968 Firearms Act. I can lend my gun to anyone as long as they're in my presence when they use it,' Hughes retorted with a sneer.

'And if we search your premises thoroughly, we're not going to find a sawn-off shotgun anywhere? Is that right?' Nick asked.

'No. Sawn-off shotgun? I don't know what you're talking about.'

Hughes put his head in his hands.

BY SIX O'CLOCK, RUTH and Nick had questioned Daniel Hughes and put him in the cells for the night. They hoped that this might scare him enough into a confession, but it was unlikely. Ruth knew what they needed was Forensics to find his and Arabella Dixon's DNA on the Stanley knife. She hoped that the stain was her blood.

Ruth had also contacted Alex and Jonathan Noakes to tell them they had made an arrest, although no charges had been brought yet. Jonathan told her that a local mystic, who claimed to have been in contact with Arabella Dixon after her death, had contacted the family. Jonathan said that he had told the woman they weren't interested and if she contacted them again he would call the police. Neither of the phone calls was easy to make and Ruth felt emotionally wrung out.

Nick was driving Ruth out to Mike and Pat's home as it was Pat's sixty-third birthday. Ruth knew she could do with a night away from her hotel room. She had bought a bottle of prosecco and some flowers for Pat. If Ruth was honest, she felt uncomfortable about meeting Nick's family, but she felt she couldn't say no to the offer. And she knew that a change of scenery would mean having far fewer thoughts about the case, and her mind wouldn't run the edited highlights of her and Sarah's relationship on a constant background loop.

Ruth looked out at the fading light and the specks of rain that were accumulating on the passenger window. She took a deep breath. If someone had told her three weeks ago that as soon as she got to North Wales she would be heading up a double-murder case, then she might have given her transfer serious thought. However, she had found her present colleagues less aggressive and intolerant than those at the Met, which was a surprise. Plus, the surroundings were staggeringly beautiful and steeped in great mythology, which Peckham lacked.

As the sun set, it cast a deep orange and dark pink hue over the sky. The steep banks of dense conifer trees that led up as far as the eye could see would be something you would expect in Scandinavia. Ruth gazed out of the window and Nick recounted some of the history and myths. He told her he wasn't fond of the Arthurian legend as he was an English king. He preferred the Welsh-based stories such as the Demon of Cerrigydrudion.

When they arrived at Mike and Pat's home, Ruth caught herself thinking it was such a simple existence. She wondered how much the little hamlet had changed since the sixties or seventies. She then hoped that she wasn't being patronising in her pleasure of its modesty and lack of pretention. She thought of London dinner parties with talk of property prices, good schools, or festivals that were a must, and how they now seemed silly and frivolous.

Pat had made traditional Welsh lamb *cawl,* which was a stew made with parsnips, leeks, swede and carrots. The four of them sat down to eat almost straight away with Pat to-ing and froing as they ate. The placemats had drawings of old hunting scenes from the nineteenth century. For a while no one said very much except how good the cawl was. Dean Martin played on the CD player.

'How long have you worked at Dinas Padog, Mike?' Ruth asked.

'Long time. Twenty-five years now,' Mike replied with a smile.

'Do you like it? Obviously not in the last week but ...'

'Yeah, nice school, like. Kids are good. Job is nice and steady. That's all

I need.'

'Nick says you're from London?' Pat said.

'Born and bred.'

'Aye, proper cockney then?' Mike said.

'I suppose so. My granddad Bill was from Hackney and born in the sound of the Bow Bells. He moved to South London when he met my nan. Battersea ... It's all changed now,' Ruth said with a feeling of resentment.

'Why's that?' Pat asked.

Ruth shook her head. 'In the eighties, my old man paid nineteen thousand pounds for a small two-bedroom flat on the Winstanley Estate. Rough as hell. It's now worth three or four hundred thousand pounds. The middle-classes have taken over.'

'What brought you to North Wales then? Apart from property prices, beautiful scenery and friendly people?' Mike smiled.

'Long story. I had family up here ages ago. Spent my summers as a kid up here. Seemed to be nice and I needed to get away,' Ruth confessed. She looked over to the framed photo of two girls grinning. Megan and Cerys.

'You have daughters?' Ruth asked. She immediately picked up on a moment of uneasy silence. She wondered what she had said.

'Yes, Megan and Cerys,' Mike said, and there was more silence.

'We lost Megan four years ago,' Pat said quietly.

'I'm so sorry to hear that.' Ruth was now regretting asking about the photo.

'She took her own life,' Pat explained.

'I'm sorry. That must have been hard for you,' Ruth said. She had encountered enough suicides in her job to know the destruction that it left behind.

'She was fragile, our Megan. Like a flower. Found things a struggle, like,' Mike's voice was low but calm. He looked over at the photo.

'But funny. Great dry sense of humour.' Nick smiled.

'Until she went all religious,' Pat blurted out. 'That's what got to her.' Pat got up from the table, visibly upset.

'Pudding anyone? Homemade apple pie?' Pat walked away from the table, composing herself as she disappeared into the kitchen.

'I'm sorry if I've upset her,' Ruth said, pursing her lips awkwardly. Even after four years, their emotions were still raw. She couldn't blame them. She knew what it felt like to lose someone.

'It's fine. How were you to know? Please don't worry,' Mike said reassuringly.

The rest of the evening was convivial as they chatted about family and Nick was teased about what he was like when he was a youngster. But the conversation about Megan hung around like an irksome ghost.

On the way home, Ruth thanked Nick for taking her. It had been a refreshing change of scene, great food and company.

'I'm sorry if I upset your aunt?' Ruth said.

'You weren't to know. She's never really got over it,' Nick explained.

'Does anyone know why? I don't mean to pry but ...'

'All we know was that she was being bullied at school. A group of bitchy girls. Something to do with a lad she was seeing. The head of year claimed she had dealt with it. She'd seen it a hundred times before.'

'And there were no signs ...?'

'We could see Megan was upset. She kept herself to herself for a while. But she was a teenage girl. Everyone thought it was just hormones. She suddenly became religious and went to church with a friend of hers who was a Baptist. Mike and Pat thought it was a phase she was going through.'

Ruth nodded. 'That's the thing with teenage girls. The raging hormones, anger, mood swings are part of growing up. It's hard to spot when it's crossed the line into a mental health issue.' She was talking from experience. She had a sudden pang of guilt about the damage she had done to Ella as a teenager.

'No one spotted it. So one day Megan drank a bottle of vodka, swam into a lake in Snowdonia and drowned herself.'

CHAPTER 21

IT WAS SEVEN O'CLOCK when Nick woke which meant eight hours without alcohol – a good sign that the tapering was working. Knocking himself out with fifteen milligrams of diazepam and ten milligrams of zopiclone, he had surrendered his consciousness and slept like a baby. Not as an ex-colleague used to joke, waking every two hours crying and wetting the bed. No, a proper dark and dreamless sleep. A sleep of the dead.

In a Llancastell detox centre, Nick and the two Scottish soldiers used to get their zopiclone early, about 9pm, and then have a competition to see who could stay awake in front of the television. Nick always lost as he would be 'nodding' within thirty minutes. He had read that Elvis and his Memphis Mafia cronies used to do the same in the penthouse suite of the Hilton in Las Vegas in the mid-seventies with Quaaludes, Demerol and benzos. Neck a handful of sleepers and downers, and the last one to sleep is the winner. He supposed it was one way of passing the interminable downtime trapped in Las Vegas hotel suites between the gigs. No doubt the sycophants would let the King win rather than rock or roll the golden boat they sailed in.

There was a growing film of sweat on Nick's forehead, which was to be expected. He gulped at a pint of water to keep himself hydrated, then reached for his notepad and studied his scribbled alcohol unit calculations. Today was a twenty-unit day. Piece of piss. People drink more than that every day on an all-inclusive holiday, Nick reassured himself. Half a bottle of white wine between now and eleven o'clock, with a five-milligram diazepam thrown in to help him and his overactive nervous system on their way. Easy.

Nick padded to the kitchen, clicked on the kettle and went about making himself a cup of tea. He made a note to eat too, as his weight was plummeting. That's the thing with alcohol. At a certain point, it completely kills your appetite and food is the furthest thing from your mind. Plus, food slowed down and weakened the effect of ethanol and cushioned the hit that addicts needed. Eating is cheating.

The last time Nick went on a proper bender, or 'relapse' as it's technically called, he lost nearly two stone. Mike and Pat had said he looked awful. When he summoned the courage to look in the mirror in recent weeks, he could see that the gaunt, grey look was returning to his face. He was glad that his current resolve to stop drinking wasn't diminishing.

It wasn't the drink that was the real problem. It was him. His head. His peculiar personality. The way the wiring of the neurones and pathways of his brain had been constructed. That unique lens through which he saw, and thought, and felt about the world. He had led a life lived in fear and anxiety.

As a child, Nick had been scared of everything and everyone. He didn't know if this was something he was born with, something genetic, or the result of having a father who was either absent or unpredictably violent. If you added in losing his mother at an impressionable age, then Nick had a potent, noxious cocktail of childhood trauma that needed self-medication. Either way, nature or nurture, Nick knew that he had thought like an alcoholic long before he had ever taken a drink.

Swimming lessons used to bring a particular sense of dread, and he'd remembered the terror of counting down the days before the horror of Saturday mornings. He would walk along the poolside, the redolent smell of chlorine, gazing at the deep end and imagining its bottomless depth. He knew for certain that if he fell in, he would drop like a stone into the watery endlessness and die, never to be seen again. It didn't help that the teacher's rather progressive idea of getting nervous kids used to the water was to throw them in.

Nick wouldn't climb walls or jump from high hay bales with his mates. Somewhere in his head, he thought he would die. And that was his default madness. Death. Not a sprained ankle as the worst-case scenario. No. He would be killed by the fall. So, he would make his excuses and watch them from afar. And that made him different – a loner.

During his childhood Nick felt he just never fitted in. He felt apart from everyone. And he envied and revered everyone around him. Their parents, their homes, their clothes and most of all their confidence. He remembered David Bennet, a boy that amazed him and seemed like he had come from another planet. He was great at sport, playing rugby for North Wales and scoring cricket centuries for the school in summer. He was bright and popular with the teachers. Yet he was also one of 'the lads', the boys that smoked and had girlfriends before Nick had any signs of puberty. Boys like David Bennet just emphasised to Nick all his shortcomings and exacerbated his crippling low self-esteem and self-loathing. Nick wanted to be anyone apart from himself.

However, one day when Nick had just turned fifteen, his friend Matt Edwards took him to a youth group at the Dinas Padog community centre on a Saturday night. When it was over, Nick went with the boys into the woods where they sat and drank from a two-litre bottle of cider. And something magical happened. The awkward anxiety in the pit of his stomach and his whirring obsessive mind just stopped. He felt relaxed, calm and by the third drink he was euphoric. *This was it! This was the answer.* His tense shoulders dropped and his stomach felt warm. He laughed and even told jokes. He had found the answer to all his prayers – booze.

For the next few years, booze was his best friend. It allowed him to walk into a party with his head held high. He could talk to girls, dance and get rowdy. His friend booze even allowed him to be aggressive, getting into scuffles with kids from rival North Wales villages. Nick knew that everything would always be all right if he had booze inside him. He was untouchable. He was a hell-raiser. Result. *Thank you, God, for the effect that ethanol has on every part of my being.*

Nick wasn't sure when he went from heavy social drinker to problem drinker. He probably drank alcoholically from his first swig of cider on that Saturday night. He drank to black out from an early age. But he knew it was time to say goodbye to his friend, and with that there was a huge sense of loss. This friend that had given him so much in the past but then betrayed and deceived him. This friend had tried to kill him and so enough was enough.

Nick stared into space, lost in these thoughts and feeling teary. He would never get away with drinking again. The warmth and confidence had been replaced by compulsion, obsession and anxiety. The good times had gone some time ago and now Nick drank alone.

The click of the electric kettle brought him back to the present. He slopped water onto the tea bag in his Welsh Rugby mug and wondered what Ruth was doing. The thought of her brought a smile to his face. She wasn't what he had expected. There was none of the arrogance that he thought she would have brought coming from the Met. Quite the opposite.

Nick wondered what she was like in bed. His mate Steve always claimed that all men think about sleeping with every woman they meet, even if it's only for a second. Not with twelve or eighty-year-olds, just with anything that was what Steve termed 'fair game'. Nick told him he was 'a pervert' but deep down Nick thought it was probably true.

SOFT DRIZZLE FELL FROM a ponderously grey Llancastell sky as Ruth marched from the car park over to the concrete, high-rise North Wales Police building. Rain dribbled from guttering and the air smelt of the exhaust of the early-morning traffic and deliveries. She sipped from her coffee, her regular flat white, thankful that for all its shortcomings, Llancastell at least had a Costa Coffee.

Ruth had already been on her early-morning run before the rain had set in, and was energised at the thought that in Daniel Hughes, they had a very viable suspect. Snippets of the refrain from *Soul Heaven* by The Goodfellas played in her head as a soundtrack to her morning.

As usual, Ruth was the first to enter the office. That's what they said about Alex Ferguson – always the first at the training ground. Lead by example and dedication to the cause. She clicked on the overhead lights. The empty rooms had the quiet peace of early morning; the smell of cleaning products and freshly hoovered carpets that hadn't yet been ruined by male sweat, fast food and coffee. Her head was clear and her mind felt sharp. Something told her that today was going to be a good day.

Before Ruth had time to log on and get the coffee machine up and running, she had had a phone call from Superintendent Jones' secretary summoning her for a meeting immediately. She felt a pang of nerves as she took the flight of stairs up to the fourteenth floor. Figures of authority always did this to her, ever since she was a child. Maybe it was because her father had been stern and domineering. Sometimes it felt that the family had spent too much time trying to placate him because of his temper. She knew that in some situations she participated in 'pleasing' behaviour and was not being true to herself.

Jones was standing by the window of his office, back to the door and hands behind his back. Ruth knocked and entered. She noticed his broad shoulders and thick neck and wondered if he used to play rugby.

Jones deliberately waited for a moment before turning. *Mind games. God, he's such a prick.*

'Morning, sir,' Ruth said through gritted teeth.

Jones walked brusquely towards his desk and turned a copy of the *Llancastell Leader* for her to read. 'Have you seen the paper?'

'No. Not yet,' Ruth replied in a concerned tone as she leaned over the desk, looking down at the latest copy of the local newspaper.

The front page carried photos of Arabella Dixon and Neerav Banerjee, which was no big surprise, but the headline *... Murders are racially motivated. Scout leader held.*

Ruth frowned. 'Shit. Where have they got this from?'

'A source in the North Wales Police apparently.' Jones was unimpressed.

'Shit.'

'Shit indeed. The media office was deluged with calls last night and this morning. Social media is awash with all sorts of allegations and conspiracy theories. The last thing we need is some kind of race war in North Wales. How do they know the name of your suspect already?'

'I don't know, sir. I can't believe that anyone on the team would have talked to the press,' Ruth said, now wondering about any members of CID that she had taken a dislike to.

'You haven't been here long enough to make that kind of judgement, Ruth. But this is on your watch and I want it sorted out. Liaise with the press department,' Jones said in a tone intended to leave her in no doubt that this was her mess and she needed to sort it out and fast.

Ruth was keeping calm. 'I'll call another press conference this afternoon so we can keep as much control of this as possible.'

'Aye, good. See if we can pour some water on this before it explodes, eh?' Jones gave her a withering look as he reached for the newspaper.

Ruth nodded. 'Sir.'

'Sodding journalists! How viable is Daniel Hughes as a suspect?'

'Sent threatening racist texts to both victims. History of racially motivated violence. He was seen rowing with Arabella Dixon on the night of her murder and has had an ongoing feud with her for a few years. We found a Stanley knife under the Scout hut which he runs. It's similar to one used to cut both victims,' Ruth said.

'That's fine, but it's circumstantial, Ruth,' Jones warned her. 'A defence lawyer would have a field day. Have you spoken to the CPS yet?'

'Just a preliminary call, sir. I thought I would wait to see if we get anything from Forensics. They've got the Scout uniform he wore the night of the murder, and the knife, which is stained. If we can get something concrete like Arabella's DNA on the knife or on his uniform, I think the CPS would go for it.'

Jones nodded. 'Okay. We could do with charging someone to calm things down.'

'Any idea if we're getting experienced officers from Manchester or Merseyside?' Ruth asked. Now she was up and running with the case, she was loath to hand it over or be replaced as SIO.

'It's Commander Tope's call. I'll keep you in the loop if I hear anything.'

'Who else is a possible at the moment?' Jones asked.

'Arabella Dixon's son Alex Noakes had a volatile relationship with his mother. We suspect that she had had an affair with Neerav Banerjee. We also think the affair might have started up again in recent weeks. But my instinct doesn't see Alex Noakes killing Neerav Banerjee in cold blood at his home,' Ruth explained.

'But you're not ruling him out?'

Ruth shook her head. 'No. Not yet. His father, Jonathan Noakes, seems to be happily married. He was around the area of the school the night Arabella Dixon was murdered. If he suspected she and Neerav were having an affair, he might have been jealous and that would give him motive for both murders. Again, that feels like a longshot. And then we have Bronwyn Wright, a teacher who was suspended from the school. When she was interviewed, she seemed to blame them for the suspension and her subsequent nervous breakdown. We're still waiting to see where she was at the time of Neerav Banerjee's murder. She claims she was at a private psychiatric unit in Welshpool at the time of Arabella Dixon's death.'

Jones nodded, taking all this in. 'There's a lot to unpick here, isn't there?'

'Yes, sir. But I've run a lot of murder cases over the years. It's nothing that the team and I can't handle.'

RUTH WALKED BRISKLY into the interview room and sat down on a blue plastic seat. She folded her legs, took her folder and opened it. Purposefully, she took her time, not looking at her suspect, as she increased the tension in the room. She knew what she was doing.

Daniel Hughes looked like he had had no sleep since the end of yesterday's interview. His skin was grey and pallid. Ruth wondered if a night of anxiety in a tiny police cell would persuade him to confess.

Hughes' solicitor sat to one side of him.

Ruth ran her finger down some notes, eeking out the silence for just a moment more, before beginning in a calm voice. 'Okay, Dan, I have to tell you again that you have been arrested on suspicion of two murders and I need to remind you that this interview is being video recorded. Do you understand all that, Dan?'

Dan nodded. 'Yeah.'

'Can we start at the beginning please, Dan? When did you first have contact with Arabella Dixon?' Ruth asked.

'Four, maybe five years ago. She picked up her son Alex from Scouts. His dad usually brought him and collected him. Nice fella. James ...' Dan said.

'Jonathan Noakes?' Ruth corrected him.

'That's right, Jonathan. He said he'd been in the Cubs and Scouts as a lad. Anyway, then one night she picked him up. Totally blanked me when I went to say hello. Snotty cow.'

'So, you took an instant dislike to her?'

'Yeah. But I'm not the only one round here that thought she was a stuck-up bitch though. And it don't mean I killed her, does it?' Dan looked at Ruth for a moment before look-ing at the floor.

'And after that? Did you see or meet Arabella Dixon?' Ruth asked.

'Only the times I already said. She complained about the cars when there was a Scout meeting and there was some-thing going on at the school. Said I should change it to a dif-ferent day. I told her to do one.' Dan smiled to himself for a moment.

'And what about Alex? What happened with him?'

'Like I told you. He'd disappear if we were doing stuff in the woods. Come back all red and glassy-eyed. High, you know? Smoking weed with his mate Tom. Always denied it. Then I caught them at it. I told his dad that Alex had to go and he understood. In fact, he apologised. Not like her.'

'What do you mean?' Ruth asked.

'She confronted me about a week later. Said her son didn't take drugs. She called me "a pathetic little chav".'

Ruth noted this down and then asked, 'And how did that make you feel?'

'I thought how dare she. She knows nothing about me, judging me like that!' Dan was getting riled.

Ruth waited for a moment and then in a disarmingly re-assuring tone, 'So you hated her for that, didn't you?'

'Yeah, I did ... But that still doesn't mean I killed her.'

Hughes' solicitor looked over, realising that his client was slowly hanging himself. 'Can I ask for a few minutes with my client privately?

'No,' Ruth answered calmly.

However, the solicitor's interjection seemed to warn Hughes that he was being far too open and honest. As the interview continued, Hughes became increasingly tight-lipped and cautious.

Ruth talked Hughes through the night of Arabella Dixon's murder but he stuck to his story, giving the bare details and no longer showing any emotion. He was adamant he didn't see her after their earlier row. He gave the times that he arrived and left the Scout hut, as well as recounted what he had done on the day of Neerav Banerjee's murder. Ruth was getting frustrated. She knew that the evidence they had against Hughes was circumstantial and that the CPS would require something more concrete before agreeing to charge him and take it to trial.

Ruth headed back upstairs to the incident room feeling deflated that she had made no progress with Hughes.

Merringer looked up as she came in. 'Boss, the nearest place to get one of those Halloween pig masks is Chester. You can buy them online very easily though.'

'Okay. Contact the suppliers and see how many they've shipped to North Wales in the past six months. Can't be many, can it?'

Nick came across the room with a computer printout. 'Boss, something's come through from South Wales Police. Last year a Muslim man, Ashiq Yassin from Swansea, was killed as he walked back from his mosque in the city. It happened at night in a dark alleyway and he was strangled. They've seen our details and they think it's got similarities to our murders.'

'It's a long way from Llancastell. I'll have a look after the press conference,' Ruth said.

'Yes, but Daniel Hughes is a distribution inspector for Welsh Water. He travels Wales looking at pipes and leaks. He's also an instructor for the Distribution department. Guess where their training headquarters are?'

'Please say Swansea.' Ruth put her hands together.

'I haven't cross-referenced the dates yet, but yes, Swansea.' Nick nodded.

Ruth took a moment. Were they dealing with a racist serial killer now? 'Jesus. Check the dates with Welsh Water. And see if you can get Forensics to get a shift on.'

Mac approached and said, 'Actually, boss, Forensics have come back with their analysis of a footprint they took from the flowerbed at Neerav Banerjee's house. A work boot, either size nine or size ten.'

'I wonder what size Dan Hughes' feet are?' Ruth said.

'We can soon find out,' Nick said.

AN HOUR LATER, RUTH felt her stomach churning as she prepared for her second press conference. Sipping water, she could feel the anxiety in her stomach. For a moment, she felt she was out of her depth. This is not what she had envisaged when she had put in for a transfer. She caught the self-pity and told herself to get a grip.

The room was teeming with national and local television, radio and print journalists. Two murders, possibly racially motivated, in the beautiful rural landscape of Snowdonia. Great story, great copy.

Ruth began the conference by giving the room the basic facts about the murder again – dates, times etc. She then discussed the crimes in more detail. She tripped over her words but remained calm and hoped that no one noticed.

'We have yet to establish a motive for these two murders and we don't have enough evidence yet to suggest they are racially motivated. However, we do have enough evidence to confirm that they are linked and that we are only looking for one suspect for both crimes. Due to growing concerns within the local community, we will treat them both as "hate crimes" and we would like to stress that there is no danger to the wider public at present. As the investigation stands now, we have one suspect in custody who has not been charged. We have other current lines of enquiry, forensic investigations, and we are also trawling CCTV.'

The press conference continued just as Ruth had hoped it would. She fielded the more awkward questions diplomatically. Jones seemed happy enough for the time being and gave her a thumbs-up as he left. In her head, she gave him the finger.

CHAPTER 22

RUTH'S HEAD WAS CHURNING. Spread out on her desk were twenty or so photographs from the Arabella Dixon and Neerav Banerjee murder scenes. Images of the dead bodies. Close-ups of their lifeless faces, limbs and other details. Was it only race that connected these two murders? Was there part of her that doubted that Daniel Hughes was a racially motivated killer? She studied the photos again, maybe for the tenth time that morning. Was there a clue in there somewhere? It was always the eyes of a dead body that stayed with her. She would never get used to seeing glazed eyes, the light of life gone out forever.

Nick came to her door with two large brown files. 'Files on the Reverend Arlo Lincoln.'

'Anything interesting?' Ruth asked.

'The Reverend Arlo Lincoln was accused of historic sexual abuse of teenagers in 2002 and then again in 2006. He was suspended from his duties as the chaplain of St Mark's College, which is a private school up in Ruthin. They never charged him but he eventually resigned in 2007.'

'Okay. Let's have another look at him,' Ruth said. 'But our focus is still Daniel Hughes.'

'Yes, boss,' Nick said.

Ruth checked her watch. It was approaching four o'clock and her team of CID detectives were starting to assemble.

Grabbing her files, Ruth made her way out of her office and into the incident room. On a new whiteboard was a photograph of Daniel Hughes dressed in military combat gear. He was grinning as though someone had just told him a joke.

Ruth looked at the photos of Arabella and Neerav on the other whiteboards smiling out at the room. They looked so happy and full of life. Both blissfully unaware of the horrendous way their lives would end so prematurely. It made Ruth angry, especially after the leak to the press that contained details that could have only come from a person working on the case or with access to how the investigation was progressing.

Ruth's tone reflected her fury. 'Right, there is someone in this building, and it might be someone in this room, who is talking to the press. You all know that you run anything to do with the media past the CCD and preferably me. It is an offence to do otherwise. If I find out who you are, I will make your life a misery, understood?'

There was an awkward moment and then Ruth took a breath. She had made her point and it was time to move on. 'At the moment, this investigation is complicated. We've had police search teams and the dog units out doing a search of Llanfihangel Glyn Myfyr – if I've said that correctly – the Clocaenog Forest, the mine and the banks of the River Afon Alwen. Unfortunately, nothing was found that would help the investigation. However, Forensics have a footprint from the Banerjee garden. A worker-type boot, either size nine or size ten. The PM will take place tomorrow morning at the hospital here in Llancastell. We have the same MO and we believe that something was carved into the back of Neerav Banerjee's hand.'

Ruth pointed to the photo of Daniel Hughes. 'We have this man as our prime suspect. Daniel Hughes. I will apply to hold him for thirty-six hours. We have to hope that Forensics come up with something so we can link him directly to Arabella Dixon on that night. Can we chase them again?' Ruth looked over to Sian who was sitting to her left. 'Sian, what did Alex Noakes have to say for himself?'

Sian thumbed through her notes. 'He has no alibi for the time of Neerav Banerjee's murder. Claims he was upstairs in Rhiannon Baker's bedroom watching football on the TV.'

Ruth thought that sounded very vague. 'Can anyone confirm that?'

'Mr Baker was out on the farm all afternoon.'

Ruth looked over at Mac. 'Anything from Bronwyn Wright, Mac?'

'Boss, she claims she was in Llancastell all afternoon. She visited the library and then visited some agencies for supply teaching. I haven't crosschecked whether she went to those agencies or at what time yet.'

Ruth nodded. 'Okay, let me know when you have.'

Nick came into the room holding a folder and looking serious. 'Boss, bad news. Forensics didn't find any of Daniel Hughes' DNA on the knife. The stain we thought might be blood is engine oil. And no DNA from Arabella Dixon on his uniform either. But the good news is he does have size nine feet.'

Ruth let her breath out. She had been confident that the stain would turn out to be blood. 'Shit! That's not going to be enough to hold him. When are we going to get a break in this case?'

'Something else, boss. The sperm found in the condom in Arabella Dixon's bathroom didn't match Neerav Banerjee's DNA,' Nick explained.

'So, she was sleeping with someone else?' Ruth said.

'Looks that way.' Nick nodded. 'I've asked Forensics to check the DNA with our elimination samples. Something by tomorrow.'

'Right. Okay.' Ruth was lost in thought.

'It might have been Alex Noakes' semen if he had sex with his girlfriend in his mum's bedroom?' Sian suggested.

'If nothing else turns up, we're going to have to release Daniel Hughes in the morning.' Ruth growled. It was always frustrating when suspects were released, but she wasn't about to take her foot off the gas. 'We owe it to Arabella and Neerav's families to find the bastard and get them justice.'

As she walked back to her office, Ruth was aware of the strength of feeling with which she wanted to – had to – get the case solved. Remembering the shocked look on the faces of the Banerjee children, Ruth knew she wasn't going to rest until they had caught the killer.

CHAPTER 23

NICK REVVED THE ASTRA'S two-litre engine as he sped up the A5 towards Dinas Padog. Royal Blood's *Figure It Out* boomed on the car stereo and Nick felt a surge of adrenaline. The sky was cloudy and the sunlight hit the windscreen intermittently.

To the right, a grey dry-stone wall separated the road from a steep drop into the Dee Valley before then heading north towards Ruthin. The countryside swept away in a tapestry of different greens, broken by clusters of darker trees or hedgerows. The road darkened as an overhanging canopy of branches from both sides cut out the sunlight. Even at this time of year, Nick noticed that cars with caravans were heading in both directions towards the caravan parks of the north and west coasts of Wales.

As Nick rounded a tight bend, the Berwyn Mountain Range, *Y Berwyn or Mynydd y Berwyn,* loomed into view. It was covered by dark heather, three feet thick, along with grassland and bracken. Nick could see the main summits of Cadair Berwyn, 2,730 ft above sea level, and Cadair Bronwyn at 2,572 ft. The Berwyn range was crossed to the southwest by the Milltir Cerrig mountain pass. Cadair Berwyn lay on a main ridge of the Berwyn range which ran north–south. The eastern side of the ridge featured steep drops and crags including Craig Berwyn. Nick had been

walking and scrambling there a few times with fellow coppers. All the tourists drove straight past it as they headed for
Snowdonia and Snowdon.

However, Nick had a real affection for the area. He loved
the history of the Berwyn Mountain range because it played
its part in causing King Henry II of England to turn back
during his invasion of Gwynedd in 1165. The English invasion faced an alliance of Welsh armies that were led by King
Owain Gwynedd. The English were beaten back by brave
Welshmen and the bitter weather.

RUTH HAD DRIVEN BACK to her hotel deep in
thought. *Pure Shores* by All Saints played on the stereo and it
took her back to a moment in time. The end of the summer
of 1999. Her marriage was over. The tail end of girl power. It
was Notting Hill before the film ruined it. Combat trousers,
vests and trainers. The end of the millennium when most
Generation X-ers were thinking about getting married or
having children. It was when Ruth first clapped eyes on
Sarah. They didn't get together until years later but Ruth fancied her. She had asked Sarah if she was a 'lipstick lesbian'
and she said that she was, but only at weekends – the rest of
the time she was a 'chapstick lesbian'. The more they talked
that night, the more they clicked. They had so much in common.

Ruth got to her hotel room and cracked open another
can of slimline gin and tonic. She took a long bath and tried
to unwind. She was reading *Into The Water,* Paula Hawkins'

follow-up to *The Girl On The Train,* but she couldn't concentrate.

She could feel the Dixon-Banerjee case slipping away from her and she hated the thought of handing over the case with lots of loose ends to more experienced detectives. It was her case now.

As Ruth wandered around the hotel room in just a towel, the carpet felt warm and snug under her bare feet and between her toes.

She took the remote and turned on the local news. A silver-haired, fifty-something male newscaster with a red tie, looked at the camera.

'*And the closing headlines this evening. Hundreds of residents from the village of Dinas Padoc in North Wales have assembled at the centre of their village tonight for a candlelit vigil for the two murdered teachers at their local school. They brought with them flowers, pictures, cards, and candles in remembrance of Arabella Dixon and Neerav Banerjee, both of whom were killed last week. This is an area of the country unused to violent crime, and locals fear that the events of the last five days may have changed their village forever.*'

CHAPTER 24

NICK SAT DOWN IN THE incident room and sipped from his steaming tea. On his desk were two take-away bacon rolls, oozing butter, that he had got from Crumbs Café close to Llancastell bus station.

He liked the stillness of the empty incident room. There was time to think and take stock. It was a fifteen-unit day and so Nick had started the day with a three-unit can of lager and a strong coffee. He was feeling somewhere close to human and noticed an increased energy and sharpness. It was at moments like this that he kicked himself and the internal dialogue was driving him mad. *Just think what you could achieve if you were continually sober? Think of all that extra drive and perception you could apply to every aspect of your life.* And yet there was always the other little voice that told him that if he just took the edge off his anxiety, he would be a better-functioning human being. And the quickest route to pressing the pause button on anxiety was booze. This was the battle that often raged in his head. He knew he was winning the war and that he shouldn't wave a white flag and surrender. However, just as he was beginning to feel positive about himself, the old enemy would nudge him in the ribs and say, *Come on, mate. It wasn't that bad, was it? Let's me and you have another go, eh? For old time's sake? Remember the good old days when we were the best of friends? We had a laugh, didn't we? We got up to all sorts, didn't we? What are you gonna do without me, you boring twat?*

Nick tried to turn the chatter off in his head, sat back and looked at the front page of the *Llancastell Leader*. The headline read: *Racist Scout leader called me 'coon' – Victim's son talks*. There was an innocent photo of Alex Noakes, aged about fourteen, in his Scout uniform standing next to Daniel Hughes. Nick wondered how someone like Dan Hughes had become such a bitter and violent racist. He re-membered Dan making comments when Paul Ince was made England football captain in 1993, but he put that down to Dan's lack of intelligence. Dan was being a prat, as always, but that was all. He knew that Dan ran with the Llancastell FC 'frontline' hooligan crew as a teenager and got arrested in a brawl with archrivals Crewe's firm, the 125s. So how he had got into a position of Scout leader with no one noticing his background was baffling? What about the DBS check? Nick finished the article, which had posed just that question. Nick knew the answer. Islamophobia was rocketing and North Wales was ninety-six per cent white. Words like *Chinky* and *Paki* just weren't frowned upon by most of the population. What was the problem? It was harmless. He wondered what locals felt now that racism had graduated from casual to murder?

Nick heard a noise, glanced up and saw that Ruth was walking in, nursing her Costa flat white. He was pleased to see her.

'Bloody hell. Since when do you beat me in?' she said in a teasing tone.

'Alex Noakes has given an interview to the *Leader*.' Nick waved the paper at her.

'Great. Anything in there we didn't know already?'

'Daniel Hughes called him a "coon" and he says that's why he was drummed out of the Scouts.'

'So, he fails to mention the dealing and smoking weed?' Ruth raised an eyebrow.

'Yeah, funny that. Fancy a bacon roll, boss?' Nick asked.

'No, I like my arteries the way they are thanks,' Ruth said with a grin before disappearing into her office.

Ruth drank the last of her coffee and put the cup down on her desk. Her brain was already in overdrive. Where to go next? She needed to talk to the CPS and confirm that Daniel Hughes could not be kept in custody any longer. Without forensic evidence, they had nothing concrete linking him to either murder, and a defence counsel would run rings around them. In fact, even the CPS and Jones wouldn't let them charge Hughes with what they had.

She also knew that she had to organise uniformed officers to provide Hughes with round-the-clock protection. There had been threats made against Hughes' life on social media, as well as a brick through a window two nights ago, so they couldn't take any risks.

Outside, the weather had taken a turn for the worse and it was grey and dreary. Ruth looked up to see Mac arriving. He and Nick shared a joke and then roared with laughter.

Ruth felt a pang of loneliness. She was a long way from home and she was feeling out of her depth. In the Met, she was always surrounded by experienced detectives who had seen it all. In Llancastell they had seen little, and certainly not a double homicide. They were all looking to her to decide what to do next and lead the investigation with confidence. And that was terrifying, though she made sure no one could see her fear.

Mac came over and knocked on her open door. He waved some printouts at her. 'Boss, details from Swansea on that murder of a Muslim man last year.'

'What have they got?'

'The man was strangled, but he was also stabbed repeatedly first. The attacker took the victim's watch, wallet and phone. They think it was a robbery, so it's nothing like ours in terms of MO,' Mac explained.

'Right. Waste of time. Anything else?' Ruth asked. She was feeling frustrated.

'No, boss. Chasing Forensics and the Tech boys.'

'Okay. Thanks, Mac.' Ruth forced a smile, leant back in her seat and let out an audible sigh.

NICK AND RUTH DROVE slowly through the centre of Dinas Padog. Ruth lit a ciggie and wound down the window even though the weather outside was grey and dismal. Daniel Hughes was in the back of the car, next to a male uniformed officer.

Hughes was his usual fidgety self, scratching or touching his face, before gazing out of the window for a moment. Nick was frustrated that they'd had to release Hughes because Llancastell Magistrates Court wouldn't extend the custody beyond the thirty-six hours.

SOCO and Forensics had already pulled Hughes' house to pieces in the hope that they would find something incriminating, but nothing turned up. His uniform had been washed and ironed so no trace there. Now they were examining the Scout hut trying to find something, anything to link Hughes to the murders.

'You do know he's still out there, don't you?' Hughes muttered from the back of the car. 'Nick, come on, mate, you know this isn't me?'

'I'm not your mate. And I know what you are,' Nick barked sharply.

'I've heard you tell racist jokes in the pub, so you can get off your soap box, *mate*,' Hughes replied.

Nick looked over at Ruth for a moment as she raised her eyebrow.

'Anti-English jokes. Rugby jokes. Not quite the same thing, is it?' Nick explained under his breath. For a moment, he just wanted to jump into the back of the car and punch Hughes' lights out.

'While you're dicking about here, there's some maniac out there and he might kill someone else, you know that?' Dan said.

'Why don't you just shut up! No one's interested in what you've got to say,' Nick thundered. Hughes was really getting up his nose.

As they turned into Abbots Way, Nick saw there were around a dozen people milling around outside Hughes' house. Two or three were press photographers. There were two uniformed officers in high-visibility jackets with *Heddlu/Police* on the back. Everyone else was there to make their feelings known about Hughes and what he had done. Some had their kids with them.

Nick saw that across the brickwork to the left of the front door someone had painted *SCUM* in red two-foot-high capital letters. He wasn't expecting to see any of this.

Hughes clocked the people and the message on his house. 'Shit!'

'Welcome home,' Nick said sardonically.

The uniformed officer in the car handed Hughes a grey, woollen blanket to put over his head when he left the car for his house.

'No way I'm putting that over m' head. I'm innocent,' Hughes thundered.

As Nick pulled the car up outside Hughes' house, he heard the noise and bustling increase.

Nick, Ruth, and the uniformed officer got out first and then opened the back door for Hughes, trying to shield him from the locals. There were shouts of 'Racist murderer!' and 'Scum!' as locals tried to get at Hughes. Someone spat at him and Nick watched a bottle sail over and smash on the pavement. He could feel that the tension in the air was growing. Police officers formed a shield, holding back the protestors and telling them to keep back.

Ruth and Nick bundled Hughes from the car and fought their way up the short weed-strewn path and into his house. Nick turned and slammed the front door behind them and the babbling noise diminished.

'Right, keep all the doors locked. Pull the curtains. Keep away from the windows. Don't answer the door or the phone,' Ruth said in a brusque manner.

Hughes rolled his eyes. 'Just piss off, will you? Oh, and so you know, I will sue you for wrongful arrest when you catch the real killer, all right?'

'That's down to you,' Ruth said coldly as she headed for the door.

'We'll be in touch when we need to speak to you again,' Nick said. Hughes was guilty as far as he was concerned and Nick was convinced it was just a matter of time before they found the evidence to convict him.

'Can't wait,' Hughes growled at them.

Ruth opened the door, stepped outside and headed down the path.

Nick stopped for a moment beside Hughes and whispered coldly, 'If it gets too much for you, you could always kill yourself, *mate*.'

CHAPTER 25

THE WIND HAD PICKED up when Nick and Ruth parked in the staff car park at Ysgol Dinas Padog. As Ruth opened the door, she could hear the nearby trees rustling as the branches arched in the strong gusts that came from the west. Then the unmistakable roar of a tractor, carrying hay bales, trundling noisily along the road.

Outside the Scout hut two white SOCO vans were parked. A handful of officers wore sets of white overalls, blue latex gloves, paper shoes and face masks. They were scouring the hall for any evidence that might link Hughes to Arabella Dixon or Neerav Banerjee. Ruth had a feeling that they'd come up with nothing. Daniel Hughes seemed the only fit, but nothing seemed to be linking him to the murder. The evidence just wasn't adding up and Ruth was getting frustrated. She was worried a double-murderer might just walk free.

As Ruth and Nick crossed the car park, Ruth noticed Nick looking over at the tree she had seen when first visiting the school. Of course, she now realised that it had been planted in memory of his cousin Megan. For a moment Ruth said nothing, but something in Nick's face prompted her to ask him about it.

'If you don't mind me asking, why do you think she did it? Megan ...' Ruth asked gently.

They stopped for a moment and Ruth wasn't sure if she had crossed a boundary in their professional relationship. The silence seemed to last an eternity.

'Kill herself? I don't know. She was a loner and didn't have many friends.' Nick's tone was reflective. 'I tried to talk to her. I could see there was something wrong. Everyone could see that.'

Ruth nodded. 'Of course.'

'But she was a teenage girl. I mean, that's what they're like, aren't they? How are you meant to know when they're in trouble and not in the midst of raging hormones?'

'Yeah ... Did she have anyone she talked to?' Ruth asked.

'There was a boyfriend, but no one knew who he was. Her friend Gwyneth said he was older. That's all she would say. I suppose she must have talked to him,' Nick explained, lost in the emotion of remembering.

'Sorry, I didn't mean to bring it up. It must be painful?'

'It's fine, boss. Honest. I think I lock it away too much and try to avoid talking about it. I just miss her, that's all. She was hilarious when she was on form, you know?'

Ruth realised the conversation was over, and nodded thoughtfully as Nick turned to walk towards the Scout hut.

RUTH WAS SITTING WITH her feet on her desk, indulging in a little bit of self-pity as SOCO and Forensics had found nothing that was any use to their case against Daniel Hughes. It felt like the case had stalled. A week ago she would have been glad that she could off-load it onto more experienced officers. After all, she had come up here for low-level crime, fewer murders, and less politics. So far, she had been met with a shit storm. But now she had got her teeth into the case, she was determined to see it through.

Ruth sat up, took her coffee and wandered into the incident room. Sian walked in, full of energy, and looked her way with a smile. Ruth felt the momentary tingle of attraction again.

'Boss, get this. Forensics cross-matched the sperm's DNA in the condom that was found in Arabella Dixon's bathroom with the elimination batch of DNA. It matches Jonathan Noakes.'

Ruth stopped for a moment as she took this in. 'What? Jonathan Noakes was having an affair with his ex-wife?'

'Looks that way, boss.'

Ruth's brain was now racing, 'The IP address for the emails sent to Arabella Dixon was due this morning.'

'Just got it,' Sian said indicating a piece of paper in her hand.

Ruth gave her a quizzical look. 'You're going to tell me that the IP address for the amorous but needy emails that were sent to Arabella Dixon came from Jonathan Noakes, aren't you?'

'I am,' Sian said with a smile.

Ruth nodded as their eyes met and she touched Sian's arm for a moment. 'Shit. So, Arabella Dixon and Jonathan Noakes were rekindling old flames but when he gets too keen, she pulls the rug from under him and tells him to "grow up".'

'Boss, I know you think that Daniel Hughes is our prime suspect, but this would give Jonathan Noakes a very good motive to kill Arabella Dixon, wouldn't it?'

Ruth took a moment as she ran through the permutations. 'Yes, it would. And if Jonathan Noakes knows anything about Arabella Dixon and Neerav Banerjee's relationship, then there is motive there as well.'

'He doesn't have an alibi for the time of Neerav Banerjee's murder. And he admits he went to the school on the night of Arabella Dixon's murder. What do we do now?' Sian asked.

'We go get Jonathan Noakes and ask him to explain why he's been lying his bollocks off consistently since his ex-wife's murder,' Ruth said.

JONATHAN NOAKES LOOKED like a shell of a man when Ruth and Nick arrived at his farmhouse in the village of Carrog, close to Corwen, to pick him up for questioning. The greying goatee beard had overgrown to a full beard across his face. There were bags under his eyes that had a purplish tint, and his breathing seemed heavy and laboured almost as though he was asleep. His mood seemed to swing between anxiety and resentment. He had been working from home, and his daughter and wife were in Spain visiting her parents. Noakes explained that they had been away for ten days and weren't due back for another four.

Noakes remained silent in the car on the way back to Llancastell except to ask if he needed to ring his solicitor. Nick said it would probably be a good idea.

By three o'clock, Noakes' solicitor had arrived. Mary Ambroise was experienced in criminal justice. She was stockily built, with a pointed nose and dyed ash-blonde hair. Her eyes were round and slightly bloodshot.

Ruth and Nick came into Interview Room 1 and sat opposite Noakes. Ruth went through the formalities. Noakes was there for voluntary questioning and could leave whenever he wanted. He wasn't being charged with anything yet. Noakes snorted a note of derision as he sat back in his grey plastic seat.

Ruth was confused about what she thought now. Daniel Hughes had been their prime suspect. Violent racist, threatening texts to both victims, ongoing feud with Arabella Dixon, knife found under the Scout hut. Ruth thought it was just a matter of time before Forensics came up with something and they had their man. Noakes had thrown a spanner in the works.

Patience, she said to herself. Patience. She remembered the advice she was given when she first started in CID: eliminating someone from an investigation was just as important as getting a positive lead.

'Mr Noakes, can you tell us where you were on Thursday afternoon between three and five in the afternoon?' Ruth began.

Noakes rolled his eyes. 'Jesus, I've been through this already.'

Ruth's tone was, as always, patient and sympathetic. 'I know. Can you just go through it again, for me?'

'I was working from home. I was on my computer, which you can check if you want. I didn't send any emails as I was doing some research.'

Nick looked over. 'You know that if we do look at your computer, we can see the time of everything you did that day.'

'And as I explained to your colleague the other day, some of my research is from books and magazines. I can't do everything online.'

'That seems very convenient doesn't it, Mr Noakes?' Nick said sternly.

'It's not convenient. It's the nature of my work. I can't help that, can I?' Noakes was getting angry.

'Mr Noakes, can you tell us what your relationship is like with your ex-wife?' Ruth asked.

'Again, we talked about this last week. I told you, we get on for Alex's sake but she is a difficult woman.' Noakes began to get emotional. 'I'm very upset that she was murdered. She used to be my wife. We have a child together. I didn't kill her because she was difficult to deal with for God's sake!' Noakes sounded distraught.

'Can you then explain why we found a condom in Arabella Dixon's bathroom that contains semen that matches your DNA sample?' Nick asked.

Noakes looked completely floored by this evidence. He closed his eyes and rubbed his temple as he took it in.

Ruth waited for Noakes to reply but he was saying nothing. 'Jonathan, were you having an affair with your ex-wife?'

Noakes didn't look up from the floor. 'Yes ...'

'Did your current wife know about the affair?' Ruth asked.

'No. No, she didn't. Oh God, you're not going to tell her, are you?' Noakes looked sick with panic and put his head in his hands.

Ruth looked through her notes. 'Jonathan, we also found a series of emails that you sent to Arabella.'

Noakes closed his eyes – his entire world was crumbling around him and he didn't know what to do.

Ruth continued. 'We have an email sent from Arabella Dixon to you on the thirteenth of February asking you to leave her alone. Can you explain why she would send you that?'

Noakes' voice was weary. 'No comment.'

Nick leaned forwards and said, 'It sounds like you were harassing Arabella Dixon. Is that right?'

'No comment.'

'What were your feelings towards Arabella when she ended your affair?' Nick asked.

'No comment.'

Ruth flicked over the printout. 'Your last email is dated the fifth of March. "You really are a cold, narcissistic bitch. I hope you die a slow and painful death and I'm there to witness it." Does that sound familiar, Mr Noakes?'

Noakes just looked at her and shook his head, as though he couldn't believe this was happening to him.

Nick looked at him. 'It doesn't sound like you were just having a little tiff about Alex. Your ex-wife threatened to call the police. It sounds like things were getting out of hand, doesn't it, Mr Noakes?'

'No comment.'

'I think you showed her exactly how you felt. You dropped your son off at his girlfriend's farm. You returned to the school and went to vandalise her car. She came out, found you pouring acid over it and confronted you. Things got out of hand, you struggled, and then you killed her. That's what happened, isn't it?' Nick asked.

Noakes let out an audible sigh. 'No comment.'

For the next ten minutes, the interview continued in a similar vein. They asked Noakes to explain exactly what had happened on the night of Arabella Dixon's murder. Why was he at the school? They asked what he knew about Neerav Banerjee and what their relationship was like. They asked again how he felt towards his ex-wife when she finished their affair. Did he want to kill her? Noakes was disintegrating before their eyes but continued with 'no comment' to everything they asked him.

At a quarter past six, they had to release him as they didn't have nearly enough evidence to charge him with either murder.

CHAPTER 26

RUTH AND NICK WERE sitting in the narrow living room of Eirlys Atkins, who had contacted Llancastell Police earlier in the day. She claimed that she had seen Daniel Hughes on the day of Neerav Banerjee's murder.

Even though she was in her sixties, Eirlys had long dyed-blonde hair and wore too much make-up. Ruth thought that twenty years ago she would have been a stunner.

There was a dark oak Welsh dresser that featured various bits of commemorative china including a gaudy 'Remembering Diana 1961–1997' plate. The house smelt of toast and cigarette smoke and it made Ruth's craving for a ciggie all the worse. She would have one as soon as they left, she told herself.

'Mrs Atkins, could you tell us what you saw on Thursday afternoon?' Ruth asked.

'It was about twenty past four. You see, I watch *A Place In The Sun* every day. I love that programme. That starts at four. In the first adverts, I make a cup of tea. I'm guessing that was about twenty past four.'

Ruth nodded but wanted to get on with the interview. 'Okay. And while you were making a cup of tea, what did you see?'

'Oh yes. I put the kettle on and got some biscuits. I looked out of that window there. And I saw Dan Hughes in his kitchen,' Eirlys said.

Ruth went over to the window and looked out. There was a clear view of the back of the Hughes' house, which was only fifty yards away. The large kitchen window was directly opposite.

'And you're sure it was Daniel Hughes, Mrs Atkins?' Nick asked.

'Oh yeah. He cuts me grass for me. And I've babysat for them loads of times. Lovely kids, they are. The little girl, Molly, loves me. I'm like her nain, really.'

'And you're certain that was Thursday afternoon?' Ruth asked.

'Definitely. I still had some shopping bags in my kitchen. And I only go shopping on a Thursday. Creature of habit, you know. I couldn't believe it when I saw Dan in the paper the other day. He wouldn't harm a fly, Dan wouldn't,' she said with a frown.

Ruth and Nick shared a look. She would make a credible witness on the stand and it would give Daniel Hughes a solid alibi. More worryingly, Eirlys Atkins was clear about when she had seen Hughes, which meant that he could not have killed Neerav Banerjee. Given the same MO for both murders, that would rule him out of Arabella Dixon's murder too. They had lost their prime suspect.

'Does that help at all?' Eirlys asked with a smile.

The irony of her question wasn't lost on Ruth and Nick.

'Yes, thank you. Very helpful,' Ruth replied.

Ruth and Nick left ten minutes later. There was silence in the car as they drove away from the hamlet.

IT WAS FINALLY SUNNY, and as Ruth looked right, she could see the beams of light coming through the overhanging boughs, casting light and dark shadows across the road ahead. The bank of shadowy pine trees stretched high above them – the whole scene looked positively alpine.

Lighting a cigarette, Ruth wound down the window as she and Nick discussed what they had learned. They both agreed that a scenario where Dan Hughes poured acid on Arabella Dixon's car, she caught him in the act, they rowed, and he chased and killed her, seemed plausible. However, did Hughes seem like a man who would arrive at Neerav Banerjee's house and kill him in cold blood? Now that Eirlys Atkins had told them what she had seen, it seemed unlikely. The details of each murder were so identical that they could only have been carried out by one killer. That meant that Daniel Hughes didn't kill Arabella Dixon. That also meant the suspicion for both murders now fell on Jonathan Noakes.

'So, do we think Noakes was having an affair with his ex, Arabella?' Ruth asked, thinking out loud.

'That's what the DNA says. Sperm doesn't lie,' Nick said with a sardonic grin.

'Thank you for putting the image of Noakes' sperm in my head,' Ruth joked.

'You're welcome.'

'When Arabella finished the affair, Noakes became obsessive and wouldn't leave her alone. Maybe she taunted him and told him about her previous relationship with Neerav Banerjee? In a fit of rage, Noakes accosted her in the car park and killed her. Noakes then targeted Neerav Banerjee out of sheer jealousy.'

They shared a look for a moment.

'That sounds more than plausible, boss,' Nick said.

CHAPTER 27

NICK WAS AT HOME TRYING to tidy up. He had necked a can of lager and now only had three units in reserve for the rest of the day. Diazepam. He went to the kitchen cupboard, took a ten-milligram diazepam from the packet that he had ordered online, and swallowed it with some water. That should do the job.

His phone buzzed and he saw he had a voicemail message. It was his dad. He took a moment before pressing play. His dad left a message for him a couple of times a year, normally when he was hammered. Otherwise, Nick went to see him at Christmas, and maybe on his birthday. His dad was full of the 'ISM' – I, self, me. He was the kind of man that was also full of the 'me toos'. He found it impossible to listen to anyone's news without relating it to himself in some way. He wasn't remotely interested in anything anyone had to say unless he could bring the conversation back to himself. Self-absorbed didn't really describe the depths of his overwhelming self-obsession.

His father's voice was deep and slurred, '*Nick ... it's me. You all right, lad? I'm struggling a bit here, if truth be known. Would be good to see you like ... Heart's playing up a bit, you know. Not doing great. Okay. Ta-ra then ...*'

The ego has landed, Nick thought. *Sod him.*

DAN HUGHES KNEW THAT his wife, Steph, and kids were going to stay at his mother-in-law's in Bala for the night. He wanted them to avoid the press and locals who seemed to have taken up residence outside their house, waiting for the opportune moment to start hurling insults. When the projectiles took on a solid form, such as the brick that had come through the window, he had agreed it was best they stayed away until it calmed down.

Dan sat drinking in his living room. He swigged another inch and then poured more Lamb's Navy rum into the tumbler. On the stereo *Roll With It* by Oasis was playing.

Hughes nodded along with the music and then finished the drink in one go. He stood and shook his head as though he was trying to clear his thoughts. He was wearing a white t-shirt that featured a photo of Jimmy from the film *Quadrophenia*, sitting astride a scooter, with the words *Way of Life* printed underneath.

Hughes walked out of the patio doors into the darkness of the night and towards a small wooden shed at the back of the garden. He opened the door and switched on the light. Inside was an orange electric mower, an extension lead and an assortment of garden tools. In the middle of the shed floor was a solitary kitchen chair. Above that, a thick rope with a noose hung from the solid rafter that ran through the middle of the shed's roof. Hughes had prepared this a few hours earlier.

He closed the shed door behind him carefully, walked over to the chair and stood up on it. He knew that the first twenty seconds would be painful but then there would be a blissful release. He put the noose around his neck. The rope felt rough and itchy against his skin.

He had read an article on lostallhope.com. The rope would cut off the oxygen supply to the brain and body, and the compression of the carotid and vertebral arteries and jugular vein would render him unconscious. The constriction of the trachea and the blood vessels would achieve death. The idea is to have enough pressure from the noose on the right side of the head, just below the jaw, to constrict the carotid artery. Interrupting the blood flow to the brain caused a quick unconsciousness, only twenty seconds, then death in five minutes. The thought of that made him happy as he kicked the chair away. It was going to be a relief to feel nothing anymore.

CHAPTER 28

NICK WAS STAGGERING around a noisy party, can of beer in hand, swaying through the familiar faces. Music was blaring and the deep bass reverberated all around the house.

Faces from school, faces from work, faces from town. He drained a can of strong cider in one go and grinned. What a great party. As he reached for another can from the pine kitchen table that was stacked high with booze, he felt a little unsteady on his feet. He pushed his toes and the balls of his feet into the tiled floor to balance himself. Better. He drank again, knowing he had had enough, but caring nothing about his slowing reactions and slurred brain. Let's get on it! If he was going to have a great time, if he was going to be the life and soul, if he was going to pull, he needed to be hammered. He needed to get to that point where all self-doubt, self-consciousness, and self-control had gone. Nothing was ever enough. Everything to excess was his motto.

Nick stepped clumsily out of the patio doors, tripped, staggered, then just managed to regain his footing to prevent a fall, and smiled to himself.

On a wooden garden bench, he saw Ruth with a man. He was handsome, with chiselled features. They were kissing passionately. She caught Nick's eye momentarily over the man's shoulder but then deliberately ignored him. Filled with acidic jealousy, Nick resolved to go and find someone to get off with.

Anyone. He'd show her. He made eye contact with a young, blonde girl but she looked away. Not interested. Bitch.

Traversing the dark, busy garden, Nick felt disorientated until he came to a set of swings and a blue plastic kiddie's slide. It was now daytime, and swinging enthusiastically was his dad, who leaned backwards and then forwards, trying to get as high as he could. His carefree abandon and laughter were darkly comic and unnerving.

'Give us a push, lad!' his dad yelled.

Nick rolled his eyes, stepped around the back of the swings and pushed against his father's back. He could feel the rough woollen material of his scarlet, Welsh Fusiliers' dress uniform jacket. You prick. I'll push you all right. *He pushed harder and harder and harder.*

Then, with both hands an almighty shove, Nick pushed his father's back so hard that he lost his grip, flew off the swing and landed in the dirt. Have that, you wanker!

From somewhere, the sound of news on the radio changed the narrative again.

'Police in North Wales have confirmed that a man believed to be St Thomas Glynn has been found dead at an address in Dinas Padog in North Wales.'

Nick woke with a start and took a deep breath. The radio next to him burbled with BBC 5 Live, which Nick often left on all night. It was both company and a comfort, and when Nick woke in the middle of the night, it distracted him from the dark thoughts that came to him and kept him from sleeping.

It was seven, and the news bulletin had just started. Nick tuned out for a moment as he sat up in bed taking a few more deep breaths.

'Police in North Wales have confirmed that they have found a body in Dinas Padog, the town that has seen two murders in the last ten days. A police spokesman also confirmed that the death is not being treated as suspicious and they are not looking for anyone else in relation to the death. An unconfirmed source claims that the body is that of Daniel Hughes, a thirty-four-year-old man who had been helping police with their enquiries into the murders of Arabella Dixon and Neerav Banerjee.'

IT WAS TEN O'CLOCK and Ruth was frustrated that the case seemed to be stuck. She and Nick had already discussed Hughes' suicide with no real conclusion. Did he kill himself out of guilt? Or was it out of sheer desperation and self-loathing after they had raked over the entrails of his life and his past?

Ruth wasn't sure what to think. The statement from Hughes' neighbour was convincing, which meant that his alibi for the time of Banerjee's murder stood up. However, if the neighbour was wrong and he was guilty, then they had allowed a murderer to hang himself, and Arabella Dixon and Neerav Banerjee's family would never get the closure and a feeling of justice that a trial and prison sentence would provide. If Hughes was innocent, they had contributed to making three children fatherless. Whatever kind of man Hughes was, his suicide didn't sit comfortably with her.

Ruth knew that the modern police force had many tools with which to gather evidence and catch a murderer. Tools she could have only dreamed of fifteen or twenty years ago. Technology had revolutionised policing. However, with all the DNA profiling, GPS data, and cyber sleuthing, sometimes the basics of investigation that had been in place for over a hundred years were lost.

Ruth's main fear was that this case could end up being unsolved. She knew so well the implications of an unsolved case, what it felt like to those left behind. She had lived it for the past four years and wouldn't wish it on anyone.

In her first year at Peckham CID, a woman's body, Leah Hart, had been found in a damp, dismal cellar of an unoccupied house on Meeting House Lane. Forensics confirmed she had only been there for a couple of hours.

Neighbours and a jogger had seen the suspected murderer leave the house and gave detailed descriptions. CCTV on Peckham High Street showed him calmly buying a bucket of chicken about an hour after the murder. There was a clear visual of his face. He was tall, white, with curly hair and was wearing a distinctive Brooklyn Dodgers white baseball cap that he'd turned round so the peak was fashionably at the back. He became known as 'White Cap' and everyone in CID was confident he would be found within twenty-four hours. SOCO found trainer prints beside the body and the roach of a spliff, so they had his DNA.

Days turned into weeks. Appeals on national and local media provided few viable leads. Their early optimism turned to a growing frustration. They had everything that a modern crime investigation should need to find and convict the killer. And yet they came up with nothing. Not one decent suspect.

For Ruth, it was an early case in her career as a detective, and as a DC she had little input into how the case was run. She did much of the grunt work such as house-to-house. But for the SIO, an ageing DCI Ian Holloway, the case consumed him like a slow but aggressive cancer. She remembered him working into the night, week after week, month after month, going over every witness statement, every piece of evidence, and then rechecking for the hundredth time. Ruth had seen DCI Holloway in the pub and noticed how distracted and discontent he always seemed. Five years later, Holloway was given an early pension because of stress and depression. Colleagues said it was the accumulation of being a detective in the murder squad for twenty years. Ruth knew it was more specific than that. It was the ghost of Leah Hart who haunted him night and day.

Two years after Holloway was pensioned off, a thirty-year-old scaffolder, Kevin Duffin, was arrested for an attempted rape in Dartford. When he was questioned, Duffin broke down and confessed to the murder of Leah Hart. She had been a hooker and something had gone wrong. He hadn't meant to kill her. He had panicked and hidden her body. Ruth couldn't help thinking that Duffin's confession had come too late for Holloway. The damage had already been done.

Ruth knew that the murder of Leah Hart was a very different case to that of Arabella Dixon and Neerav Banerjee.

Leah was a junkie, a sex worker; a rootless, desperate soul. She was on the edges of society and the repercussions of her murder were tragically minimal. However, unsolved cases took their toll on all the detectives that were involved. And the guilt of not getting justice for a victim and their family can gnaw away for many years.

A knock on her door broke her train of thought. It was Sian – *a sight for sore eyes,* Ruth thought.

'Boss, Forensics have confirmed that a pubic hair found in Arabella Dixon's bedroom matches Neerav Banerjee's DNA. This corroborates Alex Noakes' assertion that Arabella Dixon was sleeping with Banerjee,' Sian said.

'I'm guessing she was sleeping with Banerjee and Noakes over the same period. It wouldn't have taken much more than a comment from Alex to his father for Jonathan Noakes to suspect that this was true. They were close, so it was almost certain that Alex told his father of his suspicions.'

'And Noakes loses it and kills them both?' Sian asked.

'From what I can see, Arabella enjoyed playing mind games with men. Unfortunately, it might have got her killed,' Ruth said.

HAVING STEPPED OUTSIDE for a ciggie and a coffee, Ruth made her way upstairs to Jones' office. She knew that he was under pressure from higher up the command chain about the investigation and the lack of a decent breakthrough. The media were also making life difficult with daily stories and speculation. However, Ruth was feeling confident that Noakes was their killer.

Beckoning for her to sit down, Jones swigged at his coffee for a moment before sitting back. After a couple of pleasantries, Jones said he wanted Ruth to bring him up to speed with the case.

'What do we know at this stage, Ruth?' Jones asked.

'We know that the same killer had murdered both Arabella Dixon and Neerav Banerjee. It was the same MO and they had cut a Druid sign into the back of their hands,' Ruth explained.

'So, the question is what links them?' Jones said. In her head, Ruth sarcastically thanked him for stating the bleedin' obvious before proceeding.

'They worked together at the school. It is very likely that they had an affair,' Ruth explained.

'So does that put Arabella Noakes' husband as your frontrunner then?' Jones asked.

'Yes, sir. Jonathan Noakes. His DNA was on a condom discovered in Arabella's bathroom. He sent emotional and threatening emails after she ended their affair. It might be that she threatened to tell Noakes' new wife unless he left her alone?'

'What about alibis?' Jones asked.

'Very flimsy for both murders, sir. He could have dropped his son Alex and Rhiannon Baker at her home and then returned to Dinas Padog High School in time to murder Arabella Dixon. If he went in through the side entrance, there would be no CCTV. Noakes claims to have been at home on his own at the time of Neerav Banerjee's murder.

We're waiting to see if Traffic can find his car on ANPR around that time. Forensics are also trying to find a match from the Banerjee crime scene to Noakes' DNA,' Ruth said.

'And if Noakes knew about the affair between Arabella and Banerjee, then he had a strong motive to kill him,' Jones stated as he finished off his coffee.

'Yes, sir. And that gives him motive, means, and opportunity for both killings,' Ruth said. As she spoke those words, she felt that thrill of anticipation that she hadn't had for years. They were close to getting their man.

'Good ... What about these carved symbols on the victims' hands?'

'I'm not sure. I've seen people consumed with jealousy do some very dark things. It's as if they are a signature. If I'm honest, I don't know why the killer took the time to cut the victims like that.'

'Of course, the killer could want to suggest to us they were insane and provide a smokescreen,' Jones suggested.

'Yes, sir. That is a possibility,' Ruth said. For once Jones had shown some of the analytical deduction that he had possessed before moving up the chain of command.

'What about Hughes?' Jones asked.

'Hughes was a racist thug. But I just don't see him murdering two people and carving symbols into their hands.'

'And you don't think him hanging himself is a sign of a guilty conscience?' Jones asked.

'No, sir. We had uncovered some pretty unpleasant things in Hughes' life. I think he knew he was going to lose his family and get hounded out of Llancastell.'

'And the son. Alex Noakes, isn't it?' Jones asked.

'Yes, sir. I just can't see a teenage boy like Alex going to Neerav Banerjee's home and killing him in cold blood. And if he didn't murder Banerjee, then he didn't murder his mother. We can't rule him out, but he's low on our list of suspects,' Ruth explained.

'Okay. Thank you, Ruth.' Jones shifted in his chair and took a printout from his printer. 'A DCI Drake will be joining us tomorrow from Manchester's Serious Crime Division. He'll head up the case for us.'

What? Ruth's heart sank as she took in the news for a moment. After all that hard work she was being replaced.

'With all respect, sir, Noakes is our prime suspect and we're close to getting enough to arrest him,' Ruth said, trying to hide her annoyance.

'Sorry, Ruth. You've done an excellent job as SIO on this so far. But we need a result. I'm bringing in three more detectives from Manchester at the end of the week if we need them.' Jones could see Ruth's frustration. 'This is a good thing, Ruth. More experienced murder detectives can only be a positive.'

'We've done all the hard groundwork on this, sir. And someone else will come and get the credit. My team won't like it,' Ruth said. 'And I don't like it.'

'This comes from the top, Ruth. And I'm sorry you feel that way. I'd like you to get all the paperwork prepared for DCI Drake this afternoon,' Jones said.

Ruth returned to the incident room feeling deflated. She sat at her desk contemplating the mountain of paperwork that still needed to be done. She would go outside for a ciggie before tackling that. Then she made a deal with herself to do half an hour of paperwork and then go.

It was raining outside and droplets ran down the windowpanes and splashed on the sills. Even though it was only one o'clock, Ruth's office was dark and she had to turn on a desk lamp, giving the room a warming hue.

Mac knocked on her open door and she looked up.

'Boss. I've spoken to all the employment agencies that Bronwyn Wright claimed that she visited at the time of Neerav Banerjee's murder. They've never heard of her. We got the CCTV from Llancastell Library and Bronwyn Wright was not there on Monday afternoon.'

Ruth frowned for a moment as she took this in. 'Why lie to us? And why invent such an elaborate lie we could easily check up on?'

'Maybe she just panicked, boss?'

'Why panic if you've got nothing to hide?' Ruth asked, as if talking to herself.

'Fair point, boss.'

'Get her in. I want to know why she's lying to us,' Ruth growled.

CHAPTER 29

RUTH HAD GIVEN NICK the okay to drive over from Llancastell to attend the lunchtime AA meeting at St Mark's Church in Dinas Padog. Uncle Mike was doing the 'main share'.

Nick had heard his uncle do a main share at Alcoholics Anonymous before, but Mike always made sure it was different. There were always three parts, like any decent share – what it was like, how he got sober, and how he stays sober. However, some regurgitated the same story every time. Either that or they spent the full half hour on the 'war stories' – the scrapes and mishaps they had got into, rather than concentrate on how they shook their addiction and how they tried 'one day at a time' to stay sober.

As Nick approached the side door to the church, he saw Uncle Mike smoking with some others in the fellowship. There didn't seem to be many alcoholics who didn't smoke, except for him.

Mike beamed a smile that lit up his face and gave Nick a thumbs-up when he saw him. 'All right, lad? Good to see you!'

They hugged, and Mike patted his shoulders with a resounding thud.

'Needed a nap, so I thought I'd come and hear your share ... *again*,' Nick quipped with a grin. Some of the others laughed.

'Cheeky sod!' Mike said with a laugh, although Nick could see that the events at Dinas Padog were preoccupying him. He just wasn't himself.

He had heard Mike's 'war stories' before. The time he hid a bottle of vodka in the bottom of the oven and had forgotten about it. Auntie Pat had put in the Sunday roast and an hour later the vodka had exploded and taken out the oven door, shooting the chicken across the room. There were fights with policemen, nights in cells, and driving bans. There was the time when Mike tried to strangle a bouncer for taking the piss out of his orange Hawaiian shirt and it took three men to stop him killing him.

Nick gestured to the cigarette. 'Thought you'd packed that in and gone to vaping?'

'Bollocks to that. It's more addictive than real ciggies ...'

'I'm on duty at the memorial service if you're going over to Corwen?'

'Aye, lad, I'll be there.'

There were solemn nods from the others. The community of Dinas Padog wanted to come together to remember Arabella Dixon and Neerav Banerjee. North Wales Police had been overwhelmed by the number of people who wanted to turn out to pay their respects, so they had to move the memorial service from the local St Mark's Church to the much larger Saint Mael and Saint Sulien's Church, Corwen. Nick wondered whether the killer would be present at the service.

'You look tired, lad,' Mike said discreetly.

'It's this case. We're working round the clock.'

'Yeah, I've seen the papers ... Everyone's saying that Dan Hughes hanged himself. That true? Between you and me, like,' Mike asked.

'Yeah, but I didn't tell you that. He was a dickhead,' Nick said.

'He's done you a favour, hasn't he? No great big court case and media circus. Did he leave a note?'

'No. We seem to be hitting a series of dead ends at the moment.' Nick's tone was one of frustration. 'D'you know Graham Williams at the school?'

'Yeah. Assistant head. Right bloody busybody. Parish council, you name it. Bit of the old Bible basher too, if I've remembered it right? Funny bloke, though.'

'Yeah?'

There was a moment's silence and then Mike said, 'I always tried to give Arabella Dixon the benefit of the doubt. I can't remember ever seeing a coin, whether it be a dirty, filthy penny or a bright, gold sovereign, that doesn't have two sides. No one is ever just plain bad. Not in my book, anyway.'

NICK HAD LEFT THE MEETING early as he was on duty. He loved the familiar drive along the A5 into Corwen. Not because of the quaint antique shop, with its eggshell-blue-and-white painted frontage, which featured an old dolls' house, anomalous brass objects, and wooden chairs with little value. Nor the Tudor-style buildings, with black wooden beams and white brickwork. In fact, apart from the lop-sided blue-and-red Sky Sports banner that hung carelessly from the pub, there was nothing to differentiate this scene from how it looked twenty years ago.

No, Nick liked Corwen because of its famous association with one of his heroes, Owain Glyndwr, who proclaimed himself Prince of Wales on 16 September 1400, from his nearby manor of Glyndyfrdwy.

Glyndwr instigated the fifteen years of fierce Welsh revolt against the rule of Henry IV of England. Initially very successful, the Welsh gained control of large areas of North Wales. Despite the substantial rewards being offered by the Crown, Owain was never captured. No one really knew where he went, nor where, how, or when he died. Legends have him ending his days in everywhere from Scotland, through Herefordshire, to Cornwall. Wherever he was, a horse was always saddled nearby in case he needed to make a fast escape. Others have him heading to the hills of Snowdonia to die and, with him, dreams of Welsh independence.

Nick's heart swelled with pride every time he passed the life-size statue of the mighty Prince Glyndwr, mounted resplendent on his battle-charging horse, that had been installed in Corwen Square in 2007. An eight-ton, five-metre plinth of polished granite. It commemorated his unofficial status as the last king of Wales.

By the time Nick arrived at the memorial service, the church was two-thirds full, with aisles and pews all packed with people waiting quietly to sit. Many more were streaming along the lengthy stone flags outside that led up to the imposing oak doors, all in solemn contemplation.

Given the severity of proceedings, the Cathedral Council of North Wales had sent the Archdeacon of Llancastell, Dr Peter Lomas, over to read the eulogy. His hair was thick but snowy white and his nose had been broken a few times and never been reset precisely. Nick had heard rumours that if Lomas hadn't made God his vocation, he would have been a rugby player. He had that kind of stature.

The congregation sang Psalm 23, *The Lord's My Shepherd*. 'The Lord's my shepherd, I'll not want; He makes me down to lie in pastures green; He leadeth me the quiet waters by.'

Once the psalm had finished, Nick watched as Lomas ambled to the lectern. There was a white-satin silence. A sheer and complete silence. It came from above the congregation, within the grey veins of sunlight that mottled from the roof. It settled slowly around them, rising from below and then from each side.

'Today's reading is taken from Romans, Chapter 12, Verses 19-21. "Do not take revenge, my friends, but leave room for God's wrath, for it is written: 'It is mine to avenge; I will repay,' says the Lord. On the contrary: 'If your enemy is hungry, feed him; if he is thirsty, give him something to drink. In doing this, you will heap burning coals on his head.' Do not be overcome by evil, but overcome evil with good."'

Nick watched as Lomas stopped for a moment and looked out at them. He was being serious and he wanted them to listen to what he had to say and not let the words wash over them.

'"Do not take revenge, my friends," God says. He is talking to all of us. God is not saying that there were some who had more of a temper than others. People whose personalities were more sensitive and emotional, and that it was all right for them to take vengeance. That God could make an exception for them to take revenge. They couldn't help being what they were and so they were allowed to take the law into their own hands. No. In fact, they, more than anyone else, needed to change.'

Nick scoured the congregation. Families brought together by tragedy, others unused to sitting quietly together. Ex-pupils, teachers and parents. He glanced over to Ruth and assumed that she was wondering the same thing. Would the killer turn up to see their handiwork? Although some thought that would be reckless and an unnecessary risk, Ruth and Nick knew full well it was not unheard of.

In 1993, murderer Colin Ash-Smith attended the funeral of his own victim, schoolgirl Claire Tiltman, in Dartford, Kent, wearing the same beige jacket he had murdered her in. In August 2002, Ian Huntley and his girlfriend Maxine Carr helped police and residents search for Holly Wells and Jessica Chapman, knowing full well he had murdered them the previous day and hidden their bodies.

Lomas continued. 'God forgives. God has forgiven us, and so we too are to offer forgiveness to those who have treated us badly. "Do not take revenge, my friends." Revenge is ruled out. Our community has been devastated by two hideous crimes of murder. Yet in Paul, we read "for it is written: 'It is mine to avenge; I will repay,' says the Lord." We are living in a moral universe, so that what a man sows that he also reaps. The murderer has to answer to God. "It is appointed unto men once to die, and after death the judgement."

'What happens when we try to take revenge? The answer is, we almost always make mistakes. We are either too severe or too lenient. We attack the innocent. We say the wrong things and we end up making things worse. A just revenge is the speciality of God. And God has given us a conscience. An internal voice that tells us that things we do are wrong. Lying, bragging, threatening, seducing, breaking promises. God watches the motives of the heart. He knows our thoughts before we think them, our words before we speak them. He knows what we are going to do before we do it, and he knows the reason why. Judgement is God's special ministry to mankind. So, revenge is the work of God, not yours.'

Nick walked quietly across the back of the church. He looked up at the modern stained-glass window that was built into the south wall in 1979. The single-light window featured the burgundy Parachute Regiment military insignia, with poppies and grasses. To one side there was also a Parachute Regiment beret. The window had the words written: *To The Glory of God And In The Memory of Private Robert Dylan Vaughan-Jones and his comrades of the Parachute Regiment who died at Warren Point, Ulster, 1979.*

Mike had told Nick all about the Warrenpoint guerrilla attack by the Provisional Irish Republican Army who ambushed the British Army with two large roadside bombs. The first bomb exploded by a British Army convoy. Then the second targeted the British soldiers that had been sent to help with the incident. Members of the IRA, hidden in nearby woodland, then opened fire on the troops. Eighteen British soldiers were killed and six were seriously injured, making it the deadliest attack on the British Army during the Troubles.

Nick stopped and looked down the aisle as Lomas continued his sermon. He saw that Arlo Lincoln was sitting on the end of a pew close to the back of the church. Along the row, to the right of him, were half a dozen teenagers. He wondered if they had come together.

'"Blessed are the peacemakers for they shall be called the children of God." Who is Paul talking about when he describes our enemies? They are those we work with, or we are in school with, or they are members of our families. They are people who hurt us in some way or another. And if you do loving things to those who've hurt you deeply, you change hearts. You can turn your enemy right around and he becomes your friend. That's the best way of getting rid of an enemy – changing him into a friend. That's the way you get even with your enemy, not by looking for revenge. I tell you, love your enemies and pray for those who persecute you, that you may be sons of your Father in heaven.'

Nick moved around to the west side of the church. He noticed the back of the head of a woman sitting at the end of a pew about ten rows from the back. Something about the hairstyle triggered something in his memory. It was Bronwyn Wright. He was sure of it. Nick drifted towards the front of the church to get a better look. There she was. From this angle, he could see the thick, heavy lenses of her glasses that magnified her eyes. She was listening intently. Suddenly, she turned her head and looked directly at Nick – straight at his eyes. She smiled at him. It didn't seem like a smile of recognition.

'Paul ends the chapter with these words, "Do not be overcome by evil but overcome evil with good." Don't let revenge eat you up and destroy your life. We too can look at life as a kind of competition. He hit me so I had to hit him back. Tit for tat. You hurt me so now I'm going to hurt you. Getting even doesn't work. What happens when you try to get even? You unleash this whole cycle of retribution and violence. It never ends because someone else always wants to get the last word. You may win the battle, you may even get the last word or strike the last blow, but in the end, you've destroyed your own spiritual life. In the process of hurting another person, you've hurt yourself too. Anger has done its dirty work on the inside. There is malice, rage, hurt feelings, and horrible thoughts that keep you up late at night. How did Jesus survive the most awful day in human history? How could he stand there and let himself be accused of crimes he didn't commit? Why didn't he strike back? Why didn't he fight for his rights? The answer is found in the little phrase, "He entrusted himself to Him who judges justly." He believed that God was a God of justice, therefore he didn't have to say a word in his own defence. He knew that God would take care of him in the end. And he did.'

Nick moved back down the church and signalled Bronwyn Wright's presence to Ruth who was standing by a stone pillar. She nodded and moved so she could see her.

Lomas wrapped up his sermon. 'I say, go from this place in the name of Jesus, and live at peace with everyone. Go and refuse to return evil for evil. Go from this memorial service, and know that where you live, and work, and study, and play, there are people who won't like you, who will attempt to hurt you, who will mistreat you and then laugh about it. Go anyway and carry with you the love of God. Go determined not to seek revenge against those who hurt. Above all else, go with a new determination to love your enemies no matter what it takes. Don't let evil overcome you this week but go from this place and overcome evil with good. And know this much: when you go in that spirit, Jesus himself will go with you.'

The service continued with a final hymn and then Lomas made his closing comments. The congregation rose and filed out slowly and quietly.

Nick made a move to the large wooden doors and walked outside. The sun was now out and was warming up the temperature. He took up a position about halfway down the pathway and Ruth joined him there.

One of the first to come down the pathway was Jonathan Noakes, who was walking with Alex. He looked at them with thinly disguised contempt and said nothing.

CHAPTER 30

IT WAS THE MIDDLE OF the night and Ruth was finding it difficult to sleep. She had drawn the curtains so that the moonlight silvered the room, colouring the bed grey, white and black. Opening the window, she had two ciggies as the breeze whispered in. Nothing was sending her to sleep even though she had necked thirty milligrams of codeine and watched television. There was a programme about Indian frontier railways, which should have sent off the worst of insomniacs.

Rooting around the hotel room, she thumbed through a dozen magazines and newspapers. Then she picked up a copy of *Welsh Folk Tales,* something she found in the hotel's book exchange while sitting having coffee downstairs a few mornings ago.

Ruth took it – *when in Rome, eh?* – clicked on the kettle and lay on top of the duvet and read. She worried that her reading glasses made her look owlish but there was no one to see her, so who cared? Anyway, Sarah said her glasses made her look sexy.

She read of the Nanteos Cup, *Cwpan Nanteos*, which was a wooden mazer bowl, held for many years at Nanteos Mansion, Rhydyfelin, near Aberystwyth in Wales. Legend has it that it was fashioned from a piece of the True Cross. Others claimed it was the Holy Grail itself. Another theory was that the cup was used by Joseph of Arimathea to catch Christ's blood while he was dying on the cross. Medieval chroniclers claimed Joseph brought the cup to Britain and founded a line of guardians to keep it safe. It ended up in Nanteos Mansion near Aberystwyth, attracting visitors who drank from it, believing it had healing powers.

Ruth made herself a second cup of tea, ate shortbread biscuits, and turned to the chapter '*Nant Gwrtheyrn Folk Tales:* The Tragedy of Rhys a Meinir' and read the following story:

One of Wales' most tragic love stories took place in the secluded valley of Nant Gwrtheyrn, Vortigern's Creek, on the northern coast of the Llyn Peninsula, Gwynedd, in northwest Wales. A young man, Rhys, and a young girl, Meinir, grew up together in the quarrying village of Porth y Nant. They were close childhood friends, but it was not long until their bond blossomed into love. After a blissful courtship, they decided to be wed. The young couple's favourite spot was under an old oak tree, on the lower slopes of Yr Eifl. The two families couldn't have been happier at their union and so the preparations for the nuptials began.

The local sheriff of the area, Ifan y Cilie, went around the whole locality informing everyone that Rhys and Meinir would be married in Clynnog Church on the first Saturday in May. Friends, family and locals were invited down to the village the day before the wedding to give gifts to the young couple. They all came, one giving a wedding cake, another bringing some pots, everyone gifting useful things for their future life together. All the guests and family were looking forward to the joyful occasion the following day.

At this time, there were only three farms in the Nant: Ty Uchaf, Ty Canol and Ty Hen. The people of Nant Gwertheyrn insisted they kept the ancient Welsh tradition of 'The Quest For The Bride'. The custom dictated that on the morning of the wedding, the bride would run and hide. The rest of the family and guests gathered in Clynnog Church, except for Meinir who headed for the hills. Playing their part in the tradition, Rhys and his friends searched high and low for Meinir, but after several hours she was nowhere to be found. On discovering the bride was now actually missing, the guests and family scoured the whole valley. Hours turned to days, days turned to months. Rhys was wracked with worry and began to lose his mind.

Then one stormy night, while out wandering the heath, Rhys took shelter beneath their favourite oak tree. As he cowered beneath the tree, a bolt of lightning struck the trunk, splitting it in half. To Rhys' disbelief the splintered tree revealed a skeleton wearing a wedding dress. Overcome by emotion, poor Rhys collapsed and died beside his beloved bride.

There is still a symbolic tree in the village to commemorate the tragic love story of Rhys and Meinir.

Visitors have allegedly seen two ghosts wandering hand in hand on the beach - a man with a beard and long hair, and a woman with hollow sockets for her eyes. It is also believed that no birds will land on the bark of the hollow tree except the owl and the cormorant.

NICK LAY LOOKING AT the ceiling, thinking about the day ahead. He turned onto his side. The black night had fallen like a curtain and the sky was now a uniform felt grey.

The radio was debating some new government guidelines on alcohol consumption in terms of units. Nick thought that was fine, but until society changed its attitude to alcohol, there would be many casualties along the way. If you turned on the television, there would be someone loosening their tie, sitting down with a huff and saying, 'God, I need a drink.' Everything in human life is celebrated or marked with alcohol – births, deaths, significant birthdays, weddings, promotions, and so the list goes on. It was masculine to drink. And it was frowned upon if you didn't drink. It was one of Nick's bugbears. What he hated was the surrounding humour. Try finding a birthday card for someone over eighteen that doesn't make some reference to how much they drink and how hilarious that is. *If the glass is half empty or half full, that just means there's more room for alcohol.*

The radio presenter pointed out that there were 1.4 million people addicted to alcohol in the UK but only forty thousand people addicted to heroin. However, people don't stagger into work, looking and feeling ill, saying, 'Mate, how much heroin did we take last night? I was out of my head. Do you remember when you fell down the stairs in my flat? You were wasted. It was hilarious. Bet you feel ill now, eh?' If alcohol was discovered now, they would classify it as a class-A drug along with cocaine and heroin.

CHAPTER 31

ON THE STEPS OF LLANCASTELL nick, Ruth took the last few drags of her cigarette before stubbing it out in the bin. She blew out a long, satisfying plume of smoke and watched it rise. Today she was feeling anxious. She was handing over the case to – or, as Jones put it, working 'in liaison' with – DCI Drake from Manchester.

She pushed open the glass doors, waved to the duty sergeant and made her way to the lift. She was already running through the case, evidence and leads in her head. As usual, she was first into the incident room. In fact, she was so early that the cleaners were still finishing and so there was that clean, fresh smell you get from just-hoovered carpets.

However silly it was, Ruth felt like she was being inspected today. She made sure that the white evidence boards were up to date. She reorganised the evidence so it was clear. As the SIO, there were many sections that needed checking. In terms of planning, it was unclear whether the murder of Arabella Dixon was planned or spontaneous. The murder of Neerav Banerjee seemed far more deliberate. The main thing was to apply the principle of 'What, Why, When, Where, How, Who'. Then each heading could be broken down into several sub-questions.

There was also the theory of the three coincidental elements of homicide, which is a Venn diagram of three overlapping elements: location, victim, offender. The word *homicide* is written where all the circles meet in the middle.

It was gone nine thirty by the time Llancastell CID had assembled in Incident Room 1 for the morning briefing. Chief Superintendent Jones stood at the front, his hands clasped behind his back. He looked like a supercilious member of the royal family, Ruth thought.

'Good morning, everyone. First, I would like to thank you for all your hard work on this case so far. A double homicide is unprecedented at this station, and your dedication to the investigation has been outstanding. Thanks also need to go to DI Ruth Hunter who has been instrumental in the progress we've made so far,' Jones said. He then gestured for DCI Drake to come over for the introduction.

Drake was tall, black, athletic-looking with a bald head and a carefully sculpted goatee beard. Wearing a fitted blue suit, cobalt-blue shirt, black tie and brown Oxford brogues, he walked with a swagger and a strut and was the type of man who stood with hands on his hips, fingers to the front, fingertips pointing to his manhood.

'I'd like you all to meet Detective Chief Inspector Ashley Drake who has arrived on a temporary secondment from the Greater Manchester Police Force's Serious Crime Division. He will head up the investigation,' Jones said.

There were some mutterings from the CID team. Ruth could see that they weren't pleased that an outsider was coming in at this stage of the case. Nick caught her eye and frowned. Ruth shrugged at him – there was nothing she could do if Jones wanted to bring in a DCI.

'It may also be necessary to bring in some experienced homicide detectives from Manchester to help us at the end of the week,' Jones explained.

Ruth wasn't surprised that the disgruntled murmurs around the room continued. It felt as though Jones didn't think Llancastell CID were up to the task of finding the killer. They didn't want or need to have their hands held by detectives from England.

Sipping water from a bottle, Drake glanced at Jones and then looked out at the CID team. 'Thank you, Chief Superintendent. My role here is to support the investigation and lend my experience so we can catch Arabella Dixon and Neerav Banerjee's killer and get justice for their families. That's all I'm interested in. I'm not here to throw my weight around, tread on any toes or bask in any glory when we catch the person that carried out these despicable murders.'

Ruth could already see that Drake had an air of authority. She also detected a Yorkshire accent, rather than Mancunian.

Drake pointed to the photos of Arabella and Neerav. 'This is why we do the job. For Arabella and Neerav. It might be an old cliché, but we give a voice to the dead. And we work as a team to do that,' Drake said.

Ruth sensed that the mutterings around the room had quietened. Drake knew how to play to a crowd and, so far, he had said all the right things with an earnestness and honesty that she thought was impressive.

Drake looked over at Ruth. 'DI Hunter. If you can get me up to speed in my office, then I can make a start.' He nodded his head at the CID team. 'Have a safe day, guys.'

Ruth had already rehearsed to herself what she would tell him about the case. As the SIO, she didn't want Drake seeing any holes in the investigation that she had been running.

IT HAD BEEN AN HOUR since Ruth had brought Drake up to speed with the case. As she continued with her paperwork in the office, she realised how surprised she had been by Drake's lack of arrogance. It seemed to her that Drake meant what he said about working as a team. However, she would have to see whether he was just paying lip service to that in the long run.

Merringer knocked on her open door. 'Boss, Forensics have matched the two partial prints they found on the damage on Arabella Dixon's car. They compared them to the elimination batch and the prints belong to Dylan Wilkins, the assistant caretaker. Because of the oxidisation, Forensics reckon that the burnt paintwork on the car and the prints were made at the same time, and on the night of the murder.'

Ruth nodded. 'Okay. Why do we think Dylan Wilkins vandalised Arabella Dixon's car?'

'It gets better, boss. I checked marriage records on the PNC and get this. Bronwyn Wright's maiden name is Wilkins,' Merringer said knowingly.

'Dylan Wilkins is Bronwyn Wright's son?' Ruth asked rhetorically. She wasn't expecting that!

Ruth was now confused as she tried to analyse how this might affect the case. Her train of thought was broken when

Drake, who was carrying a heap of case folders, knocked on her open door.

'Hi, Ruth. I was going to ask you a couple of questions, but it looks like you've got more pressing issues?' Drake said, clearly registering Ruth's preoccupation. 'Mind if I sit down?'

'Help yourself,' Ruth said, gesturing to the empty seat opposite her. Maybe DCI Drake was serious about being hands on and supportive?

'What's the issue, guys?' Drake asked, putting the case folders on her desk.

Ruth looked up at Merringer who got the message, nodded and left to go back to work.

If DCI Drake wanted to get stuck in from the start, she wasn't going to stand in his way.

'Bronwyn Wright was a teacher at the same school as Arabella Dixon. She felt she had been hounded out of the school by Arabella's bullying and Neerav's spineless management, even though she had manhandled a pupil. She had a nervous breakdown,' Ruth explained.

'So she has motive,' Drake said. 'What about an alibi?'

'She was in the Lighthouse Treatment Centre in Welshpool on the evening of the murder of Arabella Dixon. Her car keys were locked away. It seems, however, Wright fabricated alibis for the time of Neerav Banerjee's murder.'

'What was her explanation for that?' Drake asked.

'I don't know yet. We're trying to track her down for interview this morning,' Ruth said. 'We've just discovered that Dylan Wilkins, the assistant school caretaker, is her son.'

'What's he like?' Drake asked.

'He's a fairly high-functioning autistic young man. He does odd jobs around the school, helps out in the kitchen, and assists the school caretaker, Mike Gardener. It was Dylan who dialled the emergency services while Mike Gardener was administering CPR on Arabella Dixon.'

'Okay. So Dylan Wilkins was right in the midst of Arabella's murder scene?' Drake said.

'More than that. We now have fingerprints that prove Dylan poured acid over Arabella's car on the night of the murder,' Ruth explained.

'Out of revenge for the way she had bullied his mother?' Drake asked rhetorically.

'Possibly. If Arabella Dixon caught him in the act, there might have been an altercation that got out of hand? Dylan pretends to help Mike Gardener when he finds Arabella Dixon's body and rings the ambulance, taking almost all suspicion away from him,' Ruth said, thinking aloud.

'That's pretty sophisticated for someone who is autistic, isn't it?' Drake said.

'Possibly ... It also doesn't explain Neerav Banerjee's murder.'

'Because of the same MO,' Drake said as he got up to speed.

'Yes ... Do we really think Dylan Wilkins avenged his mother by murdering the two people who he felt had ruined her life.'

'What if mother and son were working together?' Drake suggested. 'Dylan Wilkins murders Arabella Dixon and she finishes the job by helping her son murder Neerav Banerjee?'

'That's a possibility,' Ruth said, but she felt it was a stretch in terms of probability.

'Where is Dylan Wilkins now?' Drake asked.

'He's at work at Dinas Padog High School as far as we know,' Ruth said.

'Let's get a Section 18 Search Warrant signed off. Get into Wilkins' flat and have SOCO on standby if uniform find anything,' Drake suggested.

BY ELEVEN O'CLOCK, Ruth and Nick were heading from Llancastell to Dinas Padog to meet SOCO at Dylan Wilkins' flat. The school office gave them the address and confirmed that Dylan Wilkins was Bronwyn Wright's son and that it was common knowledge. In fact, it was hinted that a previous headteacher had given Dylan the job as a favour to Bronwyn a few years before Neerav Banerjee became head.

DC Merringer had gone on ahead with the warrant. DCI Drake would, as expected, stay at Llancastell station to lead and coordinate while bringing himself up to speed on witness statements, forensics etc.

Nick was eating sweets and offered them to Ruth. 'Don't take the green ones.'

Ruth pulled a face. 'Oh my God. Any sweets with apple flavouring make me heave.'

'Part of my five a day,' Nick said with a grin.

They pulled up outside a butcher's shop, above which Dylan Wilkins lived. Eric Rankin & Son appeared closed. In fact it could have closed down altogether – it was hard to tell. The old sign above the shop was worn and weathered, and Ruth thought it looked like it had been there since the 1950s. The sun had bleached the once red awning to cerise. Black and white diamond tiles decorated the step by the door. The windows, both in the shop and the flat above, were filthy.

On the opposite side of the high street was the Crown Hotel where two police cars and the SOCO van, with their yellow and blue colourings, were parked. Traffic was slowing down to manoeuvre around the vehicles and to get a look at what was going on.

'I need a ciggie before I go in there,' Ruth said, sparking up a cigarette.

Merringer came out in full overalls and purple gloves and gave them a look. 'You do not want to go in there, boss. I've never seen anything like it.'

'Why?' Nick asked.

'I don't think Dylan Wilkins has thrown away a newspaper, a cardboard box or anything much else in the past five years. There are old tins of paint. Bottles, you name it. I can't even see where he sleeps. I don't think he has ever cleaned or hoovered the flat.'

Ruth stubbed out her cigarette. 'Great! Better send in Kim and Aggie.'

Ruth and Nick went to the flat door via the dusty, threadbare red-carpeted stairs that led up from the street. There were old bits of bicycles, wheels, and bike chains at the bottom of the stairs. There were dark oil stains on the carpet.

At that moment, a female SOCO officer wearing over-alls and a mask came down the stairs with two clear plastic bags.

'Ma'am, we found this behind the television in a padded envelope,' the forensic officer said.

Ruth and Nick looked at the first evidence bag. Inside was an iPhone 6 with a cracked screen in a pink leather case. Ruth and Nick shared a look – Arabella Dixon's missing phone?

The officer then held up the second evidence bag. 'Size-ten worker boots covered in mud and pine needles. And there are two spots of blood on the toe cap.'

'Bingo!' Nick blurted out with a victorious smile.

Ruth looked at Merringer. 'Got him! Right, seal this flat off completely. Treat it as a crime scene. Everyone that comes in wears full SOCO gear. I want a restricted scene log. We don't need every bloody Tom, Dick or Harry traipsing all over the place.'

Ruth clicked on her radio. 'Control, this is DI Hunter. I want all entry and exit roads for a mile around Dinas Padog High School locked down. Suspect's name is Dylan Wilkins. Please don't do anything to alert him. Police officers are on their way.'

Ruth looked at Nick. 'Let's pick up the bastard.'

FIFTEEN MINUTES LATER, Nick and two male uni-formed officers in yellow high-visibility *Heddlu*/Police jack-ets covertly made their way across the now empty playground. At the centre were white lines painted demarking a football pitch. There were some benches and a vibrant mural painted on a wall.

The school had that unnerving quiet of somewhere that is normally frenetic. The teachers and pupils had been told to stay within the confines of the school's classrooms while they arrested Dylan Wilkins.

Ruth was with several other uniformed officers and two patrol cars at the main entrance in case Wilkins made a break for it.

Nick clicked his radio and said quietly, 'Boss, we are now making our way across the playground, heading for the canteen.'

The school office had informed Nick that Wilkins would be in the school kitchen helping as they prepared for lunch. However, none of the kitchen staff knew that he was going to be arrested.

In silence, Nick pushed open the double doors and went into the school building, past the main hall, and entered the canteen. *Why does all school food smell the same?* Nick thought to himself as his nose was accosted with the smell of overcooked peas and dry turkey. On the walls were pupils' artwork and a mosaic that reflected food, as well as slogans about healthy eating.

The canteen was empty except for a handful of sixth formers who were chancing their luck and trying to get food early. They looked alarmed as Nick and the two uniformed officers crept in. Nick gestured to them with his finger to his lips to keep quiet, and then he motioned for them to leave the canteen by the side entrance.

They started by shuffling nervously towards the exit, before breaking into a run once they were outside. Nick hoped the clatter of their feet wouldn't be heard.

The wooden shutters that separated the kitchen and queuing area were still down, and from behind them there were the metallic crashes and bangings of a school kitchen in full flow, combined with chatter and the odd raucous laugh.

Nick slowly tried a door but it was locked. He was now trying to calculate how to get into the kitchen without alerting Dylan Wilkins of their presence. He could feel the tension mounting in his stomach. They didn't want him escaping out of the back of the school site into the woods. That would then mean involving a dog unit, helicopters, and a full-scale manhunt.

At that moment, one of the dinner ladies, skinny, ruddy face, in a white coat and peaked catering hat, pushed the shutters up noisily as it was only ten minutes until the lunch bell rang. As the shutters rose, she saw Nick and the two uniformed officers and nearly jumped out of her skin.

'Oh my dear God! You scared the life out of me,' she blurted out.

Nick motioned for her to be quiet and then in a hushed voice said, 'Dylan Wilkins. Where is he?'

The dinner lady motioned towards an industrial-sized dishwasher. Suddenly, Dylan Wilkins came into view holding a plastic tray of cutlery. He saw Nick, dropped the tray with a terrible clatter and made a run for it.

Nick took two quick steps and vaulted over the serving area, his thighs skidding on the metal surface. He sprinted right, losing his footing for a moment on the tiled floor, and then saw Wilkins bolting out of the back entrance to the kitchen and into the main car park.

Nick clicked his radio. 'All units, I'm in pursuit of a male suspect, Dylan Wilkins. He is wearing a white catering jacket and heading across the main car park to the side passageway of the school site.'

Nick picked up his pace. Christ, it had been a long time since he had run around the school site like this. Not since he played tag in Year 7. Wilkins was at least fifty yards away. The two uniform officers that had been with Nick were nowhere to be seen.

Nick pumped his arms as he reached full pelt. Wilkins disappeared down the side pathway that led to the design and technology department and then to the rear car park.

Nick clicked his radio again. 'Suspect is heading for the passageway that leads to the west of the school site and then the rear car park.'

Nick was running at full speed as he snaked around the paths, dragging in as much oxygen as he could. If only he had kept himself in shape. He slowed a little to get his breath and then rounded the corner beside the art department.

He looked around. Nothing. Wilkins seemed to have vanished.

'Suspect seems to have disappeared and ...' Nick said through heavy breaths, until he saw a pair of open, green-painted double doors that he knew from his time at the school led under the school. 'Boss, I think suspect has gone into the school basement. I'm going to follow.'

Nick could see that the rusty bolt that secured the doors had been forced. He went in slowly, knowing that Wilkins could attack him as soon as he stepped foot inside. Nothing.

Usually well lit, there was a series of interconnected rooms under the school that housed the boiler room, central heating system, electrics and storage of paints, tools and ladders. However, the rooms were exceptionally dark. Wilkins must have turned the lights off as soon as he made his way in there. Nick had no idea where the switches were, which gave Wilkins a massive advantage. Nick fumbled for a moment and his shin hit a metal shelving unit with an echoing clank. *Shit,* Nick thought to himself. He'd given his presence away already.

He felt his hand along the damp wall and then turned a corner and gazed down the murky corridor. The heating system made the air muggy and oppressive. A solitary light bulb cast a long shadow down to the far end of the storeroom. Nick could taste oil and paint in the air as he moved out of the room into a black void. He waited there for a moment, trying not to let his rapid breathing make a sound.

A patch of dim red light spilt out across the floor from the boiler to show it was on and working. Its deep hum reverberated in Nick's chest. His vision was now starting to adjust to the lack of light.

From above there was the teeth-jarring sound of pupils moving chairs, and he could just about hear the deep rumble of a teacher barking orders.

Then there was virtual silence.

Suddenly, out of nowhere, a piece of metal hurtled towards Nick's face. He instinctively flinched sideways and the spanner-like object bounced noisily onto the floor.

'Dylan, you need to calm down.' Nick said quietly, while all the time checking for where the next object could come from.

'We just want to talk to you, that's all. No one's going to hurt you. I promise.'

There was silence and then the faint sound of movement. Nick braced himself for whatever was coming next.

Wilkins came out of the shadows and looked at Nick.

'I just want you to be calm, Dylan. Do you understand that?' Nick said.

Dylan looked at the floor and nodded. 'I haven't done nothing.'

Nick approached Wilkins slowly.

'Dylan Wilkins, I am arresting you on suspicion of the murder of Arabella Dixon.'

CHAPTER 32

DRAKE AND RUTH STOOD in a room with two monitors that showed Interview Rooms 1 and 2 remotely.

'Where does this put Jonathan Noakes in our case?' Drake asked her.

'Until today he was a prime suspect. But now we know the relationship between Dylan Wilkins and Bronwyn Wright, and have found Arabella Dixon's phone, and blood-stained size-ten boots, at Dylan's house, then I think that's changed.'

Drake nodded. 'Let's not take our eye off Noakes though.'

'Yes, sir.' Ruth nodded. She knew he was right. Could Dylan Wilkins really be the person they chased from Neerav Banerjee's house? The person who shot Nick in the mine? She wasn't convinced. Maybe Jonathan Noakes seemed more likely to be that person.

She liked Drake. He seemed to have a controlled energy in his eyes, as though he was always processing something even while he spoke. His ideas came out as unmediated streams of consciousness that looped around and were then explained in plain speaking. He was the antithesis to Jones' superficial schmooze.

Jones came in with an unusual sense of urgency. He glanced at the monitors.

Dylan Wilkins was sitting in Interview Room 1. They were waiting for his solicitor to arrive so they could question him.

'What do we think?' Jones asked. 'Enough to keep them for thirty-six hours?'

'Dylan Wilkins definitely vandalised Arabella Dixon's car. We have his partial prints on the primer and metal of the car's bonnet. Plus, he had Arabella Dixon's phone in his flat. We also have his size-ten work boots with two splashes of blood. They are also covered in mud and pine needles,' Drake said.

Jones nodded. 'Good. So, we're starting to build a case?'

Drake's face was non-committal. 'I think that depends on what Forensics can turn up. We also have Dylan Wilkins' coat, work clothes and a pair of gloves. SOCO are in his flat and then they will go over to Bronwyn Wright's. If we get anything that links them to either victim then I would say yes, sir.'

'Good. Good. I'm not suggesting we rush things. But there is growing pressure for us to make an arrest and charge someone.'

Ruth knew that the only thing Jones was interested in was covering his arse and keeping his job.

IT WAS ONE O'CLOCK by the time Ruth and Nick began to interview Dylan Wilkins. His solicitor, Sandra Ross, wore a dark suit and looked like she would prefer to be anywhere else in the world rather than sitting there. She pulled a face, looked through a file, and made some notes.

Ruth looked up from her case folder. Her tone was, as always, gentle.

'First things first, Dylan. Do you drive a car or have you ever driven a car?'

'No, no. I'm not allowed to. I have epilepsy so I have to ride my bike,' Dylan replied.

Ruth took a moment and then looked at him with a kind smile. 'Dylan, can you tell us why you ran away when the police arrived at the school today?'

He thought for a moment about his answer. 'I'm scared of the police.'

'Why would you be scared of the police?'

'They can put you in prison.'

'Dylan, you can only go to prison if you've broken the law,' Ruth explained.

Dylan shook his head. 'No, no, no. People can go to prison even if they haven't broken the law. I've seen it on television. On a programme, you see, there was a postman called Victor. He got convicted of attempted rape in 1996 and he was put in prison by the judge and he was there for seventeen years. Then they found some new DNA evidence on things – clothes I think – and they had to let him go. Didn't you see it? Didn't you know that? So, I get scared, see?'

Ruth shared a look with Nick – not the answer she had been expecting. Dylan's right leg was moving with a nervous jitter.

'Dylan, could you tell us what happened on the night that Arabella Dixon was murdered at Dinas Padog High School?'

'Miss Dixon? Yes, yes ... Mike, I mean Mr Gardener asked me to look at the main boiler for the school heating system,' Dylan said, concentrating on recounting everything correctly.

'Do you know what time that might have been?' Nick asked.

'Dunno. There were lots of parents and kids in the school, see. Then I went to help Mr Gardener to put away all the desks and the chairs when everyone had gone. I didn't think I'd get home until nine. That's what normally happens,' Dylan said nodding his head.

'How long do you think you were working on the boiler?' Ruth asked.

Dylan shrugged. 'Dunno. An hour or maybe longer. We've just got a Herz Firematic biomass boiler. They also put them solar panels on the roof of the school gym, and we've got a solar thermal hot water system. That's the thing that's not working properly. Only been in for a year. Should be working. I was having a look at it. I like boilers. Then we've got a Stratton wall-hung condensing boiler, which is great. I love anything made by Stratton.'

'Okay. So, you were working in the boiler room of the school. Did anyone see you there?'

'Oh yeah. Mike, I mean Mr Gardener, brought me a brew and some biscuits. He gets bourbons 'cos he knows they're my favourite. And they're only 89p from the Co-op.'

'Do you know what time that was?' Nick asked.

'No. There were still lots of parents and kids around 'cos I could hear them from the boiler room.'

'Can you tell us where you were when Mike Gardener called for help?' Nick asked.

'I was working on the boiler, like I said,' Dylan said with a frown.

'So, you didn't leave the school's boiler room until you heard Mike Gardener call for help?'

Dylan nodded. 'Yeah. I mean, no, I didn't. I was there. All the time.'

'And then can you tell us what happened when you heard Mike Gardener call for help?'

'I ran up from the boiler room. Then I went through the store cupboard, I went into the corridor and then I ran down the passageway into the car park. It was raining and I was getting soaked. Mr Gardener was shouting for help. Miss Dixon was lying there on the ground. Mr Gardener was pumping his hands on her chest, like. He told me to go and ring for an ambulance and then get help.'

'Dylan, had you seen Miss Dixon earlier that evening?' Ruth asked.

Dylan shook his head and then looked down at the floor.

'For the purposes of the tape, the interviewee shook his head to indicate that he didn't see Arabella Dixon during the evening before Mike Gardener called for help.' Ruth clarified. 'Okay. Dylan, I'm going to show you a photograph of something. Can you tell me if you recognise it?'

Ruth slid a photograph of Arabella Dixon's iPhone 6 in its pink case over for Dylan to look at. Dylan took a moment and then looked at it.

'For the purposes of the tape, this is image two-nine-three, item reference A-four-five-six,' Ruth said.

Dylan now looked pale and sick with anxiety.

'Do you recognise this, Dylan?' Ruth asked again.

'Yes.' Dylan was now rocking a little to and fro.

'Can you tell us what it is?' Nick asked.

'Is Mummy here?' Dylan asked.

'Dylan, can you tell me what you can see in this photograph please?' Ruth said quietly, aware that Dylan was now really struggling.

'It's Miss Dixon's phone.'

'Okay. We carried out a Section 18 search of your property, Dylan. Can you tell us why we found Miss Dixon's phone concealed in your flat?' Ruth asked.

'I didn't steal it. I just picked it up.' Dylan was getting very anxious.

'When did you pick it up?'

'When I was helping Mr Gardener. And we was waiting for the ambulance. I saw the phone on the ground. It was getting rained on and I thought that it might get broken if it got really wet. So, I picked it up and put it in my pocket so it didn't get any more rain on it.' Dylan explained.

'Did Mr Gardener see this or did you tell him?' Nick asked.

'No, no. The ambulance arrived and then I forgot that I had it in my pocket. I only remembered when I got home, see.'

'When you found Miss Dixon's phone, why didn't you hand it in to somebody?' Nick asked.

'I thought I'd get into right trouble. I thought someone would say that I stole it and that I would get into trouble. I thought I would lose my job like my mummy did.'

'So, you hid the phone in your flat?' Nick asked.

'Yeah. I kept thinking in my head that I should give it to someone but I was too scared.'

Ruth took out a couple of other photographs. They showed Arabella Dixon's car, a white Range Rover Evoque, and then some close-ups of the dark, burnt paintwork of the car's bonnet.

'Dylan, could you explain why we found your fingerprints on this damage on Arabella Dixon's car?' Ruth asked.

'No, no. I don't know.' Dylan was looking at the floor.

'Did you damage Arabella Dixon's car?' Nick said.

'No. I don't think so.' Dylan couldn't hide his guilt.

'Are you sure? Your fingerprints are on the part of the bonnet that is damaged,' Nick reminded him.

'It might have been an accident, maybe? I can't remember.' Dylan shrugged.

'You vandalised Arabella Dixon's car, didn't you, Dylan?' Nick asked.

Dylan just looked at the floor and shook his head. The interview continued for another few minutes before Dylan's anxiety got too much and his solicitor asked for a break.

After that, all they could establish was that Dylan didn't have an alibi for the time of Neerav Banerjee's murder. He had gone home from working at the school and watched television. He couldn't remember what he watched. He admitted that the size-ten boots were his but claimed that he used them when he went mountain biking. When Ruth asked him what a spiral shape meant to him, he seemed vague and didn't appear to know what she was talking about. Unfortunately, Ruth suspected that he didn't have a clue about why the question was being asked.

And if that was true, Dylan Wilkins wasn't their man.

AFTER LUNCH, RUTH AND Nick began their interview of Bronwyn Wright. The Tech team had tracked down both Bronwyn Wright's and Dylan Wilkins' private email addresses. From the looks of it, they used them solely to contact each other. Nick and Ruth thought the content of the emails was creepy, to say the least. Dylan Wilkins always referred to her as 'Mummy' and he was always 'Dilly' to her. Ruth said it was all a bit 'Bates Motel' for her liking, before having to explain the reference to Nick who admitted he'd never seen *Psycho*. When Ruth told him of Freud's Oedipal theory that every man subconsciously wants to sleep with his mother and kill his father, Nick thought the latter was true but the former 'bloody sick'.

Bronwyn's solicitor was a young man who was slim, balding and sat upright as he took notes.

Bronwyn peered through the thick lenses of her glasses. Her face was jowly and she wore an expression as though she had heard something amusing only moments earlier. Nick continued to think there was something deeply unsettling about her.

'Bronwyn, can you tell us why you lied to our officers about your whereabouts on Monday afternoon?' Ruth asked.

'I wasn't aware that I had,' Bronwyn replied.

'Our officers checked with the teaching supply agencies that you claim to have gone to and they have no record of you.' Nick said looking through his notes.

'Right. Well, I don't see how that is possible. I would need to check my paperwork to see which agencies I signed up with, but I'm fairly sure I gave the officers the correct information,' Bronwyn replied coldly.

'You also told us you went to Llancastell Library on that afternoon,' Nick said looking down at his notes.

'Yes, that's right.' Bronwyn looked at him with a challenging stare.

'We've looked at the CCTV footage supplied by the library. You didn't go into Llancastell Library that afternoon,' Nick said sternly.

'Didn't I? I might have got my days muddled up then. Since my suspension, one day is very much like the next. I'm not sure how I'm supposed to remember what I did exactly on one particular afternoon. It's ridiculous! I don't suppose you would remember what you were doing on a certain afternoon unless you had your notebook, or whatever you use these days. It's absurd!' Bronwyn was starting to get angry.

'If you weren't going into employment agencies and the library on Monday afternoon, can you tell us what you were doing?' Ruth asked in a calm tone.

'No. I can't. I've no idea,' Bronwyn snapped. 'Is that all?'

'I'm going to read you an email dated Sunday the twelfth of March, sent at nine o'clock at night from your email address to an email address that belongs to your son. The email reads: "Hello, Dilly. Don't forget that you promised to help me after work tomorrow. You need to bring gloves, a mask and boots. I'll pick you up at four o'clock at the usual place. Don't let me down, Love Mummy xx"'.

'Yes? What is your point?' Bronwyn asked.

'Can you tell us what you meant by that email?' Nick asked.

'Exactly what it says.' Bronwyn shook her head in disbelief.

'What did you want your son to help you with that would require gloves, a mask and boots?' Ruth asked, wondering why Bronwyn's tone hadn't changed.

'Dilly was helping clear out my attic. I'm selling my house. The attic is filthy,' Bronwyn said impatiently.

'Why a mask?' Nick asked.

'For God's sake, I've just told you. Dilly has dust masks at work. He has a slight dust allergy, so I reminded him to bring a mask back from school,' Bronwyn explained with a patronising frown.

'While Dylan was helping you clear out your attic, did anyone see you?' Ruth asked.

'I'm not sure. Yes, actually. I waved at my neighbour, Lucas Brown, when we arrived.'

'And he'll confirm that will he?' Nick asked.

'I don't see why he wouldn't.'

'Can you explain why your son told us that he went home from work on Monday and just watched television?' Nick asked.

'You are aware that Dilly is autistic?'

'Yes, we are.' Ruth nodded.

'Autism affects the memory function in the brain. He finds it difficult to store or retrieve information. He wouldn't remember what he does from one day to the next unless you remind him.'

'Okay. While you were clearing the house, did you speak to anyone on the phone or use your email between four o'clock and six o'clock?' Nick asked.

'No, of course not! We were clearing things out to be dumped or to be moved,' Bronwyn replied with utter irritation.

'Am I correct in thinking that you are an expert in Welsh history, especially the Bronze Age?' Nick asked.

'Yes. Basically, the history of Wales before the Romans arrived.' Bronwyn's self-importance was really beginning to get up Nick's nose.

'What does the spiral symbol mean to you, Bronwyn?' Ruth asked.

'The spiral? What are you talking about? What has this got to do with anything?' Bronwyn virtually spat out her words.

The interview continued in this manner for another fifteen minutes and they got nowhere with their questions about the spiral shape. Then Bronwyn reluctantly went back over her alibi for the time of Arabella Dixon's death. She claimed that she didn't think that she even owned a second set of keys to her car so could not have left the Lighthouse or got to Dinas Padog. Why didn't they check CCTV and see that her car wasn't driven anywhere on that night? They didn't want to admit that they had done this and found nothing. However, Nick also knew that if you were smart and familiar with the back roads, you could get from Welsh-pool to Dinas Padog without being detected. There weren't that many traffic cameras in North Wales, just on the major routes like the A5.

At four o'clock, Bronwyn and Dylan Wilkins were allowed to leave and go home. Ruth and Nick met with Drake. They knew that they had to wait for Forensics to find some link otherwise the CPS would never take it to trial.

The frustration in the room was palpable, especially as they knew that Jones would be on their backs first thing in the morning.

CHAPTER 33

THAT EVENING, RUTH had agreed to meet Ella in Conwy. Her daughter had never been, but she knew all about the family history and how she owed her very existence on the planet to the town. The plan was to wander around Conwy, get something to eat, and Ella would stay with Ruth at her hotel before returning to Liverpool the next day.

Ruth had spent the journey ruminating on the day's events and the two interviews. Bronwyn Wright and Dylan Wilkins had a strange relationship. She understood a mother being protective of her autistic child but there was something disconcerting and even unnatural about them.

However, plotting and taking revenge on Arabella Dixon and Neerav Banerjee was beginning to seem a stretch. Dylan Wilkins didn't appear to be like the person they had chased through Clocaenog Forest. She didn't know why. It was intuitive.

As they said in the US cop shows that Ruth loved to watch in the late nineties, she 'liked' Jonathan Noakes for the two murders. Arabella Dixon had probably made a mess of his head during their affair. Women like that played games, leaving their unsuspecting lovers hanging like vulnerable bait on a hook. One minute hot, the next cold. Ruth instinctively knew that Arabella Dixon would have manipulated Noakes and Banerjee and taken delight in the control that it gave her.

As Ruth parked her car, she realised that she had been so caught up in her thoughts about the case that she could barely remember the drive. As she went over to the parking ticket machine, it became cold and blustery, so she buttoned up her coat and tucked in her turquoise scarf. She stuck the ticket inside her windscreen, before taking out a cigarette, cupping her hands and lighting it. A nice big drag down into her lungs – *That's better*, she thought.

As she followed the signs to the centre of town, Ruth looked around. She calculated that she hadn't been in Conwy since she was eighteen. Around thirty years. Some buildings she recognised instantly, but others had been changed or built in that time. Conwy – or Conway as the English would say it – was on the north coast of Wales and faced across the River Conwy. The name came from the old Welsh words *cyn* (chief) and *gwy* (water), the river being originally called the *Cynwy*.

Ruth remembered playing with her brother in the iconic Conwy Castle and on the town walls that were built, on the instruction of Edward I of England, as part of his conquest of Wales.

Conwy Castle was a great looming fortress with eight giant towers and when Ruth was small, the castle's size made her stomach lurch when she looked up. Perched on a rock, with Snowdonia as its backdrop, it was a majestic medieval castle that seemed to Ruth to have come from a fairy tale. At night, the wall and turrets were lit and it became even more magical.

For Ruth, and her brother Chris, it was an incredible departure from the Winstanley Estate in Battersea. With its rows of concrete blocks and lines of large windows, the estate looked more like a prison. Winstanley was a working-class community, and her grandad Billy had lived there before the estate was built in the 1960s. Grandad always said that the council did a much better job of destroying the area's morale and appearance than the Germans ever did. Unemployment was high, and by the 1980s the flats were damp, and the stairwells were full of piss and foil used by smackheads. Coming to Conwy in the summers was like being on a different, heavenly planet for them.

Ruth had suggested that Ella meet her outside 'The Smallest House in Great Britain' which was on the quayside. Ella had never seen it and it was something Ruth loved coming to look at when she was a child.

The tiny house was built in the sixteenth century and was used as a family residence until 1900 when the council declared it unfit for human habitation. Since then it had been a tourist attraction. It was painted red and the ground floor room was 10 ft by 5 ft. There was a small set of stairs and a cramped bedroom on the first floor.

As Ruth made her way towards the quayside, she lit another cigarette. There was conflict in her mind. Part of her wanted to look around and take in all the blissful childhood memories. Yet the case, and the faces of Dylan Wilkins, Bronwyn Wright, and Jonathan Noakes, kept popping into her mind's eye. She climbed the town walls at the southern end of the east side. Here the tower of Llewellyn the Great's *Llys,* or courthouse, had been incorporated into the wall.

Ruth turned onto the high street and that's when it happened. A woman came out of Ye Olde Mailcoach pub about a hundred yards ahead of her. She was walking with a man who was tall and strode along with purpose. Ruth wasn't taking any notice, her thoughts were lost yet again in the case. And then something froze inside her. Something familiar about the way the woman walked. The way her body moved. The woman turned and laughed at something the man had said and Ruth saw her in profile. It was Sarah. Jesus! It was Sarah. She would know that profile anywhere. The nose, the lips, brow, chin. Unmistakable. Shit!

Ruth broke into a run but her injured ankle was still very sore from when she twisted it a few days ago in the Clocaenog Forest. Trying to run on it immediately aggravated the injury. A sharp pain shot through her ligament.

Sarah and the man were hurrying, as if they were late, and they were getting further away. Ruth panicked.

'Sarah! Sarah!' Ruth bellowed down the street but the couple didn't halt.

Ruth limped past Parsella's Ice Cream Parlour, trying to ignore the pain. Past an Indian restaurant that was closed and then the busy Galleon fish-and-chip shop.

The couple had now reached the dark, shadowy brick archway that led out onto the quayside.

'Sarah, for God's sake!' Ruth thundered.

Passers-by gave her a look and a wide berth as she hobbled on. She looked up and Sarah was now into the short archway and disappearing into semi-darkness.

Ruth wasn't looking where she was going and tripped and stumbled on a pushchair, nearly knocking it over.

'Oi, watch where you're going!' the mother said with a frown.

'Sorry ...' Ruth mumbled.

Ruth had taken her eyes away just for a second but as she looked up again, Sarah and the man were now out of sight. She had no idea whether they had turned left or right onto the quayside. Shit!

Full of panic, Ruth eventually arrived at the archway, ran through the darkness and then out onto the quay. To the left were some people sitting outside the Liverpool Arms. Other than that, there were ten or more people walking down the quay towards the smallest house in Britain. Quickly scanning them all, Ruth realised that none of them were Sarah or the man she was with.

She spun right, looking down the grey stone quayside towards the castle. In front of her an old red phone box, and then a scattering of half a dozen people. Again, no Sarah. Jesus, what was going on? She gazed again down the quay that led to the castle. No. Ruth's mind was racing. The pub.

Ruth entered the Liverpool Arms pub. That was it. They were getting drinks and they would sit outside and take in the view of the River Conwy and west, over to the next part of North Wales.

The pub was fairly bog standard, with red bar stools and dark stained tables. Ruth hastily scanned the first bar. There were some kids in their late teens drinking pints and laughing.

Alert and full of adrenaline, Ruth moved through the bar quickly and into the next at the rear. Again, Sarah was nowhere to be seen. Ruth doubled back to check. She went into the ladies but it was empty. She felt a growing sick feeling and she shook a little. What if that was her? What if she had just seen Sarah and now she had lost her again? For God's sake.

Ruth went through the pub one last time and then came out into the fresh sea air. She took a deep breath but she couldn't seem to catch it. It was the beginnings of a panic attack. Her heart was thumping against her chest. She scanned once more left and right. Nothing. How could this be happening to her? She couldn't breathe.

'Mum?' Ella had just walked out of the archway and was beaming.

Ruth looked up at her daughter, the blood drained from her face. She had lost control of her breathing and her heart felt like it would explode.

'Are you all right, Mum?' Ella could see she wasn't. Everything from her face and her stature showed that Ruth looked crushed.

'Mum? Mum?' Ella was now worried.

'I ... can't get ... my breath.' Ruth said, sucking in air, holding it and breathing out as she had been shown many times before. It was a way of stopping the panic attack. Ruth concentrated on breathing and counting, then breathing and counting again. Slowly her pulse slowed.

Ruth went over to Ella and put her arms around her.

'Mum, what's happened?'

'I thought I saw her. I did see her. I don't know.'

'Who, Mum?' Ella asked with a frown.

'Sarah. I saw Sarah. I couldn't catch up with her and now she's gone again.'

Ruth sobbed and Ella held her tightly.

IT WAS SPITTING WITH rain as Nick filled the steel wheelbarrow with earth again. He had agreed to help Mike with digging the foundations for an extension to their cottage. If Cerys was going to have a baby, they needed more room.

The outside lights lit up the whole area. Nick's boots were caked in mud as he wheeled the barrow over to a large red skip and poured the earth in. It would have been nice to have had some food and watch TV but he knew how much Mike had done for him.

Nick looked over and watched Mike shovelling earth at a rate of knots. He was in good shape for a man his age.

'Bloody hell. You do know this is my night off? I'm meant to be resting and getting fed, not humping great lumps of mud?' Nick grinned, and his simulated protest wasn't lost on Mike.

'Get on with it, lad. Do you good, bit of exercise rather than sitting on your arse, like,' Mike teased.

Nick headed towards the side door. 'Make us a brew, shall I?' Nick asked.

'You've only just started and you're half my age.' Mike shook his head.

Nick headed over to the side door and saw Cerys.

'Don't you dare come in with those sodding boots!' She wagged her finger at him and smiled.

'I'm doing this for you, you cheeky twat,' Nick exclaimed.

'Oi. That's no way to speak to a pregnant lady.'

'Yeah, and when you say *lady*...' Nick grinned.

'Make a sentence out of *piss* and *off*.' Cerys gave him the finger.

'Just put the kettle on, will ya?' Nick loved the sharp to and fro of their banter.

She wandered over and clicked the kettle on.

Nick gestured out of the window to Mike who was digging like his life depended on it.

'How's he doing?' Nick asked quietly.

He noticed as Cerys paused for a moment, thinking about how to answer the question.

'What is it?' Nick said, now concerned.

'I don't know. Something's going on. Ever since he found Miss Dixon's body. I don't blame him, it must have been horrible. But he's keeping himself to himself,' Cerys replied with a frown.

Nick knew that when he had seen a dead body for the first time in a road traffic accident, he'd had sleepless nights and, when he did eventually sleep, nightmares. It was something he found upsetting for several weeks after the event.

'I'm worried about Mam too,' Cerys said.

'Why?' Nick asked.

'And I thought I smelt alcohol on her breath the other night.' Cerys was now whispering.

'Alcohol? Don't be daft. She only drinks at Christmas!'

'I might have imagined it. My sense of smell is all over the place now I'm pregnant. When Mam's cooking, I keep having to go out and get fresh air 'cos I feel so sick. I dunno,' Cerys said.

'Did you tell your dad?' Nick asked.

'No. 'Course not. Probably just my imagination. I'll make you two a brew, shall I?' Cerys said, turning back to the kettle.

'Yeah, great,' Nick said, but his mind was ruminating over what Cerys had told him.

ONCE RUTH HAD CALMED down, she and Ella had walked down the quayside towards the castle as the light faded. Ruth admitted that, in hindsight, it might not have been Sarah. It had happened before. But there was something about the woman that seemed so familiar. It was torturous.

They returned to Ruth's hotel, ordered room service, chatted, and watched TV. They both opted for the wild mushroom and goats cheese tagliatelle, which they later agreed was better than they had thought it would be.

Ruth had a hot bath and tried to control the racing thoughts in her head. Watching the beginning of *Bridget Jones's Diary*, Ruth sat in her bathrobe and smoked out of the window, as she did every night.

'How are things? You know, after the split with Andy? You haven't talked about it,' Ruth said, aware that the whole evening had revolved around her and her problems so far.

'I think I've met someone else,' Ella blurted out. Ruth could see she was feeling anxious.

'That was quick!' Ruth said, raising an eyebrow.

'We've been friends for ages. Sorry, is it okay for me to talk about this after earlier?'

'Don't be soft. I want to know what's going on in your life. Who is he?' Ruth asked, blowing a plume of smoke out of the window. There had been boyfriends before, but nothing serious.

'Yeah, that's the thing,' Ella said quietly.

Ruth looked over at the television for a moment.

'Alex,' Ella said.

'Right ...' Ruth still didn't see why Ella was so reluctant to talk.

'Short for Alexandra.'

Ruth took a moment and then looked over at her properly. 'Okay. Alexandra.' It was a surprise, but she needed to reassure Ella that she wasn't fazed at all.

'Is that weird? I mean ...' Ella squirmed a little.

'No. If you're happy, it's not weird. It's 2017 so nothing is weird.'

'I am happy.' Ella smiled.

'Then that's great.' Ruth smiled back, relieved.

CHAPTER 34

RUTH SIPPED HER FLAT white coffee as she tried to catch up on some paperwork that was mounting in her office. It needed to be sorted. The North Wales Police logo spun slowly on her computer screen and she watched it for a moment.

She and Ella had got up at 6.30am and had breakfast together before she left to return to Liverpool. There was no more talk of Ella's new girlfriend. Ruth felt that if her daughter was happy, then nothing else mattered. Gay, straight, bi, none of it mattered. However, she could feel the emotional hangover from yesterday's events in Conwy and had taken some codeine to take the edge off. She definitely wasn't in the mood for running.

Ruth huffed as she gazed again at the mound of forms in front of her. What she needed was another ciggie but that meant getting in the lift to the ground floor and going outside, and frankly she couldn't be arsed. Half an hour and then she'd go.

The two main culprits in taking up her time in Llancastell nick were the bottlenecks in custody and the frequent delays in carrying out fingerprinting, photographing and criminal record checks. There was less manpower than in Peckham. Her paperwork included crime reports, intelligence reports, and even paperwork connected with the shift administration and overtime. It had to be done, but it was never-ending.

Between eight and eight thirty, members of CID drifted in and got to work. Drake arrived at eight on the dot, waved, and went into his temporary office. They would catch up at the briefing at nine.

Nine o'clock came and Drake sat to one side in the briefing as Ruth went through what they had learned from the interviews with Dylan Wilkins and Bronwyn Wright.

'I need someone to go and talk to this Lucas Brown, Bronwyn Wright's neighbour, to confirm he saw her on Monday afternoon. Mac, can you go and check with Mike Gardener and see whether he knew if Dylan Wilkins had taken a dust mask home from school?' Ruth said.

'Yes, boss. Dylan Wilkins doesn't seem like the kind of man to borrow things from work without asking permission first,' Mac said.

'That's true ... Check with Mike when and where he saw Dylan Wilkins on the night of Arabella Dixon's murder. When did he take Dylan tea and biscuits?'

Mac nodded as he scribbled in his notepad.

Ruth looked around the room. 'Sian, can you check traffic for Bronwyn Wright's car on the roads to Llandrillo? Forensics also need chasing for the results of Dylan Wilkins' boots, clothes and gloves but I can't see less than a twenty-four-hour turnaround on that.'

'If not longer,' Drake chipped in.

'Are we going to arrest him, boss?' Nick asked, as he uncrossed his legs and sat forward on his swivel chair.

'If anything comes up linking Dylan Wilkins forensically to the Banerjee crime scene, then we might have a case we could take to the CPS. Otherwise it's circumstantial,' Drake explained, and then turned to Ruth. 'What are we doing about Noakes?'

'We need more before a magistrate will issue us with a search warrant. But to get more evidence, we need Forensics to examine some of Noakes' things and to do this we need a search warrant,' Ruth explained, rolling her eyes.

'Classic catch twenty-two,' Drake said raising an eyebrow.

Nick looked down at his notes. 'A PC told me earlier in the canteen that Jonathan Noakes and Alex Noakes were involved in a road traffic accident yesterday. Their car was a write-off, but they walked away with only a few bruises.

'Why don't you swing by Noakes' house and see what had happened. Have a dig around,' Ruth said. She knew guilty people had a habit of acting strangely and it would also keep the pressure on Noakes until they had something more concrete. Drake agreed it was a good idea.

At eleven o'clock, Ruth had cleared about half of the reports and paperwork that were on her desk. All the time her brain whirred, going through every hypothesis in the case. She kept coming back to Noakes. She knew that crimes of passion and revenge made seemingly normal people behave in the most uncharacteristically violent and uncontrolled way. But those spiral markings? They were either done out of rage or as a neat way of hoodwinking the police into believing that the killer had psychopathic tendencies.

Back in 2003, when she was still in uniform, Ruth had worked a case in London. She remembered it had been an ordinary, dull September morning when they went to a shout to attend a shooting at a beauty salon in Chiswick, a very middle-class, wealthy part of West London. By the time Ruth got there, other officers had sealed off the crime scene and CID were arriving.

A woman in her forties with no criminal record, Juliet Morrison, had dropped her daughter off at primary school in a leafy village in Berkshire before driving into London to confront Claire Orwell, who was having an affair with her husband and was now pregnant. Her husband, Paul Morrison, had just announced that he was going to leave Juliet and set up home with Claire.

Juliet Morrison parked up outside Orwell's upmarket beauty salon, took her husband's double-barrelled shotgun out of her car boot, and went in. Orwell is said to have frowned and then laughed, 'What, have you come to shoot me then?'

'Yes. It's okay, Paul can look after our kids,' Morrison said, nodding calmly. Then she shot Orwell, in cold blood, twice. At her trial, she said, 'I wanted her and my husband to feel some of the pain they had put me and my kids through.' That's what jealousy and anger could do to seemingly sane people.

DC Merringer knocked on her open door and broke Ruth's train of thought. 'Boss, Dylan Wilkins has previous.'

Ruth frowned. 'How is that possible?'

'I dunno, boss.'

'He works in a school,' Ruth said.

Merringer wore an ironic smile. 'You're gonna love this. Turns out that Dylan Wilkins doesn't have a DBS and previously didn't have a CRB check either.'

'You're joking? He's worked at that school for years!' Ruth exclaimed.

'No, boss. I'm really not,' Merringer said, shaking his head.

'What the hell are they playing at?' Ruth said to no one in particular.

Ruth remembered when the Criminal Records Bureau, CRB, was launched in 2002 to check the criminal background of all people who work with children or vulnerable adults in schools, voluntary organisations or professional bodies. For the first time, information about an individual was collected from the police and government agencies. Their name was checked against a confidential register of all people convicted or suspected of child abuse. Police forces in every area of the country in which the applicant had lived or worked were contacted for details of any relevant convictions. Checks were also made for convictions that had expired under the 1974 Rehabilitation of Offenders Act.

Ruth and some of her colleagues felt that it wasn't rigorous enough. There were too many delays and mistakes, and the checks also meant that people were less guarded when they felt safe in the knowledge that someone had a CRB. Unfortunately, within twelve months their fears were realised when Ian Huntley slipped through the net, got a job as a school caretaker, and murdered two ten-year-old girls, Holly Marie Wells and Jessica Aimee Chapman, in Soham, Cambridgeshire.

From the mid-1990s, Huntley had targeted young girls, yet they never had enough evidence to stop him. He had been charged with three rapes, there were allegations that he had sex with underage girls, and an allegation of indecent assault on a ten-year-old. However, he was never convicted of any offence, changed his name, and then managed to gain a CRB - and a job in a primary school.

In 2012, the CRB became the Disclosure and Barring Service, DBS, with even tighter restrictions. The idea that Dylan Wilkins had been working in a school without either was, first, horrifying. Second, it was illegal, with huge fines or even prison for employers if anything went wrong. Ruth still wasn't sure whether something had gone badly wrong here.

'Turns out Dylan Wilkins has two counts of assault in 2005 and 2007. In 2005, he was cornered by two drunk teenagers in Llancastell and put one in A&E. Five hundred-pound fine and no sentence. In 2007, he was accused of shoplifting in Corwen. He punched the shop assistant and broke her nose. Suspended sentence of six months,' Merringer informed Ruth as he looked at his notes.

'Jesus! Can you ring the LEA and tell them so that Dylan Wilkins isn't allowed back on the school site?'

'Yes, boss.'

'So, Dylan Wilkins has a nasty temper when cornered or confronted and he feels trapped and anxious,' Ruth said thinking out loud.

'And we know that he attacked Arabella Dixon's car with acid. What if she caught him and threatened him?' Merringer continued the hypothesis.

'He lashes out, punches her and then in a panic of the repercussions, he strangles her?' Ruth said.

'It sounds plausible. But how do we then link that to Neerav Banerjee's murder, boss?' Merringer asked.

'"Dilly" tells "Mummy" what he's done. She tells him not to worry. Maybe Bronwyn Wright had plans for revenge already. Wilkins' murder of Arabella Dixon just spurs them on to finish the job. One murder or two. What's the difference? Just kill the bastards who ruined your life.'

AS AN OBSERVER OF THE changes in his own health, especially while detoxing, Nick would have described his mood that morning as 'bouncing'. The detox had worked and now Nick was feeling euphoric. A natural high. Usually it took a week or two for his dopamine and serotonin receptors to recover from the aggravated assault they'd had from alcohol and drugs. However, Nick wasn't going to worry or even over-analyse. He was in a positive, strong mood and that was that.

Stevie Wonder's *Signed, Sealed, Delivered* came on the radio and Nick cranked up the stereo.

The countryside rose slowly on both sides of the roads. The lower fields were a vivid green in the spring sunshine and covered by grazing sheep. Purple and brown heathered moorland darkened the upper reaches. Lines of bright, yellow daffodils that swayed in the wind flanked the roadside. Spring had arrived.

Nick arrived at Jonathan Noakes' home and banged on the door. After a moment, the door opened.

'Mr Noakes? Can I come in? There are a couple of things I need to clarify with you,' Nick asked, moving over the threshold before Noakes could say no or slam the door.

'I'm just leaving for a meeting,' Noakes snapped. He looked jittery and tired. Was that guilt or grief?

'That's fine. This won't take a moment,' Nick said with a smile as he got out his notebook. 'I understand you were in a road traffic accident yesterday?'

'Yes. Not my fault though. Women drivers should learn which lanes to use at roundabouts,' Noakes declared pompously.

'Where was the accident?' Nick asked.

'Up on the road to Glasfryn. Now if that's all, I really must get going,' Noakes said as he went and opened the front door.

'Of course. Thanks for your help, Mr Noakes.'

As he left, Nick glimpsed a business card from the Glasfryn garage on the hall table. He knew it was just down the road, halfway between Cerrigydrudion and Pentrefoelas, and decided he would swing by there on the way back to Llancastell.

The B5437 was clear as Nick gunned the Astra up to 60 mph. High up on the right side of the road, a large and powerful bird, with long blueish-grey pointed wings, and black feathers around the beak and its white face, circled and hovered looking for prey. Nick recognised it as a peregrine falcon – it liked to kill and eat shorebirds, ptarmigan, red grouse and smaller songbirds. Suddenly the bird plummeted towards the field at extraordinary speed and disappeared behind a hedgerow where it must have made its kill. The precision and velocity of the bird's attack were at once both chilling and impressive.

Nick pulled up outside the Glasfryn garage, his mood still buoyant. The garage was timeworn and in dire need of refurbishment. There were two dirty petrol pumps that looked like they had been there since the 1970s. It wasn't even clear if they had petrol in them. Above them, a gaudy blue roof was held up by a large red steel pillar in the middle. On a sign was *Glasfryn* in white lettering and beside it a grimy, yellow sign that had *UK* in black.

Nick closed the car door and looked up at clear cobalt sky and sunshine. He enjoyed the feel of the sun warming his face, took off his jacket and threw it in the back of the car. He then wandered around the back of the building and saw a mechanic in oil-stained overalls.

To one side, there was Alex Noakes' blue Renault Clio. The front driver's side had a huge dent and the bonnet was bent up so that the engine was now visible. The headlight was shattered, and the paintwork had deep scratches. The wing mirror was gone, there were abrasions and bumps down the door, and the rest of the driver's side had dents and marks on the paint.

Nick had made the assumption, from what Jonathan Noakes had said, that it was his Audi that had been in the collision. Noakes spoke as though he had been driving. Nick bet that Noakes was glad that his brand new Audi hadn't been written off.

'Can I help, mate?' asked the mechanic with a quizzical expression.

Nick got out his police identification. 'Detective Sergeant Evans. Is this Alex Noakes' car?'

'Yeah.' The mechanic looked worried, but many people reacted like that to police officers.

'Write-off, is it?' Nick asked.

'Oh yeah. Just doing an assessment for the insurance company now.'

At that moment, Nick had a thought. He knew that his cousin Cerys, who had only been driving for a year or two, had a black box tracking device fitted to her car to cut her insurance. It recorded the distance and speed of journeys made. Some of the devices also had a curfew, with lower insurance premiums for young drivers who weren't out late at night. More importantly, the box recorded dates, times, and GPS locations of the journeys made. Nick wondered whether they should have a look at the data just to make sure they could eliminate Alex Noakes from their enquiries. The assumption had been that it had been Jonathan Noakes' car that had been in the accident. But if was actually Alex's, perhaps there were a few more questions to be asked.

'Does it have a black box fitted for the insurance?' Nick asked.

'Yeah. I've just taken it out,' the mechanic said in a helpful tone.

'I'm going to have to take it so we can look at the data on it.' Nick told him.

'No problem,' the mechanic said, turning and heading into the grubby office. A moment later he returned and handed Nick the small black box, the connecting lead and the data card. 'I'll tell the insurance company that you've taken it.'

'Thanks,' Nick nodded and made his way back to his car.

RUTH COULDN'T SHIFT the nagging feeling about the spiral shapes that had been cut into both victims' hands. It was the only part of the case that threw her main suspects out of the ring. There was no reaction when the shape was mentioned to Dylan Wilkins. Based on how the interview had gone, and Wilkins' agitated responses, Ruth presumed that he would have had a strong, visible reaction if he had cut that symbol in either victims' hands. However, he didn't. He just looked baffled by the question and that was a worry.

Ruth had been researching the spiral as an ancient Druid or Celtic symbol for a few minutes just to see it for herself. However, she got side-tracked. Featured on her Google search were results that showed that the spiral symbol had been used in modern television programmes. In *Game of Thrones*, she read that the White Walkers positioned corpses in a spiral shape and that the Children of the Forest also used spiral shapes in rituals. In both cases, the spiral was used to show that a past wrong was remembered and retaliation would happen. Ruth had never seen *Game of Thrones*. It was all too Tolkienesque with its goblins, dragons and magic nonsense. She preferred her TV drama gritty and realistic.

As Ruth continued to search, she also found that a popular supernatural television series called *Teen Wolf* also used the spiral symbol in a significant way. Again, the spiral was used to represent revenge, this time amongst werewolves. Ruth didn't know the series but remembered the film from the 1980s, which she thought Michael J Fox starred in. Were they looking in the wrong place when it came to the spiral? It seemed a bit of a stretch but may be worth flagging up.

Ruth took a few steps into Incident Room 1 and she took off her jacket. The spring sunshine was burning through the huge windows and warming the room up like an oven. Ruth hung her jacket on the back of her chair and paused a moment. She needed to know where to go next in the investigation but she felt pulled in different directions and it was frustrating her.

Earlier in the morning they had spoken to the 'charming' Lucas Brown, Bronwyn Wright's neighbour. Ginger and thick-set, Brown was a barman in the Crown pub and had snorted at the idea that he had waved at Bronwyn Wright and Dylan Wilkins. He described them to officers as 'freaks of nature' and claimed that, had they tried to wave and talk to him, he would have 'knocked them out'. So, that meant Bronwyn Wright and Dylan Wilkins had no alibi for the time of Neerav Banerjee's murder, and Wilkins' alibi for the time of Arabella Dixon's death was vague and confused. Bronwyn Wright had lied yet again about what she was doing at the time of the Banerjee murder. She was covering up something.

Mac walked into the room and looked over at Ruth. He had been over to Dinas Padog High School to talk to Mike Gardener. Ruth was making sure that there was distance between Nick and his uncle within the case, just so there could be no accusation that it had been compromised.

Mac, now in his shirt sleeves because of the heat in the building, looked red and sweaty so Ruth knew that he must have taken the stairs.

Mac was a little breathless. 'Boss, Mike Gardener says that Dylan Wilkins didn't ask him if he could borrow a dust mask from work. However, he said that there were half a dozen knocking about so he couldn't tell if someone had taken one. As for Dylan Wilkins' whereabouts on the evening of Arabella Dixon's murder, Gardener confirmed that Wilkins was working on the boiler. He took him tea and biscuits at seven fifteen and Wilkins was where he said he was. But, get this, he said Wilkins had been outside because he was wet from the rain.'

Ruth took a moment. 'So are we thinking that Dylan Wilkins was working on the boiler as he says, but before seven fifteen he leaves and pours acidic drain cleaner onto Arabella Dixon's car. Then he returns to where he was, unaware that the rain shows that he had been outside.'

Mac nodded. 'Sounds about right. However, that would put paid to our theory about Arabella Dixon discovering Dylan Wilkins in the act, confronting him and that leading to her death.'

'Doesn't mean Dylan Wilkins is innocent. By the sounds of it, he was free to come and go from the boiler room all evening,' Ruth said.

'That's how it sounded to me, boss.'

'Thanks, Mac.'

Ruth went over to the water cooler and got some water. The codeine had worn off, and it had left her dry-mouthed.

Merringer put down the phone, got up and approached her.

'Boss, I don't know if this has any relevance to us, but Graham Williams has been reported this afternoon as a missing person,' Merringer informed her.

'Why does Graham Williams' name keep popping up like a bad smell?' Ruth asked, half to herself.

'Williams rang Dinas Padog High School last Thursday and said he wasn't able to go in. He said that he was finding events at the school difficult to cope with. He said he needed a couple of days to deal with the grief and stress. There was no word from him on Friday, despite the school's absence policy. Apparently, it's out of character. He failed to meet friends for a walk from Corwen to Pen y Pigyn. It's a weekly thing and he has always contacted someone if he couldn't make it.'

'Wife, kids?' Ruth asked, thinking out loud.

'Nope. Lives alone and always has. His mum, who lives up in Anglesey, has been trying his mobile for days with no reply. Eventually his sister rang the station a few hours ago because she was so worried.'

'I assume a uniformed patrol is going around there?' Ruth asked.

'Yes, boss. They should be there by now.'

'Okay, thanks, Luke. Let me know if you hear anything.'

Ruth went outside for a ciggie and some fresh air to clear her head. The irony of that wasn't lost on her but she knew the combination worked. A short while later she walked into the lift on the ground floor and pressed the button for floor six. As she entered the incident room, she saw Nick had returned and was now at his computer.

'How was Noakes?' Ruth asked.

'Jittery. And he looked like shit too,' Nick said.

'I'm sure he speaks very highly of you too,' Ruth said with a grin as she looked over his shoulder at his computer.

'What's this?' Ruth asked pointing at the screen.

Nick spun around in his chair and looked at her.

'I went to the garage on the way back just to check out the car that Jonathan and Alex Noakes were driving when they were in the accident yesterday. Turns out that it was Alex driving his car. I wondered if it had one of those black boxes young drivers use to keep their insurance premiums down.'

'And?' Ruth said in a tone that implied 'get to the point'.

'Alex Noakes did have a black box fitted to his car. So, I took it.'

'Without a search warrant?' Ruth raised an eyebrow.

Nick shrugged with a smile, 'Technically I don't need one if it's out of the car, and they didn't ask for one.' Nick pointed to the screen. 'This is the GPS data that shows every journey the car has made with the date, distance and location. Here we have the journeys for Monday the seventeenth of March. At four o'clock, Alex Noakes leaves Llandderfelm, where he is staying with Rhiannon Baker's family, and drives towards Llanfihangel Glyn Myfyr and parks here, which is a car park in Clocaenog Forest. It's used by dog walkers, mountain bikers, and there's a dirt bike trail. Alex arrives at four twenty. It's about a ten-minute walk from the forest to the back of Neerav Banerjee's house,' Nick explained.

'Jesus. And then he sits and waits for Neerav Banerjee to come home from school and then murders him? Very cold.' Ruth asked rhetorically.

'Then we chase him out the back here, up into Clocaenog Forest and up to the disused mine. He must have found a way out of the mine, waited and walked back to his car. Alex then drives over to Corwen, where his father lives. Stays there for two hours and then drives back to Llandderfel.'

'Do we think Jonathan Noakes is in on this or at least knows?' Ruth asked.

'I'm not sure.' Nick shrugged.

'Right, we question Alex now. No warning, no picking him up and coming back to the station. We take him by surprise,' Ruth said heading for her office to get her jacket.

As Ruth came out, she looked around, 'Anyone know anything about the series *Teen Wolf*?' she asked loudly to the incident room.

Merringer moved around on his chair. 'My daughter watches it and is completely hooked. She watches three or four episodes at a time. Why?'

'What is it?' Ruth said with a frown.

'Some sort of teen horror series about werewolves. Never seen it, like, but that's the gist I think, boss,' Merringer explained, looking lost as to why she was asking.

'Thanks, Luke. Come on,' Ruth said as she walked past Nick who was still sitting at his desk.

Merringer shot Nick a look as if to say, 'What is she on about?' Nick shrugged and grinned.

'*Teen Wolf*? Never had you down as a horror fan, boss. More rom com?' Nick smiled.

'Sexist stereotype.'

'True. But Richard Curtis should be publicly flogged.'

'Fair point. Who do we know who does like horror?' Ruth asked him.

Nick thought for a second. 'Alex Noakes. Horror t-shirts. Why is that relevant?'

'I'll explain in the car. You drive, I'll smoke,' Ruth said as they went down to the corridor towards the lifts.

CHAPTER 35

LLANDDERFEL WAS ABOUT twenty minutes down the A5 from Llancastell and on the way Ruth had, as promised, smoked and explained her research about the spiral symbol.

Llandderfel was a small village in Gwynedd on the Upper Dee Valley. It used to be known for its railway station, which had been on the Ruabon to Barmouth line. This closed in 1965 because of flooding when the River Dee burst its banks, and the whole line was never reopened again. Now there was virtually no trace of the station or its buildings except for the flight of steps that led from the road overbridge down to where the platforms once were. If you looked closely enough there was a small section of platform, overgrown with weeds, a few yards along from the steps.

The day was balmy and Ruth looked over at Nick, who now had on his black Ray Ban Wayfarers. What a poser! Ruth remembered when they were a thing the first time round and thought of Wham's *Club Tropicana*.

Looking out of the window for a moment, Ruth could see that everywhere seemed to be starting the bloom of spring and the sky had a soft blue glow to it. The countryside was being resurrected in splashes of bright colour. *This is when North Wales must come into its own*, Ruth thought.

Nick told her that there weren't many places on this planet that could rival the scenery of Snowdonia National Park. He told her about his mate Ben who had been travelling and went to New Zealand. He described it as Snowdonia on steroids. He said he regretted travelling twelve thousand miles and spending twenty-seven hours on a plane to get to a place that looked just like home, only a bit bigger.

Their car pulled up slowly onto the open yard of Gethen Baker's sheep farm where Rhiannon Baker and Alex Noakes now lived.

Ruth noticed that the Baker family also rented out farm cottages to tourists keen to walk in Snowdonia or fish for salmon in the Dee.

They got out of the car. The surface of the yard was uneven and full of potholes filled with muddy water and sheep manure, which Ruth tried to avoid. The smell was thick and overpowering, especially in the heat. She walked over to the farmhouse, trying to step over the muck as best she could, and found that the black-painted door was half open.

Ruth wrinkled her nose, 'Eau de sheep shit.'

'Fruity. Don't worry, you get used to it, boss.'

Nick knocked loudly, opened the door fully, and called, 'Hello, anyone in?'

Nick took a few steps forward and Ruth followed, peering in.

The kitchen was what she would expect in a farmhouse. Cold and uneven stone floor, huge oak table and chairs. To the left was an old cream Aga and a steel kettle sitting on it. Beside that there was a traditional Welsh dresser full of an assortment of china.

The place seemed silent and deserted. Ruth watched Nick as he went to the table and felt a half-empty mug of coffee.

'It's cold,' Nick said.

Ruth raised her eyebrows, 'So what?'

'Dunno. I saw it in a film once. Means that it's been a while since anyone was in here. Always wanted to say it.' Nick shrugged.

Ruth shook her head, 'All right bloody Columbo, any other little tricks up your sleeve?'

There was the sound of someone coming down the creaky wooden staircase. Before they could say anything, Alex shuffled into the kitchen in a navy dressing gown.

'Hi Alex,' Ruth said. She had hoped to startle him a little. The more scared he was, the more likely he would tell them the truth.

Instead of jumping, he looked at them vacantly, walked over to the Aga, shook the kettle to check there was water in it and placed it on the hot iron hob.

'It's all right, I saw you arrive. What do you want?' he said in a jaded tone. 'Has there been anything more about who killed my mum?'

Nick looked over at Alex – below his navy robe he was wearing pink slippers, but his heels were peeking over the edge.

'Nice slippers. Don't look like they fit though,' Nick said.

'What?' Alex growled.

'What size are your feet, Alex?' Nick asked.

'Erm ... nine,' Alex frowned, and went to get a mug out of the cupboard.

'What about your dad? What size feet does he have?' Nick asked.

'What are you talking about?' Alex said, and shook his head as he headed back to the Aga.

'Humour him, Alex. Sergeant Evans has a foot fetish,' Ruth said.

'Size ten,' Alex said under his breath, confused.

Ruth went over, pulled out a chair by the oak table and gestured, 'Why don't you take a seat, Alex.'

'Do I have to?' Alex was still half asleep and half stoned.

'I think you'd be more comfortable,' Nick suggested.

Alex went with a reluctant nod to the chair, sat down, took out some rolling tobacco and rizlas and made a cigarette.

'Alex, we know that you drove towards Llanfihangel Glyn Myfyr last Monday at around four thirty and parked in Gwydir Forest. That's half an hour before Neerav Banerjee was murdered,' Ruth explained in her gentle maternal tone.

Alex processed this for a moment and then frowned. 'No. Must be a mistake.'

'We have proof that your car went from here to Gwydir Forest at four twenty last Monday afternoon,' Ruth said.

'Well, I didn't drive there.' Alex seemed adamant as he shrugged.

'Come on, Alex. We have the black box from your car. There's a GPS tracker in there that tells when, where, and at what time you drove anywhere,' Nick explained impatiently.

'It must be wrong. Ask Rhiannon.' Alex shook his head. He lit the rolled cigarette and then looked at the floor as though something was troubling him.

'Alex, we have the evidence from the black box that is attached to the car. It's there in black and white,' Ruth said quietly.

'It couldn't have been me.' Alex was confused.

'Why couldn't it have been you, Alex?' Ruth asked.

Alex scratched the stubble on this face for a moment and then took a drag of his cigarette. He now seemed to be hiding something.

'Why couldn't it have been you, Alex? It's your car and it's fitted with a black box. The car was there and it didn't drive itself, did it?' Nick's tone was direct.

'I wasn't here. I was ...' Alex stopped again and avoided eye contact. He took a deep breath and sat back.

'You weren't here? What does that mean, Alex?' Ruth asked.

'It doesn't matter. It's fine. I ...' Alex's mind was racing.

'Come on, Alex. If you weren't at Clocaenog Forest who was, and where were you?' Nick asked impatiently.

'I was with Rhiannon. I was in her car. I ...I ... I was driving her car.' Alex seemed confused.

'And where was this?' Ruth asked, unsure of what to make of Alex's responses that seemed genuine.

'We were in Chester. You can ask her,' Alex replied.

'Can you prove you were in Chester?' Nick said.

Alex thought for a moment, 'Erm, no. I don't know. Do I have to?'

'Alex, your car was driven and parked close to where Neerav Banerjee was murdered. It was there at the time of his death. Yes, you do need to prove to us that you weren't in the car or we will take you back to Llancastell.' Ruth sounded like a reproachful teacher.

Alex put his hands up dramatically and blurted, 'Okay! Okay! I need to go upstairs then.'

'We need to come with you,' Ruth said. She didn't want him leaping from a top window or harming himself.

Alex nodded and headed for the door. They followed him upstairs and into a small bedroom that belonged to a teenage girl – soft pastel colours, make-up dresser and mirror.

Alex got a piece of paper that he handed to Ruth. It was from the BPAS in Chester. At the top of the letter was a blue letterhead: *British Pregnancy Advisory Service*. There was an appointment time for Rhiannon Baker which was printed as 3.30pm on Monday.

'I drove Rhiannon to Chester for her appointment and then back afterwards. We took her car because it's more comfortable,' Alex explained.

'She's pregnant?' Ruth asked.

Alex took a moment. 'Not anymore. That's why I had to be with her and drive her home. You can ring them and they'll tell you I was with her the whole time.'

Ruth passed the piece of paper to Nick as a sign he should phone them now to verify Alex's alibi. Nick left the bedroom and headed out onto the landing.

'You took Rhiannon to have an abortion?' Ruth asked gently.

'Yeah,' Alex muttered under his breath.

Alex seemed genuinely confused and troubled. Either he was telling the truth, or he was a sociopath with a gift for lying.

'Alex, you need to help us here. Who else drives your car?' Ruth asked.

Alex blinked as his mind raced. 'No one,' he said, but he was already processing the answer to that question in his head so his tone was unconvincing.

'Is your dad insured to drive your car?' Ruth asked.

'Yeah, of course. He bought the car. So what?' Alex replied defensively.

Nick stuck his head back into the room. 'Boss, someone matching Alex's description was at the BPAS in Chester from three thirty until about five on Monday.'

Ruth looked Alex in the eye. 'Does your dad use your car, Alex?'

'No, not really.' Alex was lying through his teeth.

'Does your dad use your car, Alex?' Ruth's tone was now challenging.

'Yes, sometimes. Only sometimes though. It wasn't him.' Alex sat down on the bed and put his head in his hands.

'Alex, do you know if your dad is at his house in Corwen today?' Nick asked.

'No, he's not.' Alex shook his head and looked at the floor.

'No? Where is he?' Ruth asked.

'He's in France,' Alex replied.

'Why is he in France?' Ruth was now worried that Noakes had fled the country.

'It's a business thing. I dunno.'

'When does he come back?'

'Sometime tonight. He said he'd see me tomorrow dinnertime,' Alex mumbled.

'Okay. We need to speak to him about your car,' Ruth explained. 'And we may need to speak to you again. Do you understand, Alex?'

Alex nodded as he flicked ash into a coffee mug on the table, " Yeah.'

AS SOON AS RUTH AND Nick got back, she alerted officers in CID that Noakes was now their prime suspect again but she wanted them to keep pursuing lines of enquiry for Dylan Wilkins and Bronwyn Wright.

Ruth ran stuff past Drake but kept Jones out of the loop until after they had spoken to Noakes. Jones was a prick, and she was going to solve this case without his smart remarks.

Clearly, they weren't going to wait until tomorrow to get to Noakes but she was relying on Alex to call his father to warn him that the police would be round the following day regarding the journey to Clocaenog Forest. Ruth told Nick that it might spook Jonathan Noakes into doing something reckless and they would be there to see what happened. They would pay him a surprise visit that evening.

Ruth contacted the control centre at Manchester Airport and spoke to an officer in the UK Border Force. Within twenty minutes they had searched the passenger lists and informed Ruth that Noakes was arriving from Nantes at four thirty that afternoon. She calculated that it would take him twenty minutes to get through customs and pick up his car. Then an hour and a half to drive home from Manchester. She and Nick would be sitting close by at six o'clock to welcome him home.

Half an hour later, Mac knocked on her open door.

'Something to show you, boss.'

Ruth got up and followed Mac over to his computer screen. There was a very grainy image, but it was some kind of CCTV footage. However, it was distorted by water.

'What's this?' Ruth asked gesturing to the screen.

'It's the footage from the rear car park at Ysgol Dinas Padog on the night that Arabella Dixon was murdered,' Mac explained.

The time code showed it was: *19.56pm Thursday 13 March 2017.*

'I thought this was unusable. And from the looks of it, it is.' Ruth looked at Mac wondering at the relevance.

'This morning the Tech boys downstairs gave me this footage. They had sent it off to a place that Merseyside Police use. It's a forensic video enhancement place that specialises in CCTV. They've cleaned it up as best they could,' Mac clarified.

The image on the screen had been paused.

'Well they've done an awful job,' Ruth said.

'Look here, boss.' Mac was pointing to a dark shape by the wall of the car park. As Ruth looked carefully, she could see that it was clearly a figure. However, there was little else that could be gained from the image. Mac forwarded the footage, and at 19.59pm, the figure moves. However, the rest of the image is so grainy that a second later all that can be seen is the fuzzy darkness.

'That was our killer,' Ruth said quietly and looked at Mac. It was chilling to see a person standing there, waiting to murder Arabella Dixon.

'Yes, boss.'

'Okay.' Ruth frowned. 'Mac, we can't see anything. It's just a black shape. Is there no way of enhancing this more?' Ruth sounded impatient.

'Sorry, boss. That's the best we're gonna get.' Mac shrugged.

'Shit! We can't see anything that helps us.' Ruth was thinking out loud.

'Wait, look at this, boss.' Mac rewound the footage back to where the figure is standing and waiting by the wall. 'Can you see that there is a white square here on the wall? That's a school sign about the use of minibus parking bays. And the figure's head is almost directly below the bottom of the sign.'

Ruth saw where Mac was going with this, 'So we can work out how tall our killer is within an inch or two?'

'Luke and I went to the school and measured the sign. It's five feet and seven inches from ground level,' Mac explained.

'Bloody hell, Mac. That's brilliant,' Ruth exclaimed.

'Luke and I think that if we consider the angle of the camera, and the fact that the killer might not be standing against the wall, it gives us a height range of five foot six to five foot nine.'

Ruth put her hand on Mac's shoulder, 'That rules out Dylan Wilkins. He's got to be nearly six foot.' Ruth's mind was racing. 'But Alex Noakes is around five eight.'

Ruth looked over at Nick and shouted, 'Nick, how tall is Jonathan Noakes?'

'Five eight, five nine at a guess,' Nick replied.

Ruth patted Mac on the shoulder. 'Great work, Mac.'

'Actually, it was Luke who saw the sign,' Mac admitted.

'Okay.' Ruth turned and headed back towards her office. It was such a bonus to have experienced officers like Mac and Merringer on the team.

'Boss?' Mac said and she turned around. 'Daniel Hughes was over six foot.'

'Yeah, I know ...' Ruth said solemnly.

CHAPTER 36

IT WAS JUST BEFORE six o'clock when Nick and Ruth pulled up close to Jonathan Noakes' house. Ruth had received a call from the control station of the Border Force at Manchester Airport. Noakes' flight was on time and he had passed through customs.

The village of Carrog used to be known as Llansanffraid-Glyn Dyfrdwy because it lay within the parish boundaries of Llansanffraid Glyndyfrdwy. It was situated beside the River Dee. Between their car and Noakes' cottage were two huge aluminium buildings attached to the adjacent farm. Old farming equipment lay rusting in the yard to one side of the buildings. Noakes' white cottage was fifty yards up the hill.

From where Ruth sat, the Berwyn mountains rose to the right and were covered in dark pine trees. Behind them, the sun was setting and the sky was starting to tint with orange and pink light.

Ruth looked out at the setting sun behind the mountain tops. There was a comfortable silence in the car for a while. The day had been busy and they'd both been on the go for twelve hours. A moment's peace was what they both needed.

'It's stunning, isn't it?' Ruth said of the view.

'Yeah, we do all right. I grew up here, so it's all I know,' Nick said.

'Lucky you.'

'Uncle Mike once said to me, "The problem with you, Nick, is that you don't look at the world. Not really look. Instead you just drive through it, while your mind makes excuses for why you should be so miserable. You need to sit for a moment and look. And even better, you need to find someone to sit with," Nick said.

'But you've never found anyone to sit with?' Ruth asked.

'No. I'm not wired properly. I'm still full of the ISM.'

Ruth frowned. 'What's the "ISM"?'

'I, self, me. It's all about me and always will be until I grow up,' Nick explained.

'I hear you. My daughter's far more mature than I'll ever be.'

'And you've never found someone to sit with?' Nick asked.

Ruth paused for a moment, thinking that the easiest answer would be no. But she trusted Nick now. 'There was someone. Sarah. But she got on a train four years ago and vanished?'

Nick frowned. 'Vanished? How do you mean?'

'Gone, just like that. Nothing. No clues, nothing.' Ruth clicked her fingers. 'I'm a copper so you can imagine I've tried everything. Every scrap of CCTV, every sighting, every agency.'

'Jesus. That's terrible. How do you deal with something like that?'

'I don't. Well, I do sometimes, but often I don't.'

Nick looked at her and she gave him a forced smile. She took a breath.

'I need a smoke,' she said, fishing for one in her handbag. 'I'm sorry, boss.'

Ruth nodded and she lit her cigarette. 'Please don't feel sorry for me, Nick. That's not why I told you. Okay?'

'Yeah, of course.' Nick nodded.

Ruth smoked the cigarette for a minute. Then she took a deep drag and blew a smoke ring out of the passenger window.

'Nice trick,' Nick said.

'Hey, and who said smoking wasn't cool?'

They both gazed out at the sky and clouds, which were now awash with hues of pink, crimson, plum, magenta and burnt orange. Black silhouettes of birds rose from the trees.

Suddenly there was a noise as Noakes' white Audi A5 came past them, up the hill and onto the gravel driveway that was to the right of the house.

Ruth looked at her watch. 'Right on cue.'

'How long do we wait?' Nick asked.

'Give him a few minutes to make a cup of tea. Then we'll go and bang on his door nice and loud and really make his day.'

Ruth's phone rang and the number recognition showed it was Llancastell Police Station. It was Sian and, listening, Ruth nodded while taking in the information and then hung up.

Ruth looked at Nick. 'Uniform went round to Graham Williams' flat. When there wasn't any answer, they borrowed a key off a neighbour and let themselves in. They found him unconscious, with a nasty gash on his head. Apparently, there was blood everywhere. He's been raced to the hospital, but he's still unconscious.'

'Was he attacked?' Nick asked.

'They don't know. Deep cut on his temple. Could have been a fall or he could have been hit.'

Nick frowned. 'Think it's anything to do with this?'

'His name keeps coming up and I don't believe in coincidences,' Ruth said and then undid her seatbelt. 'Come on, Tonto, let's go.'

'Tonto?' Nick asked.

'Oh God bless you. Too young to remember *The Lone Ranger*?' Ruth said as she got out of the car.

They walked up the hill towards Noakes' cottage. A couple of inquisitive sheep ambled over to the fence to watch them.

When they arrived there were no lights on. Nick knocked on the door. There was the distinct smell of smoke in the air, which wasn't unusual in the countryside in the evening.

Nick knocked again while Ruth peered through the window to the right of the front door. The cottage looked deserted. Where was Noakes?

Nick shot Ruth a look and then walked backwards and looked up at the first-floor windows to check for movement. Nothing. Then his eyes were pulled up into the dusky night sky and a plume of black smoke that was swirling upwards. It looked like it was coming from the back of the cottage.

Nick moved quickly. 'Boss, round the back.'

Nick jogged down the side of the cottage, unlatched the wooden gate and turned into the garden. Ruth followed close behind.

In the middle of a sizeable garden was a large fire in a steel bin. Noakes was standing beside it, pouring petrol from a can. Orange flames leapt and crackled. Noakes looked up, saw them, bent down and picked up a laptop that lay beside him on the grass.

'Don't!' Ruth shouted.

Noakes tossed the laptop into the fire and stood back to admire his handiwork.

Ruth and Nick approached and Noakes looked at them. He put his hands up in a gesture of surrender. He walked slowly towards them and looked defeated.

'I can't do this anymore. I'm too tired,' Noakes said weakly.

Ruth looked in the fire and saw the laptop, clothing, and papers. 'Jonathan Noakes. I'm arresting you on the suspicion of the murder of Arabella Dixon and Neerav Banerjee. You do not have to—'

At that moment, Noakes launched himself forwards and shoved Ruth with all his weight. She lurched backwards, lost her footing and tumbled onto the grass. Before Nick had time to react, Noakes had punched him hard in the face and Nick went down.

Noakes sprinted from the garden. As Ruth sat up, she saw Nick get to his knees, still reeling from the punch. Ruth got up quickly.

'Come on!' Ruth yelled as she ran across the lawn. Nick hauled himself up and followed her.

As they got to the side of the cottage, there was the sound of a car engine and then the squeal of tyres.

'Shit!' Ruth shouted.

Nick and Ruth were now sprinting down the hill towards their car.

Nick clicked his radio. 'This is DS Evans. In pursuit of suspect, Jonathan Noakes. In a white Audi A-five, registration J-N-one thousand, heading west out of Carrog on the B-five-four-three-seven. Over.'

Nick and Ruth got into the car. Nick turned the ignition and hit the accelerator, spinning the wheels as they set off in pursuit of Noakes.

'Let's get this bastard,' said Ruth.

'Yes, boss,' Nick said as he hit 60 mph. He was enjoying the feeling of power from driving fast as they hit 80.

Ruth gripped the door handle with one hand and the front of the passenger seat with the other as they screamed around the bend.

Nick sat forwards a little, peering through the windscreen. 'Where are you, you bastard?'

Noakes' Audi came into view, speeding up a hill about a mile ahead.

Ruth felt the Astra's back tyres losing grip and slipping as they cornered another bend.

Nick looked over at her. 'You've gone white, boss.'

'Not a big fan of high-speed pursuits if I'm honest,' Ruth admitted as her stomach lurched.

Nick smiled. 'One of the best things about the job. There he is.'

Nick went hammering up the hill, and over the crest. Noakes' Audi was now only about half a mile ahead, and they were gaining. He pulled out to overtake a car towing a caravan, which went past in a blur.

Ruth was trying to replay Noakes' admission of guilt in her head but Llancastell's Dispatch crackled on the radio.

'Three-six. Unit Tango-two-one is now heading east on B-five-four-three-seven to assist.'

'Received ... Sod that. Noakes is ours,' Nick said with steely determination, as he dropped the car into third when they reached a long hill.

'Do we think he's heading somewhere or just driving to escape?' Ruth asked as she was thrown against the door and then back again.

'Driving to escape, boss,' Nick said.

Ruth knew that Noakes wouldn't stop now and would be driven on by fear and adrenaline.

'DS Evans. Suspect now heading north on the A-four-nine-four. One mile south of Llanelliden. Speed nine-zero.'

A moment later, they screamed through the tiny hamlet of Llandelliden. They were going so fast that Ruth felt that the houses and stone walls were only inches from the passenger door.

Suddenly, a tractor pulled out of a field in front of them. Nick pulled the car onto the opposite side of the road, missing it by a few feet.

'For God's sake!' Nick said.

Ruth thought that she didn't want to die today and closed her eyes for a second as they careered around a bend. She opened her eyes again and a red sign that read Arafwch

Nawr – *Reduce speed now!* went past in a flash. *If only,* thought Ruth.

Noakes' Audi was now only five hundred yards away. It pulled out to overtake and whizzed past two cars. However, as Nick pulled out to do the same, there was a huge articulated lorry coming the other way. Ruth squinted and looked – there just wasn't enough time or space to get past the second car. Nick dropped down into third gear and the Astra roared uncomfortably, but the boost in speed bought them a couple of extra seconds and they made it past with inches to spare.

'Shit!' Nick said as he stared fiercely ahead at the Audi, which was now only two hundred yards ahead.

'Just don't lose him,' Ruth replied.

If they lost Noakes now, he might disappear and go into hiding somewhere.

Suddenly, a tractor pulled slowly out of a field in front of them. Noakes' brake lights glared bright red as he slammed on the brakes.

'Shit!' Nick shouted, as he hit the brakes hard.

As their Astra skidded, Ruth glanced out and saw that Noakes had swerved to avoid the tractor. However, he had clipped the front of it, lost control, and the Audi flipped over twice, landing on its roof.

Ruth felt like everything in her body was contracting as the car skidded at speed. She instinctively pulled her knees up and screwed her eyes closed. A metallic thud threw her forwards. The cracking sound of glass. Now they were travelling backwards. There was another bang of metal and crunch of glass and they came to a stop.

Ruth blinked open her eyes and immediately looked over at Nick. He looked back, blood running from a cut in this forehead.

'You all right?' she gasped.

'I think so. You?' he said looking dazed.

'Sore neck. Otherwise okay,' Ruth said.

Nick tried to open the door but it wouldn't open. He pulled the rear-view mirror across and looked at Noakes' white Audi that was on its roof a hundred and fifty yards behind them.

'Noakes!' Nick said.

Ruth opened the passenger door, got out and steadied herself. Nick eased himself across the gear stick, onto the passenger seat and then out.

Without speaking, they both ran towards the Audi. Black smoke was coming from the bonnet.

Nick got to the Audi first. He could instantly smell petrol and knew the car might explode.

He crouched and peered inside the car. Noakes was lying unconscious, upside down, his head against the steering wheel. His face was covered in blood. Nick scampered around to the driver's side. He tried the door, but it didn't budge. Ruth arrived.

'Get back, boss. There's petrol everywhere,' Nick warned her while frantically trying the door.

'What about you? Let me help you,' Ruth said crouching down.

'Boss, please get back. If this thing goes up, there is no point us both dying,' Nick thundered. He looked over at her. 'Please. I've got this.'

Ruth backed away and immediately got on the phone to call for an ambulance and assistance. She watched as Nick put his feet against the side of the car to give himself leverage. He then yanked the driver's door again. Nothing. He tried again and the metal gave a little.

Ruth looked at the back of the car and saw petrol dripping onto the road. The fuel tank must have fractured or the fuel line split. 'There's petrol leaking!' she yelled.

Nick wasn't listening. He yanked at the door again with all his bodyweight and suddenly the door creaked and swung open. Nick reached inside and across Noakes' body, frantically trying to find the release button for the seatbelt. Noakes' leg was in the way, and Nick knew that time was running out. He pushed with his fingers, managed to get past Noakes' leg, and released the seat belt.

The body fell from the driver's seat where it had been hanging, landing on top of Nick and pinning him down. He was stuck, with Noakes' whole bodyweight pressing him against the dashboard. There was another waft of petrol. *This is so not how I want to die,* Nick thought.

He took a breath, pushed Noakes, and slid at the same time, freeing himself out of the car. He reached back in, got hold of both of Noakes' arms and pulled him from the car onto the road. His head bounced on the metal of the car and then onto the road surface. Turning, Nick heaved Noakes to the other side of the road where Ruth was sitting on the kerbside.

Nick crouched and felt for a pulse.

'He's still alive. I'm not sure how,' Nick said, as he slumped down next to Ruth.

'Good. I want him alive,' Ruth said.

'Christ, he was heavy,' Nick said.

'Have you read him his rights?' Ruth asked with an exhausted smile.

'Piss off. Sorry ... I mean piss off, boss,' Nick said with a weary grin.

'We got him. We bloody well got him.' Ruth smiled and playfully hit Nick's shoulder.

'We certainly did. Thank God for farmers and their stupid tractors, eh? Where the hell did you learn to drive like that?' Ruth asked.

'Xbox,' Nick said with a smirk. Ruth laughed. He was sharp, she'd give him that.

Suddenly Ruth jumped as the fuel ignited. *Vump!* A ball of orange and yellow flame mushroomed up into the dark sky, followed by thick black smoke as the car crackled with flames.

Ruth felt the heat on her face. In the distance, a siren wailed. Nothing mattered now. They had their man.

CHAPTER 37

THERE WAS AN EXCITED buzz in the incident room. Most of the CID detectives were smiling, laughing, and generally looking pleased with themselves at the result. It had been an unusual and challenging case for them all, and they were exhausted. Smooth FM was playing somewhere and Wham!'s *Everything She Wants* boomed out.

Ruth and Nick, now cleaned up, were in her office having a moment of peace before heading out to join the others. As a matter of course, the Independent Police Complaints Commission, IPCC, would be investigating the crash and would ask any witnesses to come forward. Ruth wasn't worried though, as she knew there was a justifiable rationale for the pursuit. Noakes was wanted in connection with two murders and had attempted to escape. There were no failings in the high-speed pursuit, and Noakes' crash was an accident because of the speed he had been driving at.

They had taken Noakes to Llancastell University Hospital, but he was in a coma so was transferred to the Walton Centre in Liverpool, which specialised in head trauma and neurosurgery. Ruth had contacted Merseyside Police, asking that a uniformed officer be posted with Noakes. If he regained consciousness, they were to contact her.

They had also had a call to report that Graham Williams was diabetic and had developed severe hypoglycaemia while at home. He had mistaken the symptoms as being caused by the stress and trauma of losing two colleagues at school. Williams had fainted, hit his head on a table and gone into a diabetic coma, which is why no one could contact him. He was in the hospital in Llancastell and was likely to make a full recovery.

Ruth felt a fantastic sense of relief as her eye caught the whiteboards that stood to one side of Major Incident Room 1. The photos of Arabella Dixon and Neerav Banerjee at their centres.

'It's over,' Ruth said, half to herself.

'It is, boss.' Nick smiled.

'Maybe the families can get some kind of peace,' Ruth said quietly.

Nick nodded. 'At least they can start to plan their funerals now. It's a start, isn't it?'

Ruth stood up from her seat, took off her jacket and looked at Nick.

'Next week I want a stolen tractor or quad bike and that's it,' Ruth said wearily.

'A Welsh farmer was out tending his flock when he saw a man drinking from a stream with a cupped hand,' Nick started.

'Oh, here we go.' Ruth rolled her eyes.

'Listen, boss,' Nick said. 'He shouts over in Welsh: "Don't drink the water, mate! It's disgusting! There's sheep piss and shit in there!" The man just carries on drinking. So, this farmer, Dai—'

'Oh, Dai, now is it?' Ruth grinned.

'Yeah. Dai moves closer and shouts the same thing in Welsh again. But still the man doesn't hear him. So, finally Dai walked right up to him and repeated his warning. To which the man replied: "Dreadfully sorry, I can't understand a word you say. Can you speak English, old bean?"

'"Oh, I see," says Dai now in English, like. "I was just saying if you use both hands you can get more in."'

Ruth laughed and shook her head. 'Racist! Stick to solving crime, Nick.'

'Aye. Will do, boss.'

Merringer walked into the incident room with a crate of lager, followed by Sian who cracked open one bottle of prosecco, with another tucked under her arm. There were shouts of 'Yay!' and 'Get in!'

Ruth looked at Nick. 'Come on. Let's not miss the party.'

Ruth and Nick walked into the incident room and there were more cheers. Sian walked over with a can of beer for Nick and a plastic cup of prosecco for Ruth.

'Not for me, Sian, ta,' Nick said.

'Come on, Nick,' Sian persisted.

'Cheers, Sian.' Ruth held up her drink and Sian 'clinked' her plastic cup against it.

'Cheers, boss. Good result.' Sian smiled and she turned back to the party.

Nick gave Ruth a knowing look.

'Sian got a boyfriend?' Ruth asked.

'Don't think so. Why, you interested, boss?'

'Don't be a twat, Nick.' Ruth laughed, although having no boyfriend did make her more interesting.

Wham!'s signature beats faded and were replaced by Pat Benatar's *Love is a Battlefield*.

Ruth's face brightened and she shouted, 'I love this! Turn it up!' She turned to Nick. 'Before you were born, Nicholas.'

Mac walked over and cranked up the music as Ruth moved over to where all the detectives were chatting and laughing.

The song began to build to the opening lyrics, and Ruth and those detectives who were old enough to remember the song, sang and put their hands in the air.

Nick watched for a moment and smiled as Ruth and Sian danced and sang together.

Nick gave in and walked over, joining in as the voices crescendoed into the chorus.

CHAPTER 38

IT WAS A BEAUTIFUL spring morning. The watery light of dawn was being replaced by darker hues of blue as the sun burnt away the clouds. The tight pink buds on the trees that lined this section of the A5 were beginning to burst open.

The road was relatively empty at this time of the morning and Nick enjoyed the feeling of freedom he got from cycling. Plus, he was smug knowing that most of CID would be hungover today – but not him. It was mornings like this that reminded him what life was like without booze. He smiled. He was going to have a good day.

On his ride, Nick had started by passing signs to Swallow Falls. Swallow Falls was located on Afon Llugwy near Betws-y-Coed, in Conwy County Borough. Nick had heard that the English name arose from people mishearing the Welsh word *ewynnol,* which translates as 'foaming' with the similar-sounding *y wennol,* which means 'swallow'. He thought that was typical of the English.

Ten minutes later, he passed Penrhyn Slate Quarry, now home to Zip World which, according to the large roadside signs, was the fastest zip wire in the world and the longest in Europe.

Taking a tight bend, Nick was now flanked by grey slate walls on both sides of the road. As the road rose higher, he could see the sparkling River Afon Llugwy, which was a trib-

utary of the River Conwy. The dark water foamed and bub-
bled white where it rose over rocks and fallen branches. Its
source was Ffynnon Llugwy, a lake in the Carneddau range
of mountains further into Snowdonia.

Eventually Nick got to the turning for the A4806, and
within minutes the spectacular sight of Lake Llyn Ogwen
was to his right. Because of its length and width, it was
known as a ribbon lake. He could see a mountain range on
both sides, the beginnings of the Carneddau and the Glyder-
au.

Taid Davies, Nick's maternal grandfather, used to live
close to here in a village called Nant Peris, which lay in the
foothills of Mount Snowdon. Taid Davies used to tell Nick
about King Owain Gwynedd. His eldest son, and first in line
for the Welsh throne, was Prince Idwal. However, Idwal was
a sensitive, creative young man and his father knew he would
never become a warrior. When war broke out with the King
of Powys, King Owain feared for his son's safety and sent
him into hiding with a trusted adviser and friend, Nefydd
Hardd, who lived in the mountains overlooking Lake Llyn
Ogwen. However, Nefydd Hardd had always resented King
Owain, and one day pushed Idwal from a rocky ledge and
watched as the young prince fell and plunged into the icy water below. His body was never found.

Taid Davies told Nick that if you watched carefully,
there was a section of the lake where no birds would fly. Even
though it was hundreds of years ago, they could sense the
remnants of malevolence where Prince Idwal drowned. He
also said that on some dark nights, when the wind blew from
the west, the echo of the prince's screams could still be heard.

IT WAS CLOSE TO ELEVEN o'clock when Ruth and Nick arrived at the Walton Centre in Liverpool where Jonathan Noakes had been transferred. There had been a call earlier in the morning to say that Noakes had shown some signs that he was coming out of unconsciousness. Ruth didn't want to wait for a full recovery – she wanted Noakes' confession as soon as possible. She wanted him charged.

Nick and Ruth walked along the corridor heading for the room where Noakes was located. Up ahead, a uniformed WPC from Merseyside Police, an Asian woman in her thirties, stood outside.

Ruth showed her warrant card. 'Morning, Constable. DI Hunter of the North Wales Police. This is my colleague DS Evans. I take it that Jonathan Noakes is in this room?'

'Yes, ma'am. There's a doctor in with him at the moment,' the WPC explained.

'Right. And were you here when he regained consciousness?' Ruth asked.

'Yes, ma'am. It was just after nine o'clock.'

At that moment, the consultant neurologist Dr Andrew Duncan, tall, salt-and-pepper hair, handsome, came out of the room.

Ruth flashed her warrant card. 'I'm DI Hunter from North Wales Police. We received a phone call this morning to say that Jonathan Noakes was coming out of his coma.

'Dr Duncan. I'm Mr Noakes' consultant. I'm afraid he has slipped back into a coma. Sometimes it happens.' Duncan spoke with an Edinburgh accent.

'Any idea when that might change?' Ruth asked.

'It's usually a good sign. His CAT and MRI scans show that most of the damage isn't permanent. But it might take a couple more days before he can be questioned properly,' Duncan explained in a business-like and professional way.

'Thank you.' Ruth was pleased. It sounded as if Noakes would recover and could therefore stand trial.

Duncan nodded and walked away purposefully.

'Ma'am, Mrs Noakes and her daughter are down in the café. They've been here overnight. It's on the ground floor by reception,' the WPC informed them.

'Thank you, Constable,' Ruth said with a smile as she and Nick made their way back down the corridor and caught a lift to the ground floor.

As they entered the café, Ruth glanced around and spotted a woman, blonde, attractive, sitting at a table nursing a cup of coffee. She looked tired and lost in thought.

Ruth nudged Nick to show him who she thought was Mrs Noakes. They approached the table.

'Mrs Noakes?' Ruth said softly.

'Yes?' replied Andrea.

Ruth got out her warrant card. 'I'm DI Hunter. Can we sit down?'

Ruth noticed that Andrea's face had changed to one of anger as she shrugged. 'Don't suppose I have much choice.'

Ruth and Nick shared a look. What was that about?

'I understand that you've been away for a while, Mrs Noakes?' Nick asked.

'My parents live in Spain now. I went to see them with our daughter, Daisy, but we came back early,' Andrea explained.

'When did you arrive back in the UK, Mrs Noakes?' Ruth asked.

'Yesterday evening. Ironically, just in time,' Andrea said sardonically.

'Why were you coming back early?' Nick said.

'I'd spoken to Jonathan on the phone. He had taken Arabella's death badly. Then another murder.' She looked Ruth squarely in the eye. 'He said he was being hounded by the police. He said he got the impression that you had made your mind up that he was a murderer.'

'Mrs Noakes, I think it only fair to warn you that we suspect that your husband is involved in both murders,' Ruth said.

Andrea shook her head. 'No. No. That can't be true. He's just not like that. He doesn't even raise his voice when he's annoyed. You've got it wrong.'

There was a moment as Ruth waited for Andrea Noakes to compose herself. She had seen relatives unable to comprehend how their loved ones had committed terrible crimes many times before. They didn't suspect anything, or they chose not to. Some people were so scared of being alone that they turned a blind eye to anything.

'Mrs Noakes, did you speak to your husband on Thursday the thirteenth of March, the night Arabella Dixon was murdered?' Ruth asked.

Andrea was still distressed. 'Yes. We spoke every night I was away.'

'Can you remember at what time that was?' Ruth asked.

'We spoke between eight and nine in the evening normally. Once Daisy had gone to bed,' Andrea said.

'Can you be more precise about that Monday evening?' Nick said.

'I think it was later. Daisy and I had been out with my mum and dad. I put her to bed as soon as we got back. I guess it was nearer nine thirty. When was Arabella Dixon attacked and killed?'

'I'm sorry, Mrs Noakes, but we can't discuss an ongoing investigation. I'm sure you understand?' Nick said politely.

'Could you tell us if you spoke to your husband on Monday the seventeenth of March?' Ruth asked.

'Yes. We spoke that evening,' Andrea replied.

'Did your husband tell you what he had been doing that day?' Ruth said.

'Mountain biking in the afternoon. Then he had been working at home after that,' Andrea explained.

'Mountain biking?' Nick said with a frown. Noakes had said he was at home all afternoon.

'Yeah. Every Monday afternoon he goes mountain biking. Has done for years.'

'Does he go on his own?' Nick asked.

'No. He meets up with some friends there. Is that when the headteacher was killed?' Andrea asked, trying to piece their questions together.

'Do you know the names of the people that your husband meets?' Ruth enquired.

'No, not really. Will, Owen and Ashley. There are oth-ers.'

'What about surnames?' Ruth asked.

Andrea shook her head. 'Sorry, no. That's all I know. But he was definitely there.'

Ruth shot Nick a look – were their celebrations the previous day a little premature?

RUTH HAD SPENT THE last hour in Drake's office, filling him in on their interview of Andrea Noakes at the hospital. She was still confident that Noakes was their man.

Drake took off his reading glasses and rubbed the bridge of his nose. He had only been at Llancastell five minutes, but Ruth had warmed to him immediately. Comfortable in his own skin, DCI Drake reminded her of some of the best guv'nors she had worked with in her time at the Met.

'Looks like I'm heading back to rainy Manchester,' Drake said with a weary sigh.

'Sorry it's been a wasted journey,' Ruth said, although part of her was proud of the fact that Llancastell CID had solved the case before any other detectives had arrived from over the border.

'Nice part of the world, here. Manchester can be a bit of a zoo sometimes. But then you'd know what big-city policing is like?' Drake said.

'Yeah, it takes it out of you,' Ruth said. 'I can type up my notes from yesterday so you can sign them off before you go.'

'Thanks, Ruth.' Drake took a moment. 'You don't have a DCI at Llancastell, do you?'

'No. The last one left a year ago and has never been replaced,' Ruth explained.

'Well you never know. If you find the budget for one, I might be tempted to come over the border,' Drake said with a smile.

'Be careful what you wish for,' Ruth said with a laugh, but she'd be more than happy to be Drake's second-in-command.

Ruth got up and headed for the door.

'And Ruth?' Drake said as he sat up in his chair.

'Yeah?' Ruth said as she opened the door.

'Good job,' Drake said, giving her a friendly wink.

Ruth headed downstairs with an extra bounce in her step. Finishing a ciggie on the steps outside, she knew that she needed to get back to her office and fill out the paperwork to do with the case. Now they had Noakes in the frame, she needed to collate everything for the CPS and the trial.

On the drive back from the hospital, she and Nick had discussed Noakes' two versions of his story for the afternoon that Neerav Banerjee was murdered. Their hypothesis presumed Andrea knew that he went mountain biking every Monday, so he had told her that's where he had been, to avoid any suspicion. He had then told Ruth and Nick that he had been at home, because he knew that they could easily check whether he had been mountain biking with friends. Changing your story or forgetting what you've said was a clear sign of guilt. Noakes just didn't count on the GPS tracker in Alex's car.

As Ruth entered Major Incident Room 1 after her smoke break, Nick headed her way. He was holding a report and looking perplexed.

'Something up?'

'You could say that, boss!' Nick's tone was one of frustration.

'What is it?' Ruth was now worried, as they headed for her office.

'Forensics back on the stuff they took from Dylan Wilkins' flat. He had a pair of leather gloves in his coat pocket. And on those gloves is Arabella Dixon's blood and DNA!'

'What? How can that be?' Ruth was rocked momentarily as she took in the new information.

'I don't know, boss. Now I'm really confused,' Nick groaned, and sat down opposite Ruth.

'What about Neerav Banerjee's DNA?' Ruth's mind was racing.

'Nope. Just Arabella Dixon's,' Nick replied.

'Shit! Are we looking at two killers?' Ruth thought out loud.

'The MOs are identical, boss. We have to be looking for the same killer.' Nick shook his head. 'I sent Mac and Sian to pick up Dylan Wilkins about twenty minutes ago and bring him in as we've now got probable cause.'

'Good. He doesn't like interviews so he might have a meltdown and tell us what happened. What if they're working together?' Ruth suggested.

'Noakes and Wilkins? I can't think of two more different blokes on the planet. How do they know each other?' Nick wasn't convinced.

'I don't know. We've got her blood and DNA on his gloves, so we know that Dylan Wilkins murdered Arabella Dixon. We have the emails, the GPS tracker, and Noakes' confession and doing a runner yesterday. Noakes killed Neerav Banerjee. Two killers. They have to be working together.'

Nick nodded. 'You're right, boss. I mean, what you're saying is right. I'm just trying to get my head around it.'

'First things first. We've got probable cause for Dylan Wilkins. We can interview him under caution when he gets here.'

'They both like mountain biking? They could have met at a trail?' Nick suggested.

'Alex was a pupil at the school. Noakes sees Dylan at parents' evenings. Recognises him at a mountain bike trail.' Ruth was thinking out loud. 'I still don't know how that leads to them committing murder together?'

Nick nodded. 'Your wife's a bitch. I want to kill her. Oh, by coincidence so do I. And I also want to kill the head because he was shagging my wife. Well, I want to kill the head too. Great. You kill one, I'll kill the other. Right, let's go down this mountain bike trail.'

Ruth smiled and gave a half laugh. 'Nicely put. Very creative, Nick. But you're right.'

The phone rang and Ruth picked it up. 'DI Hunter ... Right. Okay.'

Ruth looked a little deflated when she put the phone down.

'Dylan Wilkins is visiting his father in Llandudno today. Bronwyn Wright has given us Morgan Wilkins' address and phone number, but she thought they would be probably be out. Dylan will get a train from Llandudno Junction to Betws-y-Coed station around eight thirty or nine tonight. She picks him up from there.'

Ruth went on to her computer and tapped away. 'Right, the eight twenty-three from Llandudno Junction gets to Betws-y-Coed at eight forty-seven. Next train is after nine. I'll get a uniformed patrol to pick him up at Llandudno Junction and bring him in.'

Nick nodded. 'Right, boss. I don't mind driving up there.'

'No. This is what you're going to do. I want you to go home. Sleep, watch a movie, eat some food. In the last ten days, you've been shot and had a car accident. I'll call you if and when Dylan Wilkins gets here. Take a few hours off, and that's an order.'

Nick was reluctant to leave. 'Yes, boss.'

CHAPTER 39

NICK HAD COMPLETELY ignored Ruth's orders and had gone straight to Mike and Pat's cottage to see if they needed help with the extension. In fact, he just wanted to see them, have a brew, and a catch up.

As he parked the car, Nick had seen his car temperature gauge showing a balmy fourteen degrees centigrade. The sun was beating down, and the sky was a clear, azure blue. In the field close to where he had parked, there were two sheep whose udders were swollen as they were about to lamb.

As Nick reached the squeaky, iron gate, he saw that Mike was working on the extension. There was a small orange concrete mixer, which was stationary at the moment. Mike was laying the foundations in the base that Nick and he had dug out. Nick felt a warm glow just watching him.

'Come to lend a hand, lad? About time.' Mike looked up, smiled and gestured to the foundations.

'What are we doing?' Nick asked with a beaming smile.

'Adding sealant to the concrete,' Mike explained.

'What do you want me to do?'

'Actually, I need sealant from the garage, mate. Polyseal, five litres. Near the back.'

'I was hoping for a brew,' Nick replied.

'You haven't done anything yet, you soft bugger.'

Nick held up his hands. 'All right, all right, I'm on it.'

As he went to the garage, he saw Cerys in the kitchen and banged on the open door. 'Put the kettle on will you, face-ache?'

'I don't think it will suit me,' Cerys grinned back at him.

'I see pregnancy's improved your sense of humour. I'll be back in a minute.' Nick paused, and saw that Auntie Pat was hoovering in the living room. He looked at Cerys. 'How's your mum? Everything all right?' he asked in a lowered voice.

'I'm not sure. She seems distracted all the time. Why don't you have a chat with her while you're here?' Cerys suggested.

'Yeah, I will. Back in a sec.'

Nick went off to find the sealant, going through the open side door to the garage. Clicking on the overhead strip lights, he saw that Mike had set up the pool table ready for a game. Maybe he and Mike would play later.

Nick moved towards the back of the garage, past ladders, bike parts and old pots of paint. Then the three motorbikes parked in a line. Maybe when he was fully sober, he would get himself a motorbike. He and Mike could ride out into Snowdonia together.

As Nick went forward, he caught the toe of his boot on a raised floorboard that had come a little loose. It was about two centimetres higher than the rest. He stumbled but didn't quite fall as he got his footing.

'Bloody hell!' Nick said to himself. He looked back at the offending floorboard. *That needs nailing down before someone breaks their neck,* he thought.

Seeing that the fixing nail at one end of the board had rusted and come loose from the joist below, Nick knew it would need a new nail. He looked around, saw an old plastering trowel on a nearby shelf and grabbed it. He pushed it down between the loose floorboards. He levered the loose board up, grabbed it and pulled it up. It was only about four-foot long and he placed it to one side. *Real man's work,* Nick thought to himself. He loved getting his hands dirty building and fixing things, and Mike had shown him how, ever since he was young.

As he went to get up, he saw an old red bath towel resting on the joists, under the floorboards. He frowned, wondering what on earth it was doing there? Picking it up, he could smell and see black oil on the towel. And then Nick knew what the smell was – gun oil. He unravelled the towel and saw the dark, wooden stock of a shotgun. Then the silver metal of the AYA 12 Gauge 28' double-barrelled gun, the break-action and black metal trigger. However, there was something wrong. Nick pulled the gun out of the towel and saw that the barrels had been sawn off with a hacksaw. It was less than two feet in length.

Nick's stomach lurched as he remembered the last time he had seen a sawn-off shotgun. His mind was racing. Why did Mike have a sawn-off shotgun hidden under the floorboards of his garage? Nick's mind began to make worrying connections that he didn't even want to contemplate. There would be a simple explanation, he told himself. Of course, there would ...

Feeling sick with anxiety, he looked further under the floorboards and pulled out a thick plastic bag. He heard a soft metallic clink as he took a moment before opening the bag and looking at the contents. Putting his hand inside, he slowly pulled out some keys. A large black electronic key fob with *Range Rover* embossed on it, and a small oval tag that was attached to the key ring. It read *Save Water. Drink Prosecco.*

Nick's hands shook a little. He didn't want to see what else was in the bag. His mind was racing and trying to put things together. The jigsaw puzzle that was forming was gruesome. He couldn't do it. What the hell was going on? He felt a tear well in his eye.

He took a breath, plunged his hand into the bag and pulled out something that was soft and rubbery. He could hardly bear to look. It was a latex rubber pig mask, and he knew that he had seen it before.

There was no doubt now in this mind.

Then the questions. Why? What had happened? Oh God, and then the repercussions.

'I'm sorry, Nick. I really am. I never meant this to happen.' Mike stood a few yards away holding an earth covered spade.

'I don't understand,' Nick said, his voice breaking.

Mike shook his head – he was trembling.

'I'm sorry, lad ...' Mike croaked as he was overwhelmed by emotion.

'I'm so confused. You killed them?' Nick asked, but he was in a surreal daze.

'I'm so sorry ...' Mike put his trembling hands to his face for a moment.

'I don't get it. This is crazy.'

Mike looked at him. Nick didn't need him to say anything else. His eyes told the whole story. He simply nodded.

'And I can't do this anymore. I can't hide and lie anymore. It's killing me.'

Nick felt a surge of emotion and tears ran down his face. He hadn't cried in years. How had this happened?

'I don't understand. We just found Dylan Wilkins' gloves with Arabella Dixon's DNA,' Nick said half to himself.

'I put them in his coat after I killed her,' Mike admitted.

'The spiral cuts?' Nick was running everything through his mind trying to piece things together but shock was impeding that process.

'To make it look like you were after a psychopathic maniac.'

'Why? Why did you kill them? It doesn't make any sense.' Nick felt the pain inside.

'It was for Megan. I did it for Megan,' Mike said quietly.

'What do you mean?' Nick sobbed.

Four years earlier ...
Neerav Banerjee's Home

It was a hot and humid summer's night. A teenage house party, at the home of Neerav Banerjee, was in full flow. It was his son Raahul's nineteenth birthday. Neerav was in the kitchen with a few middle-aged friends who were trying to be as inconspicuous as they could. His wife was away with the younger children visiting family in the Midlands. Arabella Dixon was chatting and smiling but preoccupied. She gave Neerav a look as she walked past him and touched his hand, as if beckoning him to follow. He waited a moment before slowly disappearing through a group of teens.

Teenagers were crammed in the lounge, drinking. Others smoked weed as secretly as they could. Most of them were in their late teens. The patio doors were open and kids were dotted around the long garden, laughing and getting drunk and high. Candles lined the garden path and lit-up lanterns hanging from the trees gave the scene a magical look.

Robin Thicke's Blurred Lines came on the stereo and the bass thudded throughout the house. A group of boys and girls were dancing in the centre of the lounge. They were whooping and singing along to the song.

Megan Gardener was dancing in another part of the room. With her make-up and clothes she could have been seventeen or eighteen, but there was also something about her that made her seem younger. She had heavy black eye make-up and her dip-dyed hair was in a ponytail.

She watched as Alex Noakes, spliff balanced between his lips, moved in the middle of the group – he was good. The teenagers clapped as he did some pop-and-lock moves, a drop, *and then the move from* The Matrix *with all the bravado of a high seventeen-year-old showing off.*

To complete his performance, he took a massive toke on the spliff and his face disappeared in a cloud of marijuana smoke.

Megan laughed at his antics and caught his eye. Alex smiled back, eyes twinkling. He casually danced over and handed her the spliff. She knew him by sight from school but they had never spoken. She took a toke, held it, and then let it out with a smile. She had smoked weed a few times before.

Megan and Alex carried on dancing. Alex whispered something into her ear and she burst out laughing. Cheeky bastard, *she thought.*

The opening strumming guitar chords of Avicii's Wake Me Up *blasted from the stereo.*

'Oh God, I love this!' Megan yelled as she looked at Alex.

Everyone in the room started to sing along with the song at the top of their voices, hands swaying in the air.

Alex put his hands loosely around Megan's waist as they danced, occasionally catching each other's glances. Megan giggled when she was caught, feeling embarrassed and looked away. She was so excited and happy.

As the beat of the song kicked in, Alex dropped his hands from Megan's waist and, along with the rest of the room, bounced on the spot in time to the music.

Alex and Megan jumped, hands in the air, singing as loud as they could. They met each other's eyes and smiled. They were completely lost in the moment, the sense of freedom, abandonment, and joy overwhelming.

Alex grabbed Megan's hand and shouted, 'Come on.'

'Where are we going?' Megan said, but she wasn't resisting.

They went out into the garden and Megan seized a bottle of wine from the white plastic garden table. The night air was cool and refreshing after the heat of the house and Megan took it in, looking at the candlelit path and garden. She felt so grown up. And Alex was fit. All the girls in Year 9 said so.

They wandered hand in hand and found a secluded space by a hedge. For the next fifteen minutes, they took it in turns to swig from the bottle. They talked and laughed. Alex teased her about her nose ring and she slapped him playfully.

Alex looked at her. 'Your eye make-up has a thing in it.' Alex pointed to where her thick eye-liner had clotted. She felt embarrassed for a moment.

'You taking the piss?' she asked, aware that her voice was now slurred with alcohol. She didn't care.

'No. Just close your eyes for a second and I'll get it,' Alex said.

Megan closed her eyes and Alex moved in for a kiss. Nice move, *Megan thought, as she responded. He pushed his tongue into her mouth and she reciprocated.*

They kissed more. Megan loved everything about it. The smell, the taste and sound. As they got more passionate, Alex moved his hands over her body and then under her bra and pants. Megan didn't feel scared, and let herself go with it.

Coming up for air, the pair pulled apart. 'Isn't your mum here?' Megan asked looking over at the patio doors.

Alex pointed to a first-floor window with curtains shut but a light on. Megan frowned.

'She'll be up there with Mr Banerjee.' Alex explained coolly.

'What? Do you mean ...?'

'I know. It's disgusting to think about, but it's been going on for months,' Alex explained, trying to show that he wasn't bothered.

'Don't you care? I mean, it's a bit weird ...' Megan said.

'No. He's not the first, and he definitely won't be the last,' Alex said.

Love Me Again *by John Newman played from inside the house.*

Alex stopped and looked at Megan, who was having trouble focussing. She didn't care. He kissed her again, tenderly.

Alex leaned forwards and whispered, 'Do you want to ... you know?'

Megan looked at him. 'Here?'

Alex nodded, 'Yeah, why not? If we go over there, no one can see us.' *He pointed to a patch of lawn behind a hedgerow.* 'You're so beautiful, I can't help myself.'

'Have you got anything?' *Megan was still sober enough to think sensibly.*

'Don't worry, I won't come in you.' *Alex stroked her face.*

'You know I'm not a virgin, don't you?' *Megan said, hoping this wouldn't put Alex off. Megan had slept with her boyfriend twice about a month ago but he had dumped her by text last week.*

'Neither am I,' *Alex said with a grin.*

Megan looked at him and laughed. She knew he was a bit of a player. 'You're such a twat!'

They moved a few yards right, behind the cover of a hedge. Megan lay back and let Alex slide on top of her. He fumbled for a moment, and they both groaned as he slipped inside her.

Their movements began to get more frantic and Megan suddenly realised that Alex seemed to have no intention of pulling out before he came. She stopped kissing him.

'What are you doing? No, Alex!' Megan's voice was distressed. She was starting to panic.

Alex groaned, 'Megan ...'

'No, get off me.' She could feel the anger rise in her. She could see that Alex wasn't listening, and he clearly didn't want to stop.

Megan tried to push him away, but he forced himself against her, pushed her arms down onto the grass and then ejaculated inside her.

Megan's head was swimming. She felt sick. What just happened? It didn't feel real. She felt frozen as though her limbs were not her own, as if she couldn't move them. Her thoughts were drifting away as though nothing had happened to her. It was too much to bear.

Megan looked away and under her breath said, 'Just get off me.'

'What's wrong? You're not going to get pregnant.' Alex kissed her hair but the smell and feel of him now made Megan feel sick. She felt dirty and just wanted to run away.

'Just piss off, will you? You know what you did,' Megan said without looking at him. She sat up on the grass.

'Grow up, you stupid little girl.' Alex shook his head patronisingly at her as he started to get up.

'Just leave me alone. I don't want to speak to you. Prick!' Megan's tone was full of fury.

'*Little chav bint. I hope you do get pregnant.*' *Alex sneered and then spat into the grass where Megan was adjusting her clothes.*

Tears fell down her face as Alex went back into the house. Megan knew she needed to get home.

IT WAS CLOSE TO NINE thirty and the summer sun was already hot when Mike stopped and parked up his motorbike on a dirt track leading off the A474, close to the tiny village of Druid. He had reluctantly agreed to meet Neerav Banerjee and Arabella Dixon to talk about Alex's sexual assault on Megan.

Megan had been very honest about what had happened. She blamed herself for agreeing to have sex with Alex Noakes. However, she was clear that she had tried to stop him, and that he had forced himself on her. She was in an emotional state, veering from guilt to anger, and then numb detachment. Mike didn't know how to deal with it.

Taking off his helmet, Mike batted away some bothersome midges. He looked out at the green fields that stretched away as far as the eye could see on both sides. In front of him was a huge forested hill. The nearby hedgerows had been over-managed and so lacked the natural beauty the area deserved. A ringlet butterfly, sooty brown all over, flitted across the brambles. He needed some guidance from his Higher Power.

Mike took off his gloves, pulled out a cigarette and lit it. The past twenty-four hours had been painful and challenging. It had been the closest Mike had come to picking up a drink in decades. The overwhelming fury he felt towards Alex Noakes left him wondering about the spirituality that had kept him sober. He had talked at length to his sponsor. The notions of keeping it in the day, not judging or resenting, seemed hopelessly naïve in that moment.

Mike and his wife Pat had taken Megan to the police station the previous morning as soon as Megan had broken down and told them what had happened. Understandably, Megan had showered as soon as she got in from the party but by that time Mike and Pat were fast asleep. She had also put her clothes in the washing machine.

Mike knew that both these actions might dent the hope of getting a conviction against Alex Noakes. So did Megan's assertion that she had agreed to have sex with him, even though she was only fourteen. The rape, or sexual assault, had happened as soon as she told him to stop, and although the law of consent was clear, a jury might see it as a grey area. Mike was confident that his daughter's account of events was the truth. Telling lies was an anathema in the Gardener household, and Megan was fiercely honest and truthful in everything she did. Neither of them could believe that it had happened at the home of the school's head teacher.

The police told them that Megan needed to attend Amethyst, which was a sexual assault referral centre in Colwyn Bay. When they got there, they waited while Megan talked to counsellors. Then a specially trained doctor took samples of her saliva, urine, blood and pubic hair, and swabs from her mouth, rectum and genitals. They also gave Megan emergency contraception.

After that, Mike and Pat sat in with Megan as she talked to two CID detectives, who told them that they took sexual assault very seriously. Megan was clear that she had withdrawn her consent during the sex, and that Alex Noakes had forced himself on her. That made the offence rape. Their agreement that he wouldn't ejaculate in her also meant that Megan had consented to sexual intercourse with certain provisos. The fact that Alex Noakes had gone against these was again an offence.

However, the detectives were also honest. It was her word against his. There were no defensive wounds or anything on her body that showed that he had forced himself on her. Megan asked that if there was a trial, could someone ask her about if she had had sex before? The detectives told her it was a possibility. Megan looked at her mum, who knew that she had slept with Jack.

In that case, Megan said she didn't want to press charges. The detectives skilfully tried to suggest that Megan needed to do whatever she wanted to do, but if Alex Noakes had committed a crime, she owed it to other girls to come forward and tell the truth. Megan asked them how many rape cases resulted in a guilty verdict. The detectives avoided giving numbers, but Megan knew it was low.

On the way home, Megan was adamant. She wasn't going to go to trial if it meant talking about her sexual history, and being bullied by a barrister. Pat was fully supportive of Megan. The decision was completely hers and they would both respect that. However, Mike thought that, after a few days, Megan might change her mind.

The sound of crunching tyres on the track broke Mike's train of thought. The white Range Rover Evoque came around the corner and pulled into the space where Mike rested against the iron field gate. The engine died and Neerav and Arabella got

out of the car simultaneously. They were both dressed casual-
ly, but smart enough to show that they weren't making light of
what had happened.

Arabella took off her sunglasses. She wore a suitably serious
expression as she approached.

Neerav walked over and offered his hand to Mike. 'It's good
of you to meet with us this morning, Mike.'

'I'm not sure why I'm here. But I owe it to Megan to see
what you want to talk about,' Mike said taking Neerav's hand
reluctantly. He didn't want to be rude.

Arabella was a few steps behind, with her usual hint of con-
tempt that elevated her chin at a slight angle.

'So that you know, Alex was arrested yesterday and ques-
tioned by the police,' Arabella said in an unfriendly tone.

Mike snorted. 'Well, what did you expect?'

'He's devastated. He really doesn't know what Megan is
talking about,' Arabella explained in a perplexed voice.

'I think he does. He knows what he did to her. And now, so
do the police,' Mike said. Alex Noakes was not going to get away
with it.

'My son is not a liar, Mike,' Arabella said sternly.

'Neither is my daughter,' Mike replied.

'Really? In that case, you don't know that Megan stole an
iPhone from a Year 7 pupil last year and lied to several mem-
bers of staff about it until someone found it in her bag.' Arabel-
la's tone was conceited.

Mike was mystified. He hadn't known about the event and
was angry at being made to look stupid. In the old days, he
might have tried to blag knowledge of the theft but honesty was
important to him.

Neerav nodded. 'Megan was excluded for a day, Mike. Dai Barker spoke to your wife. I suspected that she didn't pass the information on to you.'

Mike indicated Arabella with scorn, 'What, and you told her?' There was an awkward silence. 'It doesn't mean that Megan is lying about being attacked for God's sake!' Mike barked, as he felt the surge of anger in his body and face. He had walked straight into that and it gave Arabella the upper hand.

'She wasn't attacked,' Arabella said in a withering tone.

'The reason I'm here today is to see if we can resolve the situation?' Neerav said quietly.

'Resolve? Are you kidding me? In the old days I would have gone around to your house and broken your son's bloody skull!' Mike thundered. 'And where the hell were you? This happened at your home!'

'Let's not get carried away here,' Neerav said, raising his arms in a conciliatory way.

'Alex says that he and Megan had sex and that she seemed perfectly happy when she left the party. Mike, he truly doesn't understand what she is talking about. He's terribly upset.'

Mike shook his head. 'He raped my fourteen-year-old daughter, spat at her and walked away.'

'No. I'm sorry. Alex isn't capable of that kind of behaviour,' Arabella said angrily. 'Don't you see what you're going to put your daughter through?'

'Don't make me out to be responsible in any way for how she is feeling.' Mike said this but knew that it was only ever going to be Megan's word against Alex's. She wasn't happy at all about going into a courtroom.

'Mike, Megan is very young, and she is confused and mistaken. Please don't put her through a trial,' Arabella said. 'Don't put either of them through that.'

Mike knew that it wasn't down to him whether Megan pressed charges against Alex Noakes. He and Pat would support her whatever she chose to do. He also knew that his desire to see Alex prosecuted was out of sheer revenge rather than any balanced view of justice.

Mike dug deep as he clung to the morality that he had practised on a daily basis for three decades. Forgiveness was the road from resentment to connection. Hatred was the most dangerous emotion for alcoholics, and most people. It festered like a growing disease. Mike remembered a Japanese proverb: 'Seek revenge and you must dig two graves. One for the man you wish to harm, and one for yourself.' In the rawness of what had happened, Mike could feel no forgiveness. He would have to try to find a way of progress.

'It's not my decision to make,' Mike explained, holding in his anger.

'Is there a middle ground that can be found?' Neerav suggested.

'Middle ground? My daughter was attacked and you want to find a middle ground?' Mike snapped.

'I was just suggesting ...' Neerav started to say.

'Well don't. For starters, Megan will not come back to school if your son is there,' Mike said.

Arabella nodded. 'My ex-husband and I have already looked at Alex going to board elsewhere for sixth form.'

'And I want the school to organise counselling for Megan,' Mike said.

'I can't see that will be a problem. And Mike, I think we could expand your role at the school to site manager in the coming academic year.' Neerav wore an earnest look on his face.

'Piss off, Neerav. I will not be bribed into sweeping something like this under the carpet. It's insulting for you to even think that. It happened at your home, for God's sake!' Mike was indignant.

'Yes. I understand that. I'm sorry, I really am,' Neerav said.

Mike put on his gloves. 'I'll let you know what Megan decides.' He kicked away the motorbike stand and started the engine.

THE TELEVISION WAS showing morning programmes. Despite it being a warm summer's day, Megan was lying on the sofa in a fluffy dressing gown, and with a blanket. She just wanted to be covered up.

Looking up, she saw her mum entering with a cup of tea and a plate of biscuits for her.

'Maybe you should have a shower and get dressed for the day?' Pat suggested.

Megan didn't reply. She had spent the last four days swinging between numb detachment and overwhelming emotions. If only she hadn't led Alex on. She felt so guilty for getting drunk and allowing him to have sex with her. She had had nightmares and flashbacks. She was now too frightened to go to sleep. She just kept replaying it over and over in her mind. Maybe she should have made it clearer that she wanted him to stop, or she should have put up more resistance?

'Megan?' Pat said lightly.

'What?' Megan snapped, without looking away from the television. She didn't want to get dressed. She wanted the pain and shock to go away. Why didn't they understand that?

Megan felt a trickle of blood from her wrist run down onto the palm of her hand. Pat reached over and pulled up the dressing gown cuff before Megan had time to react. There were four neat red cuts on her wrist, all about two inches long. Cutting herself was the only relief, the only distraction she could find.

Pat looked distraught. 'What are you doing to yourself?'

'Nothing. It makes me feel better.' Megan pulled the sleeve back up again.

'I'll run you a bath,' Pat said gently.

'I don't want a bath, Mam. That's not going to make me better.' Megan banged her head with the flat of her hand. 'It's not going to make this go away, is it?'

'I don't know what to do,' Pat said desperately.

'I don't want you to do anything. Just leave me alone.'

IT WAS WINTER AND THE ragged hills, valleys, and lakes of Snowdonia were snowbound and bleak. This was a land that beat to the drum of Arthurian legend. The pounding heart of ancient Wales – a land of folklore and of myth.

A cold, damp and dismal morning and the lake of Llyn Llydaw was dark, deep and utterly still. Up on the flanks of Mount Snowdon, Llyn Llydaw was long and thin and had formed in a cwm[1], a glaciated valley, about one third of the

---

1.   https://en.wikipedia.org/wiki/Cirque

way up the mountain. It was believed to be the final resting place of Arthur, King of Britons. The place where a weary, dying King Arthur and Sir Bedevere threw Excalibur to the porcelain hand of the Lady of the Lake. It was a place of immeasurable power and myth.

Megan ran carelessly down the uneven slopes of Crib Y Ddysgl where Merlin is supposed to have hidden the golden throne of Britain amongst the grey stone cliffs. Letting gravity pull her down, she danced, leapt and jumped over the rocks until the ground evened out. She wore a blue parka coat, burgundy Dr Marten boots – her pretty face was reddy pink from the cold. Her hair was dirty blonde, her left eyebrow pierced twice, and her eye make-up was heavy and black.

Megan had white headphones in her ears that were attached to her phone. Sam Smith's Stay with Me *was playing, as a poignant hymn to the scene. As she arrived at the lake's edge, she gazed across its length - the water a dark, green-copper colour - and then away into the distance. The make-up from her face and eyes had smudged a little from her tears. There seemed to be a detached quality to her gaze – numb and anaesthetised.*

Megan took a silver cross that hung around her neck, kissed it, and then looked up at the sky.

NEERAV BANERJEE WAS *standing at the front of the school hall in an expensive-looking grey suit, smiling his obsequious grin. It was an after-school CPD, Continuing Professional Development, meeting and the head teacher was talking to all the staff – teaching, support, technicians – about the*

changes to the site, the new build, and the 1.2 million-pound science and DT block that would be constructed in the summer of 2017.

Mike, as usual, sat at the back of the hall. He had little interest in these after-school meetings where projections of data and results or new software would be explained and analysed. However, it was mandatory for all staff to attend and so Mike would join grumbling teaching assistants at the rear of the hall.

As Neerav Banerjee went through his PowerPoint presentation, Mike noticed the plan drawings for the extension of the changing rooms. From what he could see, the building's development would require the moving of Megan's memorial tree, and no one had spoken to him about it.

Mike could feel the sudden knot in his stomach as he shifted in his seat. How could they possibly have had these plans drawn and not felt it necessary to broach the subject with him? How could they have been so insensitive as to show these new plans to the whole staff body without even mentioning it before? Mike's anger seethed. Where were they going to replant the tree? Were they going to replant the tree at all? The resentment and racing mind of a recovering alcoholic was back and out of control.

Neerav Banerjee finished his presentation, saying that he would email it out to all staff. Mike bided his time as the rest of the staff trundled away to their cars to go home. Eventually it was just Neerav and Arabella Dixon left by the raised wooden stage, laughing and flirting.

Mike approached, trying to keep himself in check. Neerav looked up, stopped laughing, and moved a respectable distance away from Arabella.

'Hi, Mike. You locking up? Won't be a sec,' Neerav said in a friendly voice, taking his memory stick from the laptop.

'I've got to dash. See you tomorrow,' Arabella muttered, touching Neerav on the arm as she went to leave.

'What's happening to the memorial tree?' Mike asked. Arabella heard the question and stopped in her tracks.

'Oh yes. Of course. I've been meaning to talk to you about that,' Neerav said awkwardly, trying to feign confidence.

'Have you? When were you going to do that? As they were digging up the roots?' Mike's tone was verging on aggressive.

'No, it was something I wanted to talk to you about before we gave the plans the final go-ahead,' Neerav explained.

'So where are you going to replant the tree? Do I have some kind of say in where you put it?' Mike thundered.

'I'm not sure we are going to replant it. We're ...' Neerav was now squirming.

'We're not sure it's appropriate, Mike. That's all,' Arabella stated coldly.

'Appropriate? What the hell does that mean?'

'I can assure you that we'll find a way of remembering Megan somewhere on the school site,' Neerav reassured him.

'Oh well, I'm glad you've given it so much detailed thought. I bet you can tell me the floor area in square feet of the new changing rooms though, can't you?' Mike shook his head angrily.

'Come on, Mike. You know that we normally only commemorate students who have died ... well ... tragically. In an accident. Megan ...' Arabella looked directly at him with her supercilious glare.

'Megan killed herself because your son raped her. The tragedy is that I allowed her to have her wish and not press charges. She never recovered. And you're both responsible for that,' Mike seethed.

'I'm sorry that you see it that way. Unfortunately, Megan's emotional difficulties started long before that. Having consensual underage sex with my son was a symptom of that, not a cause.'

'I know this is hard for you but she's right, Mike. We can't be held accountable for what happened to Megan,' Neerav said, avoiding eye contact.

And at that moment, Mike knew. He knew that Neerav and Arabella had conspired to cover up Megan's rape to save Alex Noakes and both their careers.

In that moment, it was almost like he had a premonition. He knew that the overwhelming fury he felt brewing inside of him would lead to a relapse. Slow at first. And once Mike had alcohol in his system, with his murderous desire for revenge, all bets would be off. The battle between fate and the human desire to control was over. The struggle between what God asked of him, and what his human instinct and desire for revenge told him was right, had been lost. He could see his hands around their necks. He could feel the life leaving them. He was going to kill them and avenge his darling Megan.

CHAPTER 40

THE BMW 1200 RT MOTORBIKE was cruising steadily at 90 mph when Mike dropped a gear and took her up to 110. He knew exactly where he was going. His blood was full of rum and his head awash with swirling thoughts. But he had made the decision.

Thirty minutes earlier, Mike had told Nick just how he had murdered Arabella Dixon and Neerav Banerjee. They needed to pay for what they had done to Megan. It was their carelessness, ruthlessness, and refusal to take responsibility or do the right thing that had destroyed her life.

Mike had intended that Alex Noakes be his first victim, but he had missed him on three occasions. This time he wouldn't make that mistake. He had rung the Baker farm asking to book a holiday cottage. He referred to knowing Alex Noakes and was informed by Lynne Baker that Alex was at home. So now Mike was on his way to finish off the last of the unholy trinity.

A sign flew past – *Horseshoe Pass* – Bwlch Yr Oernant – *1367 feet*. The Horseshoe Pass or the 'Pass of the Cold Stream', was a mountain road that separated Llantysilio Mountain to the west and Marilyn Cyrn-y-Brain to the east. The road travelled in a horseshoe shape around the steep, treacherous sides of the valley.

397

There was a throbbing on the right side of his jawbone where Nick had punched Mike during a tussle. Mike had made it clear that he was going to murder Alex Noakes and Nick tried to stop him. Eventually, Mike had hit Nick on the back of the head with the flat of his spade. Not enough to render him unconscious, but enough to knock him down and daze him while Mike could make his escape.

The sky that stretched above him was sapphire blue, and the sun's white rays were refracted through a thin white cloud. Mike noticed sardonically how beautiful the world that his Higher Power had created could be. And yet so dark and deadly.

The bend slowly curved to the right and Mike's knee dropped towards the road's grey, smooth surface with only two inches to spare.

As the road straightened, Mike pulled the throttle again and quickly reached 100 mph. Up ahead, a car coming the other way had stopped as it indicated right to go down a small country lane. Mike was confident that the car had seen him until it pulled across in front of him. *What the hell are you doing?*

He hit the brakes, screaming, 'No!' and smashed into the side of the car at 115 mph.

His body sailed through the air and into an eternal blackness.

IT WAS A COLD, WINDY morning, and leafy yew and lime trees bowed and fluttered in the breeze. Llancastell's municipal cemetery was the only one that would take Mike Gardener's funeral. Several had refused because of the murders and any bad publicity that might accompany the funeral. It had taken Pat and Nick nearly two weeks to find undertakers, and a cemetery that would carry out the ceremony.

Nick stood with Pat and Cerys, whose pregnancy was now beginning to show. It had been a painful, horrific two weeks for them all. They had lurched from horror to loss to shame and guilt. Half a dozen members from the local Masonic lodge and the AA group had made enquiries about the service, saying that they wanted to give the family some support. But the family made excuses and no one else showed. Nick didn't blame them. Mike's actions were horrendous and had left two families, and many others, devastated.

Despite the destruction of so many things that Nick had held dear, he had somehow clung onto his sobriety. His sponsor, Dundee Bill, a man he had let down frequently since coming into the rooms three years ago, had been at the end of the phone with calm, wise words and no judgement. Love and tolerance was integral to the AA code. So, Nick was trying to live simply, one day at a time, even though his thoughts raced away with a regularity that frustrated him.

The undertakers lifted the coffin and brought it to the graveside. His death had been instant. At 115 mph, it couldn't have been anything but. The men took the sturdy ropes and lowered the coffin down into the deep grave. Nick studied them and their serious faces. It was easier than looking at his aunt and cousin. Beyond this grave were others, headstones that told of lives that stretched back more than two hundred years.

As the coffin moved downwards and out of sight, Pat gave a deep moan of pain and torment, and Nick took her cold hand. His throat and stomach felt the grief first. He was trying so hard to keep it together for Pat and Cerys but it was impossible. He swallowed as the tears came to his eyes and he bit his lower lip to stop himself from breaking down. Cerys shuddered with sobbing and put her hand to her mouth. How had this happened? How had they got to this point? It didn't feel real.

Nick adjusted his jacket. Thankfully he could feel the weight of a half-bottle of vodka in his inside pocket. He would have a go on that later and he would feel better. That's just the way things were.

CHAPTER 41

RUTH HAD BEEN LIVING out of boxes and off take-aways for the past few days, ever since she moved her small pile of possessions into the house she was renting in the village of Bangor-on-Dee, which was ten minutes south of Llancastell.

The ramifications of the Dinas Padog murders were far reaching, although the media storm after Mike's death had now died down.

Had Mike Gardener lived and stood trial, then the counsel for the defence would have used Nick and Mike's relationship to muddy the waters, claiming that it was a conflict of interest. However, Ruth had been very careful to steer Nick away from any dealings with his uncle in terms of statements etc. Superintendent Jones was confident that there wouldn't be a full IPCC investigation. He felt that Nick's appointment as the deputy investigating officer might in hindsight be seen as an ethical error in Ruth's decision-making but nothing more than that.

Ruth maintained that Nick's local knowledge of Dinas Padog was crucial to the case and far outweighed any suspicions of malpractice.

Ella appeared in the living room with a small lamp, 'Where do you want this, Mum?'

Ruth gestured to a small table in the far corner of the room, 'Over there please, darling.'

This simple domesticity should have been perfect, and just what Ruth had needed after the chaotic start to her life in North Wales Police. It didn't feel like that. Ruth felt that she was beginning to fray at the edges. Her insomnia was becoming chronic, and her free-floating anxiety was heightening on a daily basis.

After a few hours, Ella returned to Liverpool. Ruth probably wouldn't see her for a week or two but that was OK. Her daughter seemed happy and content, and that should have been all that mattered. But as she sat gazing at the blank walls of her new home, Ruth was hit by an overwhelming sense of loneliness and desperation. What was she doing here? Had she made a terrible mistake by moving two hundred miles from home?

It was nearly nine by the time Ruth went to draw the floor-to-ceiling curtains in the living room and looked out at the small garden that was now cloaked in darkness. The wind swirled and the light rain pattered at the glass of the patio doors.

She slumped onto the sofa and took the remote control from the coffee table.

At that moment, her phone beeped with a new text message. Ruth hadn't even read the message when she skimmed to the sender. She dropped the phone to the floor with shock.

... Sarah xxx

IT WAS DARK OUTSIDE and cold enough for most people inside the AA meeting to have coats and jackets hanging from their chairs. Nick had taken a seat at the long wooden table. He took a biscuit, sipped his tea and sat back for a moment. This was a good place to be. He felt safe here. Surrounded by people that never judged him, Nick knew that they also cared about him no matter what.

He had managed not to pick up a drink in the days after his uncle's funeral. He didn't know how. It was a miracle.

A middle-aged woman was at the other end of the table reading aloud from a book. 'We sometimes hurt those we love because they need to be 'taught a lesson'. We were full of pain and looking for sympathy and any attention we could get. This desire to hide a negative motive underneath a positive one, permeates the human condition from birth to death. This kind of self-righteousness can motivate the smallest act or thought. Learning daily to recognise, admit, and correct these flaws is the essence of character-building. An honest regret for harms done, a genuine gratitude for blessings received, and a willingness to try for better things tomorrow will be the permanent assets we shall seek.' She stopped reading and closed the book.

'Thanks, Sheila,' the room said.

There was a moment's silence and then Nick shifted in his seat. 'Hi, my name's Nick, and I'm an alcoholic.'

'Hi, Nick,' the room said.

'And I'm grateful to be here today. And I'm grateful to be sober today.'

Enjoy this book?
Get the next one on Amazon NOW
Available for £1.99 pence for a limited time.

The Harlech Beach Killings
A Ruth Hunter Crime Thriller
Book 2
AMAZON UK https://www.amazon.co.uk/dp/
B0837YSVNN
AMAZON US https://www.amazon.com/dp/
B0837YSVNN

AUTHOR'S NOTE

Although this book is very much a work of fiction, it is located in Snowdonia, a spectacular area of North Wales. It is steeped in history and folklore that spans over two thousand years. It is worth mentioning that Llancastell is a fictional town on the eastern edges of Snowdonia. I have made liberal use of artistic licence, names and places have been changed to enhance the pace and substance of the story.

Acknowledgements

I WILL ALWAYS BE INDEBTED to the people who have made this novel possible.

My mum, Pam, and my stronger half, Nicola, whose initial reaction, ideas and notes on my work I trust implicitly. And Dad, for his overwhelming enthusiasm.

Thanks also go to my incredible Advanced Reading Team. Detective Sergeant Ben Wild of the North Wales Police Force for checking my work and explaining the complicated world of police procedure and investigation. My incredibly talented editor Rebecca Millar who has held my hand through the rewriting and editing process and is a joy to work with. My designer Stuart Bache for the incredible cover design.